DEEP METTLE

FIRST *of*
—————— The Cycle Schyluscient ——————

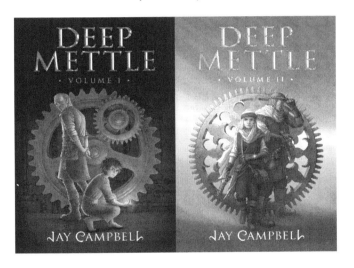

Vol. I
Pipes and Fusils

Vol. II
Tools of War

First published by
Kindle Direct Publishing 2020
Independently published

This volume paperback 2nd edition 2023

Worlds By Jay
voidstep.com

Jay Campbell asserts the moral right to be
identified as the author of this work

ISBN: 9781695536173

Text typeset in Constantia
Titles typeset in Optimus Princeps /
Optimus Princeps Semibold by Manfred Klein;
Powell Antique by Typographer Mediengestaltung
& Aquifer by JHL Fonts

Original cover art & design by Nataša Ilinčić
Text & inset illustrations by Nataša Ilinčić
natasailincic.com

Original postscript illustration & maps
by the author

Printed by Amazon Fulfilment

To: Rachel

DEEP METTLE

Enjoy the
adventure!

For Clare and Michael

I
— The Cycle Schyluscient —

DEEP METTLE

Jay Campbell

VORTH

OUTLAND OF THE INWOLD

3230R.IV

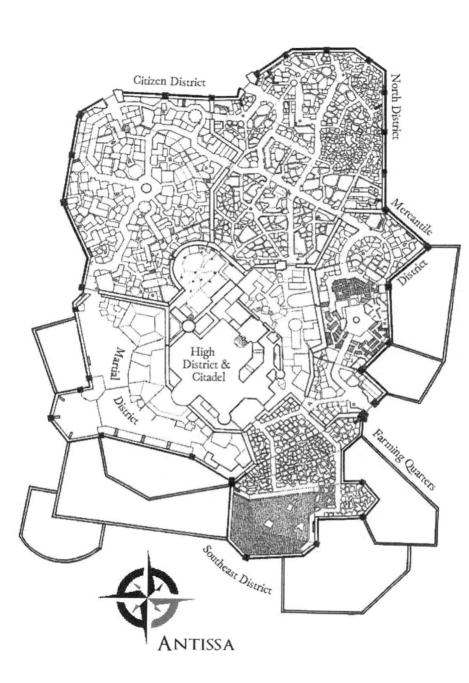

Raven

Tonight dusk fills the vale not as gloved hands over the cliffs, but thick black ichor that wells within a wound ripe for infection. Sister Cadence can feel its menace without looking from the window, but knows that it makes no difference in this room. Here, four close walls remain the charge of one candle. A night and a day she has passed here, watching. And again, Valeun's bell calls to evensong.

She will not go.

The stillness of her patient has afforded her time, more than she has had in twenty-five years, to study his face. It is not as she knows it. The skin is grey, lips bulging black, cheek split wide open in a gash where it met the chapel steps. She has smoothed his hair across the pillow; an unkempt tangle as ever, and yet changed. He is so much older now, of course: that fiery crimson gave way years ago to less vivid reds streaked through with coal. But there is a brittleness in it too, as if some other, colder fire has run each strand and doused its flame. Is he truly alive? She watches the slow rise and fall of his chest, but does not trust it. He is peaceful. And in that peace she hears a whisper. *Those wings are broken.*

His breaths are shallow.

He will not fly.

To drown the whisper in the rustle of her habit, Cadence rises, but the whisper rises with her. *It is ending.*

She schools her thoughts, steadies her own breaths and looks once more. He breathes. He lives, and that is all. Even his eyelids are still, and now she girds herself against fears of what they will contain when they open. *If they do.*

Lost in the whispers, she is deaf to the door when it creaks. Or perhaps it has creaked that note too many years. The footfall gives her a start and she turns sharply to the threshold, where the acolyte's honest eyes lift from brown vestments; a contrast to her white. 'Kendrick.'

The acolyte offers a wan smile.

Cadence sighs, 'He shows no more sign of waking than when last you came.' Her gaze floats back to the body. 'I may require more water for his hurts.'

Kendrick goes, returning with a bowl half-filled and fresh cleaning cloths. The sister sets the bowl beside the candle and again applies herself to the washing of the wounds; thinking all the while how strange it is to touch this man. She never desired it: all her life she has feared him. Now it is for his very life she is afraid, and the touch is strange only because it is not. No blazing current surges through her hand on contact with his skin; no thrum of unearthly power. The man is flesh.

Arms in his sleeves, Kendrick remains but does not sit. After a time in which the only sound is the trickling of water, Cadence asks, 'Where is the Reverend Sister?' - aware that it is the same question she has been asking of Kendrick each time he comes.

ONE

TREMORS

They came from behind us.

And below.

At least that's the way they felt to me, a child on the plains who knew nothing. They weren't real either, not as they seemed to me back then anyway. I came to know that. But it's how they *felt*, and still feel now in my dreams: like deep vibrations plunging under the mountains to reach us.

I'd feel them every time Dewar stood and stared out at those mountains, or when only those sad-slow smiles would answer my questions about *before*. In the early years, weeping would carry at night, every night, and I'd feel them then too. And I'd feel them when I learned not to ask why Mother Far, and only her in our village, was so old.

The *before*, they always told me, was a time that would be famous all through the realms, for many years. Centuries maybe. And as many miles from our plains as the other side of Ered. Just like the thing that had ended that time, that I could feel thrumming through my muscles and the soles of my feet. Not a knowing, but an echo of a knowing; that far from here, and far bigger than me, the world trembled.

But all of us would stare at those mountains sometimes. Their colours changed every day: grey, brown, black, red, blue. Always a wall between us all and *before*. There was a day when I swear they shone silver in the morning, and that was the day—I think it was—when I asked Erik if we really had come over them once.

'That we did,' he smiled back from his haunches as he kneaded a handful of earth between his palms. 'That's how we got here, to the borderlands.'

It doesn't make sense that he'd have been working that earth, just there, right outside our hut, because they never farmed so near the settlement. But it's what's in the memory.

'What's on the other side?' I asked.

'Hm? Thought you remembered all this,' he winked. I must have shaken my head. Then Erik clapped his hands of earth, pushed to his feet and put his hat on, though I saw the smile leave his chapped lips as he did. 'A sacred place,' he replied, now looking at the silver mountains too. 'The castle of an ancient, holy people who watch the gulf of the Inwold. Still do, we believe, but their doors are closed now.'

Every one of those words was like a nugget of gold; heavy as it was precious.

'What about our country?' I asked.

'That's beyond,' he said and his smile was sad-slow. With a leathery hand, he mussed my hair.

In my own memory, there are fragments of *before*. Wind on a beach and moaning boats . . . fishermen calling to one another on the gusts from a rough sea . . . When I'd describe these things to Sarah she'd always chuckle in disbelief. 'How

8

can you remember all that? You weren't even a year old in Brownport!'

Shreds are all they are. Just tiny glimpses of the place that we were from, and then had left. Flashes of a journey. Erik in the wide-brimmed hat he still wore every day, and Sarah in a shawl I'd not seen since that time, cradling a box. Wagons and faces. Arcs of high cloud above wide-open country. Distant woodlands. Sun-splashed shapes on faraway downs. Green hills that rolled forever. Then snowy drifts. I don't remember the cold of those mountains at all, but the warmth at their feet . . . that part I *do* remember. I wasn't yet a year and a half when we first reached the borderlands of Vorth, but even then I knew a difference well enough. Big skies, brown earth. And the strange, bronze-skinned people from the desert to the south.

The Vedans. In the beginning, they'd given us animals and seed so we could forge our own way in the north of their country. It hadn't been much, as Erik often remembered, but as Sarah would often remind him, it had been enough. What we had needed. Between the mountains and River Elm that flowed down from the north, the plain was fertile, good for cattle, and the foothills for planting crops. Sorghum, beets, runner beans, and other root crops in winter. Small flocks of sheep we had too, and some cows; goats in the settlements further north. Four or five of our homesteads took root in the river-plain; little specks of Naemia on the doorstep of the desert "outland."

Our own was the southernmost speck. From where our huts were clustered, on most days, we could see the ribbed blear of coastal sky, and from the foothills on a clear day the blue water of the gulf. There were few trees growing in the plain; the River Elm only named so for the elms that hugged its banks further north, in Elman.

Home was simple, like all of the memories of then: clay walls, twine-bound reed shutters, bulrush mats and coal-fires. Even in the later winters, Vedans would continue to send their hessian sacks of coal across the river. Sometimes grain too, for the chickens that would always peck at my toes. I remember how I'd learned not to be scared of our mule, or of Miss Nindry's two cows. And I remember other things, like Sarah's soups and careful ways. The rich smell of Erik's sweat when he came back from the hills, hands all marked, brow smeared. The tiny, battered book of Exelcian proverbs with which they taught me how to read, and for my numbers the counting frame of stalks and seed-husks. In the heat of the day, the shade, and hours spent splashing in the river's shallows. Rare summer showers. Even the bitterness of those nights when no amount of stoking could revive the Vedan coals against the winds that reached into the hut. The copper terrier, Scrivens we called him, then just a pup, though I don't remember where he came from. And the pallet where I slept with my fingers in his fur.

Sarah would tell me stories of our country sometimes, calling figures out of myth to walk through my dreams and back over the mountains to Naemia again. Noble kings and princes, courageous knights, the Wildmen of the woods, that strange man she called "Blue" and, somewhere in it all, the name of that holy grey castle on the edge of the gulf.

'Before the line of Naemian princes there were kings,' she would begin in that voice like crisping embers. So many times she'd told it and yet every time it was new. 'Great King Saremar was the first true king to sit the throne of our land, but he ruled other lands also. Lands as far north as Elman and south to Norwynd's horn and the islands of the gulf. These, the realms of the Inner World, were the domain of a people who had walked the woods and hills ever since the breaking of the sky. Celestri they were called; beings of the heavens bound in tall mortal forms, who dwelt within a bastion on the shore of the gulf.'

'*Fallstone*,' I whispered. That was the name of Erik's castle, the one that had fallen from the sky.

Inside her halo of chestnut hair, Sarah's smile was calm and slow. Her face, in dimming firelight, had gone the yellow of

'Is Con your brother?'

'Uh-huh, he's twelve. I'm five,' he told her briskly. I paid the boy closer attention as Sarah asked his name. Wary, he studied her face, then ogled mine. I stared back, studying him too. Skin sprayed with freckles under a mop of sandy hair, ears that stuck out, and big bulging brown eyes. He looked silly. 'Jerome.'

'A good name,' said Sarah brightly. 'A knightly name, I'd say. Do you know Florian?'

The big eyes roved over me with suspicion, seeming to try and take in everything about me at first glance for fear of needing to take a second. As he eyed my hair, I ducked behind Sarah. I knew it was blacker than anyone else's and now for some reason felt scared of what he'd think.

'Have you eaten anything today?' Sarah was already unwrapping our bread and tearing off a piece for the boy. At four I wasn't unaware of the value of things, but the kindness wasn't wasted. Jerome flung away the stick and squatted right there on our mat, grabbing the bread and trying, twice, to push it all into his mouth before giving up on that method and ripping off a bite of it instead.

Sarah asked him more questions: 'Does your brother take good care of you? It can't be easy if it's just the two of you.'

Mouth stuffed, Jerome nodded.

'Well! I dare say he's not as deft with a needle as I am. Look at your shirt, there's barely anything left of it, child.'

Jerome glanced at his clothes, then up at Sarah again with a quick, impish grin. I smiled as well, with Sarah's shoulder for cover. She was, at that moment, offering to mend his thread-bare shirt and when he nodded, she coaxed with her fingers.

'Take it off then, and keep to the shade.' He stripped it off, baring his already bronzed skin to the sun. 'And here, take some bread over to your brother.'

When he snatched it off her, I was sure that he would eat it himself. But he didn't, instead running it back to the boy he called Con. I leaned in close to Sarah's ear. 'There won't be enough for Scrivens now!' I whispered.

13

'Oh, there will,' she assured me and tutted at the shirt in her hands.

She must have worked at it long after I fell asleep that night, since it had been little more than ribbons and, when I woke, it was whole; darned from loose scraps and blanket-ends. And she would have returned it to the trading place the very same day, had the two boys not followed us back.

In Naemia their home had been a town somewhere north of the coast on which we'd lived. No one ever asked more, or what had happened to their parents, and the tremors were in that. They were lucky, Erik said, to have made it as far as they had by themselves. Since reaching the borderlands later than most, they'd simply moved about the plain, sleeping rough, stealing and begging to survive as best they could. But Sarah tamed them, and with Con old enough to help Erik with the farming on the foothills, they became part of our home.

No one ever wanted the necklaces. Mother Far, the old woman, gave us her spare hen.

One night, when I was eight, Sarah opened up our travelling trunk and took out the little box.

'I brought this with me when we left.'

Proudly I told her, 'I remember. But it's smaller.'

'You're bigger.' She sat, her smile falling so suddenly that I looked to the reeds of the doorway, fearing something had come in from outside. Leopards would sometimes prowl

Two

Antissa

'Florian.'

Not yet.

The blanket was still there, but *there* wasn't the cart anymore. Wheels were turning somewhere else now, part of a bigger, fuller noise. And it was day. I knew that even without the faint glow on my eyelids. Hot, dry eyelids. I'd keep them closed as long as I could, let nothing in, just not yet. *Not yet.*

They opened by themselves. I found myself looking at the face of a rough wall charred about as black as my own hair.

'You awake, Flor?'

Focus on the wall. I tried to do that for a while, blocking out his voice, but then he touched my shoulder. Only when his hand lifted away did I move; finding my muscles stiff and sore as I turned half-way on my back and tried to find him. My eye-lids quivered in the daylight streaming from the doorway behind him; I couldn't look at him properly.

'Here.' He nudged something at my mouth; a small skin-bottle. I took it and he helped me squeeze out what little water was left inside. It trickled over my lips, so dry I hadn't even felt them, and onto my tongue. Bitter but cool. I swallowed, but it barely moistened my throat.

'*Who has it? Where's that skin?*' someone barked. Jolting forward at the sound, easily the hardest voice I'd ever heard, I dribbled some of my second sip onto my neck. It had been a man, from outside the daylight-doorway.

Jerome snatched the skin away. 'Gotta give it back,' he rattled, voice low. On edge.

Before he went, I croaked, 'Sarah.'

He shuffled. *That* shuffle, and the shuffle told it all. And as he hurried out to daylight I was suddenly aware of all the sobbing and moaning that I'd been hearing since I woke, coming from close by, outside that daylight-door. Some of it stopped after a little while, but more started somewhere else. Then others.

My eyes were closed again when Jerome came back. He was trying to be quiet but I knew the way he breathed and he was shuffling again. 'I'm real sorry, Flor . . .' I wanted to tell him to just go, go away, but my throat had closed up. It was too dry to shout anyway. 'Sarah and Erik . . .' But he couldn't say it. I tensed up my arms to clench in the convulsions that had already started, hating that daylight-doorway. Hating Jerome. Hating the stupid sound of his voice when he tried to be gentle. 'We got to Antissa.'

'Leave me alone.'

I dragged myself, in my blanket, to the wall.

realised, I knew what had really happened. He'd been wounded by that creature when he pulled me out of the hut. *He* was the reason I was here. And alive.

Slowly, I ate the bread. It was hard and very salty, not like normal bread. Meanwhile fat flies batted my face. Acrid smoke wafted into my eyes from the stalls. And all the time the weeping lapped on and on at my back, its vicious misery like grit in every nibble I took.

As it droned on, I thought of the Vedans from long ago and the rich browns – almost golds – of the faces I remembered from the other side of our river. They were everywhere now. Not just ochre and tan and that soft, earthy fawn but deeper umber like the riverbed's clay. Some Vedans, just a few, were even blacker than peat. Most went about in cloaks of rough hessian, just like the sacks they'd sent us coal in; while others, like the shopkeepers, wore richer fabrics in reds, oranges and yellows. Some walked with cowls drawn high against the sun, others coiling headdresses or weird hats. There were hats of all colours.

The flow thickened. After a while, across the street, a kind of official came into view and strolled to stop under the shade of an awning. There he wedged the butt of his spear in an embankment of sand and stood a while, watching the traffic. I studied him. Under an open cloak, he wore black cloth with cord-bound leathers at chest and legs. His headpiece was a dome with strips of hide at the neck.

Jerome wildly shook his head at me. 'Don't!'

'Why, is he a soldier?'

'Think so.' I let my eyes drift back to the official, but Jerome was serious. He hissed, '*Stop it!* They're the ones who put us here. They're watching us.'

I risked one more look, but now the man had moved off into the crowd.

Finishing the bread, I willed the street to be louder than the weeping. To the left of our doorway, someone hammered at something that clanged a high note. I didn't like to look at his face: ruddy, scowling, beard untamed. Brutish. Wherever a stall or a shop or a merchant could be seen, people shouted. So much *shouting!* And even where they didn't, voices were harsh and accents thick.

Still, I listened.

'. . . *never half a tallan! Just look at that* . . .' Something. '. . . *five smelt, two schrod of* . . .' Something else. '*And don't go skimping on the kelp like last time!*' Another voice was all out of another unheard-of thing, but he did have—'*Khapent, very good khapent!*' Twenty pounds of that at least, and more smelt, whatever *smelt* was. '*Rubai!*' someone yelled hoarsely before demanding to know what someone took her for. That someone shouted back did she know what district this was. And on it went.

Meaningless, most of it, though it was clear to me now that the Vedans spoke the common Prate, as we did, and not their own desert language. The accents were hard, but it was better to listen to than the weeping.

Directly across the street where the official had stood, three stalls faced us, each one shaded by an awning. One was yellow, one was purple, and one had red and white stripes. The richest smells were coming from under the yellow one, where a man whose beard was black and curly sold fish and florid creatures from a pot. From under the purple awning, a woman dressed in shiny cloth sold long rolls of dyed fabric. And her neighbour, under the red and white stripes, dealt in coal. This was a gangly, grey-skinned man who I now watched as he chatted with one of his customers. The customer himself had a ratty grey beard and a green turban. I stared at him, slowly coming to realise that he was easily as old as Mother Far, maybe older. And then, suddenly, that there were many others like him here. I'd always thought her so ancient!

Before long, the old man with the green turban turned and left the coal stall. His dark brown wrinkles glistened with oil and he was chewing on something – nuts, I guessed – still cupping a handful as he went. Crossing to our side of the street, he approached the shop to our left where the brute clanged with the hammer. Looking past Jerome's shoulder, I kept watching.

The hammer stopped. '. . . fare the Guilds today, *ekh* Loquar?'

'Bah, none too worse,' the old man said in a voice that sounded choked with phlegm. 'What of the districts, *ekh* Ghalib?'

Two clangs of the hammer. '. . . at my doorstep and ask me again!'

'Aye.' Old green-turban glanced at our warehouse, his yellow teeth flashing as he chomped open-mouthed on flaky pulp. 'Sore day for 'em, sore day for you.'

'*Esha's arse*, sore day—they've doubled!'

Behind me came a moan from one of the smallest of the children in our group. A mother – young Miss Nindry, she'd made it! – began joylessly singing to calm her. The singing was almost worse, but then, thankfully, the hammer clanged harder. Through it I couldn't hear any more of the conversation between green turban and the brute, and when it paused again for the old man to make a purchase the accents seemed even coarser. The man had bought a little bag of clicking, clinking things which he slipped into the hollow of his turban. But even as he turned back into the crowds, one fell out of it. He didn't notice, and it rolled across the dust all the way to our doorway.

Jerome saw too. At first he stared. Then reached out, picked it up and lay it flat on his palm.

Metal.

I'd never seen much metal; just our rusted old farm tools, the brazier . . . some of the treasures in Sarah's box, but I rejected those memories just as forcefully as the weeping. Those things of ours had been poor examples anyway, I now saw. Hardly bigger than a Naemian coin, a hexagon of shiny yellow winked against Jerome's grubby skin. Every side of it was perfect, a hole in the middle fashioned without a flaw and finely threaded with ruts as thin as hairs. Jerome turned around to see where it had come from and, sure enough, on the ground below the clanging brute's counter many more were scattered about. But that was two yards away at least, and I saw Jerome make up his mind that it might as well be two miles. He went back to studying his own, lifting it up to his eye and peering through its hole at me. I looked away.

How little I knew about this place. Well, nothing really. They built things here, I'd once heard someone say that, but never paid enough attention to know what it was that they built. Or maybe I didn't want to think right now about who had said it.

I could bear it though, this strangeness.

Just not the weeping. Not the fear.

One more time I looked over my shoulder. I did it just as Mother Far recoiled from a movement in the street. Some Vedans had pulled their wheelbarrow almost straight over her legs, and now they were yelling at her and raising the backs of their hands. They didn't hit her, but the anger of their voices set off more of the small children. While Dewar held the old woman close and tried to steady her nerves, she trembled. Then the children wailed louder. No.

I swung my face back to Jerome. 'Where are the healers?'

'What?'

'You said they took Con to the healers. So where are they, the *healers?*'

He looked blank. 'How should I know?'

I tugged my blanket out from under myself and stood up. 'I'll find them.'

'What?'

'I said I'll go find them. You coming?'

'You *crazy?*'

'He's *your* brother!' I snapped.

'So?'

'So you coming or not?'

He swallowed his horror and glanced out of the doorway like a rodent from its burrow. Like all the rest of them. 'Better not.'

'Fine.'

I knew I looked ridiculous wearing the blanket like a robe but didn't care. If it had been with me on the cart, it might have been with me once at home. Home. Not that awful, broken sound behind me. I filled my lungs with the closest thing to courage I could find and walked out, over the blinking metal jewels and past the clanging of the hammer, into the street.

It was very different from watching. Vedans and their vehicles, mounts and beasts of burden doubled in size, doubled in speed and occupied every part of the way. Keeping to the sides to avoid them wasn't easy either, no one side ever clear for long. But I made sure to give a wide berth to the nattering women and steered well clear of the fuming man's clouds.

Up ahead were the big boys and the ball. It looked like flap of stitched pigskin, whatever had puffed it up long since beaten out by play. They were batting it fiercely at one another with their fists, elbows and knees, darting in and out of the shifting traffic, unfazed by rebukes. There was no way around the game. So I waited for the first break in the flurry of their feet, put my head down and walked through it. Immediately their yells surrounded me, as if now meant for me, which I pretended they weren't even when I knew the tallest boy had stopped to stare. Even when I'd glanced up and caught the wicked smirk on his mouth. Just keep walking.

They were only just behind me, and the plaza not far ahead, when I sensed that they had all dropped out of the game. One said something in a bitter, taunting voice. Another laughed. One gave a whistle. And then—

'Border boy!'

Keep walking, keep walking . . .

'*Eya*, border boy!' A second whistle, then more laughter. '*Eya*, talking to you!'

It wasn't so much the force of the ball as how little I expected them to throw it at me; it struck the back of my knee and I buckled. Going down, arms tangled in blanket, my cheek bit the dirt. Quick as I could, I scrambled up and turned around, only to trip on the end of the blanket. That brought me to my knees again, blanket sliding off my shoulders while the tall boy swaggered closer. Four others converged behind him like a crew of pirates.

A streak of watery red came off on my fingers when I touched them to my cheek. 'Only blood, border boy. Never seen blood before?'

Get up, I told myself, and *walk!* What did I care if he called me "border boy"?

I stood, more carefully this time, and as I did he brushed his chest into mine; only a nudge but enough to rock me back on my feet. From somewhere I found the nerve to meet his eyes – if only for a moment, fascinated by his skin: that rich gold I'd begun to think I'd imagined. I wondered if he was older, or simply taller, than me. All of them were taller. Now I looked at the grime that traced his lips, his smirk filling to a grin as he glanced down at my shirt.

'Hey look, what's *these* things?' he blurted and pulled my collar. He tugged on a button and laughed while the other boys grouped and looked too, asking each other things like, 'What's wrong with his face?' and 'Why's he so small like that?' The leader let go of my button with a flick and I touched it to make sure he'd even left it attached. 'So what you doing in 'Tissa?'

I didn't say anything. Didn't feel safe to answer.

His smile shrank back behind the re-curling of his lip. 'I asked you a question.'

The others started heckling, moving back and forth as they mocked me in their accents. Their horrible accents. One kicked a spray of sand up at my shins and I flinched. They all cackled.

'You borderlings got tongues?' gibed the leader. 'Go on, tell us why you can come running to our city soon as trouble's stirrin' up north, easy as that, huh?'

This time I didn't understand the question.

'Think you can stay?'

I thought about that. I must have frowned as I did, and he mustn't have liked it because he shoved both hands into my chest. I staggered back but managed not to fall.

'Well?'

Like a coward I shook my head, rubbing my chest below the buttons. That made him smile again.

'Good,' he said. 'Going back to your border then?'

'Don't know,' I replied, and when I said it the other boys clustered in to gawk at me, ogling my mouth so as not to miss my next reply.

'What you say?'

'I don't know!' I shouted back.

While the others jeered and clapped their hands at the show, kicking more sand, the leader raised a dusty eyebrow at my shout. Even I was surprised that I'd got cross enough to shout at him and now my chest was moving up and down at speed. I glared from face to dirty Vedish face and back to the leader just as he shoved me a second time, much harder. I fell down on my backside and it was hilarious. And even though there was no use in standing up, I wouldn't stay on the ground. So I stood, bracing myself.

'Leave me alone,' I told his ugly curled-up mouth. Then turned to reach for my blanket, but a boy darted from behind with all the speed of their ball-game. With a snigger he snatched it, snapped it away from my grasp and whipped sand into my eyes. Through the eye I wasn't rubbing clear of sand I saw him wrap it around himself and, to the amusement of the gang, fling one end theatrically over his shoulder.

'We like you, border boy,' said the leader in a chummy tone. I looked back at him, still blinking sand. It made something burn inside my chest and I wanted to shout at him again to leave off, just leave me be. But the force behind those words had gone – simply dried up in the Vedish sun – and so had the courage. 'Where's your ma?'

Who needed courage. Like a coil I sprung at his chest and brought him down. Before I knew what I was doing or even thinking, I was squared on top of his legs, fists digging into his ribs one by one. I heard the air going out of him, then struck for his nose. He turned his face aside so that my knuckles only grazed his cheek, then flailed his arms, found my shoulders and threw me off of him.

We rolled. Scraping at each other, we tussled through the street's sand and dust. But I'd only got him down because he'd not expected it. He was bigger and it didn't take him long to shove me fully clear.

I landed hard and something like a rock or piece of flagstone in the sand bit into my hip.

I heard a voice from somewhere say: 'It'll start.'

Oh it's started!

Then wheels were groaning much too close to my head. I tumbled quickly onto my feet, just in time, to dodge the cart that grumbled by.

The boys had formed a whooping circle.

When he came at me again I caught his hands and tried to push with all my strength to grapple him. But he had height over me too, not just the strength. Even so, as my sandals slipped and skidded in loose sand, I broke the handhold to grab his stupid ball and smack his head with it. *Clap!*

He let me go with a cry – the pigskin drier and stiffer than I'd thought.

'*Pelkhish rat!*' he cursed, then rebounded, aiming a high, clumsy kick at my ribs. I squirmed away, then made a low lunge at him from the side. Misjudging the distance to his legs, instead of catching both his shins, I tripped him clear off his feet and felt him tip over my back. I collapsed under his weight, and as my body went belly-flat someone else squashed my face down. I fought against the pressure, spitting dirt, and pushed free, whirling to face him. Taking his fist in the jaw.

I flopped back down with a thump.

'Like *that*, borderling!?' The street-side buildings wheeled while boys cheered on and laughed at me. I propped myself up on one elbow, panting fiercely, glaring up. 'Had enough?' he shouted. My head went all soupy and the sun was baking through my hair to my scalp, but I hadn't had enough. I launched.

But went nowhere. A strong hand pulled me from behind into hot leather and metal. 'Enough!' I looked up into the face of the official with the spear.

'He's mad, sir!' yelled the leader boy. 'Attacked me so he did! Should'a seen.'

'That right?' boomed the leather-clad man, yanking my arm so hard I thought my shoulder would pop out. I struggled against him but the hand only snapped shut around my fore-arm, pulling me closer. His eyes widened on my face. 'A refugee!'

'Yessir, from the warehouse,' chimed the sand-kicker, still swathed in my blanket. The laughter had stopped but I could still see the stolen grins. My opponent had shrunk to just another one of their number while, behind them along the side of the street, I saw Jerome creep into view.

Spear-man rattled me. 'Better watch yourself, boy. You're lucky to have this fortress for a shelter—hellish lucky! Don't need your borderland wildness on our streets, you understand?' I pulled but he shook me again, repeating the same word like an order. '*Understand!*'

Pulling even harder and twisting, I somehow came free of his grip, then tripped forward and ran. Not to Jerome or to the warehouse but away, not looking back. And without the stupid blanket, I didn't want it anymore.

Crowds were thicker in the plaza. Hard voices haggled. Square coins clattered over wood and clinked together into hands. Buyers and sellers moved in all directions and it didn't matter to them if I could dodge them in time. Nor could I get near any of the tarpaulins of merchant caravans where hagglers bustled even closer, none with a care for a twelve-year-old boy.

Or a borderland boy.

My cheek burned from its scrape and my jaw and lip itched where he'd punched it. I didn't know where I was going; had no idea where to find the healers and who could I ask for directions?

Ducking under a canopy to the side, I found myself in some kind of factory where people worked to make paint, or maybe dye. Inky frowns flashed, but I hurried between them and from there found my way out of the plaza. Walked on faster from there. Block-like apartments stood stacked on either side of the street. Crones gazed from doorways, eyes thinned to tiny, venomous slits, clutching at besoms that seemed to have teeth instead of bristles. Ahead was the big wall I'd seen above the houses earlier: rearing high over the streets, a rugged thing of sandstone rock. *That's* where I'd go.

The street sloped downward. I passed two palm trees. Under them a pump lurched and squeaked as folk drew water from below to fill their amphorae. Then there were merchants again, these selling salt and spices, dried fish, tanned hides, bundles of wood.

The studded leather of more officials with spears winked through the dust. To avoid them, I dashed for the cover of alleys but those alleys were choked with smokers of pipes who made the air even more impossible to breathe or see through. So I moved as best I could within the stream of the traffic and slipped by the door where the officials were standing. I passed a dome-shaped storehouse where people were hurling sacks into a pit and fogging the air with grainy spores. My lungs were tight, my mouth was clawing.

But at the base of the high wall there were steps, leading up. Without hesitation I scrambled onto them and climbed, now wanting more than anything else to be up and away from the streets, above the rooftops, leaving dust and noise below. It couldn't come soon enough, that clean lemony sunlight; that touch of breeze. The breeze grew stronger and fresher the higher I climbed. Sand and dust blew off my face and out of my hair as I stopped to catch my breath just two steps from the top. Suddenly alone. All there was up here was the sandstone and a clear, wan-blue sky. At least until I looked back.

Inside the confines of the fortress, the buildings I'd woven through to get here now looked like so many hundreds of barnacles, all dried-out and baking, on a rock. Their close-pressed roofs – flat, domed and tiled – climbed up the mound between smaller, intersecting grey walls. Lording the very crest of the mound, a grand palace pushed up a tower and some great big domes from behind another wall of whiter stone, sun glancing off their bronze to pierce the haze. I sucked a breath, and mouthed – *Antissa*.

Sure enough the sounds were softer from up here, floating with the smokes above the city. Some way to my right, on the walkway, stood two men holding flagpoles, their conversation now and then wafting to reach me on the breeze.

I faced the battlements: a crust of sandstone crudely hewn into squares about as tall as a man and just as wide in some places. The spaces in between them were twice that. Coming closer, I stepped into an in-between gap where the top of the wall reached not much higher than my waist, and even as my belly tightened up, I gripped the stone and leaned to look over the edge.

Much, *much* higher than the steps I'd just climbed, I realised, swaying. By a hundred feet at least, the sandstone dropped from here to meet the knuckles of the hill this place was built on. My eyes strained for focus, unready for just how high above the desert earth that was! Beyond the foot of the hill stretched open plains in dirty greys and reds and browns. I saw a powdery horizon but had no clue which one it was. No view to the sea, or any river. Nothing at all by which to tell in which direction I was looking.

My breath felt shorter. My heart beat faster. A sheet of white crossed my eyes for a moment and then my head started to throb. I winced at the pain in my cheek and my lip, then felt dizzy. Dizzy and sick.

Also, there was something in my pocket. Trouser pocket. I put my palm against my hip and felt it there. So it *hadn't* been a rock or piece of flagstone I'd landed on in the street; there was something there. Small and smooth, but definitely solid. Quite heavy. *How hadn't I . . .?* I slid my hand into the pocket and touched it. Whatever it was, it was strangely cool.

My head throbbed harder.

'Whittle's mark,' someone said.

I turned quickly, despite the dizziness, not having heard anyone else coming up behind me; maybe even more startled to see that nobody *was* there after all. The two flagpole men were still along the wall's walkway; must have been the breeze playing with their voices . . .

Nausea bloomed through my stomach. My legs wobbled a bit. All the same, I closed my fingers around the thing inside my trouser pocket and pulled it out.

All it took was one look.

Squeezing my fist closed again I reeled, grabbed the sandstone edge and pitched forward at the waist. Black speckles on my eyes obscured the plummet below my perch as my stomach heaved and I spewed whatever had been in it towards the crags far below. My sick took the fall and I slammed my eyes shut as it went. Then I heaved and spewed two more times.

As the breeze cooled the vomit left on my lips, I swayed back but kept my one-handed grip on the stone edge.

'You!' called someone. Tears clung to my lashes but through their blur I saw one of the flagmen jog towards me. I didn't have it in me to run. 'What d'you think you're doing?'

When he reached me he shoved me aside, stepped into the gap and looked down. Then at me with an expression between anger and disgust.

'Let me handle him, watchman,' came another voice.

Confused, still dizzy, I looked back towards the steps to see two spear-holding officials coming up. One was the man who had broken up my fight in the street. Had he followed me here? Now he crossed the walkway to the gap and peered down too before rounding on me with so much blistering outrage that I half-expected to be raised into the air and hurled over the battlements. Instead he grabbed me by the collar and hauled me back into the gap. I couldn't have resisted if he'd led me by the hand. He forced my head down.

'Got something to say, have you?' he brayed in my ear. 'Opinion to share with your protectors, borderlander?'

Because he seemed to be pointing, I blinked away more tears and tried to focus on *what*. About ten feet below, a pole jutted out of the face of the wall; clear enough. But what he was actually pointing at took a little longer to come clear, along with two smart slaps to my left cheek. The pole suspended a weave of fabric, heavy fabric, blue and white, which the breeze was rocking back and forth. Vaguely I could make out the emblem it bore: a circle with outward-splaying rays and streaks of yellow going down.

No, those streaks weren't part of it.

So much for the fall.

Seizing a handful of my hair, the official yanked me back again. 'Despoiling the Satrap's colours already, eh? Thought you'd add a few of your own?'

'Some start this one's having,' remarked his partner.

'He'll have manners soon enough.' They peeled my body away from the wall and I let them, thinking only to squeeze the thing tighter in my hand.

THREE

A CAPTAIN AND A COMMANDER

Boots crunched the sand on either side of me as I was pulled back through the streets of Antissa. The heat made it hard to focus on much; how far the two officials pulled me or how long the pulling took. My legs kicked just enough underneath me to stop from being dragged along the ground, but the rest of me was goop. I was down a sandal too, but at least had managed to keep hold of the thing from my pocket. I'd be sick again soon.

The ground passed into shade, though it was only when the men began to speak above my head that I realised we'd stopped. 'Taking him up the barracks,' one said. 'Puked on one of the banners.'

'He what?'

'Puked. Over the colours.'

A snort. 'That's a new one.'

I tried raising my head. There was a white wall in front, a gate, another official standing with a spear. My head dropped as someone puffed a sigh. 'Look, just give him a once-over with the crop, easy enough. Don't see why you've got to haul him up the barracks and all.'

'He's one of the new refugees off the border.' As one of my captors said this, my jaw was pinched in a grip and my face pushed up for display. 'See?'

The gatekeeper leaned in. This one had a black cape on, I saw. 'Hm, best make sure then,' he said in a more dutiful tone. My head flopped.

On they pulled me. Sand and dust ebbed away from clean cobbles that were hot on my bare foot. There were no merchants or haggling or heckles around here and the only animal sounds those of hooves clopping smartly. Buildings and balconies threw statelier shadows on the road and people passed in ones and twos. Steps took us up, then there was dimness, no more scorching sunlight bearing down, and walls touched orange by burning torches. More studs on leather and black capes moving past, and then a door that stood ajar. One of the men knocked firmly. 'Come,' a voice said.

The men pushed their way in, dragging me, then threw me down. As they immediately blocked the only way out of the room, I scampered to the first corner I could see, crouched and clenched my fist. That was an instinct – I wasn't even sure what I was holding, or why.

The walls were grey here, adorned with shields and spears and other pole-arm weapons. A small, high window weakly lit a block-like desk where papers lay in stacks that either leaned or had toppled over. 'Be brief, boys, please,' grunted the sour-looking man who sat behind it, leafing pages.

'Unruly child, sir. Vandal,' said one of my captors.

'Which one is he then?'

'Both, sir.'

A cough. 'Sure that's all of him?' The sour man flapped a page onto one of the toppled stacks, licked a finger, flapped another. 'Why else should it take all of two guards to drag a scrawny whelp up to my desk?'

Not soldiers then. Guards.

The guard who had broken up my fight cleared his throat. 'Just a vandal, sir.'

'Just a vandal,' sighed the desk-man. 'Well, we can all sleep a little easier knowing that.' He too had the accent of the people in the streets, though not as coarse. 'Go on.'

'He, er . . . we found him vandalising the colours of the Satrap, Captain,' the guard informed him. 'You know the banners on the northeast wall.'

'Mm-hm.'

'He's one of the borderland refugees, sir,' said the other guard. 'Came in this morning. Their village—'

'Left in ruins, I'm told,' the desk-man interrupted. He looked up from his paper-flapping and straight into my eyes. 'By the Rath that attacked it.'

I shied from the gaze.

'That's right, sir,' said the guard.

Eyes still on me, the desk-man tapped a finger on a page, then set it down and leaned back in his chair. 'Come here,' he said.

The guards turned, leathers creaking. 'Look alive, the Captain calls you!'

'That'll do, he heard me. There, see, he's coming.'

I had no choice. There was no running or escaping from this man, not with both guards so near the door.

The floor was cold on my bare heel, racking my body with a shiver. Or maybe that was the thought of my home in ruins, a thought that now flooded my mind. I kept both fists tight as I stepped up to the corner of the desk and stopped, a safe distance from the guards. I looked at the face of the man they called Captain. It was square like his shoulders and his desk, bristle-cheeked and wide-nostrilled. Like a bull. His hair was silvering from black, and if his brown eyes were grim, they were a sleepy sort of grim. I saw them drop to my lip.

'You've been fighting?'

I didn't answer; knew the guards would do it for me anyway: 'Attacked a boy in the street.'

'District?'

'North, sir.'

'Gutterwaifs then,' the Captain scoffed. 'Likely provoked.'

The guards fell silent.

'But the colours, eh?' the Captain went on as if, really, it must be the last thing today. 'Did you know that's what they were?' This was a direct question to me, so after a moment I shook my head, no, in reply. He grimaced: 'What exactly did he *do* to them?'

Here it came again.

'Puked on them,' said the first guard.

'Beg pardon?'

'At least, was sick on them, sir. Made a right ugly mess.'

The Captain rubbed his chin, making it crackle. 'I'm not understanding. Do you mean he was sick on the colours only *after* he vandalised them, or that his being sick was the vandalism in question?'

'Second one.'

He looked at me again, seeming a little bewildered. When I met his eyes this time, I somehow knew what he would ask and got my answer ready. 'What's your name?'

I gave it: 'Florian.'

'Florian what?'

Not ready enough; I drew a blank. Did I have to be Florian anything-else? I stared at his chin, but when his eyebrows went up in expectation, said—'Flint.' It had been *their* name, Erik and Sarah's; I'd keep it. Keep it for them. Still, it earned me a snigger from one of the guards. I didn't see anything funny, so ignored it. So did the Captain, whose eyes now shifted to the door.

There was a sudden loud scratching; I looked around just as a large beast bounded into the room – a dog, tall and blue-grey with long legs. It batted its way past the door and darted straight towards me, lunging and nosing me hard in the face.

'Tazen!'

At the shout it bounded back and came to heel beside the tall man who had also entered. A man in white. The guards straightened at his arrival and their Captain nodded from his seat. 'High Commander.'

The man didn't answer, but crossed to the far side of the desk with such elegance and poise that I couldn't help but stare at him. He wore a scabbard on his belt. It was *him*. The white messenger—the soldier on the white horse who had come to our settlement and summoned us to Antissa. Jerome had said that he'd been waiting for our carts at some dry river on the way, but I didn't remember that part. All I remembered of this man was that the last time I'd seen him, Erik and Sarah had been alive.

Without a word he now handed a small tube of paper to the seated Captain, while I gazed at the scabbard. I'd never seen one up close. Then I looked at his face; long, narrow, grave, his skin the colour of milky tea. It was framed by a headdress, the folds of which were held in place by a jewelled silver band. The jewel, blood-red.

Opening the tube and reading its contents to himself, the Captain spoke on a little absently. 'I am . . . sorry about your village, uh . . . boy, but I can't have it seen as permissible that an outsider . . . *even* a boy, uh . . . do insult of damage to the emblem of our Satrap.' He looked up. 'You understand.'

I didn't really, so said nothing. The white messenger was eerily still as he stood there; only once did he move, to make the dog stop frisking about the guards' boots, and even then all it took was a glance. The dog sat.

'You'll spend the night in one of the cells here in the barracks gaol,' the Captain went on, suppressing a yawn, 'and that will be an end of the matter. Next time, of course, less leniency will be shown you.'

The man in white cleared his throat. 'Excuse me, the crime?' And *again* . . .

'Chucked his guts on one of the fortification banners out on the wall,' said the Captain. 'Mooncircle colours.'

There were some moments of thoughtful silence before the white messenger said, 'I see,' and then paused while the Captain carried on reading his tiny paper. 'Could it not be he was ill?'

The seated man puffed, 'Of course, Commander, but he's a borderlander. I can't be half-hearted. I'm certain the Viceroy would not have me—'

'A refugee?' said the white messenger, eyes wider now.

'Yes, one of the new ones.'

Something leapt inside my body as the man they called commander looked directly at me. Down the width of the desk I could see his eyes were grey, much paler grey than his dog. Severe as they were still.

'Captain, it is one thing to punish a child for foolish damage to a flag. It's quite another to admit a border refugee to the High District when their residence in the city remains contentious.' He darted a glance at the guards. 'He should not have been brought here.'

'My men simply—'

'Your men were in error,' said the white Commander more loudly. 'It will draw attention.'

Still seated at his desk, the Captain dropped the paper and raised his palms. 'Very well. The refugees are your business after all. Yours and the Viceroy's. I'll give due instruction to the guard-force.'

'Please do. And be grateful that it was I who walked in on your interrogation, not Symphin. He is most adamant that nothing should tempt the Shield in this matter.'

His accent was even smoother and he spoke so slowly, almost a drawl. I felt power in that. He was important, that was easy; maybe more important than this Captain, but I also thought he looked younger. He began moving round the desk.

'What of the charge then?' said the Captain. I could feel my fate changing hands.

'Charge?' Suddenly huge, the white Commander stepped between the desk-front and the guards to seize my face by the jaw and jerk it sideways. Hard fingers. 'How old *are* you, boy?'

'Twelve,' I managed through the squeeze, and looked past him to the dog, whose pink tongue lolled.

'I'd have said younger. Ten at the oldest,' he corrected me. 'You would charge a boy of ten, Mondric? Wartime is having its effects on you, clearly.'

I was surprised to hear the Captain give a chuckle to this, his pen now scratching across the little tube-paper. 'I'll have you know I once relieved a lad just barely fifteen for throwing mud at those banners,' he boasted.

At that, my face was shoved away, the white-robed back turning on me. 'A Vedan no doubt, who should have known better,' said the Commander.

'There was camel shit in it if I re—'

'This boy knows nothing of our ways, our strictures.' The dog worshipfully watched its master re-circle the desk.

The Captain handed back the tiny paper-tube. 'Well, as for wartime,' he said, 'we're no longer *at* war, are we. We've the Viceroy's word on that. And your own, if you'll permit me.'

In the silence that followed, the white Commander slipped the tube into his sleeve. When the Captain spoke again, it was with less humour in his voice.

'Refuge or no refuge, *ekharan*, I have order to protect. That is rightly *my* business.'

But the Commander didn't seem to be listening to him. He pursed his lips in a low whistle that brought the dog smartly to his leg, and made to leave. 'The boy will *not* be detained in your gaol,' he said. 'Search him if you must but then see to it that he is escorted to his proper quarters in the districts.

Tomorrow morning, have your guards take him back to the wall, that he may himself wash off his *treason*.'

As the white Commander strode for the door, the Captain nodded a little order to his guards. Realising what it was, I retreated to the corner but the men grabbed both my arms, big hands all over my body as I tried twisting to escape. No amount of twisting could resist them. Soon enough they took my wrist and prized my fingers open.

For just a second, blank amazement crossed the fight--breaker's face; his grip eased. Then he claimed the thing out of my hand and let me go. I watched it seemingly float away, still in his hand, until he set it on the edge of the desk. The room went still.

An oval object lay there, no larger than an egg. An egg slightly flattened to a disc. To my mind, anyway, it looked to be made of silver. But no silver I'd ever seen or ever heard of could do *that*.

That *reflection*. Every part of the grey room was captured on its surface: not just reflected, as by a mirror, but magnified, perfected, with more crystal clarity than a mirror even ten times its size. From the Captain's frozen scowl between his papers, to the thinnest thread of sisal fibre worn by the guards, to the finely etched patterns on the handles of the weapons all the way up on the walls, to the insect—no, two insects— dancing in the light of that high window, to the grit between the floor-stones, to the orange of reflected torchlight from beyond the doorway where the white Commander had also stopped to look back – it was unnatural, surely impossible, just how completely it contained every detail around it . . . and *beyond*. My stomach turned again as I remembered the moment I'd pulled it out of my pocket on the city wall; how enormously the plains and the sky had opened; how that vastness had spun me with so much force I couldn't bear it! Far past perfection, it had summoned back the borderlands and the night, the white Rath skin and black Rath eyes. Somehow more vivid in its mirror than it was in my own memory.

As I stood there in the corner, ten feet away, and looked at the thing, I could have counted every sheet of rough-stacked paper on that desk, all the bristles on the Captain's chin, the tiny hairs sprouting from the mole just above his right eyebrow, the finest lines across his forehead. Which now creased deep as he frowned. 'What the . . . what . . . *is* that?'

'Couldn't say,' replied the fight-breaker guard, his voice distant. 'Looks . . . expensive enough, though.' He coughed, uncomfortably, I thought. 'Reckon he nabbed it or something?'

'Looks foreign is what it looks,' said the other, sounding even more ill-at-ease.

'A moment, Mondric, please.' This from the white Commander. He crossed the room again, more briskly, with the dog at his heels and waved the guards to step aside. This time he simply extended a finger to the floor to sit the dog before he stopped. His hand hovered above the thing as if it were a worrisome spider. 'Where did you get this?' he said to me.

I wouldn't say. No. Tell him nothing. What right had he or any of these people to know about the things from Sarah's box? Because that's what it was. That made it mine.

He swung his grey eyes at me. '*Where did you get it?*'

I frowned hard in full defence, but his intensity vanished. He touched the disc and picked it up, holding it near his face. I heard him exhale very lightly, and saw it too, in that mirror. The air at his mouth, I saw it *move.*

'The Viceroy has one,' he said, 'exactly like it.'

'Oh,' the Captain grunted. 'So what is it?'

'He also does not know, I gather. I believe he thinks it to be of Lackish origin perhaps, some manner of evidence that tribes still roam regions of the Dustlands.'

While the dog panted loudly, the Commander ran a finger down the disc's bevelled face. Magnified impossibly, I saw the textures of his skin in the reflection. And the guards behind him, looking away.

The Captain tapped his pen. 'Does he. Well, where did the Viceroy get his one?'

'I've never asked.'

'Same thing exactly?'

'Yes.' The Commander's finger moved beneath it now to stroke along the base. 'Same size, same shape. Same . . . metal.'

The Captain sighed. 'Well fancy that.'

'Brittle arc,' someone added.

I looked at the Commander, who must have said it, but with a sudden flick of sleeve he took a strip of cloth out of his robe and wrapped the disc up inside it. 'Get rid of him,' he ordered with a gesture at me. Suddenly I was the object in the room. 'I don't wish to see him or any other refugees in the Inner City again. This will go to the Viceroy. It may be of some interest. Tazen.'

Slipping it into some pocket of his robe, he made for the door a second time, dog up and close behind him.

Electric panic blazed inside me.

'Give it back!' I shouted.

The dog barked, silenced by a glance as the man turned back. His silver headpiece only just caught the light from the high window. His face was empty, just as it had been when he first entered. For as long as I could, I challenged the empty gaze. That thing was *mine*. A piece of home. Erik and Sarah. I wanted to scream their names at him but had yelled once now already and it had left him unimpressed, I could see. Pond-grey. That was the colour of his eyes.

Behind me the Captain's tone was almost cautious: 'You don't think . . . the boy knows more of it than he's telling? If, that is, the Viceroy's interest in the piece extends that far.'

'I don't think the boy will be leaving Antissa either way,' said the Commander. He pulled the door wide to let the dog out, then left the room.

'You heard him, boys,' said Captain Mondric to his guards, all interest gone with a last sigh. 'No refugees in this district. Get him back to his shelter. See he cleans that banner in the morning.'

From his office they frog-marched me out of the barracks, into evening light. This time I went quietly, at least as far as the white wall and district gate. Then I pulled from their grasp, kicked off my other sandal and ran for it. I'd find my own way back.

Although the air had turned cool, dark was a long time off yet. Shops were closing, keepers drawing down their awnings or canvas. The streets were a little emptier, the boys and the ball thankfully gone when I got to the plaza. The fish, cloth and coal stalls were already closed and the metal shop was silent. A lantern hung above the doorway of the warehouse now, shedding light through shuttered panes that looked different from firelight.

Inside, the shadows of my people played with amber on the walls. There was still some weeping but it had gone much softer now as people warmed their bodies around a central firepit. Some sat and watched the yellow tongues, their tear-streaks shining. Others got ready to sleep, or were sleeping. Others still seemed to keep watch, as if not trusting this new city to stay outside just for tonight. I crept around the room, over the wide wooden shelves, to where Jerome sat perched like a gargoyle. He was one of those watchers, though not a very good one. When I touched him on the shoulder, he jumped. 'Dammit, Florian!' he cursed, a shouted whisper. 'Don't *do* that!'

I crouched beside him. 'Sorry.'

'Where *were* you?'

Sleepers stirred below the shelf-ledge we sat on. 'Shh,' I warned him.

'Don't *shh* me!'

'Where's Con?' I asked, ignoring his protests. 'I never made it to the healers.'

'You've got a lotta nerve, you know that.'

'And you've got some guts standing up to those boys,' I retorted. 'Could've used some help with that.'

'I only got there when the soldier had you!' he lied urgently.

'Guard,' I said.

'What?'

'Not a soldier. A guard.'

But he only punched me in the arm.

'So where's Con?'

'You're not gonna tell me where you went?' he pushed again.

'Just explored a bit, okay.' He probably knew I'd got in trouble, and if he didn't, would find out in the morning anyway.

His eyes dropped to my lip. 'Ooh, that kid really thumped you. Right over—'

'I noticed,' I snapped, batting his hand away from my mouth. '*Is Con back yet or not?*'

Jerome looked down from the ledge, nodding at a lump on the floor right below us. The face was covered by the blanket and a crutch was lying beside.

'Is he . . .?'

'Leg's gonna hurt for a while but he's got the stick,' said Jerome. 'Scared shitless when he got back and you weren't here.' He glared at me.

I rested my mouth on my hand and watched the lump until I saw the rise and fall of slow breathing. While Jerome rolled on his side and curled up into a ball, I let at least five unwanted memories dart through and out of my head. My belly groaned. 'Any food?' I asked.

'None till morning,' he mumbled back. 'Missed it again. Just get some sleep.'

There was nothing else to do but try. And with just one blanket between the two of us, we had to share it top-to-tail. Sleep wasn't easy. And when it came, it brought the dreams: the beasts, the blood and blinding terror, spinning in chaos around me. All so bright and so sharp and so clear . . . *impossibly* clear . . . caught in the mirror of that Disc.

Four

Loquar's Crane

Con had been the first to come back from the healers. I awoke the next day to the wails of loss that met the rest; only a handful. The wardens of our shelter said these were the last. Many more were dead now, and I heard the wardens speak of some black poison which was known by Vorth's army to taint the spears of the Rath. There would be no burials. The bodies, the wardens told us, would burn in city furnaces.

They gave us food, a stodgy porridge in wooden bowls, a little goat's cheese to go with it, and water. The water here was strange – tangy and bitter, not like home's water. I gulped my five measured mouthfuls and missed the River Elm.

Outside the warehouse, the street picked up its business and traffic. And then the fight-breaker guard turned up, as promised, swinging a bucket in his off-hand. There was too much fresh grief and weeping around for anyone to notice me leaving with him. Anyone, that was, except Jerome who dared to follow at a distance.

Not far before the steps of that high fortress wall was a well. The chain being too high for me to reach, the guard attached the bucket and sent it down to the bottom. He made me pull it back up, though, then carry it as best I could, sloshing and slopping, up the steps.

'It's only water, borderlander,' he taunted from three steps behind me, but really enjoying every bit of my struggle to keep my balance. It was so full that, with each slop, the brush inside nearly floated over the rim. My arm was straining, but to swap hands I'd have to stop and I didn't think the guard would let me. I took the top steps at a skip, which was all I could do to keep hold or else tip backwards and fall.

The morning sun scorched my neck as I set it down and rubbed my arm. The guard snorted. 'Got half a mind to send you back,' he rebuked. 'Half the water's on the steps!' It was three quarters full, to be fair. But when I looked up at his face, that brown unshaven Vedish face under the dome of his helm, I realised it was talk. He'd pulled a short straw, I guessed, and didn't want to be here any more than I did.

I looked around. At the scene of my crime now sat a bulky wood and metal structure with an arm that jutted out between the sandstone battlement squares. A man was bent over behind it, peering through a hole in the arm. 'These ropes won't be wanting more molasses,' he said grittily. 'Any more an' the boy'll take best part of a week to drop a yard.'

A rheumy eye lifted from the hole. Ratty grey beard and green turban: it was the old man I'd watched buying metal clinkers yesterday.

'This 'im?'

'It's him,' said the guard.

The old man – keeper of the structure – gave me a grin, wide and yellow. 'Like your heights?' he quizzed me, but I was lost in his ugly cataracts. 'Better start liking 'em, little borderling. Long way down.' He sniffed and drove a thick black stopper into the hole in his machine. 'All in working order.'

With that, he rearranged his turban, lifted a small, sticky-looking drum under his arm, and left us, passing Jerome a few steps down, who was trying as hard as possible to look absorbed in the sandstone masonry.

The guard tapped the bucket with the shaft of his spear. 'Oi, eyes front! Thought old Loquar was here to do the job for you? There's the crane, now get to work.'

'I don't know how,' I said small.

'*How—*' Stopping short, the guard regarded the machine. Then turned and looked back down the steps the way the old man had gone. Ignoring Jerome. But the old man *was* gone. So the guard stepped up to the machine's arm and clapped a hand beside the stopper. He drummed his fingers. It was obvious: my guard had no idea either.

I looked more closely at the thing. The main body of the structure was assembled here on our side of the battlements. I saw a wheel, and a lever there. I went over to the gap through which the wooden arm leaned out, sensing a quick shade of yesterday's dizziness at the height. Well, it was easy enough to see where I was meant to go. A second, shorter pole was chained below the main arm, wound up in rope from one of the holes underneath it. The rope split into two and suspended a plank with a bucket-hole some feet above the banner. Dry now, I could barely even see my streaks of vomit.

At the wheel of the machine, I gave the lever a nudge. The wheel didn't move.

I looked back at the ropes. They looked greasy. Hadn't the old man said something about . . . 'Molasses.'

'What?' the guard nipped back.

'Isn't, um . . . isn't molasses sticky?'

'What of it?'

I knocked my knuckles on the wood of the arm: it was hollow. And there were two more metal holds, and two more stoppers, down its length. 'The ropes run *through* . . .' I thought aloud.

But my guard wasn't listening. He sighed, 'I'll call another engineer.'

'No don't. Wait,' I said, not really hearing myself, and pulled out one of the stoppers. There were two sticky ropes inside, running side-by-side, with little knots at intervals, all basted in the goo that would make them feed more slowly. Through the arm. The guard went over to the wheel and supplied an irritable shove, but it didn't move even one bit. Almost ahead of myself now, I said: 'The wheel's for pulling them *back*.'

Something else caught my eye. At the mid-point, conjoined bars ran through the inside of the arm, capped with handles at both the top and underside. When I pressed up on the lower handle, it started moving. Slowly.

Of course. *Knots.*

'Now what are you doing?'

'These bars are wider in the middle, I think. So that the knots can get through,' I told him.

He circled the crane and looked into the hollow of the arm. And scowled, 'They're not moving.'

So I pushed the double-bar all the way up, until it stopped – until molasses held it fast – then checked inside. But he was right. Even with the knots free to move, the ropes weren't feeding an inch.

'Too much,' I heard myself murmur. That's what the old man, that Loquar, had said. 'Too *much* molasses. It's sticking because there's nothing to pull the ropes out. I've got to be in the chair.'

'So get in.' He wasn't bright.

'We have to pull it up first.'

Expecting no help from him, I went over to the wheel, leaned my weight into the lever and heaved. It slowly started turning but I knew I'd never manage the full five feet of knotted rope.

'Hell's harems!' the guard cursed, batting me aside with his spear-hand. 'Just leave off, will you, before you snap yourself in half.'

He did the wheeling after that, and I went back to the gap to watch the ropes coming in. Up came the plank. The second pole, the lower one, was meant to spread the weight of the load. Surely that couldn't work very well . . .

'There—stop,' I said before the gap closed too much. When I looked back, Jerome was gaping at me. In his eyes, I guessed, I'd just given an order to a man with a helmet and a spear. I pushed the bars home. 'That locks it,' I said. 'But someone's got to *unlock* it again to drop me down, that's how it works. It needs two people.'

'Good thing you brought an assistant then!' declared the guard. He turned and seized Jerome's shoulder, pulling him onto the walkway so hard that he ploughed straight into me. Not a man who liked being shown how things worked, I supposed. 'Maybe I'm a little thick for the Guilds, but I know when someone's standing behind me. Not on the Fortress Guard for nothing. There's puke to clean, boys. I want it off in an hour.'

Soon enough I was in position with my bucket. The seat would never hold a grown man: even under my weight it creaked in ways I didn't like. And even though the face of the fortress wall was just an arm's length away, my knuckles were white around the ropes. I refused to look down, it was too high.

Our guard watched us for some minutes, then lost interest and strolled away along the walkway.

I called up: 'Ready.'

There followed the sound of the bars sliding in. I started to descend, swaying gently. Up came the banner. Down its long face I followed streaks of dry sick.

'There, lock.'

The slide of bars came again, the chair slowing to a stop at the speed of molasses. Overhead, the crane's arm squeaked.

'It s'posed to do that?' Jerome asked from above. I couldn't see him from here; he was still too nervous of the height to come all the way to the edge.

'Hope so,' I said.

'Didn't sound good.'

'Well,' I huffed, 'it's this or—'

'Or what, they chop your hands off?' Now his head popped through the gap next to the arm. But I pretended I hadn't heard him, unnerved by how right he really was. I hadn't even told him about my interrogation in the Captain's office. 'How'd you even know how to work this thing?'

'Just did,' I said, but couldn't help but wonder too. I'd never seen a crane before and yet, somehow, piece by piece, I'd simply felt it making sense. A sort of sense, at least; there must be some better way to build a thing like this.

Jerome snorted contempt. 'These people are just weird if you ask me.'

'I didn't,' I muttered back, carefully letting go of one rope to lift the brush out of the bucket. Then fished for the soap and rubbed the bristles.

Up in the gap, Jerome rested his chin on his forearms. 'Why'd you get sick on it anyways?'

'Didn't do it on purpose, Jerms.'

'Yeh I know. But if you're gonna be sick, kind of a weird place.'

'If you say so.' Aside from his patter, it was quiet. Out here, blocked by the wall of the fortress, the bustle of the districts was a murmur. Our own voices seemed muffled too, muted by the baking-hot sandstone.

'Where'd they take you yesterday?'

'It doesn't matter.'

'Where'd they *take* you?'

I pushed a sigh. 'Can't you just leave it?'

'Come on, Flor, we're best friends. You're s'posed to tell me stuff.'

I scrubbed harder. 'To the barracks.'

'The what?'

'Look, it doesn't matter. Lower me down.'

He disappeared.

Chug, slide – I was eased another foot. 'Lock.'

At first I was too careful of pushing myself off balance for my strokes with the brush to be much use. But the banner's weave was heavy. It displayed, on a pale mauve background, a yellow crescent-moon symbol over a circle of blue. Five white rays darted out from the right side of the circle. The dyes were bleached thin and the weave worn rough by the winds that must have blasted these walls to have left the sandstone around it so scarred. It was filthy as well and so were the others further along. Rain came so rarely to the borderlands; I wondered if it ever came to the desert. So I decided I would do a less-than-perfect job of it in case they noted the improvement and had me doing the rest.

The work took less than an hour, even though I'd been very, very sick and some of the vomit had run all the way down the banner's side-angled tail. There, the fortress wall retreated inwards, leaving me exposed on all sides. I was more careful again. At least it was harder to hear Jerome's annoying questions from here.

Though I'd told myself I wouldn't, I turned and looked behind my shoulder. Back across the plains of Vorth. They were so vast, brown-grey between their far fringes of gold, and scored with lines of rock striation. Yesterday the air had been too full of dust to see the dunes on the horizon, but now I could, if only just.

The "north" wall was what they called this, wasn't it? That meant the borderlands were *that* way, and home and family were out there; still out there, *had to* be out there. But no, they weren't anymore. And never would be again. I knew I shouldn't have looked. Just like the sick from my stomach yesterday I felt the ache rise in my throat, a wet-hot burning from my chest.

All that was out there were the Rath.

'Hurry up.'

Jerome's voice called me back to my body—dangling in mid-air I remembered—and I grabbed the ropes tighter. Splashing more water on blue weave, I went on scrubbing the tail. Only once I'd swallowed down that sting and thought my voice could be trusted, did I ask: 'Con know we're here?'

'Nah, sleeping.'

Scrubbing harder, now wanting to be back behind the wall again, I weighed my next question. 'Gonna tell him?'

No reply.

I kept on scrubbing but peered up, squinting in sunlight. His face had disappeared from the gap now. And it was quiet.

'You still there?' I dropped my brush into the bucket. 'Jerms?' Slow footsteps approached; they weren't the guard's.

With that same cool elegance, the white headdress and robe appeared where Jerome's head had been. The red jewel flashed. My heartbeat skipped. Without looking down, the white Commander scanned the plains. Did he even know I was here? He *had* to know; I was only here at his bidding. After another minute of silence, I reached for my brush again.

'That's clean enough.' I dropped it. 'You're to come with me now, to the Deep. The Viceroy craves a word with you.'

I wiped my forehead on the inside of my arm, staring up with difficulty, but still he didn't look down. The rapid grunt of jogging boots came from the left side of the crane.

'Begging pardon, High Commander,' puffed my guard. 'Was just a little way along the wall there, never far.'

'Yes I saw you.'

'Had my eye on him all the time.'

'I'm sure you did. In any case nothing *treasonable* appears to have happened in your absence.'

I heard the guard swallow through his panting, before the white Commander at last deigned to look down. Nothing more than a fleeting glance at me before his gaze swept on again.

'The boy is finished. Bring him up.'

FIVE

ENGINEER

My legs bounced up and down against the flanks of the white horse. I towered above the crowds that now parted ahead of us and scuttled along the sandy ridges of the buildings like mice. Shopkeepers drew back under their awnings and the guards with black capes stood to attention at the gate in the white wall. Hooves clapped on cobbles. Red granite estates looked on through latticed, balconied windows, their roofs of ruddy orange tiles pressing inward toward the palace like vying subjects. I tilted back against the Commander's chest for a better look. Up there, a shell of timber scaffolds surrounded one of the great domes. Above it the spire flashed in sunlight, the glare blinding.

He rode on past the barracks steps I'd been hauled up yesterday, through a smaller side gate, into a wide gravel yard at the side of the palace. Crowds were everywhere again. But unlike those of the lower streets these moved in lines; men and women, all filmed with grey powder, pushing wheelbarrows of earth and blasted rock from a tall doorway in the wall of the palace, to the adjacent district's gate. The tall doorway seemed to cough them into the yard on clouds of dust. That same grey dust they were covered in.

Not far from those tall doors, the white Commander reined his horse to a side-winding halt and dismounted. Then he coaxed me out of the saddle and, with firm hands under my arms, lifted me down. My bare feet landed in the gravel.

'Keep close,' he bade me, as someone dressed in a plain thobe and cowl took the reins and led the horse away somewhere else. Holding a cloth up to his mouth, the Commander strode towards the coughing doorway. I obeyed and followed him through the haze, my eyes and nose itching and stinging from the particles that floated into them. Snorting and sneezing and rubbing my face, I nearly ran straight into one of the lines of grey people. 'Keep close!'

Noise raged beyond the doors: a distorted thrash and grind of industry. Another crane arced overhead – this one much bigger than the one out on the wall – raising a massive scoop of rock that leaked hissing showers of earth and smaller stones between the claws of a seeming hand, up out of a chasm in the floor. The load rocked high above our heads, that metal-muscled arm of the crane then groaning off to one side. I cringed at the noise of the huge hand tilting forward on grating joints, and then the crash of the rubble's tumble through the chute underneath. The rubble then avalanched down through the gloom and coughed dust towards detachments of grey people and their waiting wheelbarrows.

None of this seemed to faze the white Commander, who was heading for the chasm itself. As we came nearer, I could see that it wasn't so much a chasm as a jagged-edged drop into more gloom.

Then I saw the steps: edging the chasm's inside wall, a stone spiral of steps, going down. 'Don't trip,' the Commander snapped over his shoulder. The chalky spores were still floating at my face when I peered down into the darkness and decided: I wouldn't. With my eyes pinned fast to his robes, hand to the wall, I followed down. But the spiral couldn't have made more than three laps of the chasm wall before it opened into passages of brick.

Close here. Dimly lit. More noise filled up the passages: hammers on metal, blades through timber, the gush of steam and scrape of coal-spades. Bolts stuck out above crude arches and box-lanterns dangled from them, shining with greenish, milky light. Just like the one above the door of our warehouse, there was no flame behind their shutters. Nor any time to look closer; not if I wanted to keep up.

More stairs took us deeper and the brickwork gave way to rough-hewn sandstone. Here the lanterns hung from iron lintels that spanned the width of every passage. The walls were powdery again, as if these passages were fresh, and my feet were soon matt grey to the ankles. Grey workers continued to surge past us with their gravel. Among them, suddenly—that turban! Coughing at the dust churned by the rush of feet and wheels, I glanced back and saw it bob away in the busy current. Green, I was sure.

Through the arches we passed, I saw men and women huddled in teams, seeming to measure things with angled sticks, poring over parchments broad as bedsheets. We were two levels down now, and yet I could feel in my knees the grumbles even deeper down than this. How far down did it go? And how far down did the Commander intend to take me?

As I wondered, he turned a corner and stopped, white robe-ends swaying as if they'd meant to go on. We'd come to a door that stood ajar, and through its sliver of orange light I heard two voices. Arguing.

'*One more word about the Sanhedrin's plans for fifth and I'll blow an erg-damned gasket!*'

'*You can't simply ignore them because they're not men of your Guild.*'

'I'm not *ignoring* them, I'm working *around* them. How exactly do you expect me to accommodate these plans? The Deepworks would have brought down the entire *citadel* by now had I proceeded according to the Sanhedrin's ideas!'

'The border is breached'—*that* voice I knew—'Such would justify more than a few of their concerns, I should think. This is a potential solution. We *cannot* continue to send parties to the coast.'

'I'm aware of that. But, as you are *equally* aware, we've yet to see movement south of the Empty River.'

'It'll come! And when it does, I'll not continue to place the Fortress Guard at risk.'

A sudden slam set off a mechanical rattling inside the room, which then choked out.

'Whether it pleases the Sanhedrin or not, Mondric, five years from now our pipes may well be drawing up mud.'

A snort. 'Be serious, *five years!* There's been a settlement here for five hundred.'

'Perhaps that's *why!* So I ask you again how you can refuse to see the insanity—'

'Because the Satrap decrees it!'

Beside me, the Commander shifted on his boots and tucked his little cloth away. 'Stay here,' he said and pushed his way into the room. As his body eclipsed the orange glow from inside, the talking stopped. 'I have the boy,' he said, muffled.

'Thank you, would . . .'

The door was heeled closed and the sliver of light disappeared. Alone in the tunnel, I thought of trying to sneak away, up to the surface, back to the warehouse. But could I trust myself to find my way back through the maze? Moments turned to minutes. I listened to the voices on the other side of the door, now unable to make out any words. The two who argued were the loudest, while the Commander's tone was calm and steady between them.

And then the door was flung wide open and a man filled the threshold. *'Expect me to raise my eyebrows with the rest of the viziers!'* he blasted over his shoulder. It was the Captain of the Guard.

'Raise them all you like!' the other voice shouted from inside.

The Captain saw me. He grimaced, *'You* again?' and spun on his heel to hold the door. 'High Commander, you gave me specific instruction about the border refugees.'

'Be on your way, Mondric, it is an exception,' was the reply, to which the Captain clenched his fists and fumed, but didn't say anything else. Making his exit and slamming the door so hard it bounced back on its hinge, he stormed away down the tunnel.

'Call him in then,' the voice inside said. 'The boy, I mean.'

I didn't want to go in. The other man who was in there sounded angry and far too fierce. Had I really deserved all this, I thought, whatever punishment it was I'd been brought here to receive? All I'd done was throw up! But as the door swayed half-open again, rebounding from the slam, the white Commander beckoned me in with a terse jerk of his head. My legs moved me forward as if I were no better than his dog.

I stepped around the door, and stood still.

If the crane on the wall, or the one at the cavernous entrance, had seemed like a thing from another world, then this here was that world. The ceiling was low, vaulted across with buttresses that made it look like the inside of a kiln. The russet bricks were lit by more of those strange, flameless lanterns; these ones with tan window-shutters that filtered the green light into yellow. Everywhere I looked, machines filled space: great sleeping, black-metal brutes with too many limbs, too many elbows and knees and oily, toothy pins and spines and spokes. Workbenches seemed to push their way from under heaps of metal things, towards the light where they could get it. Heaps of parts and segments of things. Joinings, plates, wheels, levers, pedals, cogs. And *tools*—so many different kinds of tools!—many still attached to the last thing they'd done or were halfway through doing. Those little nuggets with holes – the clinkers – were everywhere as well: far beyond count, they overflowed out of boxes and spilled from cups. The floor was scattered with them too, some trapped and twinkling in the grooves between the bricks. Over there, on a table, I saw some contraption of wood and silver metal, only partially assembled. It had cords like a crossbow, but also springs and gears and triggers . . .

That rattling noise had started again, drawing my attention to the far side of the room. A man was standing there with his back to us, turning a lever that made the rattle. 'That fool urgently needs his rivets realigned,' he said loudly to compete with the rattle. 'Better yet, fully replaced!'

'He's only following orders,' the white Commander replied.

'Orders meant for *me*, you mean, orders from the *tower!* How else should a man like Shandar Mondric—'

'He does not, of course, Viceroy, merely expects he might take appropriate initiative ahead of your decision. He is old-fashioned. A guardsman.'

'Then he should mind his own guard-force and leave matters that concern the Sanhedrin to me.'

The man was very cross, clearly, but the Commander's tone never changed. 'With respect, that is what he is doing, in his way. You may be glad of it yet.'

'He's being bull-headed,' snapped the cross man. 'Have we need of more oxen in this city?' The rattling went on for another minute or more while the cross man's voice repeated itself strangely in my head: clear and sharp and quick, his sentences barely broken by a breath. Nor was his accent like the others I'd heard so far. There was something else in it; something I was sure I'd heard before.

The rattle stopped.

'So I'm told you've been scrubbing down our banners. Hate to think when last those rags saw a brush. What do you think of Loquar's crane?'

This was to *me*. It was, wasn't it?

'It's, uh . . . clever.'

'It's a death-trap. A wonder your skull didn't end up the way of last year's pottery on those crags. Remember Sachin, poor girl—' He threw a glance back at the Commander who must know who he was talking about and, as he did, I saw his mustard-coloured skin, a flattened jaw, sharp-flitting eyes. This man was shorter than the white Commander but a little taller than the Captain. Older than both.

The crane. It *wasn't* clever—I'd just panicked and said the first thing that came into my head. So, 'It doesn't need the second pole,' I added, then instantly wished I hadn't.

The man turned around, rubbing a rag over his palms to lift some grease. 'And all that *erg-damned* molasses,' he agreed with me fiercely. 'I've told him much the same thing.' He rubbed a bit harder at the grease, then briefly glanced at my face.

I looked at him. His surcoat was an amalgam of dense burlap, black hide and yellow metal. It looked like a kind of armour. At his waist was a thick belt with so great a weight of holstered tools attached, I was sure that it could drown a larger man. And he wore a kind of leather cap with earlaps and a neck-guard, all pressed close to his head by goggles tied tight at his forehead. I'd never seen clothing like this in my life and, as he struggled with the grease, found it hard to stop staring.

He'd asked my name.

'Uh, Flor—'

'Speak up, the Deep vibrates,' he said.

'Florian,' I said more loudly. Adding, 'Flint,' almost too late.

'Flint, yes, that's it. Yesterday's refugees. Trusting the shelter is adequate.' If this had been a question, he gave me no time to answer it. He seemed impatient or pressed for time. Grimacing at the stubborn grease, he said, 'You'll be wondering why you're here, then. Let me assure you we need no more of the colours rubbed down.'

I cringed. How much of that story did he actually know? Here in this room full of mechanical wonders, it seemed so stupid. But now the man gave up on the grease with a scowl, pushed away from the worktop with the rattle-machine and walked into the middle of the room, his eyes on me. Somehow, although they were a kind of murky brown, or maybe green, they were piercing.

'I'm Rusper Symphin,' he said. 'I am, as you may or may not have gathered, Antissa's Chief Engineer.'

A pause. Was I meant to say something?

'In addition, during the Satrap's temporary indisposition, I hold the office of Viceroy to the throne.'

'Is this really necessary, Caliph Symphin?' interrupted the white Commander. He'd read my mind: why did I need to know this?

But the engineer ignored the question and merely gestured to the taller man standing behind me. 'You've met my martial associate, High Commander Plamen, I believe. He is official aide to the Viceroyalty at this time.' He took a short breath and pushed it out, his nostrils flaring a little. 'Something was taken from you yesterday.'

The Disc. It was here! Inside this room. I don't know how I did it but I froze up my muscles then, willing myself not to glance around in search of it.

'Come,' the man coaxed. 'I know full well that you remember. The Captain's guards gave me your name. Now I've called you here to see me quite simply because I'm interested in whatever you can say about the object.'

My heart started to race and my throat twisted shut. It didn't take long for my silence to annoy him and he narrowed his eyes.

'Are you going to stand there and gape like a cretin, or speak?' he said coldly, sounding much more as he had when arguing with the Captain before. But I didn't care, deciding in that moment that nothing of my home was theirs to know. I clamped my teeth and ground them hard.

He shot a look at the Commander. 'Plamen, you've brought me a mute.'

'Only as tasked.' Their eyes met but didn't hold.

Then, without warning, the engineer sighed enormously and turned around. 'Did you see that chain of keys?'

The Commander's calm seemed unbreakable. 'No, Viceroy.'

'*There* they are! *What in . . .*' The engineer thrust his arm straight through the eye of a cogwheel, grabbing something that jangled with a slight echo. As a ring of keys emerged in his grasp, he muttered acidly, '*That old fool at it again . . . keeps this up, by dredth . . . long walk in the desert . . .!*'

Flicking through the keys, the man called Rusper Symphin crossed the room. In the corner, that corner farthest from me, he unlocked the door of a narrow, vertical cabinet. And even at my distance I saw the Disc come out of hiding. Returning, the man dragged a stool out from a workbench to the space that spanned between us and set the thing down on its seat.

In the impossible mirror, my face remained somehow undistorted by its curve. Intensely reflected, I could trace every pore of tanned skin and every strand of black hair. How did it *do* that – make everything around it seem less real than its own reflection? Like my hair, my eyes had always been too dark to tell from black and yet in the face of the Disc it was clear—so *very* clear—that they were brown. My lip did a tremble and I saw it before feeling it move; caught the twitch of engineer's arm before he put both arms behind his back.

'Whittle's mark.'

I looked up at him, not knowing what those words meant, but he didn't repeat them. 'I've spent the better part of a lifetime behind these walls,' said Rusper Symphin more slowly. 'And I can assure you that you'll find nothing like this item anywhere else in Antissa, nor anywhere in Vorth for that matter. We Vedans are not known for our trinkets.'

So much of me wanted to tell him that it wasn't just a "trinket." But did I know that? And if it wasn't a trinket, what was it?

He went on: 'I suspect you brought it to our city. Am I correct?'

Not really listening, or trying not to, I looked deep into the little mirror on the stool. In it, behind my shoulder, I could so clearly see the face of High Commander Plamen, watching me like a predatory white bird. So easily, I could outline the pattern of sparring lions on the brooch that pinned his headdress at the throat . . .

Rusper Symphin was still speaking: 'Does it hail from Naemia, then, as you do?'

I broke my gaze from the mirror and frowned at him. We weren't having this talk, let him see it.

'Very well, let us for the moment assume that's where it's from. Is it a jewel perhaps, or a relic of some kind? Something obtained from the bastion of the Celestri?'

How dare he talk about that! That was *my* family's story, not his. I turned my frown to the floor, but now that I'd remembered them, found I couldn't unthink them again: their faces forming out of pockmarks in the bricks. Sarah. Erik. Like bile, the tears started rising.

'Alright then. If you can't, or won't, tell me what it is, at least tell me how you came by it. Did you find it? Buy it, steal it, what? Was it given to you?' Patience thinning, he rolled his eyes and addressed more questions to the ceiling. 'Is it an heirloom, a household token?'

I squeezed my eyes shut. Stop talking, just *stop*.

'I haven't the time for this,' he scowled. 'You must know something about it, boy, if it was found in your possession, so —desert take it—speak!'

Both my eyes and throat suddenly opened. I looked at him, raised my chin, parted my lips. I'd tell him something, but anything else: that I was a different boy – the wrong boy. I had nothing to do with all this. But that wasn't what came out.

I said: 'Give it back.'

Though his face almost seemed to clear of annoyance when I said it, the clever eyes held. 'Why?' he said.

'Because it's mine.'

A tiny glint happened inside the brown – or green? - eyes.

'No, it isn't.' He took a step forward and stooped over the stool. At his flat denial of my property, I felt the wild urge to dash out and snatch the Disc before he could claim it again, but he didn't even touch it. Instead he opened his left hand and placed right beside it, a twin. '*That* one is yours.'

Two.

My eyes darted between them, a race. How had I forgotten the Commander had said that yesterday? Had I simply not believed him? Well, who would? They were the same. The same *exactly*. In size and form. And . . . metal. And in ways that hurt my head to look at for more than fleeting seconds.

'I've had this for over ten years,' Rusper Symphin was saying, 'it's arrival equally lacking in explanation. If that's possible. And now, at a time when far too much is unexplained, you appear with another.' He paused with lips ajar. 'You have to understand. Many now believe we face the very same invasion to which your own country succumbed years ago. But we have enemies of our own, enemies older than your Rath, and reason to believe that such as these may be weapons of *their* making.' He paused again to put some softness in his tone. 'I have the trust of the Satrap to ensure that this fortress stands secure. Don't you . . .'

No I didn't, I decided, even before his shoulders sagged as if he'd just read from my face how pointless it was to ask another question. That thing, that Disc, was mine. Sarah's and mine. Whatever it was! It had nothing to do with his city and his problems.

Or was it that one?

'Riddle's bark.'

Before I could even bother making sense of what that meant, new voices bellowed down the tunnels outside the room. Above the sounds of ongoing industry, someone barked a string of orders. Boots drummed on stone somewhere a level above. Commander Plamen went to the door and looked out; the engineer alert. 'What is it?'

'Iron Shield,' said Plamen, returning.

'*Again?*' Rusper Symphin swept both Discs from the stool – one in each hand – and pegged the Commander with a glare. 'This child cannot be found here.'

'Perhaps put him out of sight until the patrol is over.'

He chewed his lip. 'No, can't risk it. Get him out.'

He couldn't do this. '*I want it back!*' I shouted.

The sharp glare swung. 'And you may yet have it. When you're a little more forthcoming,' Rusper Symphin replied, returning to the vertical cabinet and slamming both inside again. 'Now disappear.'

The Commander's cool fingers settled on my neck; he ushered me out. As he hurried me back through the Deep, he favoured ladders over stairs, as well as a winch-worked rising platform, to avoid the "patrol" that scoured its levels of tunnels for whatever stupid reason. Up the wide spiral of steps, back above the chasm, he pressed me on through the thick of grey people and wheelbarrows, and then lost me as I ran toward the light of the tall door.

SIX

DASKH AND THE DISC

'Where d'you keep popping off to?'

'Nowhere.'

Con skewed his eyebrows at me and drummed his knuckles on the crutch. He hadn't asked me about the cut on my lip yet; for all he knew it had happened on the night of our escape. He had a dark bruise on his forehead too. But he wasn't stupid.

'Tell me next time you go nowhere, alright? It's a big place, this city.'

Sitting on the discarded crates outside the warehouse with Dewar and Mother Far, we watched the comings and goings of the street. Con and Dewar were talking now, while Jerome's eyes fed on my face like a pair of hungry suckers. He'd always hated when I had secrets and would just stare at me, like now, as if those secrets were bugs in my hair he could pick out and study by pulling their legs off. It wasn't subtle and wasn't helping me stop thinking about the place inside the palace's hill they called the "Deep." Or the Discs. One of which belonged to me. That engineer didn't know or care about the treasures I'd lost. What if he mixed them up, or lost them?

I'd made it back to the shelter in time for midday water, but the sun was so hot I was already thirsty again. Mother Far's thirst was worse, I could tell by the way she kept on kneading her throat. Three cups a day wasn't enough, not in this heat. Dewar was, right at that moment, saying much the same thing to Con.

'How long do they expect us to go on like this?' he said, eye-balling the chutes above our heads. I'd heard them called "aqua-ducks" or something like that. 'What's their plan here? What about the elderly, and the children?'

'They've given us a roof, and food and water,' said Con. Calm, so like Erik I thought, and it stung. 'And we're safe, at least for now.'

'Yeah . . .' growled the older man. 'Come off it, you've seen the way they look at us. The Vedans don't want us here.'

'Dewar, we'd all be dead if they hadn't let us into Antissa.'

'That doesn't mean I have to trust any Antissans!'

Jerome was still staring at me. I hissed—'*What?*'—and with an awkward shuffle he looked away. Two minutes later he left his crate and came to sit by me, on mine.

'Listen Flor,' he said, using his best secret voice. 'I dunno what they want with you but you just gotta run next time, okay?'

I looked away. 'You told Con yet?'

'No.'

'Well, don't.'

'Only if you promise,' he nagged, 'to just run.'

'Fine.'

'Promise!'

'*Promise*,' I forced.

Evening came. The heat ebbed off; the street went quiet. Wardens returned, lit the lantern at our door and tumbled fresh coal into the pit. High though they were, the fortress walls didn't hold in the day's warmth long after sunset. The brown-clad men and women moved through the warehouse with the baskets that snapped and crackled as if in tune to early flames. Our people murmured, uneasy, but a little calmer than before. No one was weeping tonight, at least not at the moment. From the corner we had claimed I scanned the faces in their clusters. Mother Far as she dozed, Dewar as he rubbed her shoulder to wake her gently. Blearily she raised her hands to the food the warden gave her, and said 'Thank you.'

Something tightened in my chest.

'You alright there, Flor?' said Con.

I nodded, automatic.

When water came to our corner, we all drank it in the smallest of sips and in silence. Then came the food; four thin strips of spiced meat to a head. They didn't say what meat it was and no one asked, but it was good: better than the bread, though slightly dry and I could have done with one more gulp of water to wash it down with. But there wouldn't be any more, not till tomorrow.

Jerome fell asleep, but I stayed up with Con by the firepit. On his leg, red blotches had surfaced through the dressing he'd been given. He knew it had to be changed; along with many of the others, he'd have to go back to the healers. Our eyes met over the bandage. 'Does it hurt?' I asked him.

'Not like before,' he admitted, rolling his eyes at the memory. I didn't want to ask but knew I had to. He'd only been hurt because of me, and if it weren't for him I would be dead.

'How did it happen?'

For a while he only stared at the bloody clouds on the bandage. When he did speak again his voice sounded like it had those years ago when I'd asked about the fish carved by his father in Naemia. 'I couldn't see you anymore when I made it back to the village. And there was so much screaming I couldn't think straight.' He stopped. I waited. 'The Rath broke up and surrounded the huts. There weren't that many of them, maybe only a dozen.'

'No,' I interrupted, 'there were more. Much more than that. About thirty or forty.'

He shook his head. 'Maybe it feels that way, Florian, but it wasn't so many.'

It didn't sit right. Reluctantly, I let the bright-electric terror of the memory back into my mind's eye for a moment. Surging through the fog, I saw the blurry rabble, moving, running, and those that broke ahead sprinting on all-fours like pack dogs. It made my heart race so I fogged it all back up again quickly.

'Everyone was so scared,' Con was saying, still shaking his head as if he'd forgotten to stop it, eyes going far away. 'Some ran straight into their spears, not knowing how to escape, only knowing they had to run, try to get away, get to the river. I saw a boy fall with a spear in him and . . . well, I knew Jerome was at the carts already. I thought it was *you*.'

There was a shimmer on his eyes; I willed myself not to look away from them.

'But it wasn't.' He took a breath. 'I was almost there, at our hut, when I saw one of them going inside. So I ran harder, thinking that's where you'd be if you were anywhere. But they were so damn *fast*, those . . .' His face creased up. He bit his lip. He was going to swear, I could tell. But he didn't. 'Those *things*! And they just came out of nowhere. Bastard pulled me down and stuck my leg. I don't remember the pain—must've had a weak one or something—but I grabbed the spear off him and tried to spike him right back with it. The spear just broke though, so I threw it and . . . ran.' Only now, touching the top of his thigh, did he wince. 'You know about the poison. Guess I was lucky.'

Gloomily, I looked into the coals of the pit. Inside my head I could still hear Con's voice as he ran. Ran to my rescue, calling my name. If I didn't say it to him now, I never would.

'Thanks.'

'For what?' he said, not looking at me.

'You know,' I mumbled.

But he looked up and narrowed his eyes; those clear eyes I'd trusted ever since I was eight. He'd never been the kind of boy, or man, to brag of things, but my heart sank now that his modesty would force me to say it.

'For saving my life,' I said, embarrassed at how the words sounded aloud. 'For pulling me out of the hut. For getting me on the cart in time.' Hoping it would stop the heat from rising to my cheeks, I nodded firmly, several times. But when I looked at him again his eyes weren't only clear, but vacant. It was one of those moments when he looked like Jerome. His shoulders tensed.

'Florian, I didn't find you in the hut. That Rath had gone too. It was empty,' he said. 'Some of Sarah's things were lying over the floor, but there was nobody in there.'

I stared at his face.

'When I got to the carts at the shallows, I was bleeding really badly and starting to black out. But I saw you. You were there before me.'

Before I could think of something to say to that, he smiled sadly and reached across his crutch to hold my shoulder. Like Erik, again.

'What happened won't be easy to forget,' he said softly. 'Maybe we never will. But we're here now, and we're safe. And we're together, the three of us. That's what we've got. We'll look after each other. Okay?'

'Mm-hm,' I nodded. Automatic.

I helped him up so he could go back to our corner and sleep. Then I flopped back down and simply gazed at the coals and cast-iron rim of the pit, not knowing what I should think. On the iron, badly tarnished, was a relief of rearing lions – lions with big feathery wings. Lions didn't have wings, what was wrong with this place? Jerms was right, Antissans *were* weird.

After a while I went back into our corner as well, picked at the end of the blanket on Jerome, pulled it over my head and cushioned my cheek in my palm.

Warmth came quickly, but sleep didn't. A small dog dashed over the dust of the plain, to ready spears. There again was the monster with those blue marks on its white skin and two black eggs of eyes on me. I'd not dreamed any of it. And there was the Disc's mirror as I pulled its cloth away. Con called. He called again, again, again.

That creature *would* have killed me.

How was I alive?

Erik . . . Sarah . . . I reined those tears back with the force of anger and buried my head deeper in the warmth of the blanket, hoping harder than I'd yet let myself hope that it hadn't been too bad. I'd never know. Not *ever*. I wasn't alone in my thoughts, I knew that, as all around me now the sobs grew into weeping through the warehouse. And there they were, Con and Jerome, both by my side, as Con had said. They were like brothers to me, yet now somehow it made no difference.

My fist was slicked-up with sweat by the time I remembered that the Disc wasn't in it.

The Disc. Could it have . . . *possibly* . . . ?

Next morning, I was the first in the warehouse to wake up, Jerome's foot kicking me in the face. Untangling myself from his legs, I went to the door and sat under the lantern in the hush. The fortress wall was a shadow; one I hoped would just stay that way. I didn't want the sun to break over its battlements, flood the streets and turn the houses back to yellow. I didn't want another day. But the day didn't care. At the top of the street, through the empty plaza, a single vendor trundled his cart between the covered market-stands. Shutters opened to his first cries of 'Salt!'

Guards were everywhere in the streets between our warehouse and the big palace, making it impossible to return to the engineer's "Deep." No borderland refugee could get much farther than the plaza. Even if he wanted to.

The metal-seller next door was an engineer too, I soon learned. I figured that easily enough listening to his customers talk: they all spoke about something called the "Engineering Guild." All through the day, his bits of metal would fall and land in the dust, either dropped by mistake or discarded as junk from the counter. He didn't seem to notice or mind, though I only took and kept the ones that rolled close enough. Jerome took some as well, liking the round ones with holes and flat sides. By the end of the third afternoon he'd scored six. I was less picky, collecting ten different kinds of pieces in the same time: dark grey nuggets, threaded rods, flattened circles, tiny spheres. Bluish, greenish, yellow. Gold? Not really gold, I knew. But all of them were gems, even those rusted red and brown and fully black. And on the crates and in the sand against the wall, and in the dust, we made them soldiers in pitched battles against white stones where we could find them. It was something, anyway. A small distraction. But even then, I was only ever half distracted by the game.

Through the sandals that flapped past us, I kept one eye on the street. I watched the shops on the other side, getting to know the faces and the looks.

The three merchants who faced our warehouse would greet each other in the morning, but that was all. They never laughed or smiled or talked, not with each other. Nor would their eyes stray very far from the *fourth* stall, some way along; a stall that smoked and squawked from under a plain canvas awning inscribed with the words, "Effod's Daskh." Scruffy men and women were always sitting around about it, puffing on pipes.

The next day, our fourth day in the city, there was a change when the fish-shop didn't open in the morning. Noon came and went and the flaps of yellow canvas still hung closed.

Then I saw him again. The old man from the crane. As soon as I spotted his green turban in the crowds, I was sure. It *had* been him I'd seen down in that Deep-place. *Loquar*. Like a rodent from an underground burrow, he scurried toward the stalls I'd been watching. Then suddenly crossed back to our side, as if changing his mind. He waited a while there, looking over at the closed yellow flaps. Only when a group of customers moved from the purple fabric-stall to the red-and-white-stripe coal stall, did he cross over again, making his way towards the purple with such suspicious-looking movements that I thought he might try to steal something from her. Surely he didn't have a chance of simply melting away into the crowds with a yard of silk under his arm! He didn't try. The merchant woman caught his eye and glared with interest, leaning forward as he came.

Which was exactly when a brace of donkeys stalled right there in front of me, blocking my view. As their drivers cursed, and Jerome nudged me to get back to our game of stones and nuggets, I craned my neck. But couldn't see, not from here. So I got up, ignoring the whine of '*Flo-rrrr . . .!*' behind me, and went to where Loquar had been standing before. Across the fly-whipping tails of the donkeys, I could see him speaking hurriedly with the woman who sold the cloth. He showed her something, though they'd both turned their shoulders against any onlooking eyes. I edged forward.

'Move, borderlander!' One of the drivers took a swipe at my head. I ducked.

'Step away, Florian!' Dewar snarled, his anger aimed at the drivers as he grabbed my arm and pulled me back towards our doorway. He held me to him, waving a stiff apology to the men, though probably meant as something else. With his big arms draped over my chest, I watched the donkey-driver spit and curse his animals, then try to push them from behind. Such was his mood that if I got in his way again, I didn't doubt that he would strike me. And by the time he had persuaded his beasts to move again, and cleared off, Loquar was gone.

Leaving a strange, smug smile on the woman's lips.

News came the next day from beyond the fortress walls; we overheard it from the wardens. To the north, Rath had attacked the last borderland settlement, and its survivors were now headed for Antissa with soldiers.

Last settlement. To them it meant nothing, but to us, those were the last Naemians left alive in the whole world. The last of us. At sunset, I watched from a safe place above the gates as the line of carts climbed the rocky track of the hill. Jerome watched beside me, though his big staring eyes would drop every time I tried to meet them. There were more than forty Naemians: dirty, ragged, shaking Naemians; some so badly wounded that I was sure they were dead. No children were among them, or any as old as our own Mother Far. The sounds of their pain rose to meet us, picking at the scabs of our own and making me wonder why we'd come to watch at all.

The soldiers who escorted them dispersed inside the gate, guards barking orders to keep the new arrivals in line and moving forward. Towards the warehouse. The healers took twelve of the injured ones, and the next morning five returned.

Despite the crowding of our shelter, the engineer next door reclaimed the annexe we had used – the small stone building in which I'd first woken – and filled it up with his metal. In a blistering temper he took back all the shiny metal cast-offs we had won, screeching so loudly at me and Jerome for our *theft* that his tanned face went nearly purple. Jerome stopped sitting outside after that, although he said it was just because it was so hot.

Then things got worse. We still had food twice, and water three times, every day. But now the food was changeless: a stodgy muck of tasteless oats thickened with a very bitter oil, and no more meat or vegetables. Consistent without kindness, the wardens lit the lantern and the firepit at dusk, but didn't give us more blankets when ours would no longer go around. They never addressed any of us. Questions were always ignored. There was no privacy either. A single rat-eaten rag hung between the eyes of everyone and our more personal ablutions. Wash-water was scarce. Like Con, even the freshly injured had seen barely enough for their faces, hands and feet at the healers. Wounds had been cleaned against infection. That was all. These were my people, I knew, but they all stank of dirt and shit before long, almost impossible to bear in the full heat of the day.

I didn't care about the sun, much less the angry engineer next door. In the daytime I'd sit out on the crates and watch the flow of passing, chatting, shouting, haggling Antissans with lives that hadn't been broken yet. I envied them the vended foods they bought and ate in front of us: shelled nuts, dried fruits, salted jerky, biscuits and dumplings, boiled crab and cured fish. Mugs of beer. Rich black coffee in copper cups; served cold, I saw, but rapidly heated by a quick turn in barrel-tops of sun-baked sand. These were the district's better smells, even if I couldn't share any of their tastes. They made me think about other things. Like how crab and fish had reached the desert city, far as we were here from the sea.

And all the while I kept an eye out for the little green turban. Loquar had been in the Deep, I was convinced of it now. He was my link to the Discs.

The yellow flaps were closed again come the next morning and stayed that way. But sure enough, just after noontime, I spotted Loquar.

This time he stayed well away from the purple cloth-stall, waiting until the woman became distracted by her trade before hurrying across towards the coal-stall instead. The merchant beckoned urgently to him, but before I could see what came out of the turban, a red-and-white flap flopped closed. Almost blocking my view. I saw the string-bound bag change hands.

Loquar stepped back into the crowds.

Checking first for any backhands or kicks coming from the street, I slunk along the warehouse wall. But Loquar only went as far as "Effod's Daskh" before he wove away again to the opposite side. Right outside the stone building where our wardens kept their post, he stopped. Waited and watched. I watched in turn until, from a residential terrace above the stall, a shawled old woman came down through the smokers' fumes to hang her washing. I'd seen her do it every day so far and hadn't really noticed. But Loquar, clearly, expected her. When her laundry covered the line, forming a screen between the stalls, he crossed the street. I followed quickly and hid behind it, just as Loquar plunged his head into the smoke under the awning. 'Make it sharp, Eff,' he scraped.

Something squawked inside the stall. Then came another voice: 'What goods you got?'

I peered between a pair of shirts to see Loquar drop the coal-man's bag on the counter and tease it open with a blackened finger. There was a shuffle as the merchant withdrew into the smoke and shouted back.

'That's the one,' answered Loquar. Then the merchant said something else that made the old man cackle.

'What you laughin' at?'

'Remembered a joke.'

'You gave me lousy stuff before. Turns to ash afore it even gets into the bowl, as like!'

'So what you wanting for it then?' said Loquar.

'Six *kopechs*. That'll do me.'

'Oh, six'll do you?'

'No less'n five. Hard times, y'know.'

'Eh. Listen, Eff. You know me. You got hot competition over that there district wall, y'know that too. Can change my connections like *that*, so I can.' His fingers snapped. 'Then times get a smidgen harder, don't they. Two *kopechs*.'

The merchant called Effod gave a cough. The coughing went on for a while, as did the squawking behind him, before he spluttered an answer and some coins clattered on his counter. There was no talking after that, but I waited too long to peep out. When I did, Loquar had vanished again.

The next day I was ready. When the washerwoman came down with her laundry, I was there; already waiting on her terrace steps. And right on cue, as soon as the shirts and thobes and yashmaks formed their screen between the stalls, the turban floated through the traffic. I took a post behind the longest of the thobes hung on the line, watching as the old woman turned and achingly climbed back up her steps.

The thobe was batted aside—pegs going flying—and I faced a mouth of yellow teeth.

'I know you?'

'No.'

Loquar snatched my arm and twisted. 'Sure I do,' he said, smile widening. 'Borderling banner-scrub!'

'Not me,' I said, shaking my head and trying to wrest my arm free.

'Don't fuss now.' He threw a furtive glance over his shoulder, then another ahead at the other three stalls. Leaning in towards my face, his own creased up so deeply that the oil pooled like little rivers in his wrinkles. 'You been watching?'

'No, I haven't!'

'Course y'ave,' he grinned back. 'Got a little deal there with ol' Effod. Nothing rotten. Just good business, see, clever like. Get a good price.'

I backed away from rancid oil-stink. 'Why?'

'Got stuff he wants, don't I,' he shrugged. 'Coals. For lightin' stuff.'

'I know what *coal* is,' I retorted. 'Doesn't he have coal already? That's what he sells, isn't it?'

'Nah, not like this he doesn't. This stuff burns slow and keeps going twice the time. But he don't *use* it, no, see. Sells it the same price to his customers so they come back for twice the daskh they smoked before.'

As I took in what I realised was a dirty little trick, he screwed up his eyes so that all I could see in each one was the murky, oyster-like cataract. Then he took me firmly by the shoulder, a little companionably almost, and hustled me over to the end of the warehouse's block. We rounded that corner. There he put his back to the passers-by in the main thorough-fare and twisted off his green turban. Out of the hollow inside came a small, rounded machine: a kind of compact device made of some yellowy metal; all loops and whorls and angles edged with blades.

'Clever piece, innit?' he said. 'Chops up fish, so it does. See there and there.' He pulled a little lever while adjusting some invisible gear, demonstrating the slice of the blades that would decapitate a fish: first a large one, then a small one. It was an intricate thing, finely crafted I thought, much more impressive than his crane.

'Did you make it?' I asked him.

'Never you mind that,' he replied. 'Now for this, fishbones there could'a gave me a tidy sum. But seeing as he's closed up shop and all, I thought ol' Effy could use it for choppin' up his daskh.'

'Will it?' I said.

'Wha?'

'Will it cut that stuff too?'

'*Will it cut . . .*' he started laughing. Then cleared his face to match my own. 'No, see, it's for *fish*. Daskh's not all soft like fish flesh, it's thick and tough, stringy. It'll get all up in the gears. Like as not, thing'll bust before the week's out.'

'You mean break?'

'More like stop working.' His eyes fled sideways before he leaned in again. 'Listen, kid. Effod knows me, right enough, but not for Guild parts. I take my good parts to Rubai there, the cloth-girl. Her lad's an apprentice in the Guild.'

'The Engineering Guild?'

'Very same. Now Guild's connected with the inkers what gets her good deals on cadmium or goldenrod or some Lostrian pigment. And *she's* got special twine—that *Zeidhan* sisal— what the kindler *don't*. So I take the twine to the kindler and he gives me my slow-burning coal.'

The words almost washed over my head but it didn't matter. What mattered was what he wanted from me. This was my chance and I knew it.

'Do you want me to do it? Sell it for you?'

He beamed at this and rammed the device into my hands. 'Y'know, I like you already. Full of ideas, so you are. Eff'll think you nabbed it off the Guild or some such. See?'

'He'll think *I'm* the thief.'

'Yeh,' said Loquar blankly. 'But he's gonna want the chopper. Not gonna rat you out, is he.'

'I'm Naemian,' I said. Heard Sarah's voice echo in my head. 'He'll know where to find me when it breaks.'

'Ha!' The sour, pungent breath exploded in my face. 'Smoke-head couldn't tell a Vedan from a goat, much less a borderling.' Loquar cackled, a papery sound, and yet with those filmy layers over his eyes I wondered how even he had recognised me. 'Just go over there, try buyin' some daskh off Effy-boy and make sure he sights the chopper. You want five tallans for it. Here's one to get you going.'

Cradling the device at my hip, I opened my hand for the coin: square and rusty brown with a circular hole in the middle.

'Yes?' Loquar prompted me. When I nodded, he patted my cheek, tousled my hair and covered both with smelly oil. I winced. 'Thought you was smart, kid. Come back with the five tallans and you can keep that coin right there. Off you scoot.'

Half of me didn't believe what I was doing. Erik and Sarah hadn't raised me to steal, or con merchants. But the other half knew that this was already working. I didn't care about the tallan he'd offered. He thrived on deals, that much was clear, and if I did this thing for him – maybe even better than he hoped – I could make my own deal with him.

Reaching the stall, I looked into the vapours that came from inside; saw the rows of jars on shelves. In the corner of the gloom was a big, bedraggled buzzard that seemed to be trying to find me through its hood. Effod's face floated forward through smoke, into the sunlight; withered, grey with dewy eyes. 'What?' he retched on a cloud from his lips. 'Well, what's wantin' with you, boy?'

'Daskh,' I coughed back. 'For my father.' I could feel Loquar's eyes on the device behind my back.

Effod sucked his pipe. 'Hm, what's he take?'

My mind raced, snatching words out of the next stinking daskh-cloud. 'The cheapest one,' I said. 'I've got one tallan.'

The red-rimmed eyeballs lit with surprise. 'A *tallan*, you say! Your da gave you a whole ruddy tallan for his daskh?'

Hoping to distract from my blunder, I took that moment to put the chopper on the counter. How was I supposed to know he'd given me more than I needed? I didn't know what a tallan was worth! 'He works for the Guild,' I made up on the spot.

'Hm, could have himself a damn sight better than my cheapest with a tallan. I know 'im? City or Royal? Lot of 'em Guild boys take my Ginger Slowburn. I'll given 'im pound and a half, how's that sound?' As I answered with a nod, he noticed the device. 'What's *that* about?'

Before he could touch it, I snatched it back. But he'd had a good look.

'Looks a fine gadget you got there, boy. Royal Guildcraft is it?'

'It's my father's,' I said, now scrapping Loquar's story for my own. Maybe I was better at this than I thought. 'I'm to take it to the fish shop. For . . . for cutting . . . string.'

That was close.

'String, eh?' he said thoughtfully. 'Here now. Your da don't gotta know you showed it me. Let's have another peek.'

He leaned further forward on the counter, pipe clamped tight between his teeth, and I tried not to choke as his smoke made my throat itch. His wet eyes sparkled when I held up the device to show him, turned the little gears and pressed the lever as I'd seen Loquar do before. Carefully, I looked over my shoulder at Loquar, who winked – I think – from his post. Then at a sudden scream from the buzzard, I swung my face around again.

'String,' murmured Effod again, drawing on the pipe. 'How's about a deal?'

'I've to take it to the fish shop,' I repeated.

'Fishmonger's gone under,' said Effod. 'Won't risk the coast journey what with them Rath out on the border, so no more fish, see. Sell it *me* and I'll give your da another half-pound o' the Slowburn.'

I shook my head and tucked the thing under my arm. 'Well, the fish man was going to pay him fi—' I chanced it, '*Six* tallans.'

I'd let it slip; his face clouded.

'You was gonna say *five*,' he burred low. 'You try'na con me, son?'

From his threatening frown I took a backstep, knowing I'd have to stick to my price now or, if he was anything like Loquar, he'd drag it all the way down. Dewar used to talk to Erik about this kind of business all the time, though I'd not understood it back then.

'It's not for you anyway,' I said, 'so I'll just take it back home.' Maybe trusting too much, I turned away from his counter and began to cross the street again. Loquar gaped at me in dismay, head shaking rapidly side-to-side. But he'd been right about Effod: he *did* want the chopper.

'Forgettin' your da's daskh,' he called after me.

I turned back. Three cowhide sleeves had been laid out on the counter. Pretending to still be a little unsure, I walked back towards the stall. But when I got there and held out the tallan, he grabbed me. The buzzard screamed.

'*You want six tallans?*' Effod growled and pulled me half-way up onto the counter, so near his face that I could make out the paths his leaking eyes had made alongside his leathery nose. 'I'll give you five *plus* another half-pound o' the daskh. That's *two* pounds for your tallan. You tell your da Eff had a special on the ginger stuff today!' Letting go with a shove, he went to his shelves, returned with another sleeve and thwacked it down on the others. Then opened his purse, counted five coins and slammed them down too beside them. 'Give up the gadget.'

I did it quickly; passed him the chopper and swept the coins into my hand. Effod shrank back into his smoke and I escaped, leaving him to marvel over the contraption that would soon be useless to him. Loquar signalled me to keep walking and I followed him as far as the building I'd since learned was a brewery.

'Second there I thought you was givin' up on me,' he said as I tipped the tallans into his hands. Then I held the pouches out to him. 'What's this?' He took them, lifted the fold of a sleeve, sniffed deep and grinned. 'Ginger Slow, my first choice!' The sleeves went straight into his turban and then the coins into a pouch. 'Canny work, kid. Here, take another tallan for your trouble.'

'I don't want it,' I said.

The milky eyes stilled. He scratched his beard. 'What d'you mean you don't want it?' he said, not quite so friendly anymore.

'I want to make a deal.'

'Oh, *now* you tell me.'

'You work in the Deep, don't you?'

The eyes shrank, his appreciation for my services shrivelling fast. 'Odd job maybe. What of it?'

I told him then about the Captain, the Commander and the Chief Engineer. I described the two Discs and the tall vertical cabinet in the corner that they were locked in. When I said what I wanted, he cocked a grubby eyebrow.

'You do know you're talkin' about the Viceroy of Vorth, kid?'

'Don't care,' I stated, stern as I knew how to be.

He stared at me as the breath scraped in and out of his hardened lungs. Then, with a faraway look, nodded. 'Which one's yours?'

I stammered at that: a problem. In the Chief Engineer's workshop, even I had been fooled by the likeness. This Loquar would have no way of telling one Disc from the other.

But mine had been *taken*. It had been stolen and kept from me. Looking straight into the oysters of his eyes, I made my mind up: 'They both are.'

For another two nights, a hundred of us pressed tightly together in the warehouse shelter, trying to savour the warmth over the stench of our bodies. Both days at noon, I looked out for Loquar, hoping that I could trust him to hold up his end of our deal. But when after the hottest daylight hours, he didn't come, I would wander; making sure to tell Con where I was going. Jerome sometimes came too, but always returned by himself before long. Antissa scared him.

The people of the city seemed to like us no better. On the warehouse street, the presence of guards was almost regimented now, while trying to weave between the tradesmen and camels was not much more use. Merchants and buyers alike blasted us with their curses all the time, chasing us back as soon as seeing us. Already I was used to the look of a raised hand. Dewar was right. We weren't welcome.

The first of the Vedish evacuees came the second evening after my business with Loquar. The commotion of dust and shouting somehow carried me to the wall of the fortress where Antissans lined the battlements to watch the hundreds coming from the north.

'Verunia's emptied,' I heard someone say. 'Caliph Arif brings his people to safety.'

The wardens of our shelter had mentioned Verunia before, the caliphy of Vorth that lay to the north of the fortress, between the ergs of the desert and our own River Elm. I wondered if that meant the Rath had crossed to this side now.

In the dusky haze, the crowd climbed the hill by the road that snaked up among the crags towards the gate. Their skins were the same as most Antissans; soft browns and bronzes. Their hessian cloaks were slightly thicker. I saw the caliph himself: a man with a short, pointed beard, purple garments and a chain of silver links under his coat. He rode with soldiers at the head. No one was dead, I could tell. There were no wounds or any weeping; just the painted-on stares of people newly dispossessed. The gates were opened and their numbers crawled into the city.

Voices filled the night air. Back at the shelter, I could still hear the sounds of families all vying for space in a nearby district. Infants wailed. And yet I found that I still envied them all. Even though they'd been uprooted from their homes, they had another home to go to.

Then something changed for us too. The next morning, as on the day of our arrival, we huddled on the threshold of the warehouse in our scores to clear the way for engineers from the Guild. It had been found that, through its rear wall, the warehouse extended into yet another disused old building, and now our quarters were to be expanded into it. We'd have more room.

Both buildings, however, had warped and weakened with age. Concerns arose that to break through the shared load-bearing wall would cause the roofs of both buildings to collapse. All through the morning they came and went. Even the engineer from next door became involved in the project. Our meal was forgotten about, and at midday when still not a hammer had been lifted on the job, Dewar's patience ran out.

'They can't just leave us like this,' he fumed and shot spit onto the ground through his front teeth. I watched the dust soak up the gobbet.

Con shrugged. 'Guess they didn't expect so many so soon. Think about it, Dew, the other warehouse could've gone to the Verunians instead. To be honest, I'm surprised it didn't.'

A short-lived banging came from inside; far from the kind of banging that would open up a wall.

Dewar shook his head darkly, tamping the temper we knew so well. After the Vedans I'd encountered in the last few days, I found it strange to think that he'd once been the man I most feared in the world. I watched Jerome, who still feared him. In the ten days we'd been here, he'd taken enough desert sun to erase the freckles from his nose. But then all of us had browned from the hours spent out on the street.

'The wardens have nothing to do with the work,' Dewar said. 'They're just standing there like statues and watching, that's all, and for what? Those masons have been here for hours and not put so much as a scratch in that wall!' He gestured to old Mother Far, sitting not far from him. 'Evelyn's too weak to sit in this blazing heat without a scrap of food or drop of water. And what about the children?'

Con nodded, lifting a palm. 'Dew—'

'We've more than a dozen children here, all thirsty!'

He was right about that. And it was true: at least ten engineers were now in there, not one displaying the kind of workmanship I'd been led to expect. Especially knowing, as I did, that the head engineer ran the city like a king. And as for our wardens, surely they were *supposed* to bring us food. I was hungry. We all were. We couldn't buy it for ourselves!

Dewar pushed himself to his feet. Worried faces turned towards him, Con's first among them. 'Don't do it, Dewar. Let them finish.'

'And when will that be, when Evelyn's dead in the dust?' He started moving through the huddles.

Con stood too fast, almost dropping his crutch, then with a wince hobbled as fast as he could through the path Dewar had opened. Impulse launched me after them; Jerome behind me in turn.

Just as many people were huddled on the inside of the warehouse door, hard up against the inner wall like corralled cattle. Dewar waded through them purposefully, big hands on heads and shoulders, then strode around the firepit towards the crew at the far wall. Two masons perched there on ladders, tapping with their mallets and chisels. Others looked on, including the tan-robed wardens and a pair of fortress guards. Jerome tugged on my arm and pulled me down behind a shelf.

'Excuse me,' said Dewar.

Jerome made himself small as a warden turned around and saw the man coming towards him.

'You're to get back with the others until we complete our work here.'

'With *respect*, sir, we are thirsty and hungry,' Dewar put to the warden, more than firmly. 'There was no morning meal and it is now well past midday. None of my people are accustomed to Vorth's heat and the work you conduct here forces more than half of them to sit without shade.'

'The heat will abate,' the warden answered stiffly. 'As for your meal, you will have it when it is brought. Now step away.' The second warden glared.

I thought Dewar might leave it at that, but he didn't. 'What about our wounded?' he said, gesturing behind him just as Con caught him up. 'Our children and elders? Some didn't even get enough food last night.'

'There was food enough for all.'

'That may be. But the warehouse was crowded with new arrivals. Many were outside.'

'Then it was the fault of those who were. Do you not see the engineers sent down to double your quarters? Even now, when our city struggles to house the Verunians from the north, we offer you more space, more shelter. Are you not grateful for this boon?'

'Of course, but—'

'Of course. You'll have your food upon completion of the work, borderlander.'

'But you're not *doing* anything here,' Dewar urged. 'You're not an engineer yourself.'

The warden's eyebrows formed an arrow. The guards, alerted by Dewar's tone, sidled closer. One guard was a lot bigger than the other; a figure I instantly disliked. Jerome, I was sure, couldn't get much smaller.

'There a problem?' said the big guard.

Dewar puffed out his chest. 'Yes. My people—'

'Your *people*,' cut in the shorter of the two, 'will be one whining borderlander short if you don't get back where we tell you.'

'*We are hungry.*'

'And you will eat when we say,' the guard snarled back. 'Get on the street!'

Con risked his balance to put a hand on Dewar's shoulder. 'Come on,' he said, but Dewar shoved his hand away.

'You too!' the big guard barked at Con. 'Clear off, the both of you. Right now!'

The masons stopped their idle tapping while engineers paused their discussions. This was getting worse. Dewar stood his ground. Growing like a storm-cloud, the big guard shouldered towards him, fists like red, knotted clubs. His arm drew back.

'*Guardsman!*'

Heads turned as the bright white High Commander Plamen swept in between the huddled Naemians at the door. Two men in uniform walked behind him. The big guard took a step back, away from Dewar, and the wardens fanned out. A little sheepishly, I thought.

'What goes on here?' Plamen demanded.

Nervously the chisels took up their tapping again, which made it harder to hear what was said when the Commander got there. But I didn't get the chance to listen anyway: Jerome pulled my arm. When I looked, he was signalling me towards the door. He knew Plamen was the man who had taken me once; the man I'd told him I would run from on sight. Now I crouched close behind my friend and crept after him, never taking my eyes away from the Commander's white back at the far wall.

That was, until a rolled-up blanket caught me in the shin and brought me down.

Commander Plamen turned at the sound, though whether it was the slap of my hands on the stone or Jerome's '*Shit!*' I'll never know.

I looked at Plamen, met his eyes and then froze. Not at him, but at the oily brown face at the foot of the ladders.

Loquar. He'd been here this whole time and hadn't even bothered . . .

'Flor!' hissed Jerome.

Con and Dewar looked at us in confusion while Plamen nodded to his men, 'That's the one.'

Jerome pulled me up hard. He spun me round, pressed me through the ducking, dodging Naemians and then propelled me through the doorway. Outside, I nearly tripped over more legs, then stumbled straight into the white flanks of the Commander's horse. The huge beast bucked towards my face but Jerome was quick as always. He snatched my wrist, dragged me underneath the horse's belly, around the other waiting horses and onward into the street.

The guards on watch must have known. A few surged forward at Jerome, who skated sideways in the dust and darted left. 'This way!' he yelled.

Into the grain-store beside the warehouse. Angry curses surrounded us. Then we were out into the alleys behind the warehouse and other buildings.

Around the first corner we turned was a dead-end.

No, not quite dead. There was a ladder to the rooftop; Jerome half-way up it already. 'Come *on!*'

I leapt onto the rungs after him, taking them two at a time and, at the flat top, vaulted a low perimeter wall. We dropped behind it for cover just as we heard the sound of boots scraping to a stop below us.

'Are there two?'

'I saw two.'

'He only wants the one.' That was the Commander's voice. He sighed. 'Keep this game short, if we could, please. I tire of ferrying children.'

'Yes *ekharan*, but they could have gone—'

'The ladder.' I lurched sideways: Jerome had my arm in his grip again, and as soon as I was up he was dragging me through an open doorway. We ran into the factory building where inks and dyes were made, and sprinted down one of the upper-storey rafters. Below us, pumps were heaving and feet squelching in great barrels of the stuff. I ducked and swooped around the fabrics hanging to dry right in our path, but Jerome wasn't nearly as careful. As he tried to dodge a damp sheet by ducking past it, he grabbed and batted it instead.

His hand came of it blue.

We slammed into a door at the other end. I searched all over it for a latch but Jerome had already mounted a box under the window, now forcing wooden shutters back and smearing them with blue dye off his hand. He was through the window to his waist when, down below, one of the Commander's men burst into the factory. These men weren't guards; they carried *swords*.

Jerome grasped me by my forearms.

'Watch it!' I shouted. 'You'll get that blue stuff on me!' He ignored my complaints and hauled me squirming through the gap of the window. Ridiculously strong when he wanted to be, he even caught me as I tumbled down and out.

Another rooftop: the plaza humming just below. We looked towards a crate at its perimeter wall.

'In there!' he ordered.

I glanced at the factory window, heard shouting coming from inside, but knew I couldn't refuse him this time. He raised the lid – the crate was empty and there was space enough for both of us. So we climbed inside it together, eased the lid closed over our heads and crouched in darkness, musting up the air with our panting.

It was only seconds before I felt his nails dig into my arm. I'd heard it too: from the other end of the rooftop, the slip of hands over rungs. We tried to stifle our breathing as footfalls landed on the roof. There'd been *another* ladder, then.

The steps were slow, leisurely almost, as they neared our spot and stopped outside. Plamen, I knew.

'Jerms?' I whispered.

'What?'

I brushed my fingers over the sticky dye he'd left printed on my arm. 'Never mind.'

Again I entered the workshop of the Chief Engineer.

'Well if it isn't *ekhin* Flint,' said Rusper Symphin. He plucked the goggles from his eyes and snapped them flat against his forehead. 'Do come inside.'

Seven

Triggers

Words darted importantly back and forth over my head while the Commander explained what had just happened at the warehouse. His story was fair, at least: the wardens had neglected both our morning and midday meals, and there had been a "heated exchange" when some of the refugees had complained they were getting hungry and thirsty.

Rusper Symphin grimaced. 'Who's in charge there?'

Plamen replied, 'A man called Shamak.'

'Dock his wage. Rations to be distributed at once, no more delays. Should the evening meal be late, I'll see Shamak myself.'

He jabbed his worktop with a finger; I saw the fancy ring it bore.

'It is done, Viceroy,' said the Commander, and left.

For some moments, when he'd gone, the engineer seemed to look right through my body to the door. Then he got out of his chair, crossed the workshop and closed it. The busy sounds of the Deep were reduced to vibrations.

'Well,' he said, turning around and scratching his forehead below the propped goggles. 'That'll be another meal missed for you, er . . .' He met my eyes, clicking his fingers.

'Florian.' I was starting to get tired of saying my name all the time.

'Where are your shoes?'

I glanced down. Having now gone without sandals for several days, my feet were filthy. 'I lost them.'

Rusper Symphin's eyes narrowed; as he looked to be about to say something else, I waited, but whatever it was seemed to fold unsaid between his lips.

He took a juddering breath and left the door, passing me closely, to reach one of the lantern sconces. The tube of heavy-looking metal extended vertically, suspended some inches from the wall by a bracket. He slid back a pair of fibrous yellow panels, which widened its arc of greenish light. Through the glare I could see into the chamber; clearly enough, at least, to see that there *weren't* flames burning in there. *How did they work?*

'Say again.'

I had to stop thinking out-loud.

'Um . . . how, how do those work?' I repeated, but could tell by the way he squinted at my lips that I still mumbled and it irked him.

'What, the lights?' he said. '*Triglycerate*. Not something you'll find much of in Naemia, I don't suppose, or for that matter know what to do with in those parts.' He gestured to the sconce. 'Take a closer look if you wish.'

I started moving towards it, then stopped myself and held back. Although he wasn't a large man, something about him felt strong. And the leather and metal of his engineering uniform looked more like armour than what the Vedish soldiers wore. Marking that the sconce was too high for me to reach, he dragged up a chair. Carefully, I climbed on top of it, my legs wobbling.

'It's not hot, you can hold it,' he said.

So I tested the bracket with a touch and then gripped it, all the time trying to ignore how unnerving it was having him so close next to me. He felt vital, electric almost, as if at any moment he might pull the chair from under my feet. Trusting he wouldn't, I peered in through the window of the lantern.

Inside, between two bolts, a copper bar ran down inside the bored-out centre of what looked like a crystal; branching laterally at either end so as to fix it into place. The light itself came from that crystal, a cold light, although less green without the pane in front of it. It shone more brightly in some parts, places it seemed more tightly trapped, highlighting traceries of cracks.

'Conversion of energy,' said Rusper Symphin.

'Did you invent it?'

'Hell-sands, no!' he scoffed. 'This desert's been yielding up green halite for as long as there've been Vedans to dig it. We merely mine it and put it to use. Always have.'

'What is halite?'

'*Green* halite,' he corrected. 'A crude salt. Part of a very ancient compound. Broken down, mixed with a gritstone or loess—gritstone's better, lives longer—added to an acid, then brought to boil, moulded, set and cooked. The result, triglycerate. Light from heat. Really a very old industry.'

'So it . . . doesn't burn anything?'

'No, nothing.' He cocked an eyebrow. 'This amazes you.'

I risked a glance at his eyes—brown or green? But then he moved.

'You'll be hungry,' he announced and strode over to a table; the only surface in the room not overwhelmed with mechanical parts or tools or works-in-progress. On it, instead, was a silver cloche, a silver ewer, a silver cup, a silver knife. He lifted the cloche, releasing a cloud of sweet-smelling steam; uncorked the ewer and splashed some water into the cup. Then he hooked one of the stools under the table with a shoe and pulled it out. He looked at me. 'Come now, no need for such a face. A boy your age needs a hearty meal from time to time.'

My mouth stung to life. My nostrils almost quivered, the smell that filled them, salty and sweet. In spite of my distrust of the man, my legs moved me down from the chair and across the brick floor of the workshop. I sat on the stool and looked down into an earthenware dish through the steam. In it was stew. A hunk of marbled bread leaned into the thick mixture like an oar. There was a little side-dish as well, half-filled with a yellow liquid.

'Not quite the delicacy you've been served at your shelter, I expect,' said Rusper Symphin, who had sat down on the opposite stool. When I shook my head, he grunted. '*Shaffanful* most likely. A poor supper for even the poorest Vedish family. And if one is to judge from the good Commander's report, you'll have been lucky to have got so much as a flatspoon with which to eat it. This will be better.' With a nod, he passed me the knife.

Lentils, I recognised those. And the scent of garlic. But that was all and it must have shown on my face.

'It's called *ghutna*,' he said as if by way of a prompt. 'Goat's meat and gourd, some bitter root, cumin seeds, crushed ginger. Garlic, of course.'

I said, 'The butter's melted.'

'Yes, that's the way of butter in the desert. You soak it with the *sangak*.'

I looked up.

'The bread,' he added.

I examined the knife, a little dazed, wondering how best to start the task. Then, without thinking, stole a glance over his shoulder. There it was, that cabinet – the tall one in the far corner. The Discs would still be in there, since Loquar had obviously made no attempt to retrieve them for me. Or maybe he had. Maybe this was simply a workshop too far for his fingers. Whatever the reason, my bargain had gone to waste.

I poked the bread, dislodged it from the stew and raised it to my mouth. The tastes were strange, but at the warmth, tears pricked the corners of my eyes. I closed them and let the flavours melt over my tongue. Let my teeth glide through that soft and tender goat's meat, while seeds crunched softly with the gourd, filling my head with a spicy haze. The bread was freshly baked and warm, it tasted sweet, the butter salty. Such a simple thing, this act of filling my stomach, but it absorbed me completely. Nothing at all was in the dish when, jaws exhausted, I put the knife down and licked my fingers clean. 'Thank you,' I said.

The man had watched me in silence, but now twitched a finger at the ewer—'More?'—and splashed some more water in my cup. I quaffed it quickly and wiped my mouth dry on my hand.

A minute later, Rusper Symphin pulled the goggles off his head and let them fall helter-skelter to the table. Then he rolled up the sleeves of whatever garment he wore under all the engineering armour, and rubbed the bridge of his nose. 'I must apologise,' he sighed, 'for being so very short with you last time. It was an especially . . . problematic few days, my patience stretched thin as it was by the Sanhedrin and many more tempers than my own flying high.' He exhaled. 'And now Verunia has evacuated, with the caliphy of Laudassa looking likely to follow. As if my pipes weren't tasked enough.'

'Your . . . *pipes?*' I asked, wondering now if he was sick or something.

Folding his arms, he cocked his head towards the worktop where he'd been sitting when I arrived with the Commander. Sheets of parchment lay banked up and scattered over it. From what I could make out from here, they all showed complicated pictures. 'Something's wrong with the pipeworks. Their pressure has dropped sharply, and just when we need it more than ever.' As I tried to make some meaning of these words inside my head, he waved them away. 'Never mind.'

As he shifted on the stool, some of the golden chain-links over his chest were set to glinting. I looked at the medallion they suspended: a thick, eight-sided shape of rich brown metal with an emblem etched into the front. It was like the emblem on the banner – a crescent with rays sticking out – but somehow not. Somehow incomplete.

I was waiting for it now; waiting for him to take the Discs out from hiding and ask me all those questions again. Why else should I be here?

'It's been over a week, I believe, since your settlement was attacked by the Rath.' That hit me square in the belly. 'Correct?'

I frowned, but nothing in his face showed any remorse for the question.

'Ten days,' I said.

'My mistake.' His fingers drummed. 'Your group was the second to arrive here, in the city, but first attacked. Now I find that strange since, apparently, your settlement was that furthest to the south of the borderland region. That could mean that the Rath are entering Vorth through the mountains, the East Naemian Walls as you'd call them in your country, I think.'

I didn't like this. The pipes were better; he should talk about the pipes.

Or did I *owe* him something now? Was that the deal here, why he'd fed me? My stomach felt good for the first time in days—ten long, hot days.

'They did,' I said.

'Beg pardon?'

'Yes, they did come from the mountains.' I looked at him, saw how his features pinched with interest. 'We were in the foothills, Con and me. Rath were hiding in the rocks and we could see them from up there. The people at our huts couldn't see them, though . . . not till . . .'

'How many?' he interrupted.

Quick as I could, I thought about it, pulling those moments through the blur so I could look at them again. Con had said there'd been no more than a dozen of the Rath, but I could still see more than that. 'Twenty,' I said.

'By night, by day?'

Orange rays across the plain. Shining river. Running dog. The screams, *those* screams, they filled my head and I spoke to silence them. 'Sunset. It was sunset. Probably. It was still light before . . .' I stopped. That was enough. I'd answered the question.

'You weren't injured,' he said. I shook my head, even though it hadn't sounded like a question. 'Your . . . family, boy?'

I looked at his hands, that skin like leather browned with grease, hoping that if only held my eyes just there, their lids might hold the tears inside. The Deep's low grumbles filled our silence. But in spite of my efforts, a hot line spilled down my cheek.

'Hm.' Just a tiny sound he made, but I hated it. Pity wouldn't buy more answers from me! 'What about—'

'*They would've been at the carts!*' I blurted as two more tears ran down my face. 'They would've got there! To the *river*, in time! If I hadn't gone with Con up to the farm then he'd have got his wooden fish and come straight *back*. It wouldn't have happened the way it did! They'd be alive! Alive and *here!*'

I was only shouting because I was angry for crying in front of him in the first place. Now I folded my arms tight on my chest and kept my face off to one side, waiting for the feeling to stop churning.

In the corner of my eye, Rusper Symphin leaned forward on the table and crossed his fingers. 'Did you incite this conflict, boy? Provoke the Rath to arms yourself?'

'*Course I didn't!*' I huffed, but he raised his voice over my huff.

'It prospers no one, your shouldering the blame for such misfortune. It is not a war you started, though I confess there are those in this city who believe it. That will change.'

The tears weren't stopping. 'We didn't *do* anything!'

'I know that.' He was quiet then, and still, as if watching me try to squeeze in my whimpers; one of which then burst out all the louder for the fight. It took some time to get a hold of myself. His words went on: 'Through the ages, all through this world, invasion is a fate endured by the innocent *first*. And it is a fate that has fallen upon you and your people, not once but twice now. There are no words you or I can speak to describe that injustice.'

Sniffing, I wiped my cheek roughly. I turned my face to him and—once—glanced up, but kept my arms crossed. His eyes were softer than his voice.

'Whatever mistake you think you made on that night, it was a choice, no more than that. One choice among few choices, *made* few by those with intent to destroy you.' He paused. 'Going on, as you must, will only prove more painful if you do not let that be true.'

'Let *what* be true?'

'You were defenceless,' he said. 'Your family was a casualty of war. As you are, too.'

'Doesn't make it fair.'

'No.' He took a breath in, pushed it out. 'But there's no end to the list of what's not fair in times like these. Trust me that far, if you can. Such things befall those least deserving, always, and take things from us.'

Us? What did *he* know of the terror and ruin we'd seen, sitting up here inside his fortress with his pipes and cranes and machines? Now I refused to look him in the eyes; it would mean accepting what he'd said.

There was a full minute of my noisy sniffing. Again, I looked at his hands, then tried to check his expression without raising my face. He had been looking at the floor, but then his eyes came up quickly. 'What about the other you mentioned, this Con?' he asked me.

With another sniff, I let my arms slowly unfold. 'Con's alright, I think. He got hurt in the leg but your healers helped him. He's getting better.'

'Good. Good.'

I scowled. What part of this was *good?*

Rusper Symphin straightened. I watched his hands as he twisted that fancy ring off his finger, reached out and set it on the edge of my dish.

'That,' he said almost brightly, 'is known as the Guild-Ring-Most-Royal. I have worn it for as long as I've been Chief Engineer.'

I ran the heel of my hand over my nose and shrugged, 'So?'

'So,' he said. 'The signet-piece is wrought of a specialised alloy, very rare now in Vorth, but the band is base iron. Here.' He rotated the dish so that the ring was right in front of me. 'Take a look at it now.'

Deciding to go along with whatever he was trying to say, I picked it up. Heavy. The red-brown signet part was a cogwheel on top of a square. The band was dull grey. But what had clearly once been a perfect circle of iron was now an oval, all warped out of shape by years spent on his finger.

'Why are you showing me this?'

'Because iron is strong,' he said. 'Hard and enduring, as indeed your loss feels now. Time can prove stronger yet, as you see. It has the ability, sometimes, to alter the things we think the strongest and most enduring of all.'

I stared dumbly at the ring and shook my head. Thought of Sarah and Erik and how safe I'd always felt when they were there. Words made no difference to all this; not mine, not this engineer's. I shook my head again: 'I just . . . I . . .'

'Always will, I'm afraid,' he said.

He knew.

'Even when hardened by the rust of your years, the fact will stand that they were taken, and too soon. That will never be untrue. The question, young *ekhin* Flint, is whether the pain you now feel will outlast the likes of iron.'

He gave me a moment longer to examine the Guild-Ring-Most-Royal, then took it back and slipped it on. Suddenly I realised I wasn't crying anymore. I dared to look at him squarely. 'Can I see it now please?'

'See . . .?'

'You know.'

He smiled – the first real smile I'd seen from him – and for some reason it made me wonder if he had a wife or any children of his own. As if ignoring my request, he stretched his arms and popped his knuckles, one by one. Then he stood up, went to the cabinet, opened its door with the key and took out two small objects. A crazy gratitude exploded inside me when I saw that they were wrapped each in a cloth of a different colour. 'Red marks mine,' he told me, setting both down on the table. 'Green marks yours.' He sat again. 'I know you tried to steal them back, as it happens.'

My head shot up.

He raised a hand. 'I'm not angry. A little bewildered that a boy as determined as you would choose to rely on a man like Loquar for his dirty work, but otherwise impressed by your creativity, I suppose.'

'How'd you find out?'

'Well he told me,' Rusper Symphin replied, clearing his throat. 'Loquar's my assistant.'

Oh.

'Come boy. You gave a shifty little molerat the choice between loyalty to the Viceroy or to a refugee waif. Which do you think is likely to offer the nicer reward?'

'You *rewarded* him?'

'I did,' he said loftily. 'With a placement on the task-team currently knocking its way through your warehouse wall.'

He half-smiled. I did too.

'However,' he continued, propping his elbows on the table, 'the attempt made it quite clear how much this object means to you, truly. And now, if you don't mind, I would like to know *why*.'

No. I heard the flat refusal in my head before thinking; before considering the request or what harm it could do. None of that mattered. The Disc was my last link to my family. It was private and it was mine. I stared at the green cloth on the table, Rusper Symphin doing the same, as if we were both waiting for the thing to speak up and explain *itself*.

Eventually, he took his elbows off the table, wiggled on his stool and filled his lungs.

'When the Rath invaded Naemia'—he was going to punish me with a story—'we knew. Not, of course, in time to give the support of Vedish armed forces, even if the Mooncircle Throne would then have deigned to provide it. Here in Vorth, you see, boy, those East Naemian Walls are far more than mountains. To the Vedish they represent a line between worlds – a wall between the secular desert and the old realms of Exelcia Minor. *The Inwold*, I believe your people call them.' He seemed to wait for confirmation, but when he got none, went on talking. 'The Long Erg in the south also separates us from those realms, but that is far from Antissa, and no bastion of so-called faith stands on the other side of that. We Vedans have never had a faith. We are a practical nation, always have been.'

I raised my eyes from the cloths. 'So you don't believe the castle really . . . ?'

His expression cut me off. It said, *really*. 'Do you?'

I crossed my arms again. 'Yes!'

A shrug. 'As you wish. That's neither here nor there.' He sighed. 'But what we knew then isn't much less than what we know now, ten . . . eleven years later. The end of the Naemian principality was quick, the Saremin throne simply snuffed out like a light. The people of your nation had been wiped out already when word of the invasion reached Vorth. And then the doors of Celestrian Fallstone—your fallen sky-castle—were closed, for all time to come, according to the rumours that reached us from Ered. Naemian survivors seemed very unlikely after that. None expected refugees such as yourself to reach our borders.

'But then, that was almost a full year later. It was barely a month after the news of the fall that we received a . . . visitor here. The man was strange in every detail, though even stranger is the fact that I would be hard-pressed to describe any of those details to you now. Except perhaps to say that he was tall. Attired in some exotic fashion. He gave no hint as to where he had come from and I don't believe anyone heard him say his name. He simply arrived, lingered a week within our walls, and then was gone.'

There didn't seem anything too strange about that until Rusper Symphin reached out to draw the red cloth aside. There were both our faces in the mirror, framed instantly by far too vast a wealth of detail.

'*He* gave me this. Didn't tell me what it was, or ask for anything in return. Did not explain himself at all. All he required was that I kept it safe until such time as he returned to reclaim it. An odd request, and yet I admit the thing intrigued me . . .' His pause drew my eyes to his again. 'You've no doubt noticed how unnaturally it mirrors everything around it.'

If it was a question, I didn't answer.

'No metal I've seen before possesses any such quality, to the extent that I must doubt it to be natural metal at all. All the same, I agreed. So small a thing, I could really think of no reason to refuse him. Duly, he left . . .' He drew the red cloth back over the Disc; maybe to show that that was the end of his story, maybe to put the mirror out of sight again. '. . . and of course, has not come back.'

'Where did he go?' I asked.

'Northeast – on foot,' said Rusper Symphin, before another thoughtful pause. 'Do you know what lies northeast of Antissa?'

'Ered.'

'Not immediately. First come the Dustlands of the Lack. Those wastes stretch for leagues before even the outermost edges of the Empire. I was as decent a rider then as I daresay I am to this day. For a full five days I tracked him across those barren expanses and never once saw him flag. It was only once he'd bypassed the outer province of the Dunfinds, westernmost of Ered, that my own dwindling supplies forced me to turn back to Antissa. He travelled *further* northeast, into the unknown.'

Somewhere below us in the dark, moving intestines of the Deep, something groaned. The engineer took no notice of the sound. 'Now,' he said with a grimace, 'there are new sightings of folk in the Dustlands east of here. By all reports, not Ratheine.'

'Who are they then?'

'Can't say for sure,' he replied. 'Vorth has a long history of conflict against the Lackish barbarians, though we've not seen any of their tribes for more than fifteen years now. Most believe they've finally perished with the drying of the rivers. If that is *not* the case, however, and should they now re-emerge, Antissa cannot withstand them. A year of defending the northern border from the Rath has thinned our numbers too far.'

Confused, I asked: 'What does all that have to do with the stranger?'

His shrug was shallow but pensive. 'I know of no others but the tribes who might survive the far reaches, and that's where he went. Furthermore, that is the reason I find this . . . thing— these things—so suspect.' He narrowed his eyes at the cloths. 'The shamans of the Lackish tribes practiced magics. Mind, not the high, noble arcanum you may have heard described of Ered. Savage, ancient sorceries that destroyed great numbers of our people in decades past. And we know that they wielded such magics through *stones*.'

'So you think they're stone?'

'I don't think anything,' he said frankly. 'I don't know what they could be.'

I eyed the red cloth, then the green.

'Well I don't either,' I stated.

'You don't what?'

'Know what they are.'

'*Is that the truth?*'

At that sudden sharpness, I met his eyes. Then pushed some words: 'Sarah—she gave it to me, *alright?* It was in a box with lots of other things she brought with us from Naemia. I lost the others when the Rath came. This one's all that's left of them, the only one I saved.'

'Sarah,' echoed Rusper Symphin. Her name, in his voice, sounded more foreign to my ears than any crude Vedish word. Even though his accent was so much less Vedish-sounding than the others', and though he'd said the word quite gently, it was wrong on his lips. 'Was Sarah your mother?'

The world shifted. I'd never had to think about that; it meant so little. I'd always known it well enough, I had no memory of being told it. Ever. It belonged with the tremors I'd been too small to grasp – the huge *before* – and yet the part of the before that hadn't mattered. Hadn't made a stitch of difference. Sarah wasn't my mother, nor Erik my father. Family, yes; the one I'd known as far back as that memory of winds on those Naemian beaches, the creaking of boats and shouts of native fishermen. But now, for the first time in my life, it wouldn't do. A clever man with piercing brown or green eyes had asked one simple question, and the answer I'd always felt to be the right one wouldn't fit. I shook my head to relieve the pressure building in it, and said: 'She took care of me.'

'Fair enough. What did she tell you?'

I blinked at him, feeling off-balance. Instead of pressing for something more or something better than what I'd said, he'd simply left it at that.

'When Sarah gave you this thing,' he prompted, 'did she say anything at all about what it was or where it came from?'

I cast my mind back to the treasures, all gone, and heard her voice again. *These things are for you, pieces of home. Yours as much as ours. You're Naemian too.* Just as she'd promised on that night when I was eight, Sarah had told me all the stories of the treasures; most at least twenty times over. I knew them well.

'The things in the box,' I told him, 'were Naemian things. All of them were from Naemia. Except this one.' His face fell by a fraction at that. 'She never showed it to me, ever. She didn't know what it was, she said. Only that it had come with me when . . .'

'When . . .?'

'When my first family brought me.'

'Your *first* family,' he repeated, face quite still now. 'And what can you tell me of that first family? Do you know where they came from or where they went?'

I shook my head, no. She'd never said about that, I'd never asked. No one had until now.

It hadn't mattered.

He picked at the table with a nail. 'So, you never knew your parents, and your adoptive mother told you that only *this*, of all the things in her heirloom box, was not Naemian.' When I nodded, he inhaled. 'Surely that suggests your true family was not either.' This was too much.

'I don't know,' I said at him, letting Sarah's voice fill up my head. *You are Naemian.* So often through the years she had said that to me, as if reminding me almost. Always, without question, I'd accepted that I was. But Rusper Symphin's words had blown a piece of that away now, and suddenly, out of nowhere, I couldn't unsee the fact that my father and mother could have been anyone at all. Anyone from anywhere. And so could I. 'I'm Naemian,' I heard myself thinking aloud.

'Very young is what you are, Florian Flint,' he countered. 'Your time in Naemia was brief. So brief, in fact, that I hardly imagine you can remember much of it.'

'I do remember things.'

'Really. Like what?'

I sagged at the dubious look on his face, desperately wishing all those pieces of home didn't have to be lost. They'd prove everything I was trying to say. I gaped at his doubt; this man who'd just turned my past over on its head. My whole life up to this moment. Forget it.

Reading my struggle, the clever face tilted. 'You realise, boy, that few of us are moulded by our choices alone.'

'What?'

'Even before we're born, most men are spoken for already, our destinies decided by other powers, decisions made on our behalf. Perhaps the most important decisions of our lives. Now you, of course, believe that you have lost your true home. Twice over, indeed. But home may be defined by other things. Some take it from blood, others from the land or the city of their birth, others their trade.' He seemed to pause here for effect. 'My own father and mother were Vedish, it's true, but I am not of this desert. I was born on the mudflats of Elman, and raised there, only coming to Vorth in my twenty-fifth year.'

So *that* was it, he was Elmine!

'I am Vedish nonetheless,' he added firmly as if correcting my unspoken thought. 'Others still lead lives that allow them to *choose*, as well you might.'

'I'm Naemian,' I repeated, trying for a firmness of my own and sounding every bit the child. Even to myself.

His lip puckered. 'Very well, it's your choice. But I think you're old enough to know there's no going back to your Naemia. Even if there were a reason to do so.'

'Why not?' I rebutted, getting annoyed with him again.

'Boy, they said it was ten thousand that beset your coast in `3218. If you want my tallan's worth, I think it was more. Much, *much* more. No one knows how or why the Rath resurged in such numbers, and so long after being scattered in ocean exile by Ered, but resurge is what they did. And now our border is choked. They are moving, so much is clear from your own account, but they are slow. It will be a long time, years perhaps, before Naemia is emptied again, regardless of the war it brings to Vorth. And it may be that you weren't even born there. You see.'

'It's still my country,' I said through gritted teeth.

'You said you didn't know who your parents were.'

'I know what I said!' I snapped. 'Why do you *care?*'

'Because it would seem that your heritage links you to these.' He gestured the Discs. 'And I wish to know what they are.'

'Why?'

'I've told you why.'

My heart thudded; he had no right to be saying these things, and his workshop, for all its otherworldly content, was stifling me. 'I just want my one back.'

Rusper Symphin laughed, right in my face. 'No, Florian. What you want is to keep this little mystery all to yourself as if it belonged to you alone. Which I understand. Yours was a gift from your adoptive mother, or so you believe. But I was once a boy too, so don't think I can't read your face like a blueprint. Your eyes were like *weight-balls* when I was talking about that stranger.'

How dare he. 'You're the one keeping it all for yourself. You *stole* mine from me!'

'And you tried to steal both,' he said, cool and unfazed by my outrage. 'I've a right to my own half to treat as I deem fitting. That stranger clearly knew something we don't, and it so happens that he elected me to protect his property. Your possession of *this*, though, is different.'

'No it isn't.'

'Unless Sarah lied to you—'

'Sarah didn't lie!'

'Listen. Assuming she told the truth, then it is likely she had none of the knowledge possessed by my stranger and none of the authority to place it in your care.'

'It belonged to my first parents, I told you already!'

'So are we to believe that *they* knew what it was? Is that reasonable? To the stranger the thing was important, so why should your parents part so easily with theirs?'

'Because it's *not* important!'

'I know you don't believe that, boy.'

'It isn't!' I shouted and lunged over the table for the green cloth. But I caught my foot behind the crossbar of the stool as I did, and toppled forward, hit my chin on the dish and grazed my arms along the edge of the table, going down. My Disc popped free—I spun around on the floor, watched it hit the bricks and roll away. Underneath some gnarled, black machine I saw it wobble and go still.

Rusper Symphin kicked back his own stool and shot to his feet. 'Dolt!' he scowled. 'Now perhaps you see some of my wisdom in keeping both of them from you!'

He swept to the machine, then stopped and froze in his tracks.

'Did it break?' I asked, unable to see it past his boots. 'Is it broken?' When he didn't answer, I stood up and rubbed my arms. 'Mister Symphin?'

He murmured vaguely, '*Caliph* Symphin,' standing only a yard from where it lay.

I peered around him, almost scared of what I'd see. What I saw was the Disc, true enough. It lay just under the machine, reflecting the legs and black underside so fully and finely that, without the reflection of the bricks—just catching light—it could easily have been invisible. Maybe, I thought, if there were marks or fractures in it, the reflection wouldn't be so perfect. Who knew. But the reflections weren't the reason we could see the Disc clearly now. Even from here, I could tell that it was *glowing,* a sapphire blue, so faint a glow that had it not been for the shadow of the machine, we would have missed it. 'It'll squark.'

I glanced up at Rusper Symphin a moment too late to read his face. He opened the green cloth in his hand, crouched to reach between the under-spokes of the machine, and scooped my Disc up. He didn't stand yet, and when I looked onto his palm the soft blue sheen had dimmed already.

'Shutter the lantern,' he instructed. Obeying, I climbed up to the sconce and drew all panels. The workshop darkened; I hopped down. The Disc, still flat on Rusper Symphin's outheld hand, now gave so little of the glow it was almost . . . No. Gone.

'It'll squark.'

'What?' I said.

He shot me a stern look. 'You saw it too, yes?'

'I saw a light,' I said, confused. 'A blue light. Didn't you?'

He nodded surely. 'Just the same.' He stood and took it back to the table. There he set it down again on top of its cloth, beside its twin. Completely ignoring the toppled stools, we stared at it, silent, waiting. I felt strange, a little nauseous, but twice as curious. 'Do you think . . .' he began, 'if you dropped it again . . . ?'

'Maybe.' Lifting the corner of the cloth, I tipped my Disc off the table. Despite its weight, there was a bounce—only a small one—that sounded densely on the surface of the bricks, before it rolled over the floor and wobbled still. I dropped onto my hands and knees, almost startled when Rusper Symphin did the same right next to me. But there was nothing of that glow. Just too comic faces staring back in the reflection. My chin was bleeding from the dish and the engineer's nostrils were flared wide. 'It'll squark.'

'It'll *what?*' I said, looking at him.

'If not the impact,' he suggested, 'possibly—'

'The angle?'

'Exactly. Try it again.' He covered it with the cloth, handling the thing like some silver scarab that might escape and scuttle free, and gave it over to me. We went back to the table. 'It's sure to fall differently. Go on,' he said. And again those silly words, 'It'll squark.'

'What does that *mean?*' I demanded irritably, hand primed. But when all he did was frown back, I shook my head. 'This is so stupid.'

'They've called me worse. Come. Again.'

For a third time I dashed the Disc from table to floor.

Bounce, roll, wobble and stop.

And still no sapphire-blue glow when we went to stand above it. 'What about the other one?' I suggested. But when we lifted the red cloth to examine its twin, nothing about it showed signs of having changed in any way. As if that would have made some kind of sense!

'I know what I saw and so do you,' said Rusper Symphin. 'Two pairs of eyes don't make the same exact mistake.' He sighed a little breath and went to right the toppled stools.

His words still hanging in the air, I stooped to pick up the Disc, but what I saw in its face was far too much. That reflection too full. More than complete, the picture pulled into its curve corners and sections of the room it couldn't rightly see or know or frame. My hand filled up its mirror and magnified even the thinnest line of sweat in my palm. Which made contact.

A sound like metal tearing open filled my ears. White crackling light lanced out at me and wrapped my fingers, hand, then arm. My muscles seized. The blazing light shot up my arm, leapt to my shoulder, coiled my neck. It took my other arm and bathed it. My body burned as it took hold, the whiteness going *into* me. It spun round both of my legs, then seconds later I was blind. *It had my head!* All I could hear was metal screaming.

That and the voice inside my brain—

LITTLE SPARK!

It was going to kill me. I knew that totally, even as the whiteness sucked my body to its knees.

And disappeared.

My head went soupy. Murky spots and squiggles bloomed over my vision like rotten floaters on my eyes. And then it took me *again*—by the shoulder! No . . . it was Rusper Symphin who was holding and shaking my shoulder, looking hard into my face and saying something. His eyes *were* green. I watched his lips.

EIGHT

CROSSING

Warm water trickled over my neck and down my shoulders, chest and back. The piece of soap slithered away. When I managed to catch it, I made a lather and worked that slowly into my hair, watching the dark droplets make spirals through the surface of the water. Everything ached, as if my body had been stretched. It ached to move; it ached to think.

At the end of the workshop, it turned out, was a set of steps. Those steps led down into a chamber, almost empty except for the bathtub I now sat in, washing myself by the light of a lantern on the bottom step. Rusper Symphin had said it had been nearly an hour when I'd come to, after passing out, and when I'd woken he'd called a servant to draw the bath.

I tipped another pailful of water over my head. Suds ran into my eyes but the sting was distant. Someone else's. I felt apart from it, my senses, and what had happened to my body. Whatever that was. Even the water I was in should have amazed me: instead of having to be brought here in so many buckets, it had poured straight from a tube at nothing but the turn of a screw! Yet all I'd done was stare at it without a thought. Had it been hours or days since I'd last seen the ware-house shelter? I rubbed my knees, dulling the water.

The engineer came down the steps. Beside the lantern he laid a towel, some clothes and a pair of sandals. Leaving again. I waited for the sounds of his movements in the workshop, then eased myself out of the tub and dried my body on the towel. For the first time in many days it didn't smell; I could run my fingers through my hair without turning up those gritty sand-flakes.

A big *clap* came from upstairs.

Quickly, I slipped on the fresh clothes, put on the sandals, grabbed the lantern and went up into the workshop. It was full of smoke that stung my nose and I had to flap my hands at first to see my way. Rusper Symphin stood at the middle worktop, wearing his goggles and hard gloves. Where the parchments had been before was now an assortment of pots, jars, cups, pestles and mortars, vials and kettles, and a lamp. I saw him tip something like sand out of one jar, into another. Something popped and smouldered inside a bowl in front of him, but as I tried to make out what it was he must have seen the lantern's light coming behind him. 'Stand clear,' he said.

I obeyed.

'And put these on.' Without turning around, he prodded me in the chest with an extra pair of goggles. I wriggled them onto my head, fidgeting and nudging at the bulging eyepieces that kept on sagging from my eyes.

'What *is* that stuff?' I ask him.

'*Chrozite*,' he said. As if that helped. 'Since the beginning of our border defence, we've been testing its reaction with flame.

Something we discovered quite by chance.' He sifted the stuff inside the bowl – a chalky, yellowish gravel – then dusted his gloves and produced a short hempen cord. He lit one end of the cord on the lamp-flame, then lay it against the inside of the bowl. 'I'd advise another backstep,' he said, taking one himself.

Sizzling, the flame inched towards the gravel.

A vicious crack split through the workshop; both he and I ducked on reflex. A ball of dense white-yellow smoke billowed up and mushroomed wide across the ceiling, soon thickening the air with acrid fumes that made us cough.

'A highly . . . flammable solution,' he choked out, waving an arm to disperse the gases. 'And one, at that, which may be extremely effective if channelled.'

I kept on flapping at the smoke, but soon enough it thinned. 'For what?'

'For darning socks,' he replied, detaching his goggles to loop them over the arm of a machine. I hadn't missed the sarcasm, but he still nodded towards the worktop where the half-built contraption I'd seen earlier lay waiting. A weapon? He read the question off my face. 'Such is my work. Well, *part* of it anyway. Now,' he added with a tug on his medallion, *'everything's* my work. How do you feel?' It wasn't the first time he'd changed the subject without warning.

Unsettled again, I toyed with the hem of my fresh shirt and thought about what to say. He'd seen the white light erupt out of the Disc, and seen it vanish. He'd seen me drop and pass out. He knew as well as I did that those things had really happened an hour ago.

But the *voice* . . . the one I'd heard inside my head as they had happened . . . I'd told him nothing about that. And didn't think I wanted to.

'I'm fine,' I said.

'Hm.'

'Just tired.'

'Well,' he exhaled, then clicked his palate with his tongue. 'Whether or not what we have seen is Lackish magic, if anything is clear it's that we know none of its risks. There is a force contained here. Of its origin or purpose or strength we know nothing. Nor what it may do should we carelessly invoke it again. You appear unscathed on this occasion.' His eyes danced over my face. 'But we may not be so lucky a second time. Care must be taken.'

Somehow, even through the goggles on my eyes, he must have known I wasn't looking at his.

'Florian?'

I looked.

'Best we keep it to ourselves.'

Finally: something we agreed on. We stood quietly for a few moments longer, while chemicals simmered on the worktop. 'I should get back to the shelter,' I said at last.

'Yes.' He was chewing his mouth, eyes far away. 'Of course,' he said. 'Dark up there soon.'

There was no way to say the next thing without sounding ungrateful. 'Could I have my old clothes back please?'

Turning his head to look at me, he made a face. 'The *old* ones, what?' he said. 'They're rancid. What's wrong with these?'

'Nothing,' I assured him. 'Just I can't go back dressed like this. They'll ask me questions. The sandals are fine and really nice, and thank you, but the clothes . . .'

The engineer was still looking at me but only half-listening, I could tell. 'I see,' he said before cocking his head. 'Well, I'm afraid it's too late. While you were bathing I had them sent up to the furnaces already.' I sagged.

Rusper Symphin crossed the room, making me hope for a moment that he would give back my Disc. But he went nowhere near the cabinet into which they'd been returned. Arms behind his back, he spun around and stuck his chin out.

'It may be there's a vacancy appearing on my staff.'

'A . . . vacancy?'

'Yes, a post.' I stared back. 'A position, boy. A job. The hours are long and stipend meagre for mere assistants of the Guild, and you will not be guaranteed apprenticeship. But board and lodging are provided.'

As the words found meaning in my head, I pulled the goggles off my face. '*Me,* you mean?'

A shallow nod.

'But I'm . . .'

An eyebrow lifted. 'What?'

'Twelve!'

'Your point?'

I searched my mind for more objections – the green turban! 'What about Loquar?'

'Hah!' he laughed, flapping a hand. 'The man's been rotting from the brain down long enough, and I assure you has quite outlived his uses. He's nearly eighty after all, and smells abysmal. And he's been hawking pilfered sparts from me for years.'

'Sparts?'

'Spare parts,' he said and suddenly it occurred to me that the fish-chopper I'd pawned to Effod the daskh-man had probably come from right here. 'The coffers of the Mooncircle Throne are deep yet. Loquar will be compensated well for his services to me and further monies will go to his wife in the event of his death. You needn't worry about him. I don't.'

Outside the door of the workshop, wheeled vehicles moved through mingled voices of the other engineers, though not as many as before. Were duties ending for the day? I swallowed hard and tried to fathom what it would mean if I said yes. Access to all these weird machines, a chance to learn what each one did and how they worked, even how to build them? Maybe. They surrounded us now like bulky people listening in, waiting for my answer, while the Deep at large ached itself in through the walls. And then, of course, there were the Discs . . .

But it couldn't happen. For a start, how would I explain it to Con and Jerome? What would the others think of me – all the others who had made it here, bruised, bereaved but alive, when Erik and Sarah hadn't – that I was simply going to leave them to their fate in that warehouse? I pictured Dewar's face clouded dark. Disappointment, distrust, anger.

Rusper Symphin rolled his eyes. 'You need to think about it, clearly.' When I said nothing, he sighed. 'Understandable, I suppose. Very well then. Return here, at this same hour, in three days, and have an answer. If in that time I hear nothing, or indeed never see you again, then the offer is withdrawn. Obviously.' He spoke sharply again, as if by not agreeing at once I'd hurt his feelings, and turned to widen the wall-lantern's panels. 'Do you remember the way out? I have no one to escort you.'

'Think so.'

'Ladder, stairs, ladder. Don't take the winch-lifts, they've been sticking. From the rubble-shaft stairs, out of the citadel by the tall Deeping Door. Don't look lost.' He raised a finger. 'And if you're approached by men in blue and white uniforms, you do not speak, is that clear?'

'Why not?' I said, frowning.

'Your accent. Makes it too obvious.'

'Makes what obvious?'

'Hell-sands, boy! Is it not yet plain *enough?*' he exclaimed. As I blinked back, bewildered, his voice dropped to an urgent murmur. 'The Satrap did not open Antissa to your people, Florian. He knows nothing *about* the borderland refugees in his city, and if he *did*, well, suffice it to say that mercy is not among the virtues of Satrap Syphus the Second. Blue and white – do not speak!'

'But if the Satrap didn't let us come here, who did?'

He spun around on his heels. Snatching his goggles, he went back to the chrozite. 'Thank you, *ekhin* Flint. That will be all.'

Time to go. Back to my people in fancy, foreign, privileged clothes. I dreaded the questions they'd ask me and yet realised, even as I walked towards the door, that I wanted even less to change back into that; back to dodging kicks from the street and eating out of the scornful, grudging hands of wardens.

Back to keepers and waiting for water. Back to loss and weeping. None of that was what I wanted. But I was Naemian. An outsider, and unwelcome in this city. I couldn't stay here in this place or serve this man. 'Don't you care?'

'About what?'

I turned around. 'That I came from the borderlands.'

His goggle-lenses found me, the triglycerate light reflecting on their glass like fine green pupils.

'You're small for twelve,' said Rusper Symphin, as if he'd only just noticed. 'But you've energy and wits both quite sufficient for my trade. The rest has little bearing and I'd thank you not to raise the like again. I don't care if you came from a camel's backside.'

From the Deeping Door I stepped out into night, freshly fallen. The grey diggers had gone now and the gates of the neighbouring district were shut. The gravel yard was empty but for three men with drawn-up scarves who stood some yards away, talking very low. Their murmurs carried. Whoever they were, they didn't look like guards, and the sound of their voices made me think of the Rath; how their gibbers had echoed among the rocks of the hills. One of them glanced in my direction, drawing the others to look at me as well.

I slunk along the wall, out of the yard.

Though it was a clear sky, deep indigo, only a few handfuls of stars made themselves known. I'd always liked to watch them on clear nights back in the borderlands, and remembered the way Erik had always made fun of how I'd stand and stare upwards, not caring who was watching me. "Reel those blinks out off the welkin, you," he'd laugh, "or the tide'll take them!" Whatever that had meant – some or other fisherman's saying – I wished I *hadn't* thought of it.

Lamplight flickered tan and orange behind the estates' drawn-down blinds, while ahead, the tops of palm trees waved above the inner district wall. A cool breeze was up. It chilled my scalp, my hair still damp, and sprinkled sand across my ankles. The shirt was thin but coarsely textured and its sleeves hung down like towels. I felt stupid with it on. Clean, but stupid.

And sore. In the wake of whatever had happened, my head and body were throbbing. Had the Disc, what . . . *attacked* me? But how, and what with? Somehow the things Rusper Symphin had told me about magics didn't fit the way my body had felt right in that moment. Not that I knew how magic felt. That white light that had leapt out and grabbed me felt . . . *alive*. My muscles spasmed with the memory of how its current had seemed to search inside me while putting that voice into my head. *Little spark*, it had said. Not for the first time either.

I glanced back, hearing footsteps.

No one was there. Only shadows.

I followed the wall of the palace – no, the "citadel," that's what they called it – towards the Inner Gate. As I made my way, I passed barred entryways to the citadel courtyard. The loud conversations of some guards on duty there bounced off the stone, but I only saw their tall shadows moving in and out of lantern-light. *Triglycerate*.

So Rusper Symphin was the man who had called us to Antissa, not the Satrap. I wondered why it seemed so secret, and why he'd warned me about the men in blue and white uniforms. And what had *happened* to the Satrap that an engineer must now step in and rule the city instead? Or was it the whole country? The engineer had said the Satrap didn't want us in his city. So, if it was wrong to give shelter to the borderland people, then why had he done it? All around us I'd seen the signs that their resources were low. We had to eat, but so did they. And as refugees from a foreign land – a land to which Vorth had never been a friend, as far as I knew from Sarah's stories – it was clear that we brought trouble in an already troubled time.

Leaving the citadel wall behind, I remembered what he'd said about his own life. Although he called himself Vedish, he was really Elmine by birth. That was where he'd been born. Elman was closer to Naemia, that much I knew. Even a few of our own survivors were Elmine; could that be the reason? In some ways, I thought, he seemed just as coarse and hard and Vedish as the rest, but in others, not like them at all. Now his sarcasm came back to me, the quip he'd made about "darning socks." No one even *wore* socks in this country.

Maybe, I thought. But how would he have known that there were Elmines in our number? Even the Vedans who had sent our settlements coal and provisions from across the River Elm in those years, had never spoken much with us. There must be more. Only twice I'd met him now, and yet under that armour of leather and metal . . .

No. I gave up on the thought. Just like the rest of the Vedans, the Chief Engineer was a stranger.

I stopped and listened to the breeze. Up ahead was an estate that overarched the cobble way with three orange squares from upstairs windows. Through the short underpass I saw the brighter lights of the Inner Gate, which would lead downhill through city streets to the warehouse where I lived now. No kind of home. My mind plunged back into the Deep and Rusper Symphin's workshop. I clenched both fists, imagining a Disc inside each one, and resented the engineer. What had made him think, even for a *second*, that I could possibly be—

'Coming back?'

I shot a glance into the shadows of the underpass. From a small stable on the right side, a horse stamped the straw and whinnied in its stall while, to the left, feet scuffed the cobbles and a human head bobbed up. Big eyes gleamed out.

'Jerms?'

'What are you *wearing?*'

Embarrassed, but stepping closer, I picked at the hem of the long shirt. This was exactly what I'd feared. 'New clothes, that's all. Someone gave them to me.'

'Someone.'

"Chief Engineer" . . . "Viceroy" . . . These words would mean nothing. 'He's called Rusper.'

He snorted. 'Ruster give you food?'

'Yes,' I admitted, wishing I'd lied. 'But they should've brought food to the shelter too. Didn't they bring it? The Commander—'

'I don't give a shit about your crazy commander!' he shouted. I closed my mouth; there was never any reasoning with him when he was like this. And while it surprised me that he'd been willing to come this far all by himself, it unnerved me more the way he crouched there in the dark. He'd sat here waiting.

'Jerome, come out of there please.'

'Don't tell me what to do. You're always telling me what to do, Florian!'

'Fine, sorry,' I said.

A silence.

'You think I'm stupid.'

'I don't think that!'

'So why d'you keep lying to us? Saying one thing and then doing something else, huh? Why d'you have to keep on popping off up there?'

He was right. I had treated him as if he was stupid. And maybe, just maybe, I thought, he *was*.

'Just tell me. What do those people want with you? And don't you dare say it's 'cos of you puking on some sign.'

No, he wasn't stupid. But I couldn't tell him. Not this. He wouldn't get it. I wasn't sure I even got it.

'Look, Jerms, it's cold. We should get back. Con'll be worried where we are. I'll tell you about it later.' I waited. 'Okay?'

'Not okay.'

He shuffled up off his haunches and stepped out into the light that reached us from the citadel walls. His eyes bored into mine with a disgust I'd never seen in them before, like hatred almost, and it scared me.

'Con's my brother, not yours,' he said. 'He's not worried about you, doesn't even *care* about you!'

'Stop it!' I snapped. It wasn't true, I knew it wasn't, but my throat still tightened to hear him say it. The horse in the underpass stable stamped again. This wasn't good.

'We gotta stick together, I told you,' said Jerome.

'I know,' I said. 'We will.'

'You promised to stay away from them.'

'I didn't *promise* anything.'

'Yes you *did* promise!' I knew I had. 'But I don't care, Florian, not anymore. If you want to forget where you come from, then go ahead and forget but don't come crying back to us when they don't want you anymore.' Turning, he stalked into the shadows of the underpass again.

I followed him. 'Jerome.'

He spun back. 'We can forget about you too!' he bawled at me. 'Leave us alone!'

'*Who's down there?*'

Light-beams I now knew as triglycerate shot out of the underpass stairwell. They shone on pipes that stuck out of the wall, looping and delving into the cobbles of the road. Jerome made a dash towards the shadows of the stable on the right, but the horse veered its great head towards him. He leapt back.

A man came down from upstairs wearing a nightgown and slippers. His lantern batted on a pipe. 'What the blazing *dredth* is this ruckus?' he demanded, looking straight at Jerome who stood before him. 'A refugee, inside the Inner City? That *pelkhing* useless district watch, for all the honest tax I pour into the civic coffers, gah! Get you away and to your shelter right this *instant!*'

My friend darted away from him and out the other side of the underpass, while the man of the house crossed over to his horse. He stroked its snout protectively, but I could still see Jerome standing against the lights of the Inner Gate.

'Away!' the man shouted at him, sighting him too. 'Before I summon the guard!'

Jerome bolted.

The man swung around to face me then, lantern-light rocking on the underpass walls.

'As for you,' he said, 'servant. It is improper, your consorting with those refugee children. I might report to you to the Iron Shield for less—have your legs and arms tanned crimson for misdemeanour. Don't tempt me now. Be on your way back to your lodgings at once.'

'No sir, you . . .' I stammered. 'You don't understand.'

'Dare you answer me, you little *chidhik!*' he snarled.

I backed away from him quickly, understanding his mistake, all the while trying to think what my friend was going to say to Con. If it even mattered anymore.

'Child, are you simple or deaf?' He swayed as he barked right in my face; clearly enough he'd taken drink. 'Back to your quarters—*go* I say!'

Unable to see any other way around the estate, I ran away from his lantern and his last threatening shouts; between the neighbouring manors, only slowing when I was sure he hadn't called on someone else to chase and see me punished.

I retraced my steps.

Among the stately houses, now, there were no more people on the roads. More of the windows were dark. The air was cold and the palms swayed more ominously. Even the guards in the courtyard had moved off or stopped their talking. The gate into the gravel yard was locked and wrapped in chains; the yard empty. The shadowed scarf-men had gone too. They'd probably been the ones to shut and lock the gate, my own imagination turning honest workers into rogues who wished me harm. It didn't matter: even if it had been open, the tall Deeping Door was closed as well.

I rattled the gate for no reason. A guard stepped into view at the other end of the yard and shouted something in so heavy an accent that I didn't understand him. I took my hands off the gate, but hesitated a moment, wondering if it was best to let him arrest me right there. Maybe that way he would take me to the Captain like before, and from there to Rusper Symphin again.

Was I really thinking about that? Of going back to Rusper Symphin? The guard waved me back with his spear, and this time I understood his shout: 'To your master!'

Maybe not. I left the gate and found the entrance to the barracks by myself. But because of the dark vennel that encompassed the steps up to the doors, I didn't realise they too were closed until I was right in front of them.

Only one way was open: a road that sloped down into another, lower, district of the city. Not knowing what else I should do, my feet moved me on towards that gate, between the houses, terraced villas, long grey walls of windows with their tiny orange lights blinking inside. I heard the restless noise of many, many people in close quarters, listening as I walked, before I realised that this was probably where the evacuated people of Verunia had been put. I wandered on into the narrow, deadened veins of a marketplace. Empty, sleeping. Above the market, the fortress wall: between its fiery lights I saw the watchmen with their poles, all gazing out into the desert. None saw me passing through the market.

Behind the canvas of a stand I found a shelf, raised from the ground. A heap of tangled-up fishnets lay on the shelf. I didn't care how bad it smelled; it was dry at least. "No more fishing parties to the coast," someone had said, "so no more fish." I pulled and stretched the scabby mass until it covered my body. The warmth came slowly, but it came.

Jerome's words bled, now I was still, so I pushed them away and thought of Con. And that stung *worse*.

I couldn't think about my people anymore, I hated it.

So I forgot about them. Forgetting the world, I drifted, dreamed: not of blood spilled in the river plain, or Erik and Sarah, or monsters in the place that had been home. Not of Naemia or Vorth, or the people of either.

I dreamed machines.

NINE

THE IRON SHIELD

It was *them*—the wild boys!

I kicked the fishing nets away, tumbled off the shelf and crouched to hide behind the canvas, daylight shooting little arrows through its pores.

Not quick enough. The sheet was swept back from the stall and sunshine blazed into my face. 'Here, look what! It's the border boy!' was the gleeful cry.

As I tried to shield my eyes from the sunlight, more than two pairs of hands reached down and grabbed me up off the ground. Others joined in the effort once I was up, and I was yanked forward by my shirt. 'Ha-ha! What's he wearing today?'

'Looks fit for *greenstring*, so he does!'

'Ugh, an' he stinks!' spat one boy. 'You *smell* that?' He pinched his nose, batting the air.

Another leaned in and sniffed me. 'Awhhh yuck!' he spluttered and spun away.

Bath wasted already, then: even though I couldn't smell it anymore, I knew I stank like rotten fish. The other stalls near where I'd slept had started opening for trade, laying out their wares on boards and counters either side of the narrow way. Some early shoppers milled among them.

Another boy stepped in to grab my new shirt's collar. It was the tallest boy, the leader, the one I'd fought on the first day. He brought his face up close to mine and, as if rising to the dare, took a deep whiff of my neck. 'Mmm . . .' he mocked right in my ear.

I tried to pull away, 'Let go,' but he kept his grip on my collar. The others mimicked *let go! let go!* in silly voices. 'Shut up!' I yelled and pulled hard, angry. And came free, hurtling straight into a stall across the way. A tall amphora keeled forward from a shelf and exploded into pieces next to me.

The boys condensed, a tight pack, laughing: 'Clumsy git!' and 'Some dancer you are, borderlander!'

'*Borderlander?*' A pair of glaring eyes appeared between the still-standing amphorae.

A woman, passing a coin with one hand and holding a bag of spices in the other, turned frowning eyes at me out of her yashmak. 'Which one—*him?*'

The merchant emerged from behind his shelf of tall earthenware pots and scowled at the broken pieces. 'The feral scamp, see what he's done to my stock!'

I darted away from him, towards the woman.

'Shouldn't be any borderlanders on this side, only down the North District . . .' she was saying. 'And that shirt's citadel service, why's he . . .'

Before I could slip away past her, two of the boys jumped out to block me. They crossed their arms with fat smug smiles. 'Nah, musta stole it. He's a borderlander alright.'

'Theft *and* damages!' the amphora merchant exclaimed. 'How you gonna pay—'

'What's afoot there?' asked someone else. A man's voice. The boys who blocked me turned and looked at who was coming, as did the merchant and the woman. From around the turbans, cloaks and shawls of other shoppers, stepped an official. I hadn't seen this uniform: a vivid blue with streaks of white. On his belt and boots, silver buckles gleamed in the morning sunlight. His forearms were bound with gauntlets of silvery steel, and on his head he wore a helmet that cascaded a mane of long blue tassels down steel-capped shoulders. At his side hung a sword in a scabbard of the same blue and white. He stopped between the two boys and looked at me.

Our eyes met.

Blue and white.

I don't know how I did it: some instinct must have told me where the leader and other boys were standing. I spun around and made a feint towards the pottery shelf. That drew all three of those boys and in the split second it gave me, I was around them and running.

'*Hold that boy!*' I heard behind me through the whoops and howls of boys. The boys gave chase.

Zigzagging out of the market, I sprinted hard alongside the stacked buildings of stone, the long white ones, and then the ones with the terraces, past the curving houses with tiled roofs, across a yard of farming carts and pens of animals, then up the slope that I remembered from last night and back into the Inner City. The whoops and cries were never far. Once I recognised where I was, I made straight for the barracks – only to be cut off by *another* flash of blue and white before I reached it. I jack-knifed away from the second official, taking a new direction beside the wall of the courtyard instead. It was the way I'd come last night before turning towards the underpass. This time I just kept straight.

At a break in the wall, I grabbed the leg of a stone statue – one of two birds that manned what seemed to be the courtyard's public entrance – and stopped to catch some of my breath. I dared a glance over my shoulder. The boys raced into view, howling and yawping. And then that shining helmet too, its tassels swaying with each step.

I pushed away from the stone bird, turning left into the almost-empty courtyard, and charged across the flagstones. Ahead was the rising citadel, its broad steps climbing to grand doors. Below the steps a huge stone beast bestrode a plinth; one clawed foot raised, its wings outstretched, eyes gazing straight ahead at me. Two men with spears were standing near it – yes, yes, the *guards!* But that break for breath had cost me: before I reached them, one of my towel-sleeves was grabbed from behind and I was pulled.

I fell on my back, grunting as my head smacked on a flagstone. Above me was the beast. Down its curved beak, between huge talons, it seemed to glower over me, the shadow of its wings encompassing me and the two guards, who came closer. One of the guards shouted the boys back – and I heard them fan out, skipping – while the other looked at me as if I'd gone completely mad. 'Somewhere urgent to be, have you?'

'Please take me to the Viceroy,' I gasped as I propped myself up on an elbow. 'He knows who I am. You'll see if you just take me to him, please!'

The men exchanged a dubious glance, the first wiping a smile from his lips. 'If you've a message or errands for the Viceroy, they'll wait, lad. Sanhedrin council's to convene in an hour.'

'That there's a borderland accent,' said his partner. 'This one's a refugee.'

'If he is, why's he dressed for citadel duties?'

'*Torn your fancy dress, border boy?*' gibed one of the wild boys behind me. They'd retreated a short distance away, hopping as they circled the beast-statue. But now behind them the blue-and-white official entered the courtyard.

'Please!' I begged the two guards.

'*Hold that boy there!*'

'Ugh, now you've done it,' groaned the first guard as both leaned down, each for an arm, and pulled me up onto my feet.

'Hey, let me go! I've to go to the Viceroy,' I protested as I squirmed between them. The sound of my voice ricocheted in the cup of the stone wings, then echoed in squealing voices by the boys.

'So you've told us,' said the first guard but only turned me around to face the blue-and-white. The hopping boys widened their circle to make way for my pursuer who slowed his jog to a walk, hand resting on the hilt of his sword.

'Hand him over,' he said when he reached us.

'Lieutenant, we're under instructions from the Captain to return any strays to their shelter,' the second guard said woodenly.

'It's true!' I shouted. 'They *are!* I was there when he gave them!'

'Look, just pipe down, kid, will you,' said the guard.

As he stopped just shy of the winged shadow, the blue-and-white looked from me to the guards; a lordly look. 'My own instructions are different,' he told them. 'A refugee has no business outside the North District. As such there must and will be consequences. Mondric knows this.'

A new voice: 'Florian!'

Blue tassels swung as the helmet turned.

Two figures were coming towards us from the entrance. Fast as he could on his crutch, Con hobbled into the courtyard with Jerome tailing him. The boys threw curses.

'*More* refugees!' the blue-and-white bellowed across the open flagstones. 'Do you know the offence you commit by entering this quarter?'

Con came within speaking distance; breathless, eyes blood-shot, shirt soaked through with sweat. 'My name is Conrad Imry.'

'No one asked for your name.'

Con nodded to me. 'I came for that boy. He's with us.'

'Which, I think you'll find, is where he should have stayed,' the blue-and-white replied. 'Now he finds himself in the custody of the Iron Shield. As you will too, should you fail to quit this district at *once*.' He turned and beckoned to the guards. To my horror, their grip relaxed on my shoulders as, no longer arguing, they gave me up and thrust me out. Dumb cowards!

'It's not safe here, Florian. Come back with us.' Con reached a hand out towards me while Jerome didn't even move, staring at me blackly. I sickly felt there should be some kind of audience for all this drama, and yet apart from the ring of wild boys and a little beggar slouched against the courtyard wall, the place was empty. Con urged: '*Now*, Florian.' But I didn't want to. I knew that.

The blue-and-white took a step closer. 'It's me you'll be coming with, boy, and I would advise you to come quietly.'

I retreated deeper into the shade of the stone wings, aware that behind me the two guards had moved onto the steps, moving away. 'Only if you take me to . . . Caliph Symphin,' I said, trying to bargain with him.

'You're in no position to be making demands,' the man scoffed. 'You have trespassed.'

Not far behind Con and Jerome, the pack of wild boys had started shouting in a chant as if baying for blood. It distracted me at just the wrong moment. Before I thought he could reach me, the blue-and-white lunged and grabbed me by the neck. I twisted, slipped out of the hold, but he caught my wrist. I dug my heels into the edges of the flagstones and leaned, tugging on my forearm and flailing. But he was a wall of pure strength.

Everything slowed then, though it happened within seconds. Con's crutch fell down with a clatter as he put himself between us; wrapped one hand around my arm and the other around the blue-and-white's steel gauntlet.

Boys cheered at that.

They cheered again as my captor rammed the pommel of his sword up and into my friend's stomach. Con doubled over, limping backwards, and then the blade was drawn clear of its scabbard, the handle striking him across the face.

His fingers left me.

A broad blade sliced down through the air and stopped an inch before Con's throat as he lay prone across the flagstones. Jerome suddenly lost some of his tan, his eyes like saucers, chest pumping hard. His brother moaned but kept his chin above the tip of the steel.

'You will take greater care, young man,' the blue-and-white warned him down the blade. 'There are wills in this city that are greater than the Viceroy's. Wills not to be thwarted. This child is under arrest. You may have some of him returned to you in due course, or you may not. The decision rests with other powers.'

'*Stick 'im! Kill 'im!*' the circle cried.

'But he's done nothing!' I shouted back, looking to the guards on the steps for help. But they also did nothing—nothing but watch—and when I looked back to Con, the blue-and-white had turned to me again.

There was a moment of strange calm as he let go of my arm. Then, either side of the helmet's nosepiece, his nostrils flared with anger. Blue tassels flailing, he swung the sword and wheeled the pommel from the left. It struck me just above my temple and threw my body like a branch; the pain too pure and white to feel it when I landed.

I heard only laughter from the boys and Con's scream —'*Bastard!*' From the steps, the guards—'*Lieutenant . . .*' And then—'*Stay out of this one, guardsman.*' That voice was right above me. My collar pinched the skin of my neck as he hauled me up, ripping my shirt-front.

My vision blurred as he grappled me into a standing position, but I saw Con: he'd got up and was limping towards us again, a stream of blood down his face.

'I've warned you,' growled the blue-and-white, sword pointed at Con's chest. That metal gauntlet was now pressed up against my windpipe, but then he slammed me hard against the statue's plinth. I heard my head crack on the stone but barely felt it. 'You would do well to stand clear. I've no qualm killing the boy where he stands.'

Behind Jerome, the boys regrouped. I saw the leader striding forward. Smirking, he picked up a shard of broken flagstone and gaily flipped it, hand to hand. His eyes were fixed on Con's turned back. I tried to warn him, say his name, but couldn't speak over the gauntlet.

Con staggered closer, fading my focus on the blue-and-white who had me. There was nothing I could do.

The tall boy shoved Jerome aside, clearing a path, and slung the shard.

In that moment I think I went blind. I heard the wet thud of the impact, Jerome's scream, the wild pack's whooping. Boots of the guards rushing from the steps. That bark in my ear —'*Get moving!*'—as I was dragged onto the grand steps, past the stone beast, towards the high doors. Pain filtered through me.

When my eyes could see again, Con was lying totally still, head in a puddle that welled and ran between the flagstones. A guard was kneeling next to him. *Help him,* I willed. The other guard chased back the boys who'd claimed the crutch as a new weapon and had started closing on Jerome. Only once I was above the statue's wings could I see my friend running from them, tripping and stumbling from the kicks.

A ball of pain. That's all I was. In it, somewhere, was the hope that he'd march me to the Captain. Of course he didn't. Foolish. Instead he marched me into an ugly, dark and jagged little room and there forced me against a grille of bars. The grille was opened. Again he hit me with the pommel of his sword, this time in the back, and I tumbled forward. He slammed the grille and my knees buckled. My body had never known this much pain. Too much for tears. Too much to really feel it all at the same time. Consciousness thinned and though he spoke at me, he sounded far away.

'. . . *don't belong here . . . not long . . . pale-faced kind back in the desert at the mercy of the monsters you brought . . .*'

Couldn't look up, couldn't focus.

'. . . *regulations . . . proper treatment for thankless guests . . . learn soon enough.*'

I tried to speak: 'Captain Mondric . . .'

'He won't help you,' sneered the man before calling loudly, '*Where's the dwarf?*'

He left.

I hugged my knees and bit one hard. As the throbbing in my temple grew stronger and stronger, I leaned against the bars to cool my eye on their metal. The darkness lapped around me as I fought to keep myself awake; tried to concentrate on the rhythms of footfalls and clatters I could hear from somewhere, and tried to figure out what part of the citadel this was. Not the barracks. Not the Deep. I winced at that. Only last night had Rusper Symphin warned me about the blue-and-white men, and yet here I was: their captive. Would Rusper Symphin, or the Captain, ever come to this place? And if they did, would they recognise me? Probably not, and so I knew I couldn't afford to fall asleep.

Still, I flopped onto my side. I thought of Con lying in his blood and hoped with all the hope I still had that someone had helped him, taken him back to those healers, in time. Those guards could have done. Yes, that was something. They would have taken him to the healers like before.

But Jerome? Those boys were animals. If they caught him up before he got back to the warehouse, they'd kill him. Just like they'd tried to kill Con.

Refusing to sink into that fear, I stood and gripped the metal grille. Through the bars I looked at the room outside the cell. It was lit by a single guttering torch, high on a wall. Three ways led out: one left, one right and one by stairs leading down. Beside the stairs there was a table. It was bare but for a vice at one edge, all spattered black. I felt faint looking at it, so crouched to crawl into the darkest spot I could find, and stayed there.

And then I saw him. A short, round figure – his belly squeezed under the belt of his hessian cloak – approached my cell from the left passage. His hood was frayed, his boots were scuffed. And in the crook of his right arm something was wriggling: a wrinkled body of pinkish white; some long, translucent, hairless creature. Through the creature's skin I saw its bones and tiny, rapid-beating heart.

The little man came to the grille and wedged his face between its bars. Small beady eyes, a froggy mouth. Then I remembered: it was *him,* the little beggar who had been slouched in the courtyard when the blue-and-white took me.

I said, 'Who are you?'

His forehead expanded upwards like a swiftly rising loaf of bread, revealing the whites of his eyes. 'Hetch,' he replied in a powdery voice. Then nudged the creature's flat head into view. It had no eyes; only a vile, long-whiskered snout with two big fangs poking out. 'Heironymus.'

It was disgusting.

'What is it?'

'Sandrat.'

The man was simple, I realised. There was some dribble on his chin. Maybe he'd wandered in from the courtyard. No, he couldn't have, surely: I'd failed to get into the citadel again without first being arrested. But it didn't matter. I sighed and tried to ignore him away. He didn't go. He stayed exactly where he was, forehead shrinking closed again until his puffy little eyes looked more like folded pastries.

'He *will* come back again, you know,' he informed me. 'The Lieutenant, Jharis. Doesn't like you Naemians.'

'I noticed.'

'None of the Shield do. It's the law here, you see.'

'What law?'

'Against *you.*'

It wasn't hard to be stern with him. 'Tell me where I am.'

'Gaol of the Iron Keep.'

'I'm in a keep?'

'Well, you're being *kept*, aren't you,' he answered, lavishing the creature with a long stroke. 'Because you're Naemian, I told you. But you don't *look* Naemian, Naemian. A poor example. Tell us your name.' I looked away, shaking my head, but he bargained. 'We told you *our* names.'

'*Dwarf, there you are!*'

Suddenly the little man shrank from my grille as the blue-and-white came back up the stairs. Now cradling the helmet of blue tassels at his hip, his bald head gleamed in the failing torchlight. His lips were thin and flat and dark, his eyes ringed all around with shadows.

'Here at your service, Lieutenant,' said the dwarf as he cowered. The sandrat climbed onto his shoulder, then clawed its way down his swathed back.

The Lieutenant flicked his head towards me as if I were something a dog had done on the floor. 'You've found our borderling then.'

'The offence, sir?'

'Strayed too far, this one.'

I glared my fury through the grille.

'Can't have it, no,' said Hetch. Grinding my teeth, I showed him a share of that fury. The ugly little goblin had tried to get me to trust him.

'No we cannot,' said the Lieutenant. 'Nor should the Viceroy expect leniency from the Shield. Where he fails to contain his contraventions, he will know it. If not from the throne, then from those most faithful to it. A clear example must be made of his audacity, dwarf, or anarchy will bring the capital to its knees even before the Rath reach its walls.'

'We've seen the like before, Lieutenant.'

'But not again.' Slotting his key into the grille, the blue-and-white gave orders. 'Take a finger, bind the wound, return him to his people. Let it be a memorable warning.'

Hetch wheezed, 'My pleasure,' as the grille swung wide. The blue-and-white pulled me up, out of the cell, and at the dwarf. Though Hetch was taller than me by not much more than a foot, his pig-like limbs were more than a match for my strength. He hauled me over to the table, eyes all asparkle. 'A finger.' He slammed my arm down, sprung the vice's catch, took my wrist and squeezed it into the claw of icy metal. The vice clapped shut.

With every beat I thought my heart might rip right out of my chest, and as I hung there off the edge of the table I scrapped all pride; met the Lieutenant's dusky eyes and let my face beg them for mercy. But I might as well have begged two stones.

'The *Senera* requests my presence in council,' he said. Then lunged and seized my shirt again. 'Remember well this moment!' he hissed at me, flecking my face with spit, before releasing me to the grip of the vice and the dwarf. The right-hand passage swallowed up his bootfalls as he left the gaol, or maybe I just couldn't hear them over the noise of my heart trying to burst out.

Hetch had a knife now: playfully he stropped it over the vice, whetting the blade. I looked at my hand, pinioned and encircled by old black splashes. My heart climbed, every beat pushing it higher towards escaping through my mouth. I whimpered, writhing, but writhing was useless. I was held by iron.

Hetch said, 'Be still.'

And then the sandrat was back: it leapt onto Hetch's shoulder. An evil, wriggling spectator even without eyes, it chattered as if cheering its master on to split my flesh and break my bone and add my blood to the tabletop. The placeless echoes of the passages around us wheeled, a nightmare, while small black spots formed on my eyes, mouth drying up. He splayed my fingers, and chose. Cool steel pushed in, pressing the skin against the bone. The middle one. 'Please,' I cried, squeezing my eyes shut.

'Be *still*,' he wheezed in answer, 'if you want a clean cut, that is.' The knife left my skin and I sagged, legs going limp.

This thing would happen. It *was* happening. And I *did* want a clean cut.

He chopped—I screamed. Screamed with so much fear and rage and horror that surely that blue-and-white Lieutenant, wherever he'd gone, must have heard and smiled. Scoring my throat, I screamed before there was even any pain to scream at. I'd scream it out, all of it.

The catch sprang open and released me. I fell to the floor, skin dragging off the iron of the vice, and gripped the wrist, ready to faint. *It's not that bad, it's not that bad.*

It really wasn't.

No—there wasn't *any* pain at all. When I had the guts to open an eye, I saw a white weal marking the place where the vice had squeezed my captive wrist. But there was no blood on my hand. No ragged, belching finger-stump. I had five fingers. Had he missed? My head was swimming, body shaking and I felt sick. But I knelt and peeped over the table just in time to see the dwarf tug his knife free of the wood and slide it under his belt-strap, at no small risk to his belly. The sandrat laughed, draped on his shoulder, while the man's fat fingers pulled a cork. He tipped dark liquid from a flask onto the table, spattering.

'What are you doing?' I dared to ask him.

'You *shh!*'

He tucked the flask away and slung the sandrat, like so much laundry, to his other shoulder. Then lunged for me. There wasn't time to decide if trusting him would be a good or bad idea before he grabbed my hand, pulled me up and dragged me down the stairs of the gaol.

TEN

PLAMEN

Hetch was strong. And he was fast. He pulled me towards the daylight now, my hand squeezed so tightly in his that it almost crushed my rescued fingers.

Torchlight behind us, I felt fresh air on my face, and we were out! We made our way across a kind of bridge that spanned part of the courtyard thoroughfare, through a doorway and back into the main citadel.

Suddenly, at the sound of many footsteps, Hetch stopped. I slammed right into his back, the sandrat looping around his head to gnash long fangs towards my face. I backed away; Hetch pulled me in.

We were at the edge of a grey hall that ran between a pair of colonnaded aisles. Through it, out of a series of grey foyers, a procession of people was moving. Their footsteps whispered on the stone and murmurs echoed in a high ceiling. I saw the Caliph of Verunia, recognising him from the day when he and his people had arrived at the city. He wore purple, as he had then, but this time a finer, longer garment with red brocades. Close behind him walked a fat man robed in a cream-coloured cloth; over his head a wide tallith that jangled beads. There was a square-faced man too, with silvering hair and guardsman's—

Before I could call out to Captain Mondric, the dwarf's clammy palm clapped the word back in my mouth. Just in time. Not far behind the Captain, the blue-and-white uniform flashed into view from the same foyers.

Hetch hissed, 'Head down!' and *shoved* it down. Shunting my body to his side, he moved his grip to my elbow and pulled me on. Keeping to the shadows of the aisle, we kept pace with the procession of folk; between the passing columns I glimpsed their robes and gowns swishing, dreamlike. They were all heading towards an atrium at the other end of the hall where sunlight streamed through open doors.

Our own aisle ended in a much gloomier wall and smaller door. In place of a handle, knob or keyhole, this door bore a strange double-hexagon of tarnished metal. Hetch grabbed the narrow T-shaped bar that stuck out of it and pulled, turned, pushed in, turned, and pulled again. Swore and repeated. Then opened the door, jostled me into a stale-smelling darkness and patted me twice on the head. 'Stay here,' he said, and shut me in.

Dark and cold. I hugged my arms.

What was going on? What had happened back there in the "Iron Keep," as he'd called it? That blue-and-white official had told the dwarf – this Hetch man – to cut off one of my fingers for being in a district that I shouldn't have been in, so why *hadn't* he? Why had he spared it? Why disobey and bring me here, wherever *here* was? He didn't know me. Did he?

Blood stirred by running, my battered temple throbbed even harder. Other pains bloomed all over me. To distract myself, I reached out and felt the door, wondering if it had a proper handle on this side. It did, though I nearly knocked something over right beside it: a spindly wooden stand as I saw when I opened the door a crack. And looked out.

He was there, the blue-and-white. The arriving folk had all now stopped in front of the atrium to stand and talk, and he was there among them, discussing something seriously with some other robed person. I watched him for a little while; as my body throbbed and stung from his blows, sickly fascinated by those thin, dark lips and the deep sockets of his eyes. Then someone else at the top of the hall must have called him away; he moved out of sight. From here I couldn't see the Captain either. Or Hetch.

I closed the door. And waited a long time. Or at least it felt a long time, standing there in the dark with only my soreness to think about. But the conversations were still murmuring out in the hall when I heard firm bootfalls coming to the door. It was pulled open—wide open—and I flinched.

Then almost smiled: High Commander Plamen stood there, framed by the grey light of the hall behind him. Although his headdress was off, for the first time revealing short, wiry black hair, he was like a shining champion in white. The relief flooded my aching body. I was safe now, had to be.

But there was no softness in his eyes.

'Do you have any idea of how seriously you have jeopardised the refuge of your people?' His voice was low – dangerously low – and it wasn't what I'd expected him to say. The headdress hung loose in his hand, but as I gaped, searching for a reply, he flopped it down onto the stand and pulled a breath in through his nose. 'Shall I repeat myself?'

'No,' I said, still struggling to find an answer. 'I mean . . . I'm sorry, I know, I . . .'

'You do *not* know,' he cut me off. 'I wonder how many men of power you think there are in this city with the welfare of foreign refugees at heart.'

Though he made me nervous, I raised my voice. 'How was I supposed to know—'

'The risks were explained to you clearly,' he said, raising his own. 'Yet you parade yourself in public and provoke the Iron Shield.'

'I didn't provoke anyone!'

'You will level your tone.'

That shut me up. It was the way he said it, with that self-possessed calmness, the *knowing* that I would obey. That was his power. *Command,* I thought. He strode forward and I backed deeper into the room. A circular room: vaguely, I'd realised that it was practically empty; some forgotten bubble in the stone. Plamen came right up to me but didn't move to touch me. His grey eyes roved over the injuries on my face.

I had to know. 'Did someone help him? My friend, Con, did someone take him to the healers?'

'The older boy? He is dead.'

Of course he was; I'd known already. And if I'd been looking for compassion, I'd opened my heart to the wrong man. I stopped the feeling as it started.

'A credit to the Captain's guards, the body was removed from the courtyard discreetly. It wasn't yours so be grateful. All the same, nothing justifies the carelessness you have shown. The Viceroy believes you have a head on your shoulders. A mind fit for mining, were his words. You'll forgive me if I do not share his opinion after this.'

I shied from his contempt. But then rallied. 'Who are the blue and white guards?'

He raised his chin, slowly exhaled. 'They are not guards. The Iron Shield are the eyes and protectors of the throne. Only they are permitted near His Majesty the Satrap at this time, aside from royal physicians, and now the Viceroy of course. Nor are they military. Their order is subservient to the Satrap *alone.* As such, neither I nor the Viceroy hold any authority over the likes of Jharis—the Lieutenant Shieldman *you* have crossed.'

Frowning, but understanding, I considered this against what the engineer had said about them yesterday.

'Caliph Symphin said we shouldn't even be here,' I said. 'He said we'd be in danger if the Satrap knew about us. But *they* know we're here, don't they?'

'Oh yes, they know.' His words knocked my eyes to the floor and I stared at it miserably, again feeling the horror rising up. I squashed it down.

'I don't want to go back,' I said. 'Not now. Not now that this has happened.'

'Nor will you,' he replied. I looked up to catch the flicker of a sneer. 'Don't look surprised, child. You have now prodded at lions with a stick. If someone does not act to quiet them, immediately, much attention will fall upon that little shelter of yours. Regardless of where it should suit you to live.'

'From the Satrap, you mean?'

He sighed, yes. 'Something, in your wisdom, you may seek to avoid.'

'What about the Lion Shield?'

'*Iron* Shield.'

'If they're his eyes, won't they tell—'

'Enough,' said Plamen. I swallowed, trying hard to read some expression in his face. But I couldn't. His mouth was flat and the one eye I could properly make out in the dimness was more like a pale shell sitting in his head than anything human. As he stepped away from me, adjusting the sleeves of his white robe, I knew he'd share no more about it. Not with me.

But I still dared it: 'What will you do?'

'What I've already *done* is no concern of yours. Clearly there is so little one might leave to your discretion,' he said, adding in a mutter, 'And now you've made me late for council.'

'Are my people safe?'

He looked back. 'Yes. For now. But your time with them is finished. Symphin made you an offer of employment. You will accept it. You will also forget what occurred in the courtyard today. The deaths. The arrest. The Iron Shield. My involvement. None will be mentioned again.'

'Not even to Caliph—'

'No.' The word dropped like a hammer and I gaped back at him, confused. He shook his head with what looked like scornful pity, as if astonished at just how little of his big world I understood. 'The Viceroy's position is more precarious than yours. He stands at the centre of everything in Antissa, his every movement and decision watched by hundreds. Both his actions *and* reactions.' He paused. 'If your people are to survive here, it will be because their existence remains outside the sphere of royal notice. And if *you* are prudent—if you can possibly achieve that much for their sake—then you will allow them no closer than you've brought them already. Symphin is not to know of this.'

It made a grim kind of sense, I had to admit to myself. Just for now, anyway, it would have to be enough that Commander Plamen had saved my finger, maybe even my life.

'I understand,' I told him.

'Doubtful.'

As he turned again, the sandrat darted in across the floor towards my feet like a sudden nightmare of slithering skin. I minced away from it, disgusted. Then Hetch appeared in the doorway with a lantern, bowl and folded linen. 'All has been done as you instructed,' he said to the Commander.

Plamen looked past him at the people in the hall; they'd started to move on through the big doors.

'What of the body?'

'It burns.'

'Hm. The two guards?'

'Will hold their silence.'

'Have them advised to expect a stipend of royal merit.'

'Yes, *ekharan*,' said Hetch. 'There was . . . one *other* boy, refugee boy, in the courtyard. But the gutterwaifs tailed him. If he got as far as the North District, he'll be toothless by now, more likely dead, sir. Won't be noticed down there, shouldn't think.'

'No. Good,' said Plamen and swung his hard gaze back to me. 'You see now what comes of not heeding our warnings.'

I said nothing. The Commander took his headdress from the stand; with practiced movements he returned it to his head and rearranged its many folds while I simply stood there, staring, trying to rid my mind of the image of Con's body burning. Plamen refitted the silver band around his now covered temple, pointing its blood-red jewel forward. He was cruel. But he was right.

It was so cold in this room.

'This door will be locked. As you've succeeded in destroying the garments provided you by the Viceroy, here are new ones. Water also. Your face is filthy. Wash it, dress and be ready when I return.'

Hetch shuffled forward, although under his hessian cowl I couldn't tell if he met my eyes. He set the items on the floor and shuffled out just as quickly. The sandrat's tailless rear-end, like a puckered, rot-pocked vegetable, was the last thing I saw before the door was banged shut.

The chugs and twists of that locking block thudded through the wood. Then bootfalls mingled with the pattering of shoes and murmured voices; I heard his dull voice give some greetings, then disappear. Big doors groaned closed. And there was silence.

Silence and pain. More silence, worsening pain.

And Con . . .

No, not that. Cringing, I crouched in the lantern's shallow pool of light and peeled my shirt off. Ribs, knees, shoulders and arms all ached in different colours and my temple was on fire. There wasn't soap but I was able, if very slowly, to wash. The shirt was white like the first one, its open neck cross-hatched with lace. It too was long and so I tucked it through the binding of my breeches. My heart sank at the same silly width of its sleeves; I rolled them back behind my elbows. Surely no one would notice, or care.

The light was weak. I picked up the lantern by its handle and held it out to the curved walls; only now, as I cast shadows on the stone, noticing that there was another little door. It too was locked when I tried it, and had no metal unlocking block, let alone a handle. I set my ear against the wood and held my breath. Which also hurt.

There were voices. Arguing voices, like the hagglers of the street-markets; first one, then all at once. I rattled the door. There was a latch, I could feel it, on the other side.

I'd need a tool.

Well, the lantern was almost dead anyway. The first thing I tried to do was detach its handle, but it was too thoroughly fused to the box. So instead I flipped the catches of the panes and lifted them. Inside, the triglycerate crystal glowed meekly – like fireflies of the river-plain that used to get inside the huts in summertime. I shook that memory away and pinched the element between my fingers. Warm. The inner rods holding the crystal in place were of a metal more brittle than copper. "Undercopper," I'd heard it called. And sure enough, when I tugged it sharply, it snapped.

With the crystal for light I eased my undercopper lever between the wood of the door and the stone, and after several aching minutes of careful sliding in and up, snared just enough of the latch. I prised it clear and heard it swing, then nudged the door in with my toe.

The pale green light fell on a spiral stairway, leading up from here. The voices echoed from above.

I climbed towards them.

Eleven

Sanhedrin

The voices burst clear at the top. I ducked below a row of railings and made small.

'*Hundreds are dead and for what?*'

'*We have retreated!*'

'*At what cost when the ergish regiments were pushed straight onto the front lines? Now those caliphs cannot defend their own people!*'

'*Where then are those caliphs? Stand down!*'

At the sudden uproar of shouting that followed, I covered my ears. My climb had brought me to a narrow balcony that I figured must span the atrium and big doors. Ahead, light poured from a hole in the dome of the ceiling, contrasting the grey hall I could still see if I looked back. Crouching low, I crept forward to peer between the railings.

At least a hundred people filled the amphitheatre below, in so much colour and detail that I couldn't make sense of them all at first. I scanned for costumes I'd seen before. Some, though only a handful, wore robes like the High Commander's. There was a cluster of men in rough brown cassocks. Five very serious looking men in dark blue gowns and talliths stood at the edge of the central floor. Two men I knew were engineers by their working gear of hide and metal, sat together. Neither was Rusper Symphin.

Only one woman was here. Arrayed in flowing silks of shiny silver, head decked with many twisted braids, she sat flanked by two blue-and-white officials. It was Lieutenant Jharis himself on her right.

Plamen's voice: 'Sanhedrin gives audience to the Caliph of Verunia.' I craned my neck to better see the far right side of the floor. Over there, slightly elevated, the High Commander stood at a rostrum in the cascade of seating tiers.

'Verunia!' called a second voice, high and nasal.

The floor's central circle was flagged in mosaic: the crescent-moon-and-rays emblem I had such good reason to remember. Now a skinny-legged man in livid red retreated to its edge, while the purple-gowned Caliph of Verunia stepped in from the left.

'*Ekharaan* of the Sanhedrin,' he said, and gesturing to the woman, '*Sinarre.* I hereby call the Honorary Caliph to account upon defence of greater Vorth. Rath have now been sighted on the northern bank of the Empty River, the last hopeful frontier before the capital. There is only one fortress. Fears are growing, and rightly, for the desert communities that stand wholly undefended.'

'Arif, your caliphy is emptied and your people well protected,' said one of the serious blue-gowns.

'I speak for Laudassa and Methar,' said Arif.

'And what of Shad?' someone shouted. 'Are the people of the south not entitled to the same? Their regiments were all but obliterated in the border defence!'

'And that,' replied Arif, 'is why I should encourage Shad's caliph to join me *himself* before the Viceroy in demanding the release of his remaining forces from Antissa.'

I concentrated hard, doing my best to understand what they were talking about down there. As yet I'd still heard only seeming scraps of an older language in the desert's Prate: like *ekh* and *sen* for mister and missus; lengthening into *ekharan* and *sinarre* for more important people; names of the Vedish foods and dishes and, of course, some of the swears—but why, even in the Prate, did they have to use such long and complicated words for everything? Already, there were so many names I hadn't heard before. "Shad" was one of Vorth's "caliphies," just like Verunia, that much I grasped. But how many caliphies *were* there? Which of these men were *their* caliphs?

That same blue-gown was speaking: 'Why then do you press for defence of Methar? Should not the caliph speak for himself in this matter?'

'Caliph Bardon is not *here*, Vizier Nasser,' Arif replied, 'inconveniently.' A few in the tiers exchanged smug grins and laughter.

'Nor Caliph Khalin!'

Well, that answered that.

Arif went on for a bit then. Something about "the old Vedish way," whatever that was, and more laughter rippled on the tiers. The amusement wasn't shared by the five blue-gowns however, who huddled in, even while Arif was giving his piece, to confer with one another. As they did, a new man stood from the tier behind them. His robes and turban were black, hemmed with gold, and his face made me think of a weasel.

'Your Verunia emptied by choice,' he said archly, addressing Arif. 'Laudassa and Methar are surely free to do the same.'

Arif answered: 'I might have expected better from you, Dranz. You forget that Antissa already shelters the people of two caliphies. The streets are overcrowded, the farming quarters barely meeting the demands now bloated by our own evacuees—to say nothing of what *others* the fortress has seen fit to house here.'

My heartbeat quickened.

Plamen warned, 'Have a care.'

After a strange pause, Arif continued: 'And now we are informed that the city's pipes begin to falter. Our very *water* is at stake!' A round of jeering went up, almost drowning out another warning from Plamen at the rostrum. I saw the weasel in black and gold make a sour face. Arif raised his voice—'It is clear that few more may be accommodated here, and so it is we risk desertion of our people to the mercy of an enemy unchecked. The lives of *all* Vedans are the burden of the throne.' Another pause. 'I would thus present the clerics of the temple of Chidh Eshipas, who have travelled from Laudassa to be in attendance at this council.'

My eyes followed his purple, welcoming arm to the cluster of men in brown cassocks.

'Erg-baked madmen!' the black-and-gold weasel spat with venom, but returned to his seat when Plamen again called the room to order.

As the mingled reactions of insult and amusement rolled and peaked and washed out, I counted the clerics. Fifteen. Their skins, I thought, were not naturally so dark, but rather blackened and hardened as if scorched by the sun. Most were heavily bearded. All wore tall, square hats and placid expressions, sitting primly with their hands on their knees.

Arif was speaking: '. . . and as Caliph Bardon chooses to remain in Methar, I call upon Omran, Caliph of Laudassa, to speak on behalf of both middle caliphies.'

The purple caliph drew back from the mosaic while another stood. It was the fat man I'd seen walking beside him in the hall, his dangling droplets of amber now swaying on an awkward journey to the floor. Stepping onto the mosaic, he placed his hands on his belly and said, 'My courtesies to Verunia.'

Arif bowed.

'Indeed, it is a matter of greatest delicacy that I bring before the Viceroy and Sanhedrin. As will be well known among the *ekhars* of this most solemn council, Laudassa and Methar are home to among the last sacred monuments left by the Builders. I do not deny, of course, that the value of such sites has long since diminished among the Vedans of our age and modern thinking. However, I can no more deny that the clerics remain bound by their own tenets to safeguard them.'

'*Pelkhish* fantasies!' scoffed the weasel.

'Dranz!' a blue-gown rebuked him. 'Tether your tongue and hear Laudassa.'

'I'll have order,' Plamen drawled.

The headdress jangled again as Omran shook his head and continued: 'You may refute the clerical tradition as you wish, esteemed *ekharaan*, but those traditions do not exempt them from protection in war. Neither the clerics of Laudassa, nor those of Methar, will consent to evacuation by order of the throne or Viceroyalty. Thus is my entreaty to the Honorary Caliph at this time that measures be taken forthwith in defence of their sites.'

'Does the good caliph have intentions of *returning* to Laudassa, I wonder?' someone sneered. 'Or will he, perhaps, be taking residence in the capital instead?'

Heckles came from several directions, and Arif swept out in front of Omran as if to shield him. 'Who said that?' he demanded in outrage.

'Speaker to rise,' Plamen called.

Someone did: a man in layers of green.

'Vizier Ramed,' said Arif. The challenger raised his palms facetiously as if in answer. 'Caliph Omran should not be present at this assembly were it not that he feared for the people of Laudassa. Yet you insult him!'

'Caliph Omran is no cleric,' the green argued with a small laugh. 'Why must he persist in honouring such archaic customs?'

Omran rejoined: 'Vorth is not yet invaded, *ekharan*. There is no cause to wantonly abandon the traditions of the south.'

Up on their tier, the clerics hummed and nodded.

'Yet it would appear reason enough for you to abandon Laudassa, Caliph Omran,' said the green. 'You have not yet answered my question.'

As the green-layers grinned, Omran's cheeks puffed out ruddy, but Arif placed a reassuring hand on his shoulder. 'Nor will he. The fact is plain. The people of Vorth are not defended in war.'

'We are not *at* war,' said a new voice—*one I knew*—from the right.

Arif looked towards the source, then gently brushed his pointed beard as if to hide his own small smile. 'Begging your patience, Honorary Caliph, but Naemia's invaders are in force upon your doorstep. You cannot deny that the threat of the Rath is immediate.'

'I denied nothing of the kind.' The balcony blocked my view to him.

But it was Plamen who spoke next; briskly, loudly and clearly reminding the council that, by "royal decree," Vorth had withdrawn from all engagement in active warfare, and that by the very same decree the Viceroyalty had been empowered to do no more than defend.

'*Defence*, High Commander, is precisely what has brought Caliph Omran and his clerics to the Sanhedrin,' said Arif. 'As the capital's neighbouring caliphy, I see no reason that Laudassa should be refused its own garrison.'

'That is impossible,' said the new voice, still invisible, on the right. And now I heard movement from there.

'Council gives audience to Honorary Caliph Symphin, Viceroy,' said Plamen, and the nasal man in red announced the same thing twice as loudly.

Arif and Omran left the mosaic to make way for Rusper Symphin. As the engineer tapped down the shallow steps, I saw none of that scorched leather and metal armour, gloves or goggles of his workshop. Headgear now gone, I saw a shock of grey and white: straight, thinning hair raked back over his scalp, behind his ears. His robes were crimson, gold-hemmed, flared at the shoulders, wrists and waist. Under his collar ran the chain of that medallion. He seemed larger, even from above.

'The capital is fully aware of the danger Vorth faces,' he said, his voice crisp and vital as he walked along the edge of the mosaic. 'Our borders have been breached by Ratheine force and attempts to repel those numbers have failed. The north's invaded.'

Arif folded his arms.

'The conclusion we *cannot* draw is that the caliphies of middle and southern Vorth stand under threat. Little is known of this enemy, why they are here—indeed, why their hordes beset Naemia's coast in the last decade! And yet for all the devastation they wrought upon that realm, an unchecked force intent on conquest would have reached Antissa by now. It has not.'

Another blue-gown interrupted: 'Viceroy, they have occupied the borderlands.'

I flinched.

'Occupied. Yet made no inroads south of the Empty River,' answered Rusper Symphin.

A cough from Arif. 'Honorary Caliph, you wish to *understand* the pale creatures before defending the Satrap's realm against them?'

'The lives of more than two thousand Vedish soldiers have been claimed,' Rusper Symphin replied. 'The Satrap will hazard no more. It is by His Majesty's *decree*, not my own will, *ekharaan*, that our forces stand down, and by those same royal wishes that they muster here at the fortress.'

But the blue-gown had more to say. 'What then is your answer to the Caliph of Laudassa?'

Rusper Symphin didn't turn; simply narrowed his eyes at Arif of Verunia. 'I have not, as yet, had the pleasure of hearing a request from that caliph.'

At this, with a little bow, Arif stepped further back from the edge. The eyes of the room swung to Omran of Laudassa. The fat man cleared his throat then, turning to Rusper Symphin. 'Viceroy, on behalf of Caliph Bardon, absent from this audience, I would implore that the Third and Fourth Regiments be detached from the fortress garrison and deployed in defence of the middle caliphies.'

'Impossible,' said Plamen from his rostrum. 'Following the losses on the north border, Methar's eight hundred constitute the Mooncircle Army's most integral unit now. Caliph Bardon himself would be hard-pressed to withdraw it from the fortress, all the more so should he station it *south*.'

The fat caliph's hands abandoned his belly to flap the air as if it were suddenly too hot. 'My clerics must have protection!' he exclaimed. 'Honorary Caliph, I beseech you, an engineer of this city. If harm should befall the monuments of the Builders —'

'Thank you,' said Rusper Symphin as he took a step towards Omran. 'As you quite rightly suggest, I am only too well versed in the legacy of the Builders. But I fear the High Commander is correct. As caliph, you may withdraw and deploy your territorial regiment at will. Know however that such an action would be acutely displeasing to the Satrap, at a time when I am certain you should not wish to invoke his displeasure. Nor will I authorise such deployment. For the present time, defence of the middle caliphies, and indeed their temples, hinges upon our control of central Vorth and the capital. Your clerics are encouraged to accept the temporary refuge of the fortress should they lack faith in that control.'

Suddenly a cleric shot to his feet from the cassocked throng. 'The Stones of the Builders will not be defiled. We will stand by our temples to the last!'

'You will do as you think best,' Rusper Symphin said patiently. 'But until the Rath move south of the Empty River, there will be no pledge of outer garrisons.'

Arif argued further for a while; saying something about decentralising forces, wider control, evacuees to come . . . Just as I'd been thinking I was keeping up, it threw me off. Plamen shook his head to all of it, anyway.

'But surely . . .' Omran stammered.

Plamen was firm. 'The capital will *not* provide Laudassa with forces. By decree, Methar's Fourth Regiment will remain in Antissa. If the Rath advance south, contingents may be stationed in the middle caliphies. No sooner. *Nor,'* he added to compete with rising heckles, 'have we cause to believe the Satrap will relax his concentration of defence.'

The heckles lost their momentum, turning instead to a general hum across the tiers. The two caliphs spoke to one another urgently. So did the huddle of blue-gowns. The clerics were quiet, their hoary faces all blank. Even the one who had stood and protested sat silent with his hands back on his knees.

'And yet,' said green-layers, 'have we not just now heard the Viceroy's word to Laudassa to protect the middle caliphies once the Rath make that advance?'

'*Ekharan,'* said Plamen. 'Do not presume to feign ignorance of the constraints under which the Viceroyalty must act. The Viceroy endeavours, weekly, to steer His Majesty's stance.'

'Endeavours of the kind have been received with further displeasure,' Rusper Symphin added. 'In his present condition, anticipating full-scale siege of the fortress, the Deepworks will remain the Satrap's foremost priority.'

And just like that I felt it—that missing piece slot into place. Of course! The Deep, all those levels under the citadel, were being built under this "royal decree." Whatever it was that had happened to the Satrap of Vorth, he'd pulled back his full army from the north of his country and, instead of fighting the Rath, begun to dig out a shelter. At least it made a *kind* of sense. It was why, I supposed, the Chief Engineer was in charge.

'How many times must we listen to this same song?' Arif complained. 'At every call to council the Honorary Caliph tells us all that his hands are tied by decree, and yet we know that he dispatches armed scouts in the desert. What, I wonder, might the Satrap think of *that?*'

This won a big burst of applause, full of more jeers and heckles. I couldn't help but be impressed at how Rusper Symphin didn't flinch; how still he stood as it ran its course.

'Armed yes,' he replied, 'but under orders to avoid any and all confrontation. There is no other way to acquire knowledge of Ratheine movement beyond the confines of the city.'

Up leapt the black-and-gold weasel. 'Well!' he cried. 'If the liberty may be taken to *interpret* decree, why not make good your solemn promise to Laudassa and Methar without further wasting of words?'

Several around him started clapping, but it petered out before reaching the same climax. I wondered if I actually had *any* clue what all this was. Hadn't the black-and-gold said exactly the *opposite* before?

The Viceroy faced him. 'Vizier Dranz, you would have me countermand sovereign orders?'

Black-and-gold flashed a smile. 'Viceroy. It is for *you* to assure *us* that our sovereign's authority is absolute.'

A man surged to his feet on the lowest tier – it was Captain Mondric. 'Of course it's absolute, you craven *earthworm!* Rest your faithless pipes, and while you're at it, your—'

'Captain!' Plamen warned.

Black-and-gold stood his ground. 'I would hear it from the Viceroy. Honorary Caliph?'

'Commander!' blasted Mondric.

'Peace,' said Plamen.

As well as I could, I studied Rusper Symphin's face. Though he was calm, or looked it, his forehead shimmered. The heckles died. Once they had stopped altogether, he answered: 'The rule of Satrap Syphus is *still* absolute.'

What came then sounded worse than all the eruptions so far. A single laugh. A hollow sound, almost metallic, it came from the silvery woman. She didn't stand or try to speak; merely smiled where she sat while the two blue-and-white officials of the Iron Shield mimicked her smile. Eyes darted about and met each other across the mosaic. The silence held, the air so charged I felt the hairs creep on my neck. Black-and-gold remained standing. The Captain slowly took his seat. Had I missed something? *What had happened?*

'The *ekhars* of the Sanhedrin are justly concerned,' a blue-gown said into the hush. 'The Deepworks alone progress too slowly for the liking of the First Circle.' His blue companions all nodded with their fancy talliths. 'Caliph Symphin, how long until this decreed shelter is prepared?'

Rusper Symphin rounded on his heel. *'If I may correct the speaker—'*

'Vizier Basra,' hailed the nasal red man in a spare split-second.

'—who has most *evidently* not been in attendance at this council of late, by reminding him of *facts*. Those facts being that in spite of recent piping complications, our Deepworks have been progressing *precisely* to schedule!' His eyes, now blazing, swept over the heads of the council. 'Nor will I stand for further claims to the contrary. If the work is too slow for the *ekharaan* of the Sanhedrin, I would invite them to consider the true scale of that work. My engineers are forging a fortified, self-sustaining habitation twice the size of this district within the hill of the fortress. Not since the time of the Builders has Antissa even *attempted* so vast a construction!' He was seething. 'But perhaps it is the citadel's failing foundations that *ekharaan* would prefer to a death at enemy hands? Because, you mark me, that is how your pedantry will be rewarded, Basra!'

He glared at the blue-gown, who had the grace to look sheepish, at least.

'That is but one of our concerns, *engineer*,' said black--and-gold. 'Your ability to defend even this fortress stands in question.'

'You will apply the correct terms of address in this chamber,' Plamen admonished.

Black-and-gold gave an over-indulgent bow. 'Begging the Honorary Caliph's pardon.'

'*Pelkhish* toad,' Mondric cursed. Soft, but it carried.

'You too, Captain.'

Mondric folded his arms.

Still with that oily little smile, the black-and-gold weasel continued: 'Need I make repeated mention of how wary the *ekhars* of the Sanhedrin have grown of one's exclusive royal audience?'

Rusper Symphin squared his feet on the mosaic. 'You are aware, no doubt, Dranz, that the Satrap commands my presence alone at this time. Precisely to allay such misgivings as this, I have on occasion persuaded His Majesty to admit the High Commander in my stead, yet even that arrangement is fragile.'

'Ah, Viceroy. But it is the High Commander's admission to the tower that *compounds* our misgivings. Begging his pardon, of course, he works too closely with your interests for his presence to assure the Sanhedrin that your orders represent sovereign will.'

A short silence.

'Interests?' repeated Rusper Symphin.

'This is dangerous speech, Dranz,' growled Mondric, rising slowly again as if preparing to take a leap across the floor. 'Choose your next words with great care.'

'My words are chosen,' said the weasel.

'The Captain is to be heeded,' said Plamen, low. 'Vizier Dranz, you will resume your seat directly or be removed from this chamber.'

But the weasel, Vizier Dranz, seemed less than interested in his seat, declaring loudly: 'But I am standing for the proper way of things, *ekharaan*. As such is my right, High Commander, I would call for a vote of no confidence in the Chief Engineer's aptitude to head the capital's defence!'

'Guards!' barked the Captain.

The chamber suddenly erupted with so much noise it seemed to stretch the marble walls and fill the dome. From under my balcony walked two black-caped guards. Rusper Symphin stood back as they crossed the mosaic, climbed up the tiers and pulled the black-and-gold weasel from his place. Through the ongoing roar of voices, they marched him down across the floor, back through the atrium under me, and out into the grey hall. As he was released I saw him stumble and snatch his turban from the floor. He tugged his robes straight and pointed a finger back into the chamber.

'You will have to do better than this, Symphin!' he hissed. Then turned and blustered away between the columns.

'Council to order!' Plamen sounded through the chaos. 'Verunia and Laudassa to withdraw, you have your answer.'

Rusper Symphin faced the storm. 'So there are *ekhars* among you who lack faith in my ordinance. I fault you none of your doubts. Were it not for the High Commander as my aide, I should share them. But perhaps I might beg your indulgence.'

He glanced left—I ducked down.

When I peeped through the railings again, none other than Loquar scurried into view from the atrium, nervously tugging at his turban as if fearing the council might throw things at him. He carried a long box under his arm.

Engineer again, Rusper Symphin addressed the council and described what he had showed me in his workshop: that flammable reaction of the chemical *chrozite*; that yellow powder. I tried to follow what he said, but the council never once silenced. They shook their heads and swapped their gibes. The two caliphs looked bored, and the blue-gowns began their own conversation. The engineer persisted, turning to the box. Loquar lifted its lid – perhaps with just a little too much ceremony – and Rusper Symphin took out its contents. It was the weapon of wood and metal I had seen. Only now he gave it a name. "Fusil," he called it.

Longing to be closer, I pressed my face up to the bars just as Captain Mondric heaved a sigh and slapped his knees. 'Might we, please, Viceroy, be spared another gadget in this chamber?' More laughter followed. Another smile from silver woman, as well. Men pointed, mocking and taunting, and I hated all of them. 'The Sanhedrin can afford to spare no interest in your cogwheels!' one blue-gown scoffed. Green-layers flung his arms wide: 'They won't win us a war!' And in moments, the amphi-theatre was ringing with demands that his futile contraptions be taken away.

The shimmer on Rusper Symphin's forehead had now run down to his temples. He clapped the box shut again—not noticing as Loquar yelped and sucked his fingers—then panned the faces all around him.

He tossed and caught something small that caught the light from the ceiling. Then left the floor, Loquar following.

Time to go.

I crept away from the railings and went back down the stairs.

'Roll down those sleeves.'

I obeyed. And Plamen watched me, steely silent. I'd been waiting for another half-hour and now the council had broken; footfalls flowing through the grey hall again.

'Follow me.'

As I shadowed him out of the room, Hetch re-appeared. 'She will see you, High Commander.'

'Then you may tell her to expect me,' said Plamen without stopping. The dwarf disappeared into the grey gloom behind the columns.

Plamen was a tall man and his strides so long that I had to jog a little to keep up. Servants greeted him smartly as they passed, but always frowned back at me. Through a doorway at the base of the citadel's spire, we stepped into the open air of an outside terrace. Sunlight streamed into my eyes, sensitive after so long in that dark bubble, and Plamen's bootfalls became a beat. There were columns here too; stouter ones with tilted friezes of those winged creatures I kept seeing every-where. Low hedges flanked the terrace walkway with gardeners tending to them. Through the V of his parted shears, one looked at me, then just as quickly looked away.

It was almost too green here, like a roofless house of leaves and bright grasses, even bushes tamed to form the rooms and corridors between them, spotted all over with flowers. In tiers and partitions, the gardens were bordered inside a half-circle of the citadel's wall; raised in turn from the streets of the district another level below. Beyond that, over the orange roofs of the Inner City estates, Antissa tumbled towards the battlements and sun-bleached blue that skipped the desert. The life I'd known felt far away and very, *very* long ago.

As Plamen's pace began to slow, I saw the fat Caliph Omran ahead. With him, Rusper Symphin: 'We will do our very utmost for the clerics. Meanwhile you must try to take our full national predicament into account.'

Omran bowed, rattling his headdress beads. 'Verunia holds a banquet this night at his estate. Will the Honorary Caliph be attending, I wonder?'

Rusper Symphin smirked. '*Ekharan* should be cautious of his questions,' he said pleasantly, 'always assuming that the Honorary Caliph has not in fact been invited.'

'Forgive me.'

'Never mind.' He smiled. 'I have, as you know, matters of my own to attend to. You will find Caliph Arif to be an exemplary host.' Seeing me with Plamen then, he nodded to the caliph. 'You will excuse me.'

'Of course.'

The figures parted. As they did, a hot wind reached the terrace from the desert and flapped Rusper Symphin's crimson robe. Though it had only been a night and a morning since I'd seen him, I'd forgotten how searching those green eyes were up close.

'Two days early,' he said to me, his tone more formal than before. 'There can hardly have been much to . . . *hell-sands*, what the *dredth* happened to your face?' It was hard to meet those eyes today; he was like a king.

Plamen shifted his weight and I remembered his instructions. 'I was fighting,' I said.

'Fighting with whom, please?'

'Gutterwaifs,' Plamen said into my silence. 'You know the urchins that harry the crowds around the wall.'

A moment's pause. 'Yes . . . yes, I do.' He cast a gaze over my wounds, glanced up at Plamen, then back at me.

I swallowed. Con-on-the-flagstones flashed from memory and I tried to pretend that there was something in my eye. Too late; he could see my tears spilling and I knew, if chance allowed, Plamen would have probably cuffed me for it. I dragged an armful of new sleeve across my face and waited. Waited for someone to say something.

'Well, you've been fittingly clothed,' puffed the engineer. 'Again.' He ignored my sniffing. 'Might I assume you're here to accept a certain offer?'

From Con-on-flagstones, my mind leapt to Jerome-running-from-kicks. I squeezed my eyes shut.

'Florian, I realise it's a warm day and a bit of an effort, but I'll need a yes or no.'

I opened my eyes, let them clear, looked into his: belying his tone, steady and patient.

Family dead. Con dead. Jerome . . .

An ibis cried out over the gardens.

'Yes.'

His face gave a moment's twitch. 'Good. Your lodgings are prepared in the lower chamber of my workshop, with additional clothes. Looking at you now, you may just pass for a Vedan once attired in the swathes. High Commander, your thoughts?'

'He must be wary of speaking,' said Plamen. 'He may not look as Naemian as the others in shelter, but his accent is strong.'

Rusper sucked his teeth. 'That I grant you. Very well, let us fall upon a pretence. Let us say he is Elmine. At present there are Elmines who do serve in the citadel, so it's hardly a great stretch. Do you understand, boy? If confronted, you're not Naemian. You're Elmine. Agreed?'

Like him, in a way. Again: 'Yes.'

'For all *you* know it's true,' he added, before raising a hand at the change in my face. 'Argue later. For now . . .' He delved into his robe, then grasped my hand a bit roughly and pushed something into its palm. A key. My heart made a different kind of jump. 'You know what it opens, I trust.'

I nodded and said, 'Yes,' one more time.

'Get to work, Flint. I want to know what they *are*.'

The bathtub was gone. In its place, under the pipe that had filled the bath for me before, was now a low-set bedframe with a mattress and quilt. A little table stood beside it; also a pot, a brass mirror and a stand of hooks at the end. On one of the hooks hung a sling-bag of the kind I'd seen servants carrying around. I took off my sandals and hung them on the hook beside it. A box-lantern was mounted on top of the stand, but it had no element, so the room was dark. The clothes were laid out on the quilt: a second pair of breeches—fancy ones—a second shirt and a blanket.

No, not a blanket. Now I recognised the hessian cloak worn by so many Antissans. "Swathes" they called it. Despite my aching, punished body, I tried my best to get into the thing, but it was all flaps and pointless folds without any holes for my arms, so I gave up and hung it up with my sandals instead.

All of this, I thought, he'd put together before I'd said yes.

The Deep shuddered around me and I went back up the steps. The wall-lantern shone low there, dimming the vaulted rows of russet bricks while big machines peered out from shadows. Rusper's papers swamped the table, piled high and furled like parchment mountains, weighted down at the foothills by heavy tools. Some bore screeds and screeds of writing, others complicated pictures: rows of circles like so many slices of sausage. Meaningless. And it made no difference when I brightened the lantern to see them better.

At Rusper's worktop, abutting the wall, was a contraption I couldn't begin to figure out in the slightest. A tall, broad box of hardwood and metals with horn-like finials on top, it looked like a cupboard at first; the worktop's surface cut to fit around its sides, leaving the larger part below. The section above the worktop's surface had a kind of dial on its front panel. Set about an inch into the wood, it was a half-circle of pale parchment inscribed with symbols and pictures. Some of them I knew, some I didn't. There was a sort of arrow fashioned on it, made of brass, and pointing upwards. And at the base of the half-circle, a kind of toothy gear, or wheel. I crawled under the worktop to investigate some more, finding that a pair of narrow pipes protruded from its side and disappeared straight into the wall. There were little doors under here too, almost as if it really were a cupboard. All three were locked.

Whatever. Just leave it alone.

Walking the room, I studied containers here and there, and opened a few. One contained at least a hundred tiny metal balls, heavy when I rolled them on my palm. For a while, not knowing what else to do, I simply sat down on the floor and rolled them up and down the grooves between the bricks.

A small girl came later. She had wide eyes, a head shaven so closely it was almost bald, and wore a little yellow jacket. I stood up quickly when I saw her and put the metal balls back inside their jar, but she didn't seem to care what I was doing. In a valley of the parchments on the table she set a tray of food and hurried out without saying a word.

I ate alone. Then sat, chin in my hand, fondling the key. Nothing stopped me now, I knew that, as I stared across at the tall cabinet. All I needed to do was open that door and take it out. But I didn't. They fascinated me, of course they did. But they unsettled me even more than that. Mine had *done* something to me, something unnatural. And painful. I'd seen and felt it, and even *heard* it speak words inside my head! I'd been so close to being sure that it had saved me from the Rath. Maybe it had. But maybe . . . had it also tried to *kill* me?

At last I willed myself to move. Trying not to think about it too much, I went and wriggled the key into place, turned it and let the door fall on its hinge. A chill began at my ankles, crept up my legs. My eyes scaled the shelves; the stacks and rows of his letters and broken seals, a strip of lace. And there they were on the highest shelf, the two little coloured domes that made my stomach freeze.

I wasn't ready.

So I went back down to my chamber and crawled onto the bed. As I lay there, staring at the pipe in the ceiling, I tried to count the bruises I'd find tomorrow morning. Now I was still, the pain doubled and I started to wonder if even a bone or two was broken.

If I slept I didn't know it, but after some time the triglycerate upstairs brightened a bit. Through the cracks under my eyelids I watched him look in from up the steps; a reptilian outline of flares and collars behind the beams. Only when his lantern withdrew into the workshop did I remember that I'd left the cabinet door open. *Stupid.* Softly as I could, I crept upstairs and peered back in.

But he'd closed it. Not seeing me, he shuffled off the crimson robe he'd worn in council and threw it over a machine. Eased down into his chair at the worktop; cradled his temples and raked his fingers through his hair a few times. When he raised his head to look blankly at the wall, the eyes I saw were lined and raw. The king of the Sanhedrin wasn't there: this man was tired and old.

I went back to my bed and slipped under the quilt. It was a black and white motley of squares that had little red birds stitched in a few. The weave of its cross-hatch was warm but open enough to let cool air reach my skin. I pulled it close and made up my mind, as the Deep breathed in and groaned again, that it was mine.

Twelve

Traps and Triglycerate

It was too early for this. I was barely awake yet, and the woman they'd sent down to help me get dressed in my Vedish swathes was impatient. Even though my body still hurt from my beating, she tutted crossly and smacked my arms when they weren't where she wanted them.

Belt and buckle-ring, they came first. Once fitted to my waist, she dropped the full sheet of hessian over my head. Pulling it back to form a hood, she aligned my head between two hooks, then tugged either side of the upper edge down over my chest so the stitches followed my arms. From behind my right shoulder, then, she brought a brass frog to fit the clasp that had to match it on the left; that made a collar. With another hook she guided the lower quarter over my right leg and secured it on the buckle-ring. The same was repeated on the left, but not before *another* hook was used to raise the flank off my left side. All of this done, the swathes covered my body from shoulders to knees, my shirt pockets reachable between the overlapping flaps that came together at the buckle – the ring of which protruded from the hessian like a wheel. Buttons, it seemed, had not occurred to Vedish tailors. I'd need practice.

She pinned a green ribbon to my collar; there was one just like it on her own.

'What's that for?' I asked.

'The *greenstring*. All servants of the Mooncircle Throne must wear the greenstring.' So that's what I was now. It made sense: if Rusper Symphin was now known as the "honorary" caliph, then I must be an honorary servant.

At first there wasn't any time for me to study the Discs, and the vertical cabinet stayed locked.

'Am I correct in assuming you have never had duties before?'

'Duties?'

'Mm.'

I gave it some thought. 'Well, I used to collect the water from the river,' I said.

First morning in the Deep, and still so early that it hadn't even started to grumble, Rusper was sitting at his workbench. Forcing a smile.

'And fed the chickens,' I added. 'Helped milk the cows too, sometimes.'

He bowed his head. 'Anything else?'

'No, nothing else.'

'Well. Your duties here, under the Engineering Guild, will be quite different from all that. The work harder, you understand. Then again, by the look of you, a little stiff labour wouldn't go amiss.'

I glared at him.

'Your arms, boy. They've barely an ounce of muscle on them.'

I crossed them on my chest.

'Oh come, we'll build them up, you'll see. At your age I was made of matchsticks too.'

Over the first few days, he placed me under Loquar's supervision; the old man not yet having been dismissed from the Royal Guild. My first task: building rat-traps needed in the citadel above. 'A Deep is not without its scourges,' Rusper said before he left us to our work. 'I get no end of complaints about the vermin these days.' Adding, as he left, that Loquar stank of stale daskh.

His mysterious "piping" problem, as well as his business as Viceroy, would take him away from the Deep for hours at a time. But he always came back eventually, often with loud groups of engineers, massive piles of parchment and complex conversations about pipes that were hard to ignore. I tried my best to mind my business, while also trying to ignore just how badly Loquar *did* smell.

We stationed ourselves at the worktop farthest away from Rusper's team and began with the trap assembly blocks. Wood had been sent down from the first-level joinery. Strong but springy, Loquar said it was yew.

'Yew trees in the desert?' I quizzed him.

'From Elman.' He winked knowingly at me.

'I'm not Elmine,' I said. 'You *know* that.'

'Chief says you are.' There were five four-foot planks of yew wood, each one an inch or so thick, and three baskets full of thinner strips. With saws we cut the planks down into useable segments, having stacked almost forty on the worktop by mid-morning. Then we sanded them down, using coarse grindstone slabs.

Meanwhile, behind us, the engineers discussed their piping riddles . . .

'How many aqueducts affected?'

'All of them.'

'No, not all. The outer farming quarters remain at full supply.'

'Stands to reason, they're fed off fourth.'

'Circuit Two. Fault must be there.'

Rusper: 'No, that isn't feasible. Look at the dribble through the Martial District and upper Mercantile. The troughs under that wheel have never stood so low.'

'. . . Kid . . . *kid!*' Loquar rasped in my ear. 'I said *sand* 'em, not wear 'em to nowt but dust!'

'Sorry,' I said.

Two to a trap, the assembly blocks formed roof-and-floor of each container. We combined them with strips, cut to length and nailed with hammers. After I got my first purple thumb, Loquar found me a glove. By far the most awkward part of the job, this took the longest. And when I tried to cheat by spacing the bars just a little wider, the old man chided me for it. 'You ever *seen* a rat, kid?'

I thought of saying something clever but stopped myself.

'Reckon a critter couldn't creep outta *that?* They squirm and squeeze, kid. Space 'em *close!*'

I slammed mine down on the worktop. 'Why don't you just make boxes then, what's the point of the bars?'

'They gotta sniff the bait!' he said in a shouted whisper. I blanched at the smell of his breath, then fished more strips from the basket. But his oily fingers snatched my effort away and cast it into a corner. 'No good. Start over.'

So I did. Rolling my eyes.

The engineers argued on behind us . . .

'Too much coming off the upper zone. Too many primary lines. The Deep can't get much bigger than this on a mere two containment systems. The outer sluices—'

'Gudge, it's a closed circuit. Nothing to do with the sluices. And none of that explains why distribution to the North District—'

Loquar banged his hammer over the words.

'—these diagrams,' someone finished saying; I scowled at Loquar from my work.

'But they've never once given us cause to doubt the transcripts before. Scores of the original lines have been unearthed in the last decade, and with every one Meck's proven right.'

'We still cannot be sure whether or not the four arterials operate independently of one another.'

'Pint's right, Chief. The roots may yet be interlinked near the aquifer. How would we know?'

'How could Meck himself have known? He never entered the Hub.'

'Obviously.'

A thoughtful pause. In it, Loquar experimentally tapped his trap and I pretended to do the same.

Then I heard Rusper speak again: 'I'm not convinced. Why would the Builders leave so extensive a network, only for it to be impervious to civic expansion? Antissa's population has always fluctuated.'

'Yet never reached *these* numbers.'

'Not according to records anyway.'

'Meck too will have faced this problem, Rusper.'

I heard the Chief Engineer deflate with a sigh, but missed his answer.

Next came the rods. The metal for these came from the junk-piles, Loquar told me. 'We recycle,' he explained. Each rod was cut down to two inches. Then we dragged out the big bulky machine he called the "lathe"—the screech it made as we pulled it over the bricks earning us dark looks from Rusper and the other engineers. Powered by pedals, we used the lathe to twist the rods into curves. I worked the pedals myself while Loquar attached the twisted lengths to brass-wrought girdles that had been sent down to us from the smelters. These had already been fashioned with holes for our bolts, so that the process of fitting each piece to a trap was made simpler: the rods hammered fast under the metal so that they pointed inward from the mouth of the cage.

It was a basic idea. A morsel of food would be left at the end of the box, to lure a rat. Rats having flexible bodies, as Loquar kept reminding me, they could easily wriggle between the inward-pointing rods at the entrance. Once inside, though, the rat would find the rods curved back towards its face, making it impossible to wriggle out.

By the end of the day, we'd made five traps.

'Let him finish,' murmured Rusper. Loquar left; the other engineers had gone already. The Chief Engineer sat by himself in another corner, hunched over the umpteenth page of parchment, making scruffy notes along its margins. Far too tired to disturb him, I ate my supper and turned in. And while I lay under my quilt of the red birds, eyes on the pipe above my bed, the lower reaches of the Deep gave up their final groans of the day. I wondered how long I'd be down here, and when next I'd see sun.

Cold water splashed me in the face.

I tumbled off my mattress, spluttering, and crawled away from the deluge coming down. Looking back, still half-asleep, I saw the pipe above my bed still belching splashes from the ceiling. When it stopped, the quilt and mattress were soaked through.

Confused and groggy, I wiped my face and shook it out of my hair. Then he arrived.

'Wouldn't do to have the Viceroy's hand oversleepin', now would it.'

'*You* turned that on!' I yelled up the stairs at Loquar.

'Smart kid,' he sniggered and held a bowl into the light of his lantern. 'Here, get dressed and eat your *tashi.*'

'What's the time?' I groaned.

'Hour afore sun-up. Chief's got you a new job, gotta be up extra early for this one. Shake a leg, kid!' He sat and waited in Rusper's chair until I was ready, then pulled on his green turban and led me out of the workshop at a scurry.

The Deep's passages were black but for his lantern's bars of light, and quiet too except for the deepest grumbles. A tunnel and a ladder going up from the workshop were the furnace rooms where yesterday's embers were still glowing. Loquar shovelled some coals out of the bed of a forge to half-fill a small scuttle. He passed the scuttle to me. Then swept up a tool that looked more like some kind of weapon and squeezed a trigger: black tongs with nasty double claws. 'From now on, kid, this'll be your task,' he said.

'What task?' I asked, to which he drove the tongs down into the coals like a sword. I recoiled from the sparks.

'Lighting the Deep. Come on.'

Most industries were here between the red granite walls of the first and topmost level; joinery, foundry, metalworks and smelters, vellum-tanners, parchment-mills, rows upon rows of rooms for scraps and spares and storage. The walls bore their bones on this level: big pins of iron from which the box-lanterns hung. I could only just reach them to turn their latches back, open their windows and apply the hot pincers to the undercopper stems. I was mesmerised by the first, the second, the third; how the triglycerate element flashed on first contact with the heat, flickered, then basked the wall in its light. Loquar called it "hotting."

Our way scribbled under buttresses as the tunnels grew and shrank, zigzagging, backtracking, becoming rooms and passing them by. One wall was never far from sight. Different from the others, its stone was greenish and slick. But I didn't ask about it. I wasn't sure I trusted Loquar, or all that many of his answers.

When we came to the place where the rubble shaft opened in the floor, I inched in closer to look down but Loquar thumped me in the chest. So. I couldn't quite trust him for facts, but at least he wasn't going to let me jump into a hole.

All lights now lit on first level, we took the stairs back down to second. Two nights I'd now slept here in the Royal Guild headquarters. The level was bigger than that above and though its layout was similar, the sandstone passages made more sense. Here the lanterns were bolted fast in sconces. Just as before, the chasm of the rubble shaft cut its way through floor. And again, all ways and passages met at the central green-stone wall.

Rungs brought us down to the third level, the broadest level of the Deep, where the arrow-straight corridors divided sand-stone, leading inward. The air was warm and full of powder, making me cough as we went. Many parts of this level were still being built, I soon realised.

We ghosted on, now only lighting the lanterns that were positioned at the ladders. Soon, more ghosts joined us. The diggers of the Deep—"sappers," Loquar called them—overtook us in threes and fours with their own shallow lights. Grey faces, grey hands and grey clothes, as if painted. We followed them down to the fourth level, which was less than half built; barely more than a muddle of masonry and struts within rock pockets. A trembling started from somewhere, and sappers passed in larger groups. By the time we reached the last lantern, vibrations shook the floor we stood on.

Noise blasted up. Through a manhole, a ladder simply dropped away into nothing; a nothing in which human voices fought with thrashing metal echoes and mechanical moans. I hotted the lantern at the ladder and the triglycerate brightened, its glow waxing over bedrock and worming skins of buried pipes. I leaned forward and saw some lanterns blinking down there.

'Someone's already hotted those lights,' I shouted to be heard above the noise, though secretly nervous of going any deeper.

'Digging starts early, tight schedule,' Loquar shouted back to me. 'Gotta keep 'em lit through the night down on fifth.' He rattled his lantern at the manhole; then seeing my hesitation, put it down, took my scuttle and tongs, and went first. I watched and waited until he was something like ten rungs below me, thinking he'd not be too impressed if I squashed his turban, then gripped the poles. I started down.

Rock swallowed me. From all sides, pipes loomed like fat, sleeping reptiles in the earth. The noise got louder, became so loud that I couldn't hear my hands or feet moving over the wood. Down, down and down . . . just don't *look* down.

The earth and rock drew back around the ladder. Space opened up. I passed a dangling lantern, squinted in its light, and kept on going. Foot—hand, foot—hand. Deeper, deeper through the gloomy openness and noise, until my sandals met some surface and Loquar clapped me on the shoulder. I stepped off the ladder but, when I turned, so did my stomach.

Here gaped a cavern like some big, foul, rotted mouth. Lights on the scaffolds gave it half-form, rocks grinning out between the pipes that shot across the open. They weren't a wall or a ceiling but a face of gritted teeth, gnarled-up brows, rearing lumps and jagged spines, mostly dark despite the lanterns.

My guide led on. Up, down the ladders, over, under scaffold platforms. Lantern to lantern. The dust was overwhelming here, thick in the air, a chalky sweetness that filled my throat. The scaffolds followed the curve of the green-stone wall, which now stood fully exposed some hundred feet or even more. Shadows lapped its edges and my stomach did another turn. Instead I looked at where I was putting my feet.

They were down there, the sappers, scores and scores of them now. Under the scaffolds' iron legs and that messy cable webwork, the bottom of the Deep was a crawling, grey morass of digging. And there was Rusper! Impressively, he clambered about through the work, far too busy to see me. I heard the high rasp of his voice calling instructions, but all the hammering and smashing and screeching of machines drowned out his words.

Loquar and I made our way back up again, a final ladder and a manhole bringing us out of the cavern. 'Think you've got it?' he quizzed.

'I think so, yes.'

'You'll needs be back here come dusk time to hot fifth level for the night.' Not something I was looking forward to.

Back at the traps, I soon got faster, and by the early after-noon was keeping pace with Loquar. We didn't say much to each other; from him there was barely ever more than 'make a long arm for this' or 'make a long arm for that.' Other engineers came and went; consulting, collecting, exchanging charts. Rusper didn't come back that day.

Glancing at the tall cabinet in the corner, I thought again of the Discs. And then the Rath. The council had said that none had been sighted this side of the Empty River yet. But that had been two days ago; they could be closer by now. Was I really safe behind these walls, within this rock, inside this room? And were my people? Forget the Rath—were they still being fed and given water and enough blankets to keep warm?

And what did they think of *me* now, the boy who had left them for something better?

There were six more traps by evening.

THIRTEEN

ARTERIAL-III

My third day in the Deep started the same way—splashed awake. Again I rolled onto the floor, sat and waited out the splashes. The pipe stopped splashing. But when Loquar didn't come, I dressed, went to the forges for the coals and made my own way through the levels, hotting the lights by myself. When I got back to the workshop, all our rat-traps had been taken from our station and a bowl of steaming tashi had been left at my bench.

All that day, the Deep was teeming with noise and busy movement, and yet I saw almost no one. At some point of the morning a pair of "overseers" – a man and woman – discussed some plan at the table, but mostly the workshop was empty. Loquar did come eventually, but built only one trap before making some lame excuse for a break, and simply not coming back. So I worked away on my own: sawing, pedalling and knocking in nails the way he'd shown me. Purposeful feet thrummed back and forth outside the door, while whatever was happening far below on digging level shook showers of stone and grit and dust from the ceiling bricks. The hours were slow.

In the evening, as instructed, I took my scuttle of coals and hotting tongs down to that lowest level and lit the fading lights there. It was a changed place in the hush after the day's work was over; the great, clawed hand of the rubble-raiser lying still among lax cables like a sleeping, captive ogre, and only a few weary sappers climbing out of the pits. The two overseers I'd seen in the morning were there, talking on the scaffolds, and when one looked in my direction she seemed to recognise me. Pintle and Gudgeon I'd heard them called, though those didn't sound like real names.

A steaming supper was waiting in the workshop again: a meal of minced beef, diced okra, some other Vedish white vegetable I'd never eaten, a wedge of peppered bread. The Deep went quiet. No footfalls or voices in the tunnels; even the grumbles of the hill all around it turning sleepy, it seemed. I finished my supper and widened the panes of the lantern.

I wasn't tired, not just yet, so I went over to the box-contraption that had so puzzled me before – the one with the half-circle dial. It was called a "clepsydra" - a *hydraulic* clepsydra – and now I knew what it did. Loquar had showed me how a mechanism of gears, floats and stoppers, as well as a steady feed of water from the pipes, would make the dial slowly rotate behind its pointer. By means of pictures on the dial – suns, stars and moons, birds, lizards, lions, giants and mythic creatures – the device would tell what time of day it was. Useful down here, where you'd have no other way of knowing. I found its keys behind the finials, unlocked one of its tiny doors below and, just as Loquar had showed me, opened the valve to refill its tank and keep it going another day. It was still a miracle to me that, in this city, water flowed at the mere turn of a screw.

Hands to myself, I walked the room. The "fusil" I'd spotted on my first visit to the workshop, and which Rusper had tried to present to the Sanhedrin council, had been moved to the workbench where he most often worked alone. I lifted its cover. The thing still undergoing constant changes to its design, he'd both added and removed since last I'd looked. Soldered to the front was now a lateral metal bar. From it, cords of hide stretched from each end to the very back. He'd taken grips off, handles too, but I guessed that was only to make it a bit easier to work on. Other parts like levers, triggers, wheels, chains and gears lay scattered around it like so many organs he'd pulled out. A yellow dusting of chrozite lay on the surface as well, and one of the jars of leaden balls was sitting open on the side. He called them "schot." It was tempting, but I didn't touch. Didn't dare. He'd know for sure if it was tampered with or moved even an inch. I dropped the cover and stepped away, towards the middle table.

The piping parchments had been left a little tidier today. I looked more closely at the pictures, all drawn in different mediums: ink for the lines and the labels, graphite for shading, some kind of stain, I guessed, for grades or types of pipe? I didn't know. My reading was slow anyway, but here the handwriting made words impossible to make out. Almost. That one word "Transcript" was always clear in the headings.

Transcript Four, Transcript Five . . .

The smaller sheets were even harder to make sense of; crowded so thickly with corrections that at first glance they looked little more than a mess of silly squiggles. I challenged myself to understand at least *something* from those pages. Knowing I probably shouldn't, I started leafing through the sheets. Slowly, through the tangle of the levels I saw depicted, I started finding landmarks, points of the city I knew. There were outlines of the districts in what were called the "circuit grids." And maps made up entirely of criss-crossing lines, showing the "aqueducts." And yes, that's what they were, I realised: *updated* versions of the Transcripts.

'Any ideas?'

I spun around.

Rusper wore a thobe of olive-green with grey brocades; Viceroy again. He stood with his arms behind his back and I felt a fool that I hadn't heard him come in.

'Bored with traps, I take it.'

'I've used the wood up,' I said, flustered. 'The metal too. Nearly, almost.'

'How many today?'

'Eight,' I said and motioned towards my station. His eyes followed my hand without much interest.

'Where's Loquar?'

'Had to leave.'

'Leave?'

'This morning.'

He cocked an eyebrow. 'You built eight traps by yourself, then. In a day.'

'Well, seven,' I confessed. 'The eighth was Loquar's.'

He stared at me; I looked away, then back in time to catch his glance at the piping parchments I'd disturbed.

I took another step away from them. 'Sorry, I was—'

'Curious? Don't blame you,' he said. 'It's a most curious problem.' He came over to the table where I'd been standing before, hands still clasped behind his back as if restraining himself.

I had to ask: 'What *is* the problem?'

'Hm?' His eyes stuck to the pages.

'The pipes . . .' I prompted. 'Is the city running out of water?'

He turned and looked, not at, but through me. Had he heard what I'd said? Then, 'No, I don't think so. Not yet at any rate. Though some of my planners have begun to fear as much.'

I remembered the quarrel I'd overheard. 'You told the Captain that the city had five more years.'

'Well remembered. I was trying to shake him.' Only now did he put a hand towards the sheet that I'd been studying, but jerked it back as if stopping himself just in time. He shook his head. 'The real problem, Flint, lies in the loss of a legacy. These pipes, they are unique, the system that feeds Antissa from beneath the desert unlike anything you'll find in all the realms. Not even Ered, with its renowned crafts and high science, has anything to match it. As far as we know.'

He left the table and went to where I'd eaten my supper. From the ewer of water, he filled my cup and walked back, drinking deeply.

'The pipes were here before our time,' he went on, licking his lips. 'Before my predecessor's time. Before the founding of the Guild. Before the first dynasty of the satraps or the chieftains before them. They are the product of far greater, ancient masters. And the more our city changes, the more obvious it becomes how little we've retained of that mastery.'

It was only when he pinned me with his eyes that I realised I was gaping as he spoke. 'You're talking about the Builders,' I said, to take control of my face. 'The builders of the fortress.'

The stern eyes softened. 'So you've been listening.'

'And the pipes?'

'*Especially* the pipes,' he said. 'The Builders were the first. Unrivalled engineers and true perfecters of the industry on which they founded our city.'

'So how old *are* they?'

'The pipes?' Rusper raised the cup and sipped his water. 'We've made additions of our own, but for the most part at least five hundred years. That's the delivery circuits. Chamber's older.'

'What chamber?'

'This one.'

Setting his cup down, he fished a sheet out from the mass by a corner almost black it had seen that many thumbs. As he laid it between us, I recognised the rows of sausage-slice circles from before. And realised, too, that I'd come back to the table.

'The Hub Chamber,' he said, a little grandly, as if the words were sacred. 'The nucleus of the system on which Antissa depends. And not just our pipes, mind. Building a Deep where we did would have posed a rather steeper sort of challenge without the Hub's structural advantage. We believe it could be as much as two hundred years older than the network around it. And now, very likely, the root of our problem.'

That wall of slimy green stone—*this* was that wall, the one I'd seen at the centre of every level of the Deep, and which towered enormously over the scaffolds and pits on digging level. With new eyes I scanned the page of weird circles, each one presumably representing a cross-section of the cylinder that ran down through the Deep like a pillar. The first pillar. Giant and hollow, seven hundred years old.

I had a worrying thought. 'Um . . .'

'Don't mumble.'

'Only, was . . . was I meant to hot the lights in there too?' I asked.

'What?'

'Light the lanterns, I mean. Inside that chamber.'

He fixed me with a frown as breath seeped out of him slowly. 'There aren't any,' he replied.

'No lanterns?'

'Not to my knowledge.' He looked puzzled, and I returned the puzzled look. We shared it like that for a moment. Then, 'It's sealed, Flint. There's no way into the Hub from outside. Didn't I say?'

'No you didn't.'

'How remiss. Well, there you are. It's impenetrable. No way into the Hub.'

'So, it doesn't have an entrance?'

'How many ways would you like me to put this?'

'But why not?'

'It just doesn't,' he shrugged. 'Not anymore.'

'So how d'you know about that?' I said, pointing at the sausage circles.

'*That*,' he said immediately, 'is the copy made by Meck, the Chief Engineer before me, of renderings the Builders themselves left behind. Parchments no longer available to the Guild, regrettably. Almost all our estimations are based on what Meck believed to exist behind that wall.'

That couldn't be right. 'But how . . . how do you—?'

'We don't,' he said, guessing my question. 'The system has never so much as wobbled until now.'

''Cos now there's too many people?'

Rusper answered with a scowl. 'If that's what you think. I disagree. The so-called legends of early Antissa continually lead us to believe that a population this size subsisted here long before the delivery circuits were complete. Which would suggest—*strongly* suggest—that water was conveyed to more than ten thousand people directly from *these—four—channels —here*.' He jabbed a finger into the four largest circles displayed inside one section.

No, inside *all* the sections.

'Artan . . .' I tried to read. 'Artor . . .'

'Arterials.'

'They draw up the water?'

'From an aquifer more than three miles under the hill, according to the Transcripts. Now, after seven hundred years, I call that proof of a capacity to sustain greater numbers than have *ever* lived here.' He cleared his throat, seemingly aware of how intensely he'd been speaking. 'The problem's balance. Somehow, from the outside, we've offset central pressure.'

I peered in closer and tried to make more sense of what I was seeing; the cryptic numbers, codes and symbols. Every section was unique, but on each of the sections lines made exits through the circumference of the circle I now knew to be the green wall. Suddenly, I had to know what was inside.

'Can't you turn them off?' I heard myself ask.

'Turn what off?' he said.

'The pipes.'

'Some pipes, what of it?'

'I could go in. Through a pipe.'

'*Wha—?*' he gushed. 'No, Flint. Sadly you could not. Even the largest of the laterals are much too narrow for that.'

'But I'm small.'

'Not small enough,' he said, shaking his head. 'You'd end up trapped in the line. Besides, there's no way to open the pipe once inside. And even if you did squeeze yourself as far as the Hub interior, you'd only plummet to *pelkh* knows what death at the channel elbow.'

I persisted. 'Aren't there spaces?'

'Spaces, what do you mean?'

'Inside that green wall, around the pipelines.'

For just the tiniest moment he studied the air above my head. 'There . . . are cavities around some of their entry-points, yes. But they're inconsistent, very unlikely to penetrate the estimated forty feet of that wall.'

'Let me follow them then,' I said. 'I'll find out for you.'

I caught the way he sized me up; he saw me catch it. 'No, much too narrow.' He was firm. 'Too dark, too wet inside those cracks and likely choked full of rust.'

He drained the cup and strode back to the ewer, refilled it with a splosh and quaffed a gulp. Eyes faraway, he stood there tapping the cup with his guild-ring, chewing the inside of his mouth. Well, that was that.

'And unpredictable!' he blurted, coming back to himself. 'Meck never finalised the routes those pipes take through the Hub wall, never had enough to go on. We know where they go *in* and can be fairly confident of where they come *out*. In *theory*. But between those two points . . .' He scratched his scalp. 'Flint, we don't even know if the circuit zones align with the levels of the Deep. Probably not!'

'You said you wanted me to help you,' I pushed.

'And you will, but this is—'

'Dangerous?'

'*Deeply.*'

We locked eyes. His single-minded glare was the first to soften, if slowly, leaving in its place the same hungry look he'd given the Transcripts. As he kneaded his knuckles, something made me think of Erik; hand on my shoulder as he told me to be brave.

Danger. I'd seen it. And survived.

I could do this.

Rusper flattened his lips and breathed out through his nose. 'The Guild has never sent children into the Hub. For good reason.'

'It's never had to,' I reminded him. 'You just said so.'

After hotting lights next morning, I pored over the charts on the piping Transcripts and soon began to understand what Rusper meant when he said *proof*. A walled city Antissa might have become, but it seemed that at any time in its history its inhabitants could have migrated to the gulf coast. They never had. Instead, the city's builders had chosen to remain here in the harshness of the desert and plunge pipes into the earth.

By noon, the diagram of the Hub Chamber was back inside its tube, secured to Rusper's belt, and bobbing against his thigh as he walked. I had to skip to keep up.

'What's a Deep for?'

'Hm, what's it *for?*'

'Uh-huh.'

'A range of things. We owe the first level to Meck himself, of course, fifty years ago, to make room for the expanding industries of the Royal Guild under his ordinance. As for the extended Deepworks that we've since undertaken, they are royal decree. The Satrap commands we dig, so we're digging.'

'But digging for what?'

'Protection.' He almost spat it. 'It's to be our shelter should the Rath move further south. We're no longer fighting a war, as you know. The army is withdrawn by royal command. Engineering having been thus pushed to the fore, that makes me Viceroy in wartime—I saw you up there in council, weren't you paying attention?'

I dodged his glance.

He sighed, shaking his head. 'But even without the threat of invasion'—he looked behind us, at Loquar who shuffled with his scuttle of coals—'the Satrap is not as he was.'

We came to a room full of pipes, here all exposed. Brown, red, pink, orange and flaking, and ribbed with clefts like fishes' gills, they delved through the floor and through the ceiling from the face of the green wall. One of them Rusper followed to where it passed through a seal of iron, which he knocked with his knuckles.

'*Two-bee-three,*' he named it. 'A common lateral feeder. Pipes such as these enable us to regulate a marginal degree of water-pressure.'

I came closer, eyes glued to the seal encircling the pipe. *II-b3*. That seal was barely wider than the length of my arm, and now Rusper raised an eyebrow at me as if to ask what I'd expected.

Loquar arrived and put his scuttle on the floor. 'Chief,' he said, gritting yellow teeth. 'It's off the *boil* sending the kid—'

'A hand please, Loquar.' Rusper shoved the scroll-tube at my ribs—forcing me to catch it—and stooped to get a grip on the seal. Then Loquar also pushed a bundle at my chest—I caught that too—and stooped to help him. 'You still *reek* of daskh, man!'

'Sorry, Chief.'

With a jerk they freed its wheel, spun it three times, then slid it out over the pipe. Damp air rolled into our faces and we stood back together, staring after the peeling line that ran on and disappeared through the crevice. It was tight: *very* tight.

I swallowed, steeling my nerves. 'What do I do when I get in?'

'*If* you get in,' Rusper corrected with a severe look.

He snatched the tube back from me and popped its lid, pulled out the scroll. Spreading the sheet on Loquar's back, his finger guided my eye across the plan of "Circuit Two."

'Entering from here, you *should* be able to reach this zone. From there . . .'

'*Three-ay-one* and *three-bee-seven*,' I recited from memory. He'd already versed me in the laterals he suspected.

'Correct. Should be open. What else?'

'Everything on the sixth zone,' I replied.

A nod. 'That circuit's been obsolete for decades. Try those valves. Should any be open, seal them. If you can do that, it may increase pressure on this channel over here, *Arterial-three.* If we're lucky.'

Arterial-III. I tried to memorise its position before the scroll was put away.

I became a knight with two squires who prepared my armour for darkness. Loquar coaxed off my sandals; I'd need my toes for grip, he said. Meanwhile, Rusper used the strap of the scroll-tube to attach it firmly to my back, a bit too tight, but I said nothing. They had me sweep back my hair. In Loquar's bundle was a small globe of glass that he had threaded with an undercopper stem and a triglycerate crystal. It had been fused to a cloth which, when tied around my fore-head, set the globe facing front. Aside from the lenses of Rusper's goggles, the only glass I'd ever seen had been in Sarah's box of treasures: that vial of Naemian earth.

Forget that now.

'Don't come easy in 'Tissa,' Loquar grumbled as if peeling the thought right off my brain.

'Not even for the Guild,' Rusper added.

'So mind yer way,' Loquar warned me. He raised the hotting tongs towards my forehead.

'Hold still,' said Rusper.

I winced at the heat, heard the undercopper sizzle and blinked in the glare of greenish light.

Between more stern warnings not to break the glass if I wanted to live, I wheeled a leg over the pipe called *II-b3* and bent down low to look in. The headlight played eerily in the curdled crevice, my nose twitching at the smell. I'd get used to it, I hoped. My hands, at least, were free.

Rusper was still talking: 'I want to know about anything that might indicate deterioration. Not just *Arte-III*, anything at all. Not even the finest engineering lasts forever.'

I nodded understanding, then shimmied my body under the lip of iron framing the hole. It was a difficult squeeze and, once inside, immediately harder to move than I'd feared. I tried not to let it scare me, but knew it wasn't going to be easy. Before I'd made it in three feet, my knees were scraped by the rough stone. But the pipe was dry, luckily. Holding to its gills, I could pull my weight along its topside with the help of my legs. It would be slow. And so I pulled, the headlight barely separating the darkness up ahead.

The pipe curled left, the crevice with it. The hiss inside the iron under my body was almost human. Except it never took a breath.

'Still hear us, kid?'

'Course he can hear us!'

The echo of their voices was wet.

'I'm fine,' I answered, pushing calm, wetly echoing too.

'Flint, just be—'

Silence.

I froze. 'Caliph Symphin?'

Not only had Rusper stopped short in mid-sentence; he'd stopped without echo. I said his name again, louder, and waited for him to answer. But he didn't.

'Loquar?' I tried to steady my breathing and stave off the panic that slid in with the thoughts I couldn't help but start to think. Would they have sealed me inside? Was this a trick? Why would they do that?

This had been my idea, I remembered. And no, there hadn't been a bang of any iron slamming shut, although now even the seeping breath of the crevice had gone silent. It was as if the green wall had swallowed me up, sound and all, leaving me alone with my own breath and that soft hiss of running water.

Just stay calm. Whatever had happened back there at the opening, there was no way of crawling back now. Only forward. So I did that, all my muscles taut with extra care, and almost blind. The crevice curled right, the pipe's hiss growing louder underneath my belly, and my elbows, knees and shins all sticky with blood before long.

What was I doing? Just two weeks ago, I'd been a child of the borderlands, running and playing in the river-plain. Now I was here, behind the high walls of a fortress city, and crawling through its pipeworks! Serving its lord! Had Erik and Sarah ever existed?

The scroll-tube snagged on stone, the crevice suddenly shrinking tight around me. I was about to get stuck, I could feel it, and at the instant terror I tugged too hard and scored my back on the ceiling. My stupid yelp sounded so strange, contained so tightly by the space, and when the tube *did* come free I lay forward on the pipe. I panted there, collecting my nerve and remembering what Rusper had said. *The Guild has never sent children into the Hub, for good reason.* I knew I'd have to be more careful from now on.

But then, a few yards further in, *II-b3* made a different kind of turn. Instead of bending left or right, which I was getting good at, it elbowed *down*. The space around it just as close, if not closer.

He'd warned me.

I felt the panic surge again, now with the added dread of knowing that I couldn't turn around. Would it be possible, even, to shimmy my way backwards if I had to?

Not if I did it. *Did* find a way to crawl down.

I pulled my way up to the elbow, the water's hiss becoming urgent and aggressive at the curve right where the current hit the change and veered and fell who-knew-how-far. I stretched and twisted through the curdled stomach walls of the crevice and, gripping bolts, let my light peek over the slope.

The pipe went vertical from here and dropped a distance I could stand in. The line then straightened and went on.

Also the crevice, at the bottom, looked slightly wider where it turned: wide enough, I thought, to crouch and re-adjust my position. Or my direction, if need be.

Going down, I first made sure to splay my hands against the stone of the far wall—if any wall in here was *far*—in such a way that I was balanced with my belly on the curve. Then it was slowly, slowly, *slowly* angle down until the drop between my hands and the straightened pipe when I slipped forward wouldn't be too far to fall.

No sooner was I face-down and vertical than the panic rushed through me again and made me want to squirm back up. I tensed, off-balancing my grip, and dropped.

My hands slapped lateral iron. Under my weight, both my arms buckled but didn't buckle all the way. My own bones, bending outward in collapse, slowed down my fall, wedging me in by my own joints, which sent relief gushing down—or *up*— the length of my body. It was only well after I'd wriggled myself down into the lower space, and realigned, that I could feel how it had carved the skin right off my elbows.

The farther on I crawled into the wall, the harder it became to tell what kind of distance that was or how many minutes it had taken. The air got colder. I sucked it in between my teeth, tasting a tang. At least my light showed that the crevice had widened a little up ahead; enough, at least, not to have to worry about getting wedged and stuck again. Through the glare, a lipless circle then appeared around the pipe. Air touched my ears. I dragged my body further on, more careful than ever not to crack the globe against protruding sides.

But then the sides simply weren't there. My light fled out through open darkness, my body's sounds lost in echoes. Surging water, moaning metal, things that plunged and gonged and gurgled. Yawning space. My fingers clawed into the gills. I breathed and waited out the thudding in my chest.

I was inside.

And straightaway, my light seemed pointless. Just ahead, a larger pipe passed over *II-b3* – left to right, darkness to darkness – that was all. Of the Hub Chamber itself there were only sounds of moving water and its echoes, and echoes of its echoes. Behind me, the ancient green wall dropped from my heels into pure blackness. I felt my breakfast move inside me; that blackness seemed to lick and suck my soles.

There were no ladders, no steps, no terraces. As far as I could see, no way of getting through the space but by the pipelines themselves. So much for the legendary Builders. How many of them might have fallen to their deaths here? I shuddered, thinking about their bones strewn on the floor, and then again at just how far away from me that floor could be.

Reaching behind, I worked the scroll out and spread it under my headlight. The Hub was easily as huge as Meck had made it look on parchment—I could *hear* it. Dauntingly huge. And yes, the pipe up ahead was *II-a7*, meaning I'd come out in the right place: Circuit Zone Two.

Alright. Breathe.

At least, *III-a1* wasn't too far.

I slid the scroll back into place, balled up my guts, hugged *II-b3* with arms and legs, and edged out slowly.

Extremely slowly.

When, after something like ten minutes, I got as far as *II-a7*, I carefully climbed on top of it and just sat still there for a while. Volumes of water rushed inside, the surge vibrating at my legs. To test the hugeness all around me, or just really to bolster my courage, I drew a deep breath and shouted out the first thing in my mind.

It was a swear.

Maybe it echoed, maybe it didn't. It was impossible to tell. The hissing and surging of invisible currents to every side owned all the echoes in this place.

I started off then, to the right.

The curving pipe followed the green wall, my light touching nothing else at all.

Yards farther on, I ducked to shimmy under the belly of a lateral, then went more slowly towards what I knew was coming up not far ahead.

Knowing it was coming didn't prepare me.

Arterial-III. It entered my sphere of light like the back of an enormous, peeling pig. I couldn't move for a few moments. Then, on nervous joints, I dared to tilt my neck back and look up its rusted hide of girders. Fifteen feet wide, at least, full height a secret of the dark. I heard its hiss, though strangely faint, then leaned back slightly with my light. The monster seemed to mimic me, leaning back into the gloom that it had come from, and I shuddered. I'd never felt as small as this; alone under a fortress with the giants in the dark.

Checking again to be sure of my way, I continued to crawl along the line. *II-a7* ran under some criss-crossing laterals, large and small, and I spotted their valve-wheels as I passed. Then, from the other side, Arte-III reared up again and displayed its own row of gills.

Like a ladder.

I touched the gills, lightly, almost nervous of somehow waking the beast, but they were dry and deep enough for both my fingers and my toes. I was now so keenly aware of what a single slip would mean that it took me several minutes to manoeuvre my body into a position that felt right for the step; another few minutes after that before I was ready to do it.

I sent a shaking leg down.

And then another.

The gills allowed for good grip, I soon found, but even with that there was no way I could afford to move faster. One wrong foot, I knew, and my bones would be the next down on that distant, ancient floor.

It was a long, *long* way down; fifty feet, I guessed—fifty of those shaking downward steps—when Zone Three's laterals came into view. There was *III-a1* below me. I gently stepped down on its valve-wheel, took hold for balance and eased myself into place with my back against the giant.

The water that moved through this pipe wasn't strong. When I set my hands to the wheel's outer bar and tested it, I half-expected it to stick. But it didn't. The vibrations were firm, and the wheel turned. *III-a1* was open.

Which left *III-b7* still to test.

Another check of the chart first. Though on the same zone —just parallel, in fact—getting to that one would be risky. As if any of this *wasn't!* The only pipe that led to it from here was thin, about a yard off.

So I took my time, measured the distance and crossed with a wide step. Immediately I dropped, landing hard, wrapping my legs around the line and knocking the globe. Its *clang* went on for what seemed like a hundred miles of metal and for the first time I wondered if this wasn't, as Rusper had possibly said, a bad idea. Then again, I'd come this far already, and so far my only hurts were scrapes to knees and elbows.

At the first lateral to undercut my way from there, I changed pipes. Then I went on, following the curve of the green wall. Another arterial – *II* – passed through my light. Unlike its sister, the sound of its surge was enormous. Pressure, I thought. He'd been right about pressure.

It could have been an hour in the dark, or even two, when I reached the clustered pipes around Arte-I. Struggling to make sense of how they curled and converged, I clambered over the laterals until they pressed closer together, closing the gaps between them. By the time I found *III-b7*, the second of Rusper's suspects, I was able to stand, and then walk to where it stemmed into three. Like a mushroom the valve-wheel seemed to sprout just before the vertical downturn. I balanced my way towards it and took hold, instantly feeling the current coursing through the metal. Open.

I sat and slumped against the wheel over my clammy fore-arms. My clothes were damp, too. I shivered. He'd been wrong on both counts.

But even as I thought about it, staring out at that dense gloom, I realised that I was looking at something that shouldn't be there. I narrowed my eyes against the glare of my headlight, but it was too much for me to make anything out properly. So I wriggled the light off my head and held the globe out by its cloth.

Cables?

Still not enough light to really tell. Carefully, I mounted the valve-wheel and leaned forward on my knees. Yes they *were* cables, a kind of web of cables, surrounding what looked like a cluster of lines. And not pipes like the others; more like thin, vertical tubes. Whatever they *were*, they weren't on the chart; right now I was looking directly into the centre of the Hub, which I had studied all morning. This wasn't marked.

But there was something else. Something *behind* the tubes and cables . . . I reached out further. A bridge? *A stone bridge!*

The cloth slipped.

I swiped and missed and lost my balance. Dropped to the wheel.

Heart thudding lead into my veins, I clung on tightly with my body. '*Shit, shit, shit!*' This time I *did* hear my echo and felt the huge pipes judge me too. Zone by zone, I watched the light shrink away into the depths, calling the hall of iron arteries obscenely into being on its way, almost hitting some lines. Slamming my eyes shut, I fought to turn the gauge on my fear and push calm back through my nerves.

But when I opened them again, the dot was there. Still there, unmoving. As if the globe hadn't smashed, but simply . . . stopped. I stared at it, my heartbeat slowing, but the dot stayed right where it was. *How?*

How didn't matter. I had no choice now but to climb down to the bottom and get it back, or in the dark I'd never get out of this place.

Blind, I felt my way back to Arte-I. Touched its face. Patted a path and found its gills. Holding on tightly, I hoisted myself up against its side, though my feet slid about before finding their place. Another panic. It was a long journey to the bottom of the Hub, and soon measuring the time became an impossible thing. Counting the gills meant less and less. Twice I glanced down between my feet just to be sure the dot was at least a little bit bigger than the last time, almost ready to believe the Hub was infinite now. If there was no light in a place, maybe it *could* go on forever . . . ? By the time I could see the gills in front of my face again, my count had overshot three hundred.

Down here the gills were wet, however, so I slowed down before dismounting. On a thin lateral feeder, I braced myself between another of the verticals, just as thin, and Arte-I. Shadows closed off everything above me, and although the light had taken on the green tinge of the wall, lit by triglycerate, it was too weak to read the chart. This was Zone Six: apart from the ongoing surge of the four central arterials, it was completely shut off—as it should be. Pipes were still.

All of that was half-noticed, though. For a few eerie moments, it seemed that my headlight hovered in space. Reflections played on the pipes. And then I realised that the globe wasn't hovering, but floating on the surface of a lake, beaming down through clear water into the narrowing zones. Through those zones, spindly verticals reached down like skeletal legs to disappear into the murk all the murkier some-how for being underwater. The globe's glow was dimming. The undercopper stems that powered the crystal had cooled, which meant there wasn't much time left.

A lateral led me to the northeast side of the water, curling around a fat Arte-II girder.

From there I balanced to Arte-III. The globe floated close enough just there, the cloth that floated beside and underneath it giving it the look of a luminous jellyfish. I lay on my belly and started stroking the water towards me. It was icy!

Something was wrong. No way could this be the city's water-source. Below, I could see, all four arterial channels turned inward with the green wall and plunged down deeper, deeper, deeper. Rusper had told me, anyway, that the source—the "aquifer"—was three miles down.

Water shouldn't be here, I decided. Not on Zone Six.

The globe drifted towards my fingers on the current I'd made, fading as it came. I stroked more quickly, not liking how it made me feel to look down through the surface of the water. Each time I did, I felt the fear that something old, deformed and curdled by its rust and stygian algae would swim up and grab me by my arm.

And then I saw it. A dark eye.

I froze and stared back for a moment, then made a grab for the globe and plunged it down into the water. The weak light waxed over jagged edges—it was a hole. Though hardly bigger than my hand, it was as if a chunk of Arte-III's metal had been ripped out of its side. A thrill rolled through my body. *This was it:* the reason for the system's drop in pressure. Even now, if I looked carefully, I could make out the quivering of water rushing from the fissure. How long had it been like that? Long enough, obviously, to fill Zone Six, but how long was that? How fast was the water level rising? How long would it take before it flooded the Hub? I was no engineer, but it didn't take one to know that the channel had to be sealed. At least until the real engineers could do something about it, I figured, as I pulled my arm out of the water.

Tying the dripping cloth back around my head, I looked up. So much darkness, but at least this time it was a darkness I'd been in. Hands to the gills, I started climbing.

The first sub-gauge was on Zone Five—two levers—and the surging current fought me back as I forced them flush against the girder, narrowing the floodgates. Zone Three had the second; I forced it too. And then climbed higher, faster now. The light was sputtering inside the globe, and total blackness closing in. Another sub-gauge on Zone Two: under my hand the stream *was* thinning.

Disgruntled bellows of the pipeworks rising with me as I climbed, I pressed for the top of the Hub Chamber. There, my light flickered just enough to show a broad, vaulted ceiling that put another shudder through me. Some feet shy of a colossal iron girder, affixed with bolts wider than my face, was the Mains Wheel.

Anchoring my fingers and toes into the gills as best I could, I gripped and heaved.

A juddering groan was what came first. Then everything the channel still had power to raise raged back at me. Vicious, outraged, the wheel spun against my strength but I held tight and kept on pushing. At least as long as I could bear before the force of the valve plucked me clear. I grabbed the wheel, swung down and jolted.

The Hub shook all around me.

Arterial-III trembled and roared. Then gurgled, shivered and went still.

Rusper drummed his nails on a feeder and bristled as if he might eat me alive. 'A *leak*.'

I nodded, for the third time.

'Desert take it!'

Crouched on the bricks, I used the headcloth to dab my knees and sliced elbows, smarting at the grit that had got into the cuts. They weren't as bad as all that.

I looked at the misty globe. The triglycerate had died on my return through the green wall, though after its time in the cold water I'd been lucky it had lasted even that long. Had I really just done that: sealed one of the central piping channels of the city of Antissa? Whatever I'd done, I'd reported everything in full detail to Rusper. He was intrigued, instantly, about the stone bridge and tubes and cables that I'd seen, but after my mention of the hole in Arte-III, didn't care.

'That settles it.'

'What?'

'I'll have to halt the Deepworks. The risk's too great, digging this blind to what's in there.' As he grimaced, I knew he wasn't really speaking to me. '. . . have to redirect the aqueducts. As of now the entire North District will be drawing up the dregs of its reservoirs. It's *midday*.'

I thought about my people. 'So I'll go in again.'

'Don't be stupid. Won't have you dropping to your death in that tomb!'

'But I already went.'

'No.' He looked at me and read my face. 'You did well, Flint. Sealed the arterial, stopped the flood, balanced pressure for the moment. It needed done.'

I swelled a little. 'So how will you fix it?'

'By opening the Chamber,' he said. 'We can admire the Builders until the ergs drown this fortress in sand, but our trust in their legacies must be tempered. It's time. Antissa's needs have now changed.' A white strand of hair fell loose over his eyes. He was silent for a while, gazing ahead at the green wall as if making mental calculations already, before I dared to interrupt.

'Where's Loquar?'

'Dismissed.'

For the day, I thought he meant, but I was wrong. The next morning, even though this time I'd pushed the bed well out of its range, that pipe didn't open to splash me awake. It didn't open again.

Fourteen

Deepwork

Six days after my run-in with the Iron Shield, I stepped out into the sunshine of the courtyard. My blood ran cold, even in the heat, and when I saw the group of children playing around the citadel columns, challenging each other to wrap their arms all the way around each one, I nearly went back inside.

But they weren't the wild boys.

Pigeons fluttered off the steps as I made my way down, under a wing of the great stone beast on its plinth. The creature had parts of both a lion and an eagle and they called it a "gryphon." The shadow of its beak ended right on the flagstone where Con had been struck down by that boy, and bled to death; now scrubbed white and clean as if nothing had happened on it at all.

I looked around in the mid-morning quiet. The guards on duty barely saw me; just another swathed boy of the Mooncircle Service, and none of the passing viziers shot me looks.

I could walk without fear now.

In the weeks that followed, the workforce of the Guilds was diverted from the Deepworks. All digging stopped. For the first time in centuries, the Hub Chamber of Antissa's famous pipe-works would be opened.

Even so, with the Sanhedrin pressing for progress, Deep preparations continued. The City Guild was now charged with the planning of advancements to be made to the Deep's lower levels, and it was under this arrangement that my official duties began. I could read, I could write, I was good with my numbers. In Rusper's words: 'Now I can avail myself of *four* hands when no hands can go spare!' Trusting my hands almost too quickly, it seemed, he assigned me the duty of checking drafts as they arrived from the city engineers. A job which anyone could do, he told me, but which took up precious time – time that could be put to better use by his more skilled engineering staff.

The City Guildhouse was at the centre of civic engineering industry, found at the edge of the North District's upper quarter. Jumbled stone and timber buildings seemed to lumber over the downslope of the hill there, as if they were sagging out of bed, while a dome of loose and lifting tiles stretched to bind and hold them all together like a lumpy patchwork quilt. Business poured out of its shade into the streets at every hour of the day, and it was through that business that I elbowed every morning to collect the drafts from the foreman. In exchange, I'd bring him messages from the Royal Guild. If these weren't yesterday's *amended* drafts, they'd be routine manifests for materials and supplies to be sourced from the district artisans, signed off as royal quota by the city quartermaster, and later dispatched by wagonload to the Deep. Transporting such cargo wasn't part of my duties – at least not in the beginning – and only when Rusper included orders of his own was I expected to return with them in hand. Sparts, as he called them.

His right-hand overseers, Pintle and Gudgeon, weren't willing to squander their time on the basic flaws for which the city engineers, or so they told me, were famous. So it was my job to make sure that every draft that was submitted by that Guild was good enough for Royal standards before reaching their desks.

And so it went. Perched at my workbench every day, embanked by parchments, I'd scour for obvious mistakes, correcting whichever ones I could correct, sometimes copying whole diagrams from scratch when corrections simply weren't enough. I'd redraw plans, table measurements, work out the figures called "controls" from a set of formulas I quickly memorised. There wasn't place for invention; only precision.

It wasn't hard, and I learned fast; becoming quick and methodical and a steady hand at drawing. Before too long the overseers were finding so little fault with my work that they started sending their own drafts to my bench from time to time. Halfway through the second week, I was sure, the odd scrap of Rusper's work had found its way to my station as well! None of these, at first, helped with my curiosity about the Hub; little more than proposed scaffold plans for the entryways. Like the City Guild plans that made up the bulk of my daily bundle, they offered fragments, at best, of bigger things.

Soon my bundle was reaching the overseers by noon or before. But there was always more work to be done, and my hands easily put to more physical duties. After mornings spent alone among my parchments and pencils, I would fall in with the tasks of the novice engineers. Most days I'd reach the wagon depot in time to help offload the cargo. Then I'd push my wheelbarrow down along the underpass roads, then down the spiral of the rubble-shaft and through the levels of the Deep. All kinds of rounds I made with that wheelbarrow, loading it high with broken parts and used equipment, surplus tools; wheeling them to the smelters where the metal was melted down, reborn, remade. I collected buckets from utility rooms, to be emptied down the drainage ducts, stacked and returned. At this I also grew quick and soon was running other errands for engineers throughout the Deep; filling up their clepsydra tanks, ferrying their wood and their metal, their parts and tools, letters, replies. The sling-bag was handy for all these jobs, fitting lightly at my hip as if it wasn't even there.

I was no one's apprentice and didn't pretend that I was. But as a hand of the Guild I became used to my routines, comforted by the rhythms of the labour. Not only did the screams from the borderlands go a little softer in my head, but when they were loud again at night, I wouldn't have to try and muffle them under my red-bird quilt for long.

Sleep had never come so easy.

Given the evenings to myself, I'd watch Rusper at his work on the fusils. I'd seen first-hand the explosions that his chrozite could produce, wanting nothing more than to believe that some mechanical weapon could channel something like *that* against the Rath. Rusper didn't often notice me sitting beside him at his bench, but he always muttered when he worked. And because I listened to his mutters, I knew he was still far from satisfied.

The weapon was too clumsy, he believed. The mechanism that he'd created to make it do what it must was complex; because of that, it got too easily jammed. As for the chrozite itself, it was still a far greater danger to the wielder than the target. Which was, I had to agree, not much use in the field.

'The wrong amount and the whole erg-damned thing'll blow up in your hands. Not to mention the fallibility of the catch-mech. See just there? Trap enough grit when that opens and the same thing'll happen.'

The little balls of leaden "schot" had now been coated with chrozite. As far as I could tell, the weapon should work by drawing the schot from front to back on tensile cords, where a sort of spinning transmission thing made up of wheels, flint and hammers set them alight. A trigger squeezed by the wielder's finger would then eject the schot at breakneck speed. But it *was* intricate mechanics to make all these things happen smoothly and, as he said, it *did* keep jamming.

Many mornings I climbed the steps from my room to find the workshop bestrewn with pieces of fusil underneath a settled storm of sketches. Rusper would be there, somewhere among them; hunched, half-sleeping on his arms. I'd always try to read the notes, but his writing turned all words into scribbles.

Other nights I'd lie awake, under my quilt, to the claps of chrozite far below. I'd imagine him down there in the gloom of digging level, firing away at granite walls, and be awake when he returned, muttering again.

And still I'd be up before the dawn to hot the lights.

It couldn't have been more than a week before I opened the tall cabinet again. It took some time to admit it to myself, but now that the mystery of the Discs belonged to me, I didn't know what to do with it. Or where to start. There they lay, their twin reflections perfectly mocking the spiky black mess that was my hair.

Had it been real, that blue glow and white blaze? Of course it had. Rusper had seen it too, he'd said so.

But he hadn't heard that voice. He knew nothing about that, and I wouldn't tell him. Not just yet.

Nervous of releasing the white blaze a second time, I never touched them with my hands. Handling mine only with its cloth, I repeated what we'd done on that day to make it glow; dropping it on the bricks in the same way, from the same height, reversing the pattern of knocks and trying others, mixing them up. I tried the same on Rusper's one, eventually just dislodging one of the bricks from the floor to ease the task.

Strange forces existed, I knew. My knowledge of Ered was hazy, from Sarah's tales, but I knew that there were men and women of that empire who could craft what seemed like miracles out of air and will alone. In Ered such things were understood as a kind of science, I gathered, performed by learned old men I always imagined with bald heads and spectacled noses.

There were the druids - the Wildmen - of the faraway Westreach, and their woodland magics that had been practiced once in Naemia too. Some druids even my family had known by name: men Sarah had said could command the earth at their feet, heal the sick and the dying with the warmth of their hands. Talk with the trees . . .

As impossible as such things seemed to me, they were real. I could accept that they were real because they were just as far beyond me now as the tremors of *before* had always been. And those tremors, too, had come from something that was real. Our home. I believed all Sarah's tales. And I believed Rusper's tales too. Neither brought me any closer to what I'd felt from the Disc.

If I sat completely still, I could still bring back how it had felt in that moment. It had moved *inside* me, through my body, even through the thoughts inside my head. *Wanting* something. To fear it felt right, but the more I remembered the blaze and the voice, the farther away I stepped from any kind of answer.

Would I recognise a magic? Did a magic feel *alive?*

The Discs weren't machines, that much was clear to me, at least. And here in Antissa, where surely few things could be *less* real than a magic, I could understand why Rusper wanted them kept secret.

So I went looking for clues.

Up in the citadel there weren't many maps to be found of the lands beyond Vorth, and those that showed the realms of the Inwold at large were sparing with names. Elman—that was commonly marked, I later learned because of the logging trade that Vorth had depended on for decades. Now ended. I found only one map marking Naemia and Norwynd. Together, these were the countries of the Inwold; known in Ered as "Exelcia Minor" because of the religion of Fallstone that had once bound them together. Parts of Ered, also, followed Exelcian beliefs and that, I guessed, was what made up the rest of "Exelcia." Some of Ered's western provinces were shown on those maps: Cless, Creach and Crippin, Nem, The Dunfinds . . . all these were parts of the region of Ered called "Lostor."

I thought of my family's little book of Exelcian proverbs, but none of the proverbs had stuck. Vorth, I remembered, had long ago broken away from Fallstone's religion, becoming known by Naemian people as the desert "outland" because of that. Not that it mattered anymore which lands were in and which were out. Not with Fallstone's doors closed for all time. Not in a world full of tremors.

The Lack was marked on all the maps I looked at; the cartographer always making it very clear that whatever bit of it he'd had space enough to add was but a scrap of the expanse that stretched away to the northeast. Barren and empty, rivers dry. I struggled to believe what Rusper suspected of those wastes and just how unforgiving they were: that because of one stranger who had gone there, the Discs proved the tribes were out there too. Roaming, preparing, re-arming. Did he believe that the stranger himself had been one of the shamans of those tribes; that he was watching the Vedish now through a magic window of that Disc? And how did that explain *my* one, then?

It didn't make a lot of sense.

And yet it was my task, by order of the Viceroy, to find in them some kind of truth. I was a link, that much was certain, but a link that knew nothing.

Why did I have one? Why had Rusper's stranger?

The task stared back at me, silent.

Adjustments to the aqueducts around the Inner City wall began only a day after my journey into the Hub. Cutting off water supply to the North District hadn't been on purpose - I'd had no choice! Not unless I'd wanted to let the Hub Chamber simply flood. But now, for as long as Arterial-III remained sealed, water to the surrounding districts would have to be diverted and siphoned into other reservoirs. The work was swift though, and those reservoirs already rising by that evening. I told myself that my people couldn't have gone thirsty for too long.

The engineers set about forging their channels through the green wall; masonry so old it seemed a crime to scratch a mark into its face. Or perhaps it would have seemed that way to a less practical people. Planning took a week, Rusper conferring with his architects and picking apart citadel maps in search of the safest place to weaken the very struts that held it up. It was under this unspoken threat of levelling a district and crushing everyone who lived inside the palace that I began to admire the true precision of the Chief Engineer's work.

'You're *sure* Meck's Transcripts were correct?' he asked me at least half a dozen times. I could only shrug and repeat what I'd told him already: that what I'd seen by my small light had matched the charts. Except, that was, for what I'd found in the centre of the Hub – the bridge, the cables and those vertical tubes. Those things were missing from Meck's Transcripts, and they unsettled Rusper.

Frustration peaking, he began the work half-prepared.

I kept as close an eye on what went on as I could without getting in the way. Both entrances were to be located on the second level of the Deep, facing one another across the diameter of the Hub. Measures were taken to support the load from above, cavities bored into the top of both points, threaded with poles. These stuck out to allow for vertical posts to be secured underneath. New masonry was cut to make lintels above them in order to sustain the enormous pressure of the citadel bearing down. Only then could the temporary posts be removed, and the first green stones cut from the wall.

The tunnels would be wider at their openings, squared into rooms that extended just under a third of the full thickness of the wall. Great care was taken to avoid damage to the pipes in the process, but still the progress was crude. Often, I'd hear Rusper's voice rasping above the chisels: 'Don't mind how it looks, we'll border the boundaries—give me a hole I can push a barrow through!'

Surprisingly, the ancient green stonework ended after only five feet. Beyond was *sandstone*—and I hadn't even noticed as I'd crawled my way through it!

'The more we uncover of their works, the more the Builders amaze us,' Rusper mused one night over his cup of black coffee. 'Don't you see, boy? We are *built* upon sandstone. It's as if the Hub was constructed within unbroken, natural rock.'

'Is that possible?'

He made a strange face at me.

The teams picked on through the sandstone. More holes were bored and more poles threaded, rough buttresses installed in the corners of the entry-rooms. I watched. The burrowing continued now at half of the original width. Then new tunnels were formed, bolstered in turn. Planning for the bridges was begun. As soon as they gained access to the Hub, construction would begin on a network of cantilever bridges: one bridge to span each of the zones that made up the column.

Designs were sparing. I was consulted more often now, and even dared some plans of my own. These never met with approval, either from the Chief Engineer or his architects and overseers. Rusper's disdain for imprecision made him a hard man to please, and it only took one botched measurement to set him off on a tirade.

'You've muddled up all your formulae!' he would complain, when in fact I'd only switched a pair or forgotten to add one in. Then it was my coding that was wrong: '*Black ink* for adjustments, *wash* for foundations!' And when I'd mastered as perfect a draft as any City Guild diagram approved by the likes of Pintle and Gudgeon, he'd no longer want to see it at all. 'A practical example is worth *ten* rendered plans, boy! You know were the scrap is. Build me a model!'

They were never accepted. But Rusper was always attentive to what I could tell him of the Hub interior, and always listened to me closely. As long as I could speak fairly quickly. The space inside, I knew, was easily as huge as Meck had claimed it was, and gaps between the pipes were impossibly wide in many places. A bridge to each zone, even built at speed, wasn't going to be enough.

'What of the clefts in the piping . . . the gills, as you call them?'

'Too dangerous,' I said.

'Hah! You'll recall I recently sang you that same song,' he chided me. 'Let me worry about dangers. Will the gills get my men to the haemorrhage or not?'

'No. You'll need ladders.'

'That demands too much metal. And we can't use timber in there. Air's too wet, it'll warp.'

'What about rope?'

'I'm listening.'

'There's heaps of it lying around down here,' I said excitedly. 'We could connect the pipes with nets while you work on the bridges.'

This plan he approved, almost at once, and I overheard his muttering about not having thought of it first.

Eight days after the first stones were loosened, sandstone gave way to green again. We tasted moist air, close now. That tang I remembered. Then the ends of both entry-tunnels crumbled open, and the teams could call across the cold dark to each other. Hands were dispatched into the chamber with many lanterns, and behind them came Rusper.

And me, by his side.

We watched from the tunnel's edge as the lights pricked their tiny ways into the huge hollow. Between the four giant arterials, the central pipeworks revealed themselves to us all with a kind of grudging majesty; far more than I'd imagined had been there while I'd been groping around in darkness. 'An engineer's dream,' Rusper said on a sigh.

Some way down from our lookout was the bridge—that stone bridge I had discovered. From the southwest wall it arced inward towards the central tube cluster, and then stopped short as if severed. Around the tubes, at four points, a boundary of cables was suspended. So I hadn't made them up. Those tubes ran all the way down through the lights of the lanterns; lights which now, far below, began to play on the water. It made me dizzy to look. 'What now?' I said.

'Now we work, *ekhin* Flint,' Rusper smiled.

Over a hundred triglycerate lanterns were needed to give shape to the sacred vastness, and even that was just enough. Many were pulled from digging level, which plunged the Deep floor into blackness and cut my morning rounds short. Others came from the citadel grounds and servant quarters. But Rusper also made demands upon the estates of the viziers, most of whom favoured open fires and scented lamps anyway. Assuring them all that the inconvenience would be short, he sent sappers back to harvest the green halite mine on fourth level.

But getting the workers through the Hub was a challenge in itself. The pipes could be scaled using the gills, I had done it myself. But my fingers were smaller than those of the men and women whose job it now was to carry tools and materials across a drop of nearly four hundred feet. On the second day of access, Pintle reported that a man had fallen to his death from Zone Three. Rusper must have seen something in my face when she brought that news; if more deaths followed after that, I never heard about them.

He doubled the workforce. Up and down the interior of the ancient green wall, lanterns were mounted on poles that reached inward through the half-light. In the concentrated triglycerate, pipes shone green. Faithful to my advice, everything that could hold it was covered in rope, trellises suspended across all zones, hammered to the wall with ten-inch pins and clamped to the iron pipes themselves. The Hub became navigable, if only just safe by the time we climbed down to Zone Six to inspect the damage.

Workers sank a lantern-pole through the surface of the lake and I knew, the second I saw it, that the hole had grown bigger. Now gaping out of the arterial's side, it was wide enough to fit a man in a suit of armour. Full-plate Naemian armour, the way Sarah once described it.

'It's bigger,' I said, squinting through the greenness of the lanterns. Their glare obscured all detail above and below the water; even Rusper's gloved fist as it knocked on the iron.

'Can't be,' he said. 'You sealed it yourself. There's been no pressure on this channel since you were here two weeks ago.'

I shook my head. 'I'm sure it's bigger.'

'Trick of the light,' he replied, clapping the glove on my shoulder.

But there was more than just the haemorrhage to inspect. Now more than ever before, it was clear to the Guild that Meck's Transcripts of the Hub had been correct. Almost perfect, in fact, except for three missing features I had discovered myself: the stone bridge that extended from the wall of the chamber—*so out of place*—the cluster of thin, vertical tubes that descended from the ceiling, and the web-like vane of black cables suspended symmetrically around them. There seemed no explanation for these things, or even any purpose.

Pintle and Gudgeon, both experts in such things, examined the cables themselves and found them to be made of some material unknown to Antissa: a coarse yet malleable fibre that would stretch but never break. Each of its intersecting lines was anchored to the wall at opposite sides of the Hub, with closed hooks which wouldn't—*couldn't*—be loosened. Nor could any of the Guild's industrial saws cut through the fibre, even slightly. So for the time, Rusper decided to simply leave them alone. There was other work to be done.

Fifty foundrymen and a score more hands were conscripted for the bridges. Sappers were mustered to drain the water from the bottom of the column. Cranes were installed at the edges of the tunnels to raise buckets on ropes, assisted by a conveyor-belt of hands along the gills. Deepworkers ferried the water in barrows to the reservoirs of the city. And after five days of steady labour, the haemorrhage I had found broke the surface.

Repairs on Arterial-III were begun.

Meanwhile, my puzzle went on.

The Discs *had* to be something.

I turned to the tools of the workshop, often sharing it with Rusper in the working hours of the day. Though their smoothness made slippery grips of even the tightest of vices, I'd secure them in place as best I could and, with whatever I could find – ratchets, chisels, files, scrapers and a growing bewilderment – prize for any tell-tale, proud edge that could be hiding in their elliptical mirrors. Hands always gloved.

They couldn't be perfect! But no matter how fine a tool I used on them, there were no edges to be found. Not anywhere, however small. I tried all strengths of magnets too. But magnets had no effect on them at all.

Something had to make them do what they did, or what at least mine had done to *me*. Was it inside them, *trapped* inside? And if it was, how could I reach it? Did the metal exterior open? It seemed it couldn't be broken. Or maybe it was the metal itself, if it *was* metal. *Magic metal . . . ?*

'Will you stop grinding your teeth, please.'

'Sorry.'

That had turned into a nervous habit now, along with squeezing my thumbs or frowning so hard and for so long my forehead ached. But the Discs absorbed me so fully, even as their surreal mirror-images mocked my focused frown. Somehow I ignored those reflections, though it was much harder to ignore the two perfect copies of Rusper hunched over his fusils-in-progress. Without having to look up, I could watch every little thing he did; every snib and node his fingers tweaked, as if through the fingers themselves.

And what proved, after all, that there was anything behind or underneath the impossible faces of the Discs? They were heavy enough to be solid right through, so why did I suspect something hidden inside them? What, within a tiny metallic oval, could unleash a white fire and put a voice into my head?

Did I dare touch it, unleash it again? Would it work a second time? Would the other do the same, and if I risked it, touched it, would it—?

'Flint—the *teeth!*'

Work went on at a pace.

The Transcripts became indispensable to progress. Daily I was tasked by Gudgeon – now in charge of Hub "Reconditioning" – to search out old pages of codes or coordinates penned by Meck long ago. With the reclaiming of the original core of the pipeworks, the Royal Guild had now entered a new engineering era, so it wasn't long before I found myself raking into Meck's uncategorised papers: hundreds of drawings and notes without place.

Something about his material entranced me. Among the endless stacks of sheaves, were plans for things that seemed unlike anything the Guild had ever done. One drawing I kept coming back to – graphite on water-damaged parchment – showed a circular figure with a divided interior. The sections were shaped like the axle of a wheel, and yet it couldn't be a wheel because the spaces within the axle opened onto heavier lines. It seemed to *turn*, and even *open*, as I looked. He'd put no labels on the drawing but left a side of it blank as if he'd meant to come back.

More obscure were the scribbles: entire notebooks full of scribbles. Most of them were meaningless shapes, mostly circles or variations. Over and over, they seemed to reach for a form just out of his grasp. Here and there I'd find a label or random number, rarely a word. And while his penmanship was flawless, his writing easy on the eye, on every few pages at least one word or figure would be looped in desperate whirls.

Had Gaspar Meck simply gone mad? In less roughed and damaged notebooks, the shapes were more detailed and the circles crossed with thin, bisecting lines. I delved on deeper, the figures becoming less and less like scribbles now, more like preliminary sketches. Bisecting lines more like pronged arrows: sometimes four, sometimes six. Most were haphazardly labelled with some kind of measurement or other, but never anything to tell me what it was that it measured. Nor could Rusper shed any light when I brought them to him with my questions.

'Much of Meck's material was never archived after he died,' he said, regarding the mass of paper behind me like a chore he'd been quite happy to avoid until I'd gone and brought it up. 'And that's only because he himself left it unclear or unfinished. Most of what you'll find there will be ideas that never worked. If there's anything new of use, it's not worth searching it out.'

But I was hooked. It was those circles. I relished every chance I got to leaf into the notebooks I hadn't opened yet, too often losing track of the time. Gudgeon's requests would reach him late, and on one such occasion he brought complaint to Rusper. Who gave me a stern dressing down.

The Royal Guild expected, and would accept nothing less, than full attention to the tasks with which I was charged. That's what he said, quite cross with me. So, after that, I put aside my own time for chasing Meck's circles.

And yet, just as the circles seemed to be floating away, becoming little more than doodles on the edges of discarded transcripts, I found the thing that they'd been floating towards. At last, hard lines at the end of the meaningless scribbles.

Someone had cleared away all his papers but left the scroll-tubes behind, thinking them empty. I'd thought so too. But when I looked into one, a sheet of rotten parchment was stuck fast to its inner lining. I pulled it gently, tearing only a narrow strip of its margin, and spread it out. Whole, I guessed it twenty inches by thirty, though a wider strip had disintegrated from the left side as well. Moisture had bloated the rest, leaving it brittle and brown with many patches of mould. But while the inkwork was cloudy, it was clear enough to me that I was looking at a finished diagram.

It showed a complex circle. Like the rings of a tree-trunk, it repeated itself in blurred double lines. Eight radial spokes in pitch-black ink sprang from the centre like horns. They gave it the look of a hoary old compass, but that wasn't what it was. No. At the end of the spokes, I could make out the remains of more detail, now faded. Only near the top of the page had any true detail survived: a weird extension of one spoke, angled away. It was furnished with another, different shape and a few fine labels, although most of these had gone with the left-most edge.

I rummaged for a lens to magnify the script, took up a pen and found myself climbing right onto the table. Nudging the lens over the page, I copied fragments to my arm:

SPHERE FRAME / . . . using arms / Anchor claw [?] / [NEUTRAL] / [REST + NEUTRAL / 90 degrees / . . . drical / . . . pipes

I threw down the pen. *Claw?*

What had Meck been trying to build—a machine or a monster? And had he built it or not?

Carefully, I rolled up the sheet, put it back inside its tube and slipped the tube under my bedframe. It would keep. Rusper was too busy anyway, and my own tasks piling on.

The metal of the Discs was unbreakable, inflexible, reactive to nothing.

'*Rhaum*,' suggested Rusper. 'Hardest substance I know. At least, before . . .'

I guessed it: 'Those black cables in the Hub?'

He nodded vaguely as his thoughts were drawn back to that mystery. The "Polymer," as we'd since taken to calling it. But he shook the thought away.

The Discs couldn't be *rhaum*, he eventually decided, because rhaum had a very distinctive smell and the Discs didn't. '*Esmum?*' he offered, then changed his mind about that too. The colour wasn't right: esmum was known for its yellow tinge. *Haematite?* No. They weren't grey, or for that matter, any colour at all. They were manifest reflections, with no visible quality that belonged to just them alone, seemingly. They didn't make sense to the eye or to the brain, and if I looked at them too long I'd get all anxious and giddy. It almost hurt, in a way, and I knew Rusper felt it too.

'Lead?' I ventured, not really serious about that idea at all. The weight was right, I supposed, but lead didn't reflect. He didn't bother to answer.

'Glass would have cracked or shattered by now, we know that,' he thought aloud, 'and not even the artésans of Ered can forge unbreakable glass.'

'What are mirrors made of?' I asked, though I knew – for all their clarity – they were no crafted pocket mirrors. Even the word we'd been using all this time for what it did—*reflect*—was wrong somehow.

'Here they are made from silver and brass, which we add to a substrate to stop them corroding,' Rusper said. But he was doubtful of the theory. If the Discs had been made in the same way as Antissan mirrors, the outer substrate would be flawless and likely too hard. That presented a problem. Without flaws it would be difficult to test the substrate's qualities.

'Can we try anyway?'

He equipped me. I sat through the evenings with both Discs set before me, armed with wire brushes and jars sent up from fourth level. I caressed the perfect mirror faces with every possible catalyst – liquids and powders with names so obscure that they might as well have been codes on piping charts – coaxing them to speak. Say or do something. But they wouldn't.

Some evenings into the process, Rusper suddenly exclaimed: 'Have you tried *water?*'

I hadn't.

Filling a bowl from the workshop's tap, I dropped them in and, as I waited, Rusper watched me.

But . . . 'Nothing,' I pouted.

He pouted back. 'Still, worth a try. Some metals do react with water. *Aqualumium* for example. Rare now, but once mined in Laudassa.'

I'd never heard of it before; at least I thought I hadn't. He crossed the workshop, pulled off his Guild-ring and dropped it straight into the bowl. The reaction was quick. While the Discs played weirdly with the reflection of the ring's band, the red-brown cogwheel crest transformed. Specks of yellow peeped through the metal and then suddenly the whole cog shone bright enough to light the interior. It was easily the most beautiful thing I'd ever seen in my life. Rusper gave a smile at my amazement and fished it out with a shake. Back on his finger, the gleam faded.

What he had said those weeks ago about my loss and the pain, and the strength of iron, came back to me. I caught his eye. He caught mine too, but if we were thinking the same thing, he didn't say anything about it.

Not long after that he sent down Meck's "blister" catalogue, which detailed how to apply various chemicals to a metal, provoking reactions. It was done with delicate looped wires and special lamps, creating bubbles of solution from a subject. Or so we hoped. The bubble was held to the flame of the lamp and studied through the dark lenses of goggles for any changes to the colour of the flame. Colours would tell of all kinds of properties contained in metals, and Meck had made long lists of these. I tested hundreds.

'Progress?' nudged Rusper on the sixth or seventh night.

Slumped on my workbench, I looked up and rubbed my face, drawling, 'No *nyphon*.'

'Come, show me.' He dragged the transcript page out from under my arms and skimmed it fast. 'In that case, cross off copper and cobalt as well. Elimination's half as good as discovery, Flint.'

No it wasn't. 'That's if anything came off on the wire in the first place,' I moped and sank back into my arms. My patience with chemical tests had run out. But then, so had the Deep's chemical stores.

FIFTEEN

BUILDERS AND BLUE

It took me a while to understand how it all worked. That is, what exactly my service to the Viceroy really meant, and how it bound me to both the Caliphate and the Mooncircle Throne.

As a wearer of the greenstring, I was allowed to move freely through the Inner City, or High District as some called it, and all the other city districts. As one who served only *one* master, I was also permitted in the upper halls of the citadel. But I had to be careful. There were those who regulated the duties of the Mooncircle service, of course, but there were also the guards. These were the citadel "black-capes" of Captain Mondric's Fortress Guard, all of them quick to cane any servant who stepped out of line. The backs and legs of all the greenstring servants were a webwork of scars, the children's too, and in the mornings I'd hear the cracks and cries of pain from the underpass roads where they took beatings. The guards didn't look down on those they punished, or so it seemed to me anyway, and the servants didn't hate them either. At other times, servants and guards would talk and laugh with one another! It was, I soon learned, the Vedish way. It wasn't kind.

There were exceptions. If seen wearing the swathes, or tailored jackets that came of working for just one master, a servant could often escape the guards' notice. I was one of these few. The swathes took getting used to, but eventually I could put them on without help. Their itch did wear off and soon I was wearing them wherever I went. They were a blessing in the sun.

Other servants refreshed my washpot every morning after breakfast, but I washed my own clothes. To clean myself, now that the bathtub had been removed from my chamber, I used the steams where all the servants went to bathe. There wasn't much privacy there. But the others were wary of me: with most of my time spent underground – or at least, under the surface of the city – my hard-won desert tan was fading. And as I became the pale-skinned Elmine that I was rumoured to be, they gave me space to bathe alone.

From the uppermost halls of the citadel, it was possible to reach some of the towers. Curious about the tower with all the scaffolds around its dome, I went exploring.

Whatever work the scaffolds were there for had since been paused, or even cancelled. Musty from disuse, and dim inside, I found the winch that worked the skylight in the dome; except it kept on sticking with rust or lack of oil or something, and opened less than halfway. The light that shafted from the gap revealed a spiral of murals in pinkish stone that climbed the full height of the tower's interior walls. By taking to the sloping, winding walkway I was able to study the sculpted tales they told of Vorth's history. Or try.

There were no written descriptions of anything here; only mute, graven figures of the Vedans from the past. So I guessed.

As I climbed alongside the murals, I marked instatements of satraps and caliphs, with thrones and mapped regions to tell which ones were which. The maps consisted of little more than jagged borders and chiselled textures of sea or sand or hills or rolling dunes. Scenes grew more detailed near the top, as if events were clearer in memory but now a challenge for sculpting tools. After another map of Vorth's coast came the scene of a throned man who pointed to another man, who knelt. The kneeling man was on the side of the coastal map, and his hands were raised. As if begging. In the next scene, his head had been cut off – that was *very* clear. And in the next, a great host of people could be seen walking away from the throne and the pointed finger; away from the coast and from the dunes, northward it seemed, to judge by the squiggles of the rivers I counted. Yes: the Empty River and the Elm.

These scenes felt angry, somehow, and stayed with me for days after that. Why had no one written down, in words, what they seemed so eager to tell?

Abandoning that mystery, I went back down to look more closely at the murals near the floor. These were the earliest tales. Scenes showed, quite clearly, an early fortress being built up on a hill. They showed some structures, old machines and early pipes as they were laid. But most enchanting of all were scenes where groups of early Vedans stood facing another, stranger folk. These strangers were sculpted as if far larger than the Vedans: great square titans of men with huge eyes and even huger hands. Another scene saw them raising bricks of huge size from the desert and placing them atop the hill. Ancient Antissans of legend, I knew. The Builders.

Had they been giants, then? It was thrilling enough to imagine. But if so little was known about the Builders, then was it not simply more likely that these sculptors had guessed? Or made it up? I knew how stories worked, I realised, and thought about the more fantastic of Sarah's tales: like the mysterious Blue Man and some of the things that he was meant to have done in Naemia. And now I wondered when exactly my love of hearing those stories had left *believing* them behind.

I dared to explore a little further from that tower of murals. Not far, on the same floor, was a grander hall, floored all in marble, that looked out onto the city from tall windows. Servants in the steams had talked about it as the "Dynasty Hall." Along its windowless wall was a long display of regalia. No crowns, but sceptres and staves with coloured jewels; lustrous cloths, bright golden medals and links of chains. I even found the little hook under which the word VICEROY was engraved. Of course, no medallion hung there now.

Here were also likenesses of the satraps; largest being the four who had ruled under the name of *Aysattah*. The statue of Syphus the First, founder of the Aysattah Dynasty, reached almost all the way to the ceiling, raised on a plinth which one could climb by spiral steps, and there surrounded by four snarling lions. Near him, though smaller, were his sons: Hyphet the First, Hyphet the Second.

Last was the man who ruled today: Syphus the Second. Or at least, that was his royal name. His was a bust of head and shoulders, although I instantly thought his sculptor must have had nerves of stone as well. The face was warlike and cruel. If a mouth had been carved into it at all, it was invisible under the beard-cones that splayed outward from his sharp cheekbones and made his bald head look like an egg wrapped in a pleated napkin. The nose was big and fat and flat with wide-flared nostrils, like two tusks. Temples broad and sloped. Brow folding forward, a curling wave the moment just before it broke and crashed. And empty eyes that glared contempt. Hating me.

I didn't go back to the Dynasty Hall for a while. Too close to the tower of the Satrap himself, and the blue-and-whites never far. For me at least, being overlooked by the Iron Shield wasn't so certain. I'd learned first-hand what they were willing to do with half a chance, and for a while couldn't shake the fear that they'd spot me on my errands and drag me back to their sneering Lieutenant. There were much fewer of the Shieldmen, and yet some days I saw them almost as often as the guards. So it was strange, unsettling too, that they ignored me every time. Soon, I stopped drawing my hood up or dodging behind the nearest pillar. Whether or not they did know better, which they did – I *knew* they did – I had become the Elmine boy.

Rusper's personal living quarters were on the same floor as the steams, although at first I found it strange that a man who held the rank of Viceroy didn't live in more . . .

'More what? My rooms were here before the Viceroyalty was instituted,' he explained, 'and I've no desire to move them now. Just how much sleep do you think I'd get with the Sanhedrin for neighbours!'

They were comfortable, if simple. He slept in the smaller of two rooms, reserving the larger as a study. Unlike the cluttered, low and lantern-lit workshop, it was bright and airy. A window overlooked a fully ivy-coated wall above the courtyard under-pass. There was a writing desk he never used, and a bureau. A sheepskin chair. A plain rug. A very boring tapestry. A pipe-fed triglycerate oven that shone shallow green at night-time and, somehow connected to its pipes, a tall brass samovar that he used to boil his coffee. He had no wife or children. Nor did I believe any of the gossip I heard in the steams that he courted a *harem-senah* from the lower districts. I never saw a woman in his rooms.

He would invite me here sometimes to eat with him in the evenings. Sometimes we'd talk, and sometimes not. When we did, he would ask about my duties and tasks and was I not overworked? Was I comfortable in my lodgings? Was I eating enough and did I like Antissan food? Was I aware that I was not held as a prisoner in the Deep and could freely return to see my people at their shelter? I'd nod to that, but say nothing. He didn't know it wasn't true.

Piece by piece, he told me of how the Guild had been founded, describing some of the greatest feats of engineering of the past, and how a famous mathematician named Albastra Azal had been involved in some of them. In turn, I did my best at reciting Sarah's stories as she'd told them to me: great King Saremar and his reign and his knights, the holy Celestri of Fallstone Bastion, the untamed druids of Culn Forest. The ones I told best *were* of the Blue Man: that weird, wise hero of our lore. He'd been over a hundred years old, the legends said, had advised the great princes of Naemia and even held conversations with the Celestrian Archons.

All these stories entertained him, but to me they still weren't right. Not anymore.

On other evenings the High Commander would be there, delivering reports and conferring as the aide to the Viceroy. To begin with, Plamen showed reluctance to speak in front of me, as if disapproving of my presence or worried about what I might hear. So when he was there, and they were talking, I'd simply play with his dog Tazen. That gave him reason enough to ignore me, just as he would wherever else we crossed paths.

Captain Mondric, as unlike Plamen as it was possible to be, was rough but good-natured with me, in his way. Every time we met anywhere he'd grip my neck in one hand and screw my hair up with the other, booming out, 'If it isn't our little Elmine tool-boy!' Heads would turn.

It was better, I realised, to stay in the Deep and eat by myself in the workshop. A meal in the morning and another meal at night, always brought by the same bug-eyed, bald girl with the yellow jacket. Her name was Zeek; she smiled sometimes, but never said anything to me.

The food was simple: stewed ramsons, spiced asparagus, or yams with sesame *tahina*. Beef *kibhin* on a good day. And in the mornings always tashi, that bowl of sweet and frothy oats, currants and caraway seeds. The Vedish ate no poultry, keeping chickens, ducks and geese only for their eggs and feather down. The meals were good and I was grateful; just like my clothes and nice warm bed with its red-bird quilt, a better fare than that afforded to my people.

News of the Rath came through the High Commander's scouts out in the desert. Under the Satrap's decree, which forbade the deployment of martial forces, the use of these scouts had somehow upset the viziers of the Sanhedrin. This in spite of strict orders that the scouts engage no enemy; not to mention the fact that the council seemed only too happy about parties still risking fishing journeys to the coast. That arrangement didn't last though, and before a full month was out, there was no fish to be bought or eaten anywhere in the city. Things were changing.

Western Verunia, in the northernmost caliphy of Vorth, was overrun, and the people of its "shen" villages crammed between the Southeast and Mercantile Districts. All the borderland settlements were now empty as well. Unless a pocket of Naemians survived somewhere else, away from the desert, then the ninety in the North District were the last of my people in the world. That was strange to think about sometimes. And I found myself feeling sorry for the Verunians too, all the more when I worked out that they'd been the ones who had helped us, sending seed and livestock and coal over the Elm those years ago.

I listened closely to Plamen whenever I could. The Rath, who would only ever attack in small groups, never occupied the sites they laid to waste, but instead moved back again to greater numbers every time. As to where those greater numbers were, there were no reports.

The scouts were led by a soldier called Kathris – an "Artabh" of Antissa's regiment, whose soldiers were called "vortans" –

charged with observation of the Empty River's banks for any sign of southward crossings by the Rath. Kathris, I heard, had erected a flag-line from the coast in the west, all the way to the edge of the Lack in the east – some fifty miles. But the flags had not long stood up to the shredding night winds of the desert.

Heavy, intricate sparts from the stockpiles of the Deep had been positioned at the flagpoles after that, and Ratheine movement tracked by where and how often the items were disturbed. Rath moved by night, ranging through the north. And soon enough, as revealed by the reports, their groups began to breach the flag-line. Kathris and his party would sight up to thirty at a time on the dunes of the Northern Erg. Growing bolder, it seemed. And although, as an enemy, Plamen said they showed no clear purpose or direction, the image of the Rath at city walls was never far from my dreams.

Those on the border could do it . . . mount an advance on Antissa. Even without the thousands yet to cross out of Naemia, through the mountains . . .

To my comfort, I'd also heard Plamen's outline of defence in the event of facing greater numbers. Since the retreat from the northern border, the Mooncircle Army was garrisoned here at Antissa, again under the Satrap's high decree restricting defence to the fortress alone. East and west of Antissa, Plamen explained more than once, a front could be formed that would stretch from the coastline of the gulf to a place called Calvallagh in the east: a front fully manned and provisioned from the fortress. This, he advised, was the Viceroy's best chance of holding back siege of the fortress, or worse an invasion of the middle caliphies. The Bronze Coast, then Laudassa, Methar after that . . .

The Sanhedrin, I understood, was watching the Viceroy very closely. Everyone knew only too well that before a single soldier was prepared for deployment beyond Antissa's sandstone walls, the Satrap himself must lift decree. Any less would mean high treason.

But the Satrap, high up in his tower, remained silent. And the Viceroy's hands tied to that decree.

When I remembered Meck's scroll, I spent more nights poring over it. And the harder I tried to make sense of that weird diagram, the more intrigued I became by what the former Chief Engineer had been doing in his time heading the Guild, and the more fascinated about the ancient Builders of Antissa. I asked to see their parchments; the originals Meck had copied for the Transcripts, but Pintle said that those parchments had been the property of the throne for more than a generation. That was annoying. It made me only hungrier for what *was* known about the Builders.

'Precious little,' Rusper told me. Nestled in the big sheepskin chair of his quarters, there was a mood of sedation about him tonight. Stars stood clearly in the window behind him while the triglycerate oven cast green shadows on the rug. One of the shadows was mine. I sat at his feet, my legs crossed under me, and snapped my magnets together.

'But why?' I said, showing my frustration.

'Because,' he said, fluttering his eyelids, 'once you've separated all the mechanical and architectural engineering, Antissa's written records are scant at best. That makes our history obscure. And even then, what we have now is only what survived the great onslaught.'

'You mean the fortress was attacked?'

'' 2760. Four hundred years ago,' he replied. 'Sacked by Lackish barbarians, and their shamans of course. The city was left so devastated that now true Vedish nationhood is only taken from that date. The barbarians were repelled, but at the price of many lives. And much history.'

'So that's what happened to the Builders? Barbarians killed them?'

Rusper pondered. 'No account of their disappearance links it to death by any means. But it's possible. We don't know how many there were, after all.'

'Barbarians?'

'No, Builders,' he said. 'A thousand, a hundred . . . a mere dozen perhaps? Little more than speculation exists about them now. That and their works.'

From my rapt gaze he must have clocked my true interest in the subject. He sat forward.

'Whoever the Builders really were, what has always been clear is that they were regarded as superior by the people of the desert. It may be that they ruled here, and yet to claim a fortress by the sword and then abandon it does not make much sense. Yet that is the lasting belief.'

'That they left?'

He sat back, yawned and nodded. 'Legend has it that they followed the river and never came back to Antissa. The clerics, however, believe they *did* return some decades later to erect their monuments in the desert. The stones at Calvallagh, Laudassa and Methar are the sites of their temples.'

'I thought you didn't have gods.'

'We don't,' he said. 'The temples stand to venerate the Builders themselves, in the form of the gryphon: a sigil gleaned from the stones, though winds have worn them away now.'

'I've seen the gryphon.'

'Of course, hard not to. Gryphons have obsessed our sculptors ever since the old days.'

'So what do the clerics believe about them?'

'About the gryphons?'

'No, about the Builders.'

He picked and brushed lint off his thobe. 'They are devoted to the Builders' legacy, as they see it. That and the prospect of their future return. Few have any use for such ideas in our time, you understand, even if the first clerics are supposed to have been engineers themselves. Nevertheless, to this day, the ergish Vedans of our desert retain ties of deep trust in the clerics. Ironic, perhaps, that such should be what most divides us from the southern communities now.'

'Do you think they'll come back?'

'The clerics?'

'The *Builders*.'

'Ah.' He gave a wistful smile. 'Flint, it's a legend. We know they were masters of engineering-craft. We have the proof all around us. We also know that, after their time, the inevitable occurred here. A population, which may or may not have been as Vedish as they were, took governance of the city and pursued the engineering that had been practiced behind its walls. One cannot deny that it is the pivot on which Vorth's identity now turns.'

Frowning , I thought how that hadn't really answered my question. And I was disappointed because none of this was helping me at all. 'Was Vorth even *called* Vorth back then?'

'Probably not.'

'And does . . .' I began. But shook the question away; it was only going to sound stupid to a man like Rusper Symphin.

'Out with it,' he said, resting his cheek on his knuckles.

'Does the gryphon exist?'

My magnets snapped together sharply, and the engineer simply smiled. 'The clerics hold it to be the ultimate Arbiter of Justice. A beast with the body of a lion, head and wings of an eagle by most depictions. I've never seen one!' he laughed.

I'd wander.

Surrounded by masters and tasks almost all of every day, the hours I could claim for myself were somehow sweeter. I wouldn't stay in the High District. Stately dress and clopping hooves reminded me too easily of my place as a servant, so I would venture away from the Inner City altogether.

Fascination overtook the fear I'd felt on first peering out of that bright warehouse doorway. Slowly, I grew more at ease with the noises and smokes of the bustling North District. With coins from my pouch – the small stipend of seven kopechs a day that I'd been promised – I bought handfuls of nuts, bags of dates and currants, salted jerky. Before they cut off the coast to the fishing parties, I ate pot-crab right from its shell. A meal that was once the common Vedish man's fare, it cost ten kopechs—almost a tallan. I drank cups of frothy goat's milk and a few tankards of *braehg*, the weak beer made out of oats that the lay Antissans all drank. I didn't like it very much, realising to my surprise that I'd got used to the city water's metal tang. Maybe even liked it.

Hood drawn, I breathed Antissan life on the fumes of the streets; listened to the whine of *duduk* flutes, pluckings of the *rebab* and the *zither*. I thought how human the crowds looked now; made of families like I'd had. People who lived, just as we'd done, day to day and chore to chore. People who maybe only now started to fear for the future. They'd been so frightening to me before – so hard and rough and unlike us – and they still *were* those things, I guessed. Dismissive, brusque and unkind. It wasn't easy to like them, even now. But did I hate them? Vedans had been kind to us once, when we'd first reached the borderlands. Perhaps not these Vedans, alright, but just how different could they be?

Those had been Verunians, I remembered. Far northern Vedans. Probably *very* different.

When the bustle got too much, I'd go up to the citadel gardens and stroll among the hedges that overlooked the districts. There I soaked in aloneness and the peace of green things under the sky. Often I saw the clerics there too, at least often enough to know that they remained at the fortress for no more than two weeks before returning to their temples in the desert. And whatever fate awaited them there when the Rath moved further south. Their fat Caliph Omran, I heard, *did* stay behind.

Steps from those gardens led down into the Citizen District, where some evenings I would walk between the better, white-walled houses. I watched the women and girls from the capital harem-houses: dark, outlandish creatures from southern caliphies, arrayed in silks and speckled gems. They sang and danced, enticed, but never broke their nymphish charm. I had my own giddy ideas about what wonders of the body awaited their suitors behind the closed doors of those secretive houses, though in time would learn that this was not the way of the harem. They were not whores.

A crust of sandstone fortress wall was now the edge of the world. From the eastward walls, I'd sometimes watch the practice-fire of war machines; the catapults and trebuchets that flung great loads of broken masonry and rubble over the heads of the Verunians in the Mercantile District, to smash into the sandstone of other, long-ruined buildings below.

To the south were the farming quarters that clung to the crags like shelves of crops. Built to fit the ledge of each rising crag, they climbed the hill like shallow steps toward the rear-most gate of the fortress; soldiers always on patrol along the lower walls that hemmed each one from the drop. I'd stand above them, looking down, watching the labour and the beasts. Or close my eyes and let the warm, still, bleating air take me somewhere else. Far from the fortress and the desert. At least until some watchman came to tell me off and jostle me away.

More often, I'd stand on northern walls and let south winds blow dust and powdered brick and chrozite out of my hair; face to the borderlands. *Overrun*. So full of memories that hurt. No going back there, now I knew. No home to go to. I thought about returning to the warehouse; a piece of me knowing that I still belonged among those people, and not with strangers. Did they have enough of what they needed, as Rusper always assured me? Were they warm when they went to sleep? Were they safe, and were they treated, if not kindly, then not too cruelly by those wardens?

Who was there for me now if Jerome had died that day? Dewar, maybe, and Mother Far. A grumpy butcher and an old woman. Even so, the dread of just how disappointed they'd be in what I'd done made me feel sick.

Not that it mattered. Plamen couldn't have made his rules more clear on that day without threatening the removal of one of my fingers himself. And I knew he was watching. Whether or not by the grace of the Satrap of Vorth, I was a citizen of Antissa now and couldn't rejoin my people.

But then one evening, just as the dusk light was starting to fade, I climbed the steps from the gardens to spot a face I recognised. A name leapt straight out of my memory. Shamak. The warden. He'd been at the shelter on the day when they'd knocked the warehouse wall down, dismissing Dewar's request for food. I caught him up.

In a cool silence he listened to me as I described the boy I hoped still lived among the refugees at the warehouse. Bulging eyes and lots of freckles, sandy hair . . .

'If he's a borderlander who did not die of his injuries, the shelter is where he will be,' Shamak replied in clipped tones. Daringly, I offered him a tallan in the hope he'd double-check, but he snorted at the coin and stalked off.

And then it came to me—*Hetch*. The little man with the sandrat sent by Plamen to rescue me. I'd thought him the Iron Shield executioner that day, and maybe he was. But he was more than that. He seemed to be everywhere and doing everything, probably the reason Plamen found him useful. And if he was useful to Plamen, he could be useful to me.

For a man who was everywhere, however, Hetch proved a challenge to find now I was actually looking. But after three days of keeping an eye out for him, I found him loafing in the steams.

'You were there that day, in the courtyard,' I said, addressing the half of his head that was visible above the water of his bath. 'You saw my friend escape those boys, the boys who killed Con.' The hairless head too deep in water to nod, the eyes widened. So I described Jerome again.

Frog lips surfaced: 'That's more like it.'

'More like what?'

'More Naemian. More than *you* look, Naemian.' The lips dipped. I stared blankly. Little bubbles popped in front of his nostrils, followed moments later by a larger bubble near the middle of the bath. I blinked back steam. I should correct him, say I'm Elmine, but the words wouldn't come out. He knew the truth anyway.

The dwarf emerged, slopping water on the tiles. Looking away from his pink naked skin, I stepped back and nearly tripped over the sandrat as it scuttled behind my heels. I shuddered when its nude flesh brushed my ankle.

'Watch it, Naemian!'

It wasn't easy, this; getting any answers out of Hetch. He didn't seem in the mood. But as he wrapped himself in towels, a beady eye peered at me sidelong.

'Tomorrow I bear a missive to Senera Amyra's estate. I shall go to the North District after, and seek this boy of whom you speak.'

He was as good as his word. The next day, when I got back with my drafts bundle from the foreman, a note was waiting on my workbench. The words were small, just like the man, but the message wasn't a long one. My heart lay down as I read it:

Boy not there — h.

Empty of ideas, I took to pacing the floor of the workshop, idly flipping and catching my Disc. For about a week now, I'd not been scared of its touching my bare hands, and when it had, nothing had happened. Nor was it going to break if I dropped it on the bricks.

I'd taken hammers to the thing and hurled it at walls with all my strength just to make something *happen*. Even the pain of that white blaze, I figured, would be better than this. But nothing. I'd almost started to hate it, but couldn't.

Now I paced some more, flipping the Disc. Then flopped myself into Rusper's chair and set the Disc down on his workbench. A minute later, I picked it up again and knocked it twice: once on the brick, once on the wood of the worktop. I ground my teeth and, in the mirror, watched my magnified jaw muscles clench.

Enough.

Yes it was late, all lanterns low, but now I knew these levels well. I took the winch-lift and a ladder up to the furnace rooms. All the foundrymen were gone, but forges gleamed as they would all through the night; some higher flames licking their overhanging canopies and baking the shadows around them. My fist was just as tight around the Disc as it had been the day the guards first marched me to the door of the Captain. Years ago that felt now, though it had only been a month I'd lived and worked here in the Deep.

The task of the Discs was separate. Even if Rusper did believe them to be the magic talismans of Lackish shamans, forewarning attack from the northeast, I couldn't say why he even thought it important. I didn't care. The riddle was so much more mine than his. It took root in the beginning of my life, it seemed, and was without a doubt what had brought me to this place. Not only was it why I found myself wearing Vedish swathes, an engineer and Viceroy's hand—it was the reason I was alive. That it had power, that much was easy. But what was it *for*, that power? Why'd it been released, and why at *me?* These questions had always been the main ones, the most important of all, but now they bubbled to the skin of my brain on the heat of anger.

Give it to the fire. That's the one thing I hadn't done. The flames could peel back its secrets, melt them all the way down.

There'd be one left.

At a forge, I climbed brick steps and stood above a roaring fire. Like a caldera at my feet, it tossed up sparks. I held the Disc out. Its mirror *became* the flames below it, as if it truly contained them, and so bright it burned my eyes. I looked away.

Heat seared my fingers.

Something gave way—

—Had I just fainted?

I *had* fainted . . . from the heat?

My head was spinning. I was lying on my back, and it was sore. I let my eyes adjust; focus on the ceiling, but when they did it was . . . wrong, that ceiling. It had been all shadows when I came in, but now the buttresses were close. *Too* close.

I sat up on the floor.

They were too close because I wasn't *in* the furnace rooms. I was back in the workshop.

How?

The Disc lay on the bricks between my legs, unscathed and perfect as always, reflecting my confusion. I put my hand out, watched my fingers growing huge inside its face, then disappear behind the gleam.

The Disc shone *blue!*

Jerking my hand back, I tried to scrape some of my thoughts back into order, but couldn't do it, they just kept slipping and sliding out of focus. I could barely trust my legs to support my weight when I stood up. Something felt different; very different, in the room. Eyes dragging weirdly as I moved them wall to wall, worktop to worktop, I realised everything was in its proper place, just as I'd left it. Nothing wrong. Except that something *was* wrong, and how had I even got back here? Had the light dipped there? No. It hadn't. Triglycerate shone cleanly behind a lantern's partial shutter.

Was someone coming to the door? The door was closed . . . *How had I got here?* I watched the handle, which didn't turn. Of course it didn't! *What was I doing?*

I was exhausted, overworked, confused and who knew what else. I'd been at this too hard. But then, this *was* a result: the Disc still glowed there on the floor, that eerie aura even brighter than last time.

A little gingerly, I bent down to pick it up. Ignore the glow. Ignore the glow.

Ignore the—

YOU!

I keeled back into a stool and went clattering down with it, no sooner on the floor than I bolted back onto my feet. *That voice!* Same as before, like a clap on the shoulder in my head.

Someone *was* coming. I heard no footsteps, voices, movement: I just knew. The light *had* dipped. And something at the workshop door, I simply understood with some new sense, was going to *happen*. I stared and waited.

Waited until the wood's grain warped and parted in front of me. An oval pressed in through its surface like hot wax through thinnest paper. The shape was pale and featureless but for two almond-shaped mounds embedded in it. The mounds both split then and peeled. Colourless circles *looked* at me. I looked at them too, willed them away. Willed away the whole shape— away and back into the door!

It floated forward instead. A head was birthed out of the wood, behind it a body. A figure, tall as a man, stepped onto the bricks without a sound. I wanted to drop onto the floor, hide my head under my arms and unsee it, but the muscles I needed to do those things were frozen.

The Disc was pure blue fire, no reflections.

The figure's circles were still on me. It moved the line that was its mouth. Then raised an arm. And made words.

'*Little spark.*'

I clapped my hands flat over my ears.

'*Little spark, come.*'

The eyes, if eyes they really were, changed after that. The circles emptied, sank inward, then vanished altogether. The face-shape softened like so much butter and seemed to melt as if from heat. Heat from behind. The raised arm fell, dissipating, and then the body caved in on itself like a hollowed candle. And then it simply wasn't there.

With an armful of papers at his chest, knitting his brows at the overturned stool next to me, Rusper stood where it had been. Door open behind him.

'Productive evening?' His voice was muffled, so I took my hands away from my ears. His frown zoned in on my face. 'You look a bit ashen, boy.'

When I looked again, the Disc wasn't glowing anymore. Sensing my muscles might obey, I ducked and grabbed it off the floor and slammed it back inside the cabinet with its twin. Turning the key, I looked fierce daggers back at Rusper. 'It's not Lackish magic.'

'You've found something?'

Icy pebbles dropped and slid down the back of my swathes. 'Something's found *me*.'

Sixteen

Sight

Black mud.

Through it, flames.

Something moved in front of a hearth, something barely a man, with a thin white gown clinging to his bones as if soaked through. Withered he looked. A cool air seeped from him, somehow. In his hands, more like the scaled feet of a chicken, he held an object. And when he spoke the voice was weak: 'Come, little spark.' The scaly hands opened up, but that black mud closed in around them. Mud that blotted out all sight.

Pressure was growing. Something was stuck. No air, no breath. Breath wouldn't come. Mud was a taste.

Light broke and, with it, icy cold. Teeth of rock enclosed a narrow cave. Outside, through a fissure, the snow was falling.

Within were men who moaned from pain; men gaunt and streaked with the black mud . . . or something like it. A dripping hand hung in the fissure as the moans grew loud, and then began to fade, becoming bubbles in the mud. Moans washing in, then ebbing out.

The mud wave surged. It came to life—spun, swooped, plucked, pulled at human skin. And still that pressure, squeezing, choking.

Again, light!

This light lanced out of an open hand—five bright white knives, each to a finger. It sliced the mud. Behind it, eyes shone wild and gold. A shadow flew. A bird beat wings, whipping a storm. It was a raven. Though not as dark as that black mud, the storm-wings blasted mud away.

What was left of it went dry, and cracked, and crumbled.

And there was stillness. The desert. Dull browns and yellows stretched away to each horizon, while above them grey skies loomed. Here there was peace.

I was dreaming . . . now I *knew* I was dreaming, but still held onto the peace. If I was still, I might stay here. *Behind me, gypsum crunched. I turned.*

White skin, black eyes, jaws parting—I grabbed my quilt, clutched at my throat and pawed my skin.

Slick with cold sweat.

Throwing the quilt away from my body, I wheeled my feet onto the floor and sat there, catching my breath. I rubbed my face and raked my hair. Then touched my throat and kneaded it, still aware of the sensation of choking.

Red bird, red bird, red bird . . . I nailed my focus to one of those red birds in my quilt, as I calmed down.

I'd never dreamed like that before—actually *felt* the cold air on my skin or *tasted* blood. Yes blood, not mud! Where had I ever seen a cave like that? Not in the Deep, not even down on digging level. And falling snow? I'd been a baby the last time I'd been anywhere near a snowfall, crossing the mountains with my family. I could barely remember it!

But then, that man. He'd used the same words as the ghost I'd seen appear in the workshop hours ago. That same voice, too! And much as I wished there was a way he could have simply been a dream I could forget, I knew he wasn't. I'd seen him pass straight through a door to stand before me and say words. He was as real as all the rest; all of the unexplained things that had happened since the Disc. As real as my impossible survival.

I fumbled my shirt on, took the lantern and went up; the workshop dark. When I cleared away the day's papers from the clepsydra's face, the sun symbol had not even begun its arc across the rising dial: only a single curly ray could be seen chasing the tail of the gryphon that flew before it. It would be hours still before any movement came to this level.

My eye slipped to the vertical cabinet, key sitting in its keyhole as I'd left it. Last night, once Rusper had got me to sit down in a chair and take some breaths, I'd evaded his questions; said I was tired and not thinking clearly. He'd wholeheartedly agreed.

Now I went back to the cabinet and reopened the door, finding the two coloured cloths with my light. I took my own to the workbench and rolled the Disc out on the wood, lantern light dipping as dregs of heat left the triglycerate crystal. I didn't sit, though, piercing the Disc with a glare that dared it to defy me one more time.

Up at the forges last night, I'd almost thrown it in the fire. But I hadn't. *Had* I? I'd . . . passed out, or something. Then woken up back in the workshop. And that was where that face, that man, that . . . ghost . . . had appeared. Was this a magic? Or had the answer I'd been looking for all these weeks, the Disc's true nature, woken up? I held my breath and touched its mirror.

The blue light bloomed, outshone the lantern. No white blaze. No voice. No ghost. Just the blue glow and tiny tingle in my fingertips and knuckles.

I drew back—the glow faded and the dizziness I remembered from the wall rocked my whole body.

It was *answering!*

So I swept it off the workbench, held it chest-high in the cup of my hand so that my skin pressed from all sides except the top. Immediately my face's reflection disappeared, blue glow rising. I heard my pulse. The tingle came, coursed over my wrist and up my forearm, and I swayed: now it was stronger. My body's instincts said to drop it.

No, don't! This wasn't really pain. It was something else, so I refused to ease my grip as the feeling moved. Up it climbed, curved at my elbow, reached my shoulder. Now it came sliding up my neck. I tottered on my heels and, squeezing tighter, slammed my eyes shut.

Or thought I did. Closed was how they felt because *close* was what I'd made them do. And yet, if closed was what they *were* . . . The force filled me up, flowing like a stream from the tips of my fingers right down to the pads of my toes. It tensed every muscle and I wasn't sure if I was remembering to breathe. Not because of pain—there wasn't pain—but because I knew my eyes were closed. My eyes *were* closed.

But I could see.

I saw the workshop all around me, all in halos of that blue, except it wasn't made of shapes or things or structures anymore. Furniture, machines, objects I knew stopped mattering, as if the presence of a thing were just the absence of nothing. Floors, walls and ceiling became boundaries as fragile as thin mist, all threatening to retreat at my touch.

My will dissolved them. Above, below and all around me, my awareness expanded as if my mind were its own torch, impossibly bright. I saw my bedchamber behind me and straight through its wall to the room beyond. The weapon-works. Through *that* wall a sparts-tip followed, the disposals above, fresh units of sandstone a floor beneath *them*. Awareness expanded every time I put a touch to what I thought was its limit, and the Deep unfurled on that command as though its stone and brick were even frailer than so much water-logged parchment. Tunnels and rooms, holes and cracks. Ladders, trapdoors, scaffolds, winch-lifts, pipes. Wider it ranged, unveiling secrets, laying claim to more and more, and then more still. While high above me, the citadel shimmered full of life like a massive painted ceiling.

Gasping, I let go. Opened my eyes. The current left me with a suction on my guts that made me almost double-over, and the Disc, going dim again, dropped onto the workbench. It wobbled there in a sliver of light from the lantern.

My throat was dry, the walls too close. I stood there, trembling a little.

How much *more* could I have seen if I'd dared to look even further? The whole of the Deep right down to digging level? Could I have followed the pipelines to the aquifer itself or delved into pockets even deeper underground? Could I have peeped into the chambers of the citadel estates; watched the High Commander and the Captain asleep in their beds; or stepped into the tower of the Satrap himself?

And was this the secret I'd been chasing—the answer to the power of the Disc, at last? Would its twin do the same? Or was this all still a dream?

As I pinched my left ear between my nails, just to be sure, the triglycerate died.

Yes, it was real.

It changed *everything*.

SEVENTEEN

METAL AND MESSAGES

Before anything else, I tried the same with Rusper's Disc. But his did nothing, didn't answer. Even though the two looked and felt alike in every way, it was as if his were still . . . fast asleep.

I pocketed the key to their hiding place and headed out to hot the lights.

The way the key shifted in my pocket as I made my morning circuit through the Deep made it almost impossible to think about anything but the *sight*. By the time I got back to the workshop, the sun symbol was fully visible on the dial of the clepsydra. So I pulled a comb through my hair—useless as always—then put the Disc into my sling-bag, wrapped up in a flannel probably last used to dust chrozite residue. Buckling the strap, I slipped out.

The Deep was waking up to its early groans and bangs and clicks, familiar now. Sappers going down into the Hub passed me as I jogged up the steps of the rubble shaft. Surfacing, I entered the citadel and threaded my way to the kitchens. In front of their wide doors, cooks were laying out hot rolls of *tesak-radhan*, a ruddy sourbread from the Bronze Coast. Crisp on the outside and spongy in the middle, it had a bittersweet taste. I took half a roll and ate it standing in a corner of the foyers, watching the cooks bustling about among their agas. Still brushing crumbs from my swathes, I climbed the stairs from the foyers.

Voices reached me.

'. . . will expect more than a mere handful of newfangled crossbows, Ezra.'

'You must be patient, *sinarre*. Those armaments may yet prove to be of some . . .'

I rounded a corner. The corridor had one lantern, and by its light I clearly saw the High Commander's white mantle. He stood with a woman who wore a caftan of dappled grey and sea-green, its pattern like snakeskin. Her own skin was rich and her braided hair collected into coils. It was *her*. Her from the council—the one who had laughed that chilling laugh into the silence.

Claws scratched on stone. The blue-grey body of Tazen stood to attention and looked straight at me. He barked—I jumped. Both man and woman turned their heads. Plamen's eyes found and pinned me, so I put my head down and moved on, wondering if he'd ever warm to me at all.

When I knocked on the door of Rusper's quarters, it opened partway and Zeek peered through the crack.

She blinked at me.

I blinked back. 'Um . . .'

'Flint! Good you're here,' exclaimed Rusper who suddenly appeared in the gap, then disappeared just as fast. 'Step in, step in, we have to speak.' Zeek made a dash around my body and scurried from the door like a mouse from under a wardrobe; stepping in, I leaned the door closed behind me.

A large breakfast, one of the few luxuries Rusper had not declined as Viceroy, steamed on the desk through the morning sunlight. Zeek must have just delivered it. Rusper was dressed, not in working gear, but a sleek, green-gauze thobe and turquoise headdress. Riding boots too.

'You'll need the papers on my desk,' he said through the mouthful he was managing.

But I had to tell him what I'd found before he had a chance to get started. 'Caliph Symphin, I need to . . .'

'The papers, boy!' he flapped. So I crossed the room to the desk. Some leaves of parchment were there, bound with twine, and a scroll-tube. 'I'm to see Vizier Dranz in half an hour, and after that the rest of the First Circle. Then I ride for Methar where Caliph-Archimandrite Bardon expects to receive me at Chidh Uribb by nightfall. I need you to take charge of things for a day, two at a push.'

As he ladled another flatspoon of tashi into his mouth, I turned around. He must be joking. 'Take *what* of things?'

He raised a hand, disarmingly. 'Don't worry, those documents include all my official instructions and they'll enable you to act on my behalf if you must.' He swallowed, took a breath before the next spoonful. 'Now most pressing is the metal . . .'

My news was bursting! 'Please, Caliph Symphin, I—'

'You'll have to check on the Hub first. See Gudgeon, he's in charge there. I want progress reports on both repairs and cantilever construction. You'll write them yourself, understand, so ensure no detail is spared. *No detail.*'

I bobbed my head for his attention, fidgeting with the scroll-tube in my hand and probably looking like I was aching for a piss.

'Then go to the metalsmiths. They expect *me*, of course, but there's no time. I want you to deliver my blueprint for the *jezail* frames.' Swishing past me, he tapped the tube in my hand.

'That includes the dispatch for immediate commission, signed and marked with my seal. You're to oversee it.'

Oversee. I didn't like that word, but ignored it for the moment, desperate to change the subject.

'Foundrymen are feisty,' he warned me. 'Make sure that they commence construction on the jezails without delay. *No excuses.* And alter *none* of those designs—Ghulzar's been known to tweak at will, given the chance. Then, when the jezails are ready, I want them transported to the northwest wall of the fortress. Again, you have my seal on—'

'Caliph Symphin!'

'Yes what is it boy?' he seethed.

'I've worked it out.'

'Worked *what* out, Azal's Theorem?'

I stammered. 'What's Azal's—'

'Never mind.'

For just a moment, I stopped thinking about the Disc and the Sight. A name Rusper had mentioned suddenly snagged in my mind. *Dranz.* Wasn't that the black-and-gold weasel vizier who'd been thrown out of the council that day? I studied Rusper as he now dusted his mouth clean and patted his sleeves. He was on edge; always was when obliged to hold these talks with the viziers and high officials of the city, but there was more to it than that. Why was he meeting Vizier Dranz, a man who obviously didn't want him as Viceroy? And why so suddenly riding off to the caliphy of Methar? That was south, I remembered, so at least he wouldn't be in danger. Hopefully. But still.

Whatever the reasons, he wasn't ready for my news. And as he picked up the thread of his instructions again, forgetting I'd interrupted him at all, I realised I didn't have to tell him. Didn't *need* to. Not yet.

Fastening a broad silver torque around one of his wrists, he glanced at me. 'I've a horse in the courtyard. Everything you'll need is in those papers. Flint, do this for me and at noon in two days' time I shall meet you at the wall.'

I nodded, his servant.

Then without warning he attacked his wrist, unclasped the torque and flung it down on his desk. 'Damn thing's too tight!'

I don't know why. But on some impulse, once he'd gone, I put the torque into my bag.

And so the Disc would wait again.

Luckily for me, Rusper's instructions were just as thorough as ever; I only hoped that the two days would be enough time to carry them out.

Gudgeon was stationed at the Hub's south entrance where his workers were bricking the tunnel, and I caught the nod he gave me. Being acknowledged in the Deep wasn't so strange anymore. While just another servant in the halls of the citadel, down here I was becoming known by some as the "Chief's boy."

'Where's Symphin?' he shouted over the shoulder of a mason.

'Called away,' I shouted back.

He cupped his ear. 'He called a what?'

I repeated it over the din of the work and he rolled his eyes dramatically.

'How's Arte-III?' I asked louder.

'Higher with that cornice!' Gudgeon ordered the masons before looking back to me, scratching his nose. 'Can't say, boy, I've been here since sun-up. Pintle's heading the repairs. You'll just have to go down.'

I wove between the busy masons, down the length of the new tunnel and came out in the cold, moist air of the massive Hub Chamber. A finished cantilever bridge now spanned its breadth here, joining the north and south entries. I swayed on it a moment, suddenly horribly aware of the high-hanging darkness, yawning depth. Who could ever get used to this? Gripping the railing, I reminded myself that I'd been here before, alone, in darkness. Lights blinked below, through the confusing criss-cross of pipes and rope-nets that muddled up the descending zones. The other bridges were also close to being finished by now, although today all five were dark and I couldn't see any workmen at them. That was strange.

Far below, a tapping echoed. The flooded sixth zone was fully lit and there were movements down there; I could tell by the way the shadows and reflections played. Leaving my sandals on the bridge with my bag, I scaled down.

Where the chamber walls narrowed there was still enough water to swim in; the damage to Arterial-III standing some five feet above the waterline. Pintle watched me come down and step across the wide lateral. 'Where's the Chief?' she said, on cue.

'Seeing viziers,' I replied. Deciding not to say anything about the ride to Methar, I asked after the progress.

'Work's almost done here,' she told me. 'And I'd wager the Builders themselves would be proud.'

Another trellis of rope hung below the primary lateral we stood on. Pintle's repair team dangled in it like spiders around the place where the haemorrhage had been. A new girder of fused timber encircled the arterial now, five hands high and three hands deep; boards conjoining at angles to increase its capacity and endure the pressure when reopened. Behind it, I knew, were sheets of hard Vedish alloys. I watched the team driving bolts home through the girder, then looked up again through the bridges and webs.

'Why aren't there any workmen on the bridges?' I asked.

'Reassigned,' Pintle frowned. I rubbed my forehead and wondered if I should have known that. 'Something about a new arms-construction dispatch.' She gave a shrug, but I knew. The jezail frames.

'What's that?'

'No it's nothing,' I said.

But on my way back up the nets, a fresh chill slid down my spine. If work on the bridges in the Hub had been halted for these "frames," then Rusper's defensive preparations were more urgent than I'd thought. So I picked up the pace, made my way out of the Deep, left the citadel and reported to the City Guild-house. The foreman rebuked me for being late, but it couldn't be helped and today, at least, the bundle of drafts from him was smaller. I returned with it to the Deep, and found the metalsmiths on first level.

Hot air blasted my face there, but I gasped and pushed my way through it. The space was bricked and veined with pipes. Another clever piece of engineering: these pipes delivered water that was heated by the furnaces to the rooms of the citadel levels. That was what powered the triglycerate oven and samovar in Rusper's own quarters, although I still wasn't sure whose invention that had been – Rusper's or Meck's. I tugged my collar. The ceiling wasn't high enough to disperse all the heat here and it smelled of sweat and braehg. About twenty metalsmiths stood in a wide ring around a barrel, all bare-chested and shining copper-brown in the firelight. They spoke in hard, mannish voices as they washed down bread with their beer. Waiting for Rusper.

I looked at my papers, found the name of the man in charge, then with my heart in my hand, slipped between the shining bodies and admitted myself to the braehg-barrel meeting.

'*Ekh* Ghulzar?' I said.

Big arms unfolded and the talking petered out around me. A bald man at the barrel turned with a quart in his hand and foam on his dagger goatee. Not tall, his frame was tightly muscled and there were faded tattoos marking the tops of both his shoulders. His neck was thick and bore a collar of studs like a mastiff's chain.

'Who the *pelkh* are you?' he said, foamy spit flecking the bricks at my feet.

'My name is Florian.'

He didn't have any eyebrows, but four ruts formed in his forehead as he looked me up and down. I was out of place here. Someone grunted, 'Symphin's boy.' 'Elmine apprentice,' said another.

I tried to harness at least some sense of my duty, some importance: 'I work for the Chief Engineer.'

'Join the clan,' replied Ghulzar, and took a swig of his braehg. His men exchanged their grins.

'And I'm not his apprentice. I'm his assistant.'

''n that case,' said Ghulzar, 'shouldn't you be a mite older? Just a smidgen, mind. Yeller teeths, milk in your eyes, breath like the desert's arse-crack?'

All twenty men brayed at that and knocked their quarts together while my cheeks filled up with heat.

'Loquar's left the Royal Guild,' I said and coughed to hide my voice's croak. I knew it hadn't worked when they laughed again.

The crow's feet deepened around Ghulzar's eyes. Ice-blue eyes. 'Wondered where he'd buggered off to,' he said. 'Aye, I've seen you potterin' round, well enough. Anyways. Got told the Chief would be here. Not assistants.'

'That's because I'm here in . . .'

But the metalsmiths had started going back to their own talk, drowning my voice out. I was disappearing. So I remembered that I was servant to the Viceroy, straightened my back and took a deep breath.

'*The Honorary Caliph*,' I said more loudly—talk subsiding —'has other business. That's why he sent me instead. I've got the blueprints for the job he wants done.'

I held the tube out.

Ghulzar sniffed. When he strode forward to take it from me, it took all my nerve not to step back. Then, with a tug, he freed the parchment and went back to the barrel where he spread it with a quart to pin its edge down. I hurried in before the chests could lock me out.

Just tall enough to see, I looked across the sheet and knew I'd never be good enough to use ink and stain so brilliantly. Every line was needle sharp, every detail precisely clear. A series of diagrams showed a triangulated shape with four legs, a "gutter" and a "gunrest." Smaller diagrams down the margin detailed other components: a ball-bearing and axle, a line of rollers, a "pull-back" stem. And something that looked like a fusil, but bigger. Much longer. I glanced over the measurements, the list of metals to be used. But the foundryman's eye was so much quicker. 'He needs nine,' I said before he could make any comment. 'He wants them started straightaway.'

'That's clear enough,' Ghulzar replied. 'Be on your way.'

'I'm to stay,' I said flatly. Any warmth that had crept into his crow's feet now vanished. I was dirt. Then made it worse—'And oversee.'

'*Oversee*.' I looked away.

'I know the way he wants them.'

'And I'm looking at the prints.'

Couldn't argue with that. Still, I had my own orders and, handing over more papers, showed Ghulzar the page on which the words "*Overseeing: F. flint*" were penned in Rusper's windswept flourish.

'Stay then,' he snorted, 'if it's his will. Only keep out from under the feet of my men. That's if you don't your own feet-fingers broken.' He drained his quart and gathered the blueprint as if it really were none of my business.

But I wasn't quite done. 'How many men will you need?'

'What of it?'

'For the frames. Gudgeon needs metal men in the Hub. It's the bridges, they're still not finished.'

He clapped his mug to the top of the barrel, making me flinch. 'And *this* here dispatch says to ferry nine of these frames to the fortress wall in two days!' But he had seen Rusper's seal. He knew my words carried the authority of both his own Chief Engineer and the Viceroy of Vorth, and so snarled: 'I'll send five.'

'Thank you,' I said, nodding as respectfully as I could. The nod was lost on his back.

I stayed for an hour, choosing a post well out of their way: a table near a forge no one was using. From here it was easy enough to watch the work without needing to dodge whenever Ghulzar made to walk. As for making sure he didn't stray from the plans, my job seemed done. I'd got his back up. Or maybe Rusper had achieved that by sending a child to relay orders to a master craftsman instead of some more senior artisan like Pintle or Gudgeon. Either way it had worked. Ghulzar wasn't about to be corrected by a savvy hand of twelve years old, and now would probably stick even closer to the plan than if Rusper had been there, looking over his shoulder. I got on with my reports on Arte-III and the bridges.

But there was another job to do. At first it sounded strange: arranging three days' provisions to be delivered to the Deepworks. As far as I knew, only engineers and artisans were fed at the expense of the throne. Even then, those provisions would come from the citadel supplies, not ordered directly from the city's farming yield. Besides, the Deepworks were suspended and had been that way for a month.

I read again, slowly:

> *Of import to: the fortress YIELDMASTER*
> *1 x Halfweek rations {prov. Workers approx.90}*
> *6 vat: 300 lb shaffan-ful*
> *45 lb cornbr. / lavak*
> *dasheen / mooli – if avail.*
> *10 ½ gal (pump) water*

3 sack brickcoal
2 x wagon (heavy cover), destin: Deep
Arrival 3rd hr/noon hereafter
~ DISPATCH & BURN
R.s

I read it several time over, in fact. If I understood it right, this dispatch letter was to authorise two wagonloads of rations to the entrance of the Deep. Right enough, it was signed by Rusper. There was his seal. But why would he want ten and a half gallons of pumped water delivered to workers already at the pipeworks? And why brickcoal? Nor did I understand the need for food rations in—Wait.

That word, *burn*. That stood out.

Burn what—the coal or the message?

But there was more; a second message:

Of import to: the CAPTAIN, Fortress Guard
LOAD IS DISPATCHED
[Crop Yard—Deep]
/ Intercept & redirect as prev.
/ Escort to wardens: N District
~ BURN
R.s

Just as cryptic, it bore the seal.

As for my own instructions, they were simple: deliver the second message to the Captain of the Guard only when the first message had reached the Yieldmaster. The two messages were linked, that much was obvious enough. What took me longer than it should to understand was that whatever was bound for the entrance of the Deep wasn't meant to get there.

Redirect, I read again. *Escort to wardens. N District. Ninety workers.*

Ninety.

And it clicked.

I took the ladders and the stairs and left the citadel again, this time making my way down through the byways of the Mercantile District. Following Rusper's directions, I found her in the Crop Yard among her baskets and trugs and panniers; the wizened old woman they called the Yieldmaster. She had skin like beef jerky. It was this woman, though she looked far from any kind of official, who ran the distribution of the farming quarters' crops to the citadel and wider network of city markets. She ogled me from out of the yashmak she wore over her swathes and made me stay and watch the message burn to nothing on her cooker. As it blackened and flaked, I wondered who they'd got to bring the last directive. 'Supplies will come,' the woman said, picking her teeth, and let me go.

Retracing my steps, I thought again about the urgency for arms. Nine of these "jezail frames" for the wall, each to be issued to a team of two field-engineers trained in the use of the fusils. That's if I understood the blueprint back in Ghulzar's metal foundry. But why? There was only one man I could think of who might give me a reason, and that man was unlikely to see me, much less answer any of my questions. Or was there someone else, maybe?

Hood up, I climbed the wide steps of the barracks' vennel, moved through the corridors of guards and rapped his door.

'Come.' As I entered, Captain Mondric barely lifted his chin. 'Tools,' he greeted blandly. 'Do something for you?'

'Sir, I've a request from the Viceroy.' My voice surprised me. Efficient.

'And what'll it be today?' he smiled wryly, just before thumping some parchment with a heavy sealing press. When he looked up at me, he made a noise at my hood. I pulled it back, my hair snapping with static from the hessian.

'He needs the most recent of the scouting reports,' I lied to him.

'Not my department,' Mondric sighed. Then drew together his silver-black brows and focused his eyes. 'Not got it yet?'

I hesitated. 'The Viceroy has been . . .'

'Busy. Yes, well. It's the High Commander Plamen you'll need to see about those reports.'

His eyes seemed in a hurry to usher me out, and so I held my papers close, choosing the next best lie to tell him. 'The High Commander won't see me.'

Well, he probably wouldn't.

Mondric laughed out loud. 'Ach, don't take it personally, Tools. High Vedish family, the Plamens. All tall horses and such.'

'Please sir, only I have other duties,' I said.

'Oh you have, have you,' he scoffed. 'And how d'you suppose *I'm* mouldering around? Knitting the wife-mother a new scant-thobe for her name day?'

I fished through my papers for any sheet inscribed heavily enough with Rusper's handwriting and held it out. 'This is a message from Caliph Symphin.'

'Bah, keep it!' he grimaced, waving a hand at the reams just as I'd hoped. 'I don't have eyes for that damn scribble, can see the seal clear enough!'

I hung there, waiting, until he puffed out his chest and stood up from the desk with a wince.

'The best I can give him is a copy of the last one.' He shuffled through some little scrolls on his shelf. 'Here.'

I came to the edge of the desk, where he'd examined me that first day, and took the tiny scroll from his hand. Looking at it, I stayed faithful to my story; made a face. 'Sorry, Captain, but this won't . . .'

'I'm sorry too, Tools. I am. But we've each got parts to play right now, and the war, or lack of one, isn't mine.'

'Yes, Captain.'

'Is that all?'

We locked eyes. I took out the second dispatch message: the second link in the chain that would feed the refugees. My people. And by the look on his face, it was what he'd been expecting when I came in. He gave the note a cursory glance – not the first one he'd seen, clearly – then struck a match and dropped them both into a bowl. We said nothing as it burned. He then nodded me to the door and so I thanked him and left. Heading straight for the workshop.

Now to find a message that matched it.

Rusper didn't use the desk in his quarters, besides I was already holding the only papers that had been there. The reports would be *here*, they'd have to be. But when I opened the high cupboard that he used to store his general paperwork, the scrolls of decades came tumbling down towards my face like an avalanche of old news. I slammed them back behind the doors as just a few leaves fluttered out. No—not in there!

My key in hand, I went to the vertical cabinet. I'd seen some scrolls in there before, but as I looked at the shelves now, found only personal letters. At first, apparently, to the wrong person: "*Ekh Semafin . . .*" one began.

"*Semafin, brother . . .*"

"*Firmest friend . . .*" But all too old, their parchment marked and yellow now.

I fingered through some others: "*Of import to: Symphin . . .*"

"*Rusper, a warm greeting from . . .*"

"*Belov . . .*" No, not official.

I closed that door and turned the key, grinding my teeth. The scroll from Captain Mondric was small and compact with a seal of blue-stained undercopper about a nail's head in size. Though cracked now, it bore the emblem of three towers in a circle, whatever that meant. Important though. Secret? Maybe. Scouring his workbench turned up nothing but his rough sketches for the frames.

I racked my brain, impatient: *Scouting reports—fortress defence—new weapons—fusils!*

Stacking two stools, more than a bit dangerously, I climbed to reach the fusil cases stored up along the gantry. There I found one lid ajar. Unlike him to leave things open, I thought, especially the fusils. But when I looked into the case, it was there. The weapon's barrel shimmered with violent possibility while the mechanism seemed to glint at me with hunger. I looked in on them all, one by one. There were no scrolls.

Another case in the same fashion had been stored under my own workbench. This case was longer, however, and more secure than the others. I crouched to rattle its heavy lock and then stood up with a sigh.

Right there, on my worktop, lay a slender folio of hide.

Can't be. Can it?

Hoping anyway, I untied its knot of twine, unwound the loops and there they were. Those cracked blue seals. Had Rusper really been in such a hurry this morning as to leave them right here in open sight? Strange too that I hadn't seen the folio this morning, simply lying on my station. Had he been here *after* me, while I'd been hotting the lights?

Thirteen reports. Artabh Kathris, I was lucky, had a readable hand, and they were dated. But Rusper had muddled them up, and having been raised on the Exelcian calendar, I struggled a bit with the order of the Vedish *wyles*. I wasn't even exactly sure which *wyle* we were in at the moment. *Zeidhat. Ospa'fon. Fon'verun.* Mondric's scroll was dated *Fon'verun-3.* So all I needed was the next one.

I leafed. There, that one! *Fon'verun-8.*

Hurrying, I stuffed it into my sling-bag, put the folio up on the gantry and went back to the metalsmiths. There I read them, slowly, in order:

Of import to: the HIGH COMMANDER; Plamen
& VICEROY; Symphin
~ 12th Reconnaissance REPORT of the North
~ DATED to: Fon'verun r.3 / `3230

> *Observation lines, equidistant from fortress at
> 30 miles, breached at ALL flag points. Over 20
> Ratheine parties in 3 days [size uncertain—
> night sightings]. As yet no indication of
> movement closer to fortress. Caution advised:
> Pattern forms clear NW ARC around Antissa.*
>   *~ATB. Kathris*
>   *Antissan Regiment / 3rd Battalion*

The words were chilling.

Now imagining all the things I didn't want to imagine, I looked up from the report to watch the base-poles of a jezail frame being assembled by the smiths. Nine frames, I thought. Nine teams trained to fire them from the walls . . .

I combed through my other papers and found the wagon dispatches. Yes, it was the *northwest* wall that Rusper wanted them transported to.

Who knew about this? Obviously the High Commander. But what about Captain Mondric? Other viziers of the Sanhedrin? The Satrap? And yet, Rusper was about to arm the fortress wall with the best he believed his Guild could throw at an advancing enemy: the chrozite. Why only now? This report had come a full five days ago.

There must be more. More, as well, behind the sudden need to travel to Methar. I tried as hard as I could to call to mind what I had heard about that caliphy and its regiment, but just couldn't remember anything.

Bating my breath, I opened the last one – the most recent report.

A different hand:

> *Of import to: the HIGH COMMANDER; Plamen
> & VICEROY; Symphin
> ~ 13th Reconnaissance REPORT of the North*

~ *DATED to: Fon'verun r.8 / `3230*
   Telmadh assuming charge of Company
   following disappearance of ATB. Kathris & 2
   accomp. failing rendezvous at NW passage of
   N Erg [21 hrs]. Search unsuccessful—KATHRIS
   BELIEVED DEAD. Requesting 3ʳᵈ Battalion
   Mounted Vortans immediate return to fortress.
   Ratheine movement IMMINENT. Awaiting
   orders.
                  ~ *TMD. Hafsar*
                  [Adjutant to ATB. Kathris]
                  Antissan Regiment / 3ʳᵈ Battalion

Three more words were in the corner; I recognised Plamen's thorny letters: "*Party recalled – Respond.*"

Gut going tight in my belly, I folded the message. Rath on the move. A northwest arc. Three scouts missing, Kathris among them . . . Then I unfolded it again and tried to flatten out the crease: I was going to have to put it back, shouldn't have even read it in the first place.

All over again, I felt the fear stirring in my body as if all I'd done was push it down into a pot and put the lid on. The information in these reports now lit a flame under that pot. The safety I'd given myself permission to feel here in Antissa could be taken away.

And yet what could *I* do about it?

No. Rusper Symphin was the Viceroy. I told myself that several times. It would be fine. Everything would be fully under control. I was sure. This was a fortress, high on a hill! And those sandstone walls were *really* high.

Quicker than ever, I completed my checks of the drafts and ran them to Gudgeon. Then came back.

Somewhere above us, the sun curved across the desert sky while work went on in the foundry. Blueprint now up against a wall, it was more interest than distrust that lured me in for a closer look. Ghulzar eyed me in turn from his own frame-in-progress, but then shook his shining head and went back to work. Nothing left to do, I simply sat at my post and watched them working away.

Little spark.

I jerked my hand back. It had found its way down through my sling-bag, to the bottom where the Disc was, and brushed its metal with fingertips. The voice had happened inside my mind, just as the Sight's living tingle had thrummed up my joints. Not here, I thought.

But as I moved my hand away, down at the bottom, my fingers brushed another metal. Rusper's torque. I took it out and turned it over several times. It was broad, the silver polished, plain but for one thin, looping line. I slipped it over my wrist and found it fitted my forearm. Then I rapped it with my knuckles.

Hmm . . .

Taking every care not to annoy any of the smiths, I went and found myself a cutting block and mallet. Sliding the upper part of the torque's band into the block, I hammered at the cylinder until the silver gave way and the sharp edge bit down through it. A round fell out.

I had a hole.

Next I'd need a chamber. Some kind of box, but not too big. There was scrap here in great towering heaps and the rummaging took time. But eventually I found something small enough to be a fit, shaped more or less like the oval of the Disc. Made of brown pewter, it might have once been used for snuff or perfumed powder. It was old, yes, but not so tarnished as to black out the engravings of curling leaves along its sides, or on its lid, a lion's face. The inside was rusted a bit, but that didn't matter. Through the base, I cut another hole.

Opening the lid, I took the Disc out, in its flannel, and put it in. The fit was snug. And just as planned, the curving surface of the Disc stuck slightly out of the hole I'd made. Not by much, but just enough.

By now, the metalsmiths were downing their own tools for the day, and storing frames.

I took my things and left the foundry.

Rusper's second day of absence went much more smoothly than the first. I hotted the lights, ate my tashi, reported for drafts at the Guildhouse, and at my post in the foundry made my checks through the morning. Pintle had her bundle before noon.

But something wriggled in my mind. It was like a dream only half-remembered, almost impossible to place. An itch I couldn't reach to scratch. Had I forgotten a task? A message? I couldn't have: all my errands were right here in my sling-bag, penned down by Rusper himself. Everything else was now routine. Whatever it was, though, the nagging worry wouldn't go away, lingering like a spider that had only crawled down the back of a bed. Out of sight, but still there.

Trying to distract from the feeling the best way I knew how, I inspected the jezail frames. They were taking proper shape now and so I dared to come closer. Two were almost complete and stood as tall as my shoulders. Over there, a gunrest's bearing was being fused to the hinge of a pull-back stem. That would let the fusil swing in both a vertical path, through the structure of the frame, and around. The gunrest itself was over three feet in length. So *that* was what had been locked inside the long case under my workbench. A *longer* fusil.

Catching Ghulzar's eye, I became aware that I was smiling to myself, and wiped the look off my face. He sat through a little arch; legs wide apart, an empty mug hooked on a finger. And as I shied from his hard face, I saw the hammer by his shoulder. By far the biggest, meanest hammer I'd ever seen.

I went back to the task I'd set myself yesterday. Attaching the box to the torque's band would be a challenge, I realised, and I returned to the towering scrap heaps for something like a winch or lever mechanism. For hours I sorted through those junk-piles, scraping and cutting my skin on the sharp edges of metal, before turning up a prong of steel plate five inches long. Wide at one end, with a pair of raised cusps on the rims, it had probably been part of a gear of some kind.

I found a vice. Prong-plate held fast, I took a file to its edge. Then I removed it and put the torque in its place. My plan was for the lever to run under the holes, enabling a side-to-side slide that wouldn't stick against my arm. The Disc itself was smooth, of course, and the edge of the plate could be filed down to stop it snagging. Even so, I'd need a finer blade than this one, a larger tool, and *much* more strength.

As if summoned, Ghulzar shambled out of the firelight and shadows. I knew he'd been watching me since noon, and now he nudged me aside. A blade flipped into his hand and he set it to the vice, sharp edge primed just above the torque. He glanced a question back at me.

'Erm . . .' I stammered. 'Down a little?'

He moved it.

'Left a bit.'

Again, and . . .

'There. Yes, just there.' As I was thinking it might be good to step away, the hammer swung and struck the blade with so intense an impact that I thought my teeth would crack from it. Ghulzar bounced back on his heel, turned the hammer in the air and slammed its head against the vice as leverage. Freed the blade. In the silver of the band was now a narrow, clean-straight slit, like a staunched gash.

This done, he shambled back to work without a single word to me. Those tattoos on his shoulders, I now realised, *weren't* tattoos after all. They were brandmarks: each weal of heat-blackened skin displaying a symbol over a circle with a number-figure in it.

A little stunned by his help, I pressed on. Filed down the inside of the band where the silver had ruptured inwards, then the underside of the prong so that they wouldn't scratch or pierce my skin. I slid the prong into the slit. Again, tried it on. The lever held, firmly now, at least until I could find some kind of catch to secure it.

Meanwhile, I mounted the box onto the band of the torque. That was easy enough with just a poker from a forge. I positioned the box so that the two holes were aligned; smoking and smouldering, fused them together. A messy join, but still a join. While the silver bubbles were cooling, I found a nugget of brass and made a stop-catch.

It had come together better than I'd hoped. I popped the lid, peeped through the hole, slid back the lever and smiled.

Just one more thing. From the workshop this morning, I'd taken one of Rusper's gloves. Now, with a pair of heavy-duty shears, I sliced off all of its fingers, then chopped the thing clean in half. All I needed to do was seal each half around a rim of the band, to form a gauntlet. It might as well be comfortable.

Midmorning of day three.

Nine jezail frames were ready and I set about having them moved to the fortress wall. My dispatch papers authorised three delivery wagons from the depot on the citadel's west side, with teams to load and offload them; so that all I had to do was climb aboard beside the driver, bringing only my papers. I couldn't help but feel important.

From the depot, the wagons made their shaky, rattling departure. They trundled through the underpasses, across the gryphon courtyard, through the baking Inner City and out into the districts. Sounds and smells thickened. I pulled my hood up, not just to shield against the blistering heat, but in case someone recognised me. Then I realised that our ox had overshot my people's shelter. Even so, the beast laboured slowly under the weight of all the metal, three foundrymen and a boy. We rolled between the clustered, coloured awnings and shouting bidders. One led a stubborn camel in our way, forcing the driver to stop while it pissed there like an open pipeline. It went on pissing for a while, but we were well ahead of schedule. While the driver shook his head and cursed at the traffic and the camel, I simply sat and watched and waited. Watching everything that moved.

Something chattered. I looked left to see wild rodents inside wooden cages, gnawing at their bars, desperate for freedom. And suddenly knew what had been stuck in the back of my mind since yesterday!

What was it Hetch had said that day when I had found him in the steams?

A missive . . . *I bear a missive to Senera Amyra's estate.*

Amyra. That was *her*. The silvery woman from the Sanhedrin council. The same woman I'd seen talking in the corridor with Plamen. Surely it was her!

Another memory soon followed; the one I hated the most. Well, almost. Lieutenant Jharis of the Iron Shield glaring down his sword at Con. *There are wills in this city that are greater than the Viceroy's.* That's what he'd said.

Hetch had been watching all of that. He'd seen it all, from Con's bloody death to my arrest. He'd nearly chopped off my finger, but then had helped me escape. And why'd he done that? Because, as I'd found out soon enough, he served the High Commander.

Just as Jharis served . . .

The Senera, Jharis had said before he'd left me to the knife, *requests my presence in council.*

Hetch.

The little man tied it together, from my arrest to the ease with which Plamen had released me from the gaol of the Shield.

And as they'd been doing since that day, Plamen's instructions rang coldly: *None is ever to be mentioned again. Not even to the Viceroy.*

I'd obeyed him. Said nothing. Not to Rusper, not to anyone. I had complied with his wishes, to protect my own people, as he'd advised. But was there something else behind that warning—something *more* than that protection?

My brain hurt.

She will see you, High Commander. That's what Hetch had said to Plamen after council that day. There'd only been one *she* in council. And now, as the stream of camel-piss came to an end and we rolled forward again, I thought about her talking with him two days ago. Plamen and Amyra . . .

These sticky thoughts were still clagging and clawing in my head when the fortress wall rose up ahead to block the full light of the sun. Our wagons stopped beside a braehg-house. From here, a casement of steps climbed the fifty feet of rugged sandstone to the battlements above. Offloading the frames, the team began to carry them up. I followed them, climbing via the wall's long, arched extension, then final steps onto a gangway.

Hot wind out of the northern desert grazed the crenels as I presented my official papers to the watch. They said nothing, merely nodded to show my teams had free run of the thirty yards of fortress wall between the left and right turrets. I looked around to see that the left turret adjoined the North Gate. It wasn't far from here that I'd been sick on the banner.

Some minutes later, wheels and hooves approached below, and I heard orders being shouted as more people climbed the steps. 'Sir,' the watchmen greeted, and 'Viceroy.' He replied to few of these greetings, putting almost all of his attention into berating the team who bore his cargo up the steps. Just as suspected, one of the cases was the long one I had found locked in the workshop. 'Carry it straight!' Inside the casement extension, Rusper appeared and looked up. I nodded a greeting but he'd looked away, snapping at the men for bumping the case. *'Can't you—'*

I flinched on their behalf. They carried it, more slowly after that, onto the gangway, along the wall and into the turret to the right, along with several other cases I recognised from the workshop gantry. Fusils, each one. The foundrymen were ordered to assemble the frames in position along the battlements and, once this was done, Rusper walked the line of nine evenly spaced metal structures, making his inspection like a general. In each frame he tested the axle, the ball-bearing and stem that raised the gunrest in such a way that they pointed almost directly down from the crenels. He was an engineer again, though only wearing one glove today. I tugged on the left sleeve of my swathes.

'No difficulties, I hope,' he said, walking towards me. 'I'm sorry for having to foist my duties on you, Flint. Urgent matters needed attention.'

'I know. I *mean*—I understand,' I said and quickly asked him how his business had fared. How much would he say?

He stepped into a crenel and took the air into his lungs. 'Not unfavourably,' he said, letting out the breath. 'One might now, perhaps, assume a fragile loyalty from Dranz. A man easily ignited. The First Circle is another box of screws altogether.'

It was all he gave me. I studied his face as it gleamed in the sun and realised that he wasn't going to tell me anything about his journey to Methar.

So I grabbed my doubts by the neck: 'Who's Amyra?'

I saw the whites in his eyes. '*What?*'

'Amyra, who is she?'

'Where did you hear that name?' he snapped. I stammered, without a ready explanation for my question, wondering if it was only anger that I'd just heard there in his voice. Whatever it was, something slid over it. 'She is a *senera* of Shad,' he said stiffly. 'Shad caliphy. The wife of Vizier Zimran.'

'Is she against you?'

He folded his lips, then grabbed me by the arm and pulled me four crenels further down the battlements. Away from the watchmen and smiths. When he looked into my face, it was as if he didn't trust me. 'What's this about, Flint?'

Now or never. 'I've seen the High Commander speaking with her. In private.' He lifted his chin and pursed his lips. Relaxed slightly. Into his silence I asked, 'Who's Zimran?'

'Head of the Iron Shield. One of the Satrap's most trusted.'

'More trusted than you?'

He narrowed his eyes. 'Yes, I should think so.'

'So why's *he* not the Viceroy?'

'Because of royal decree. Defensive engineering. You know all this. Besides, Zimran no longer leads a public life. The man is . . . *housebound,* has been for months. Lackish Cochineal Fever . . .' There he paused as if choosing words with care. '. . . The Senera you mention presides over his estate and acts as his advocate both in office and council. You may think of them as one. And as *your* worst enemy.'

'Mine?'

'Your *people's*,' he said. 'The Iron Shield is subservient to the Satrap. Directly. And the Satrap does not care to make a Naemian refuge of his city.'

'So Amyra *is* against you?'

He sighed. 'Yes. She is against me.'

'Because of *us*.' I said it as a fact; let him deny it.

But he didn't, only slackened his shoulders tiredly as if this was all silly childishness. 'Is that all?'

I shook my head. 'No it's not. It still doesn't make any sense. Why doesn't she tell the Satrap that you've let us into the city?'

'She's not permitted near the Satrap,' he replied. 'Again, I was given to believe you understood this.'

But the answer skipped over my brain. 'And what about the High Commander? He's supposed to be your . . . your aide, and I've seen him *with* her! They've been talking. Don't you believe me?'

'I believe you.'

'So why—'

'Because you've made a mistake,' he cut me off. 'Politics is a dangerous dance, boy, and one learns to meet a threat on its own turf, you understand. But no, you don't and why should you. You're a boy.'

I showed all my outrage on my face. But I really *didn't* understand and was getting angry now as well.

He spoke calmly. 'Plamen still serves me, I can assure you of that.'

'He's having little secret meetings with her, talking about you and the fusils and the Deepworks and—'

'I know. I *know* all that, Flint. I am *using* him to blackmail the Senera with certain sensitive information. Information which, exposed, will levy greater transgressions than my own upon her head. Like I said, she and Vizier Zimran are one and the same voice of the Iron Shield.'

He paused again and bit his lip. Whatever was on the tip of his tongue, he didn't want to say it.

I watched his eyelids fall, hold closed, open again. Then he slowly squared himself in front of me and spoke, very softly, over the top of my head. 'She's his widow.'

'He's *dead?*'

'*Keep* your flaming voice down!' Rusper snarled and whacked his glove against the crenel.

Practical, I thought. Just like the look in his eyes now. Make sure of the Senera's silence and, in so doing, keep my people safe from the Satrap.

'Zimran's death is not yet *known*—all of this *city* thinks he's sitting up in *bed,* running the *Shield!*' he said, voice low and urgent. 'As for the reason for that, you'll have to work it out for yourself. *In your head.* You've fitted several of the pieces already, the last is hardly a leap.'

Perhaps it was just how he'd said it, but as his eyes rolled away to look over the battlements again, the truth slotted into place like a sheathing dagger. My mouth dropped open. 'She didn't—'

'Flint!' I snapped it shut.

So that was it: she'd killed him. Her own husband, Zimran, a man loved and trusted by the Satrap, murdered by the Senera herself. And now she was pretending to speak on his behalf in the Sanhedrin, using his powers for . . . for *what* exactly? How long could that last? And how did Rusper know the truth if no one else did?

Reading my face, he gave a smirk I didn't like. 'For far too many reasons, there are things I cannot tell you, *ekhin* Flint. Most would name me a fool for trusting a foreign child as far as I have trusted you already. Now I've no doubt of your good faith, but there are limits.'

I bowed my head away and thought through what he'd told me. 'I'm sorry,' I said. 'Guess I shouldn't have said those things about the High Commander. I just thought—'

'You wanted to help,' he conceded. 'But right now, the best way for you to help me is by trusting my judgement. There is work ahead of us. Work for which I brought you into my service.'

'But . . .' I could see him deflating, but I needed to know. 'If you're the Viceroy, why can't you just tell the Satrap what you know about her, the Senera?'

Rusper pulled at the fingers of his glove. 'That's where it's clear you know nothing of our Satrap, dear boy. Would that it were so simple. An accusation such as that would excite the man to fury, even sway him to remove me from my office for slander. *Both* my offices, perhaps! Amyra happens to be one of his personal favourites. Not to mention that the Shield has a firm hold on his physicians. An important fact, I'm afraid.'

He shook his head, his face bitter. We were quiet for a while. The team of foundrymen was now making its way back to the steps. I caught one smith's eye, raising my hand half-way in thanks or goodbye. I got a nod; more than expected. 'Will I ever see the Satrap?' I asked, not really sure where the thought had come from.

'I rather hope not,' said Rusper, still panning the desert view. 'To him you're an invader. An enemy of Vorth.'

'I'm twelve.'

'Small matter. You hail from Naemia, as do the Rath. Hand him a butter knife and he'd probably—'

But something must have popped into his head. His body stiffened, his neck erect like a rabbit alert in tall grass. His gaze was fixed.

'Caliph Symphin?'

'Follow my eyes please.'

I stepped into his crenel and looked out. My own eyes watered even as I shaded them and creased them up into slits against the glare. Rusper's chest was close at my back and his arm brushed against my temple.

'There,' he said, pointing past me.

I followed the gloved finger across the barren expanse, left of northwest, where whorls of earth reared brown in grey. The plains were darker in that region, spotted with the skeletons of trees. My pulse was rising.

'Scope!' Rusper shouted down the wall, making me jump, before he hurried along the crenels to the right. 'Look at the trees.' I scanned them slowly. But they were trees. Had something moved? No, just the wind sweeping a haze of dust across a ridge; it was always stronger out there. Then another movement. A hawk this time, riding an updraught.

Rusper almost ran into a watchman. 'Viceroy,' said the man, holding out a brass rod.

The Viceroy took it without thanks and pulled it open to three clicks. 'Do *you* see it?'

'I do, sir.'

The rest of the watch, here when we arrived, was now perched along the battlements, pointing out in watching huddles. Rusper pressed the telescope to his eye, jerked it down. Then up again. 'Lost it!'

'Sir!' shouted someone to the right. This wide-eyed watchman might as well have thrown a noose around us for all the persuasion he needed. Rusper jogged towards him, others opening a way and then closing. I was cut off, but it didn't matter. Everyone could see it and so could I.

Eighteen

Phantom at the Wall

A figure stood on the plains, not two miles from the fortress hill. The earth was grey over there and fewer bony trees disguised it. I squeezed my way between the men around Rusper, to that crenel. Heat blazed from the sandstone and leather jerkins of the watch, their pole-flags fluttering above our heads in the light breeze. Now, while I stared out, Rusper made his study of the figure through the glass. It faced the fortress, I could tell, and even at a distance its shape brought back that night full of horror. The shape, not its stillness. The stillness was wrong.

From the turret to our left, three guards in tabards and swathes jogged out to meet us. Two carried spears, the other had a sword at his hip. Rusper looked to the sword-man. He nodded smartly, '*Ekharan.*'

'What do you make of it, guardsman?' said Rusper.

'Sheriff,' the man corrected. 'Sir. Northgate Sheriff Arras.'

Rusper passed him the scope. 'My mistake, Sheriff.'

'A scout perhaps?'

'They've never scouted before, not like this at any rate. Nor ranged so close.'

Once Sheriff Arras had looked through the glass for himself, Rusper surprised me by tapping the scope on my shoulder. I took it and put the hot brass against my eye. A smudgy circle was inside: grey and brown, flashes of blue. Earth—sky—earth —sky. Then I felt a hand guiding the end, and the circle blackened with detail. My body tensed. Like a beetle appearing at the bottom of cup, it was *there*, as if standing only ten feet from me.

This one wore cobbled scraps of hide and ratty rags. Its hands were bound with ropey cloths, its head and shoulders by the shabby upper half of an old cloak. The cloak might once have been green. Spoils of its kills, I imagined, and wondered just how much of what it wore might be Naemian. I dared to meet what I could of its eyes: oily black under their cover.

'It's not moving, just watching,' I said.

Then it did move. Through the smudges on the glass I saw it stoop, drop a white arm towards the ground and lift a spear. It straightened slowly.

'The scope please,' Rusper said.

I gave it back, and the Rath shrank to a tiny mark on the plain; a mark that was still again. Too still. How could Rusper be so sure they'd never been this close before? They were night-crawlers, he knew that, and the watch on the walls wouldn't be able to see them through the darkness. I thought of the reports and that "northwest arc" of Ratheine movement.

'Could be curious,' offered a watchman.

'They're invaders, Kereth, not banqueting guests,' another chided. Sheriff Arras shot a reprimanding glance at both of them.

'Curious,' mused Rusper, softly, as if considering it himself. 'Well, it doubtless makes Kereth here as uncomfortable as it makes me to think of the Rath as dispatching their own scouts.'

I twisted my neck to look back at the watchman called Kereth. Bright brown eyes, a few days' stubble. Like the others of the watch, he wore the cream-coloured headdress and red jerkin in his swathes. His grip was tight on his flagpole. The man beside him looked like him, a little older. Brothers, maybe.

'It's backing off,' said Arras.

'I can see that,' murmured Rusper.

'Look, *another*.'

The scope swung left, with all our eyes. About a mile west of the first one, straight ahead, there was a second. It stood as still, its spear held out and away from its body. 'Head and hands covered again. I don't like it,' Rusper marked.

'Does it mean something, *ekharan?*' asked Kereth, leaning a little forward.

'Planning perhaps,' said Rusper. 'They avoid the sun where they can. Few would have cause to cover their bodies quite so thoroughly as this. It would suggest that any journey that brought them here from up north was deliberate, not mere wandering. That they *mean* to be here.' I looked at him: his forehead glistened below the cusp of his cap.

'Our view is clear for leagues,' said Arras. 'We'd have surely seen larger numbers. And the gates are well manned.' Rusper didn't answer. He collapsed the scope under his palm to a triple-click, and took a breath.

Then—'Another, Viceroy!' blurted Kereth. 'To the north!' The scope clicked open again. I ducked as it swept over me and then looked, seeing—'No, *two* more!' I shouted.

'Where's the other?'

Further off, more like three miles, on a gypsum rise. I couldn't make out much detail of this one, but it was obviously there beyond that one Kereth had sighted, and I pointed until Rusper and Arras could find it.

Others appeared. A fifth and sixth, each new arrival isolated from the last by at least a mile. Then, after the seventh, farthest of all from the fortress hill, we saw something else. Leagues away, just east-off-north, towards the mustard haze of the Northern Erg – too far to pick out single figures – a dark mass contrasted the slopes of the dunes. It seemed to be moving.

'How many?' said Arras.

Rusper aimed the scope, setting his teeth. 'Hard to tell,' he said, straining. 'Sixty, eighty . . .' In a lower voice, 'Bigger than any group we've detected in Verunia.' A nasty hush fell over us. 'They might have been there all along, we'd have not seen them at all without first sighting those nearer.'

He was right. It might easily have been a cloud's shadow or belt of scrub over the dune-side.

Still, I didn't like the tautness in his voice: 'If more appear, I want Captain Mondric alerted and all district guards posted at the two northern gates.'

'All of them?' said Arras. He sounded doubtful. '*Ekharan*, begging pardon—'

'There may be more massed beyond those dunes,' said Rusper. 'Where did *these* seven come from so quickly, hm?' Though his glance back at the two watchmen lasted no more than a second, it was enough to make them lower their eyes in some shame.

Meanwhile, Arras turned and squinted back across the city to the towers. 'Such numbers would have been sighted by the sentinel spire. The alarum would have sounded.'

'Not if the spire's manned with such complacency as yours!' Rusper snapped back.

He could be such a bully sometimes.

'Viceroy,' said Arras, also raising his voice. 'From here we command a full view of Antissa's north and west surrounds.

With respect, sir, whatever greater number that may be marked from the spire will be ten leagues from the walls and small threat to the city. And I must warn you, such a rally of the guard-force may cause unrest in the streets.'

They looked away from each other and back over the plains. The seven Rath held their positions, perfectly still. Watching. The scope was compacted again and returned to its owner. 'Thank you,' said Rusper. 'Your name, watchman?'

'Uh, Gareth, sir.'

Brothers for sure.

Getting too hot inside the huddle, I backed out to the edge of the walkway. The metalsmiths and their wagons had left, back to the Inner City, and only Rusper's wagon was below. Its ox was still yoked as its waiting driver slaked his thirst on a quart from the braehg-house. A man and two women stood chatting on the porch of that house. Men rolled big barrels from the brewery, between the buildings around it, and under the casement extension. The sound of stacking rose up from that side, below the gangway. Wood was sanded somewhere, hide was slapped, metal hammered. Right below me, a peasant in a dusty cloak began to climb the sandstone steps. I wasn't feeling so good. Behind me I heard Kereth mutter, 'What do they *want?*'

'I don't know,' Rusper breathed. 'It's as if they wish to be seen.'

A disapproving sound from Arras. 'We're within shouting distance of the gate.'

'You needn't keep repeating yourself, Sheriff.'

'But sir, there's no other way into the city from the north.'

No other way. My eyeballs jiggled in their sockets. Around me, suddenly, things felt much smaller. Not just the wall, us standing on it, or the district below. But the whole fortress. Along the walkway, to my right, another standard-bearing watchman and other guards had come up from the turret for a view of the arrivals. The ragged peasant had reached the top and gone to look out from a crenel. Through the city's daytime smokes and dust I looked back at the rising citadel; white, grey and bronze from the Inner Wall. Not far from here. My gut clenched up in a big knot. Antissa was tiny.

The word dropped out of my mouth; I turned around. The huddle opened up enough to let me back in, and at Rusper's side I said the word again, this time with force—'*Pipes*.'

'Flint, you shouldn't even be here,' he said without looking at me. 'Gareth, escort my assistant to my citadel quarters. This is no place for him.'

'I haven't a horse, sir.'

'Take my wagon, it's below.'

The watchman took my arm. I shook his hand away from me and glowered at Rusper while the guards and watchmen stared at my defiance. 'If I go, then you come too. Someone has to get soldiers to the *Hub*, don't you see. That's how the Rath are going to get in—through Arte-III!'

When Rusper looked me in the face, his own was plastered with sweat. 'That leak's been sealed,' he said curtly. 'I have it in a report that *you* wrote. And even if it wasn't, how could such a thing be possible?'

I grasped for explanations: 'Maybe it . . . *wasn't* sealed. Not fully.'

'Flint, it doesn't make—'

'Please!'

'They're gone,' Kereth said. Rusper and I looked to the desert. Kereth was right: as quickly as they'd appeared, the Rath had vanished off the plains. All seven, gone. I strained my eyes towards the dunes and even the shadow had disappeared.

'I'm not waiting,' said Rusper as he looked to Arras. 'Have a guard convey instructions to the Captain. I want men on all the northern gates and walls.'

'Yes sir,' said Arras, all duty now. 'What of the alarum?'

'Not yet. It may provoke them.'

'What about the *Deep?*' I pressed, refusing to be ignored. 'What about sending soldiers *there*? Caliph Symphin, you have to do that. Or at least close the Hub Chamber!'

'I'm staying here.' He shot impatient eyes at Gareth who took my shoulder this time, harder.

'Let go!' I yelled, trying to shove the hand away again and failing. 'Caliph—'

'*Nor will I suffer further argument from you!*' Rusper seethed at me. '*You've a place,* boy, lest you forget it—*well* beneath mine!'

That checked me, if only for a second. But he was a man pushed to anger by his fear. 'What if I'm right?'

'Do you *wish* to be? Can you even *conceive* of what that would mean?'

'That's the point!' I shouted.

'*What* is?'

'I *am* right!'

He snapped fingers at Gareth. 'Get rid of him—now.' Eyes hard, as if I were nothing but a nuisance, he glanced over my head along the battlements. 'And you, Kereth, yes? Get that peasant off the wall.'

Kereth coughed, 'Sir, that's a soldier,' while his brother pulled me away towards the steps. No sooner had Kereth said those words than I saw the peasant's sword-hilt through a hole rent in his cloak. The cloak was torn and shredded in many other places too, but there was an emblem on its shoulder, I saw that clearly: three towers in a circle. The man was scanning the plains, frayed hood in profile to us.

Behind me, Arras: 'That's a Fortress Regiment sigil. Third Battalion, I think.'

Gareth nudged me towards the gangway.

'Soldier,' called Arras.

The peasant-soldier didn't move. This felt wrong.

Third Battalion . . .

'I'll get him, sir,' said Kereth, who then strode past me and Gareth with his flagpole in hand. I twisted in the grip to throw a glance back at Rusper, who had taken Arras by the arm, saying something urgent.

Kathris!

Couldn't be—Artabh Kathris was still missing in the desert, or dead. *Wasn't he?*

'Watchman . . .' called Arras, his tone more stiff.

I looked ahead. Kereth reached a hand out to the figure and took his shoulder.

The cloak opened as the figure whirled out of the crenel—faceless in the hood—and steel swung with it. In an instant the blade had moved across Kereth's throat, a white mask sprayed livid red as the flagpole clattered to the stone. Neck spurting gouts, Kereth listed on his heels and crumpled forward.

'*TO ME!*' bawled Arras.

Gareth let go of my shoulder with a sound that seemed to come out of his stomach, then roared. He lowered his flagpole and ran forward, spear-tip pointed. I watched the sword deflect the charge, hook the spearhead, drag the pole and sweep up fast to slash his jerkin. Gareth retched. His muddy insides slopped out on the hand that had just held me by the shoulder. '*Florian—back!*' someone shouted. But I couldn't tear my eyes away from Gareth: moaning, he knelt in all the blood that was still leaving his body, the tubes and ropes of his belly, then keeled and slumped over Kereth's legs.

The white-masked figure took a step and carved a swift line through the air, dashing blood on the sandstone. The watchman brothers both struck down, I stood with less than five yards to the sword that had killed them: a Vedish shortsword, I noticed in vivid hyper-awareness. My eyes met holes in blood-flecked leather. Someone shouted something.

On the other end of the walkway, behind the phantom, guards readied spears. The phantom ignored them to take another step towards me. It leaned forward, bizarrely, neck extended. There was no question that those eyeholes were pointed at me and only me, but I couldn't look away. Or run. Or move.

Three men charged past me—Arras and his guards. One shoved me back.

The phantom flailed.

Someone grabbed a handful of my collar: with more strength than I knew he had, Rusper wheeled me behind him, yelling something.

A spear went flying. A man fell screaming. More disgusting splashes wet the stone. Steel rang and clashed. That was Arras' sword now, meeting the phantom's as others with spears rushed from behind. The shortsword was spun from the phantom's hand and then thrown clear. It clattered down in front of two more rigid watchmen.

The rear guards closed in. Disarmed, the phantom turned and struck the first a blow to the head, and then leapt. Impossibly high, it vaulted right over the men who had come in from behind and landed on its haunches next to one of the jezail frames. Gripping its gunrest with both hands, the creature ripped it free of the hinge and took the ball-bearing with it.

Rusper forced me back another step, facing the fight, but hands all over me as if a second were too long to be sure I was still there. Then he turned and shoved me back, hand at my chest. 'Go! Into the turret!'

I ran and crossed the turret threshold. Muscles flooded with white panic, not running straight, one of the crates tripped me up and I flew over it, coming down hard on my arms. The screams outside shot me to my feet and I darted for the opposite door. I yanked the handle—no, *locked! Of course it was, I'd been here often enough!* The watch never kept more than two adjacent stretches of wall open at a time.

Hopping the crate, I sprinted back.

Now not far from Rusper, the phantom wheeled the metal gunrest into the head of a guard, the bearing smashing his face into bloody pieces. The man fell down. I grabbed Rusper by the arm but he shook me clear and pushed me away from him, harder. '*The turret! Go, boy! Now!*'

'Other side's locked!' I cried. 'We'll be trapped in there!'

I'd been trapped with the Rath once before and only a miracle had saved me. Not again. Now I searched the face of the wall below us, distantly aware of the shouted reactions around the brewery and braehg-house, but it was sheer drop, too far to fall, we wouldn't make it. This was really happening again.

Two more were dead when I looked back. Arras raised his sword; the phantom ducked and circled round, spinning the gunrest into a downward thrust that disappeared into the Sheriff's back. Kicked from the metal that I'd overseen in construction, the man slid and fell onto his face with a cracking noise I shouldn't have been able to hear at this distance.

There was nothing between us now. Only two watchmen stood behind the phantom, and its shortsword still lay only a yard from their boots. '*Take the weapon!*' Rusper urged them, voice cracking. '*Take it!*' One of the watchmen took a step forward, but fear had turned his legs to wood.

The gunrest whirled. Leaping again—further and higher than I'd known they *could*—it crossed the length of the walkway to make a three-point landing at the sword. The blade swept up and carved a face. I looked away from the open head, but heard the burbled scream and blow that silenced it.

Another shove from Rusper.

I shoved back.

Rage in his eyes now, hard to tell from the panic, he pushed away—'*You foolish child!*'—and strode for the turret.

I heard its door slam.

Sheeted crimson, the last two watchmen had now fallen to the stone. There was no escape from this creature; Rusper only waiting for his death behind that door. Somewhere below, I heard barked orders and people running in the streets. Boots beat on steps and, at the sound, the phantom's mask darted towards the casement. Then swung back to me.

It walked towards me.

A wounded guard stood up, groaning, with a spear in his hand, as if to stop it. The phantom swiped its sword like a warning, and when the man tried to strike out, his spear was swiftly dragged aside. The shortsword's hilt crushed his nose, the guardsman spluttered, dropped his weapon and toppled onto the gangway. There the blade entered his chest, slid out and slashed his neck in half. I saw the head leaving the body as it was kicked clear off the gangway, and heard it crash into the barrels those men had stacked below the wall. More people screamed.

The phantom came. Extending its neck in that weird way, and making sounds . . .

No, it was speaking.

'*Nemae il veru deh gossa kerak . . . nemae il veru deh gossa kerak . . .*' The language was like mud. The sword was almost within reach.

What was I doing?

I turned and bolted for the turret.

But never got there. Before my hand could reach the handle, the door flew open, nearly hitting me directly in the face as it swung and smacked against the sandstone. I tripped and fell at Rusper's feet and rolled on my back, out of his way.

Never stopping, the phantom carved the air in rotating mock-slashes. Rusper, clearly insane, walked out of the turret towards it. And raised his arm.

Chrozite smouldered at eye-level.

With a crack, a flash, a spray of sparks and yellow smoke, the burning schot spat from the fusil. The phantom's feet left the stone as it flew back.

The fusil fell. Hand to his face, Rusper swayed a moment and sagged down on his haunches. My ears pealing from the noise, I shuffled forward to brace him, but he flopped against the battlements. Through char-blacked fingers, his left cheek fizzed and bubbled: blood *and* chrozite. My voice, sounding faraway, shouted his name, but either he couldn't hear me or was in too much pain to answer, eyes tightly closed. I shouted for guards. I shouted help into the street. I kept on shouting.

The phantom lay still, feet away. Yellow fumes rose out of the hole that had been made in its head. The stretch of wall was a red mess.

Then boots were thudding towards us. The Captain of the Guard was on the wall; six, eight, ten more guards behind him. Ten guards too late. His face dropped at the sight of the bodies on the walkway and, somewhere in my heart, I thanked him for marching straight to where we crouched. And then his men were over us, bringing shade from the sun. Mondric elbowed me hard in the chest and knelt in front of Rusper.

'Symphin?' Whatever he said was still too muffled for me to make out as he tried to peel the hand away from the sizzling burns. But before I saw how bad they were, Mondric took a cloth out of his jerkin and pressed it firmly to the cheek. Rusper's eyelids snapped open, lips moving.

My ears popped.

'. . . backfired . . . fusil backfired . . .' he was repeating, his eyes wide on Mondric's knees. 'Backfired . . . thought it was fit for purpose . . .'

'Symphin? Symphin!' Mondric shook him.

'. . . need to . . . must . . . to the citadel.'

Mondric nodded. 'I'll say.'

Eyes still on the knees, Rusper spoke in fragments. 'Find the High Commander. Tell him . . . battalions on every gate . . . every wall, artillery . . .' Then, 'Captain?'

'It's done,' Mondric replied and mouthed a stern *find him* at the guards. Three broke away at a run. 'Now let's get those burns seen to properly.'

'Forget the *burns!*' Rusper choked. Chrozite had got into his throat. But he wasn't staring, even looking. The eyes were glazed, red-rimmed, unblinking. '*I can't see.*'

The Captain glanced at me blankly. Almost stupidly, I thought, he passed a hand over Rusper's face but the eyes didn't blink or move at all. So he slid an arm around his waist to help him stand. They would have trodden on the fusil had I not darted to pick it up. Not that there was much left of it: still hot, charred black, cords sizzled off, mech ruined.

Rusper squeezed his eyes shut, weeping yellow-black fluid. '*Florian?*'

'I'm here!'

'You shouldn't be,' he croaked. 'Get to the pipes, that's an order.'

Nineteen

Haemorrhage

Alarum duduks wailed along the walls of the fortress, as if Antissa was screaming. I shared the saddle with a guard who rode the Captain's own horse at a canter to the Inner City. Militia was moving. Citizens were bustling everywhere, afraid, not knowing why. I didn't care about that right now. I'd had no choice but to leave Rusper on the wall with Captain Mondric, hoping he'd get safely to a healer. I had been given an order.

We clattered over the flagstones towards the statue of the gryphon. Here in the courtyard, martial detachments were assembling out of the underpass roads: vortan soldiers in black uniform with leather tabards and greaves. Two groups were mounted, the front rider of each holding up the banner of his battalion; that three-towered symbol I'd seen on the reports, and on that phantom. Fortress Regiment. The High Commander had clearly received the news already.

As the horse swerved near the gryphon, I let myself lean with the motion and drop out of the saddle. My knees almost buckled on landing. My escort followed me down a lot more smoothly and acknowledged the High Commander now emerging from the ranks in a fluid stride. 'Where's the Viceroy?'

I volunteered: 'At the northwest wall, he's hurt.'

'I was addressing the guardsman.' Plamen didn't so much as glance in my direction.

'Boy's right, sir. Northwest wall,' said the guard. 'The Honorary Caliph sustained an injury in confrontation with a Ratheine intruder.' Plamen's face didn't change. 'He's bound for the citadel now with the Captain, *ekharan*.'

'What of the intruder?'

'Dead, sir. Dispatched by the Viceroy himself.'

Just a twitch of Plamen's eyebrow but I caught it. Behind him, six mounted men rode through the courtyard, leading a much larger white horse by the reins. Plamen's horse.

'Please,' I broke in, begging his attention. He sucked and held in a breath as if to show precisely how much time he'd grant me to speak. 'I've orders from the Viceroy too. I'm to inspect the Hub Chamber.'

'Be about it then. Guild duties have nothing to do with me.'

'You don't understand,' I said before he turned away. 'The Rath are *coming* that way, through the Hub, through the broken arterial.'

Only now did he regard me. 'I thought that problem had been dealt with.'

Again, unsure of how to answer that, I settled for: 'Maybe not.'

'Are you asking for men?'

'Yes.'

'*Say again, boy?*' The jolt ran right down through my body and I felt my shoulders straighten. Until now, I'd only ever heard him raise his voice to the dog. Suddenly, with the regimental rank and file mustered behind him, I saw him as he was: a commander. Over the white robe and mantle, a hauberk of steel mail braced his chest; a finer mesh reinforcing the folds of his headdress. If only I could remember the titles when they mattered.

'Yes, High Commander. Sir.'

'Out of the question. I'll spare no men until I know what we face at the wall.'

'Nothing!' I urged. 'There'll be nothing when you get to the wall. It wasn't a scout. It wasn't a real attack!'

'Ten men are dead,' said the guard beside me.

Plamen's voice levelled. 'You're wasting my time, child. Guardsman. Escort the Viceroy's hand to the entrance of the Deep. From there he may attend to his *orders* by himself.'

Quadrants of soldiers began to leave the courtyard, bound for the fortress gates. I was swung back into the saddle. Plamen mounted his beautiful horse and looked back at me, just once, as we rode left of the gryphon. The crunch of marching, blare of nasal duduk sirens and shouted orders fell behind.

In the shade beyond the Deeping Door, the guard helped me down and left me at the edge of the rubble shaft without a word. I went down quickly, returned the ruined fusil to the workshop, then made my way towards the Hub. I passed the sappers in the tunnels, but around the green wall, almost no one. So when I heard a pair of feet doubling my own behind me, I spun around—'Who's there?' I snapped.

I was on edge, which figured. But something *was* there, in the passage. I unhooked a lantern and raised two of its shutters to see better.

'Who's *there?*' I said again, holding it out.

He didn't try to hide. Tiny eyes catching the light for just a second through the converging folds of flabby skin, he waddled into view and raised fat cheeks in a spongy smile. No sandrat with him today.

'Were you following me, Hetch?'

'Yes.'

Hard to say much to that. And I couldn't just ignore him – couldn't *ever* ignore him, he'd saved my sentenced finger. 'There's been an attack,' I told him fast.

'Casualties?'

'Guards and watchmen,' I said. 'The Viceroy got hurt too.'

'The *Viceroy*, indeed?'

'Yes, the Viceroy,' I nodded seriously, then made a show of my hurry. 'Hetch, I have to see to something. *Now.*'

He made an ushering gesture at the tunnel ahead. 'Of course, Naemian.'

I moved on. And Hetch tailed me. Even well ahead of him, I could hear the shuffle of his sandals, did he really think I couldn't? My lantern beams stroked freshly bricked passages, then from the southern access tunnel I stepped into the hallowed hall of pipes. Heart of Antissa. Where the Rath could slice up through her veins if I was right. There were lights on some bridges but none lower than fourth zone. Just below, on third, a metalsmith team was on shift. Ghulzar among them.

'Don't half like this room,' murmured Hetch, beside me. 'Goes a long way down.'

'It goes *all* the way down,' I said, not looking at him.

Our words were soft, but the Hub carried them. Ghulzar looked up. 'You needing something?'

I called back: 'Pintle. I'm looking for Pintle. Where is she?'

'Repair work's done.' He shrugged his ball-like, branded shoulders. 'No one working down there anymore.'

Not good. '*No one?*'

'Summat stuck in your lugs? Aye, no one!' He shook his head and spat over the cantilever railing.

Not happy with that answer, I jogged to the midpoint of the bridge where a metal ladder had been installed to join Zones Two and Three. Careful with the lantern, I started down.

'Here he comes, lads, look sharp,' Ghulzar mocked me to his smiths. When I reached his bridge, he strode towards me with that huge hammer in hand. I leaned over the railing and looked down but it was impossible, even from here, to see any-thing of sixth zone. Just too dark. 'Told you, no one down there,' said Ghulzar, slowing his step as he looked up and frowned at Hetch clumsily navigating the middle rungs on the ladder.

'I've to check on Arte-III,' I said. 'It's urgent. There could still be something wrong down there.'

'Pretty damn set on this *overseein'* business, aren't ya?' said Ghulzar, and sniffed.

I widened my eyes at him. 'It's *important*. There's been an attack.'

His face fell. 'What kind of attack?'

I didn't answer straightaway. As Hetch came down off the ladder, I simply yanked off my sandals and made him hold them. If he had to follow me around, then he might as well be useful.

'Kid, what *attack?*' growled Ghulzar, fist going tight round the hammer's grip. Some of his smiths turned their heads.

I was aware of my mouth making some words about what happened, but couldn't hear them. As I spoke, I tightened my grip on the lantern's handle, slipped a first foot into the ropes and started to work my way down. Outside my head, I think, Ghulzar got some other pieces out of Hetch, then maybe sent one of the smiths to find out what was really going on.

The clicks and squeaks of the others' work carried on, then; a little slower, eerily magnified by space. Ghulzar's sniffs, echoing, took on the likeness of industrial metal scraping coals. Invisible water hissed through the intersecting pipes around me, but so much louder was the silence that ruled this place—big, fat, waiting silence that made me queasy—merely *allowing* worldly sounds to find half-voices inside it. Thirty feet down . . . forty . . . fifty . . . The nets worked their route around the fourth zone laterals. I bypassed the fourth zone bridge. A hundred feet, and colder . . . Laterals got fewer after that, and without their company to fill the Hub's diameter, I avoided looking at the verticals I was left with: thin, ghostly trees standing in the void like staring strangers.

Guessing at something like two hundred feet below third zone, I stopped and steadied myself. And then leaned back off the ropes, reaching out with my light. Just as always, Arterial-III made me shudder. I breathed cold air deep into my lungs and let it pass. A little further down from here was the big new girder where the rupture had been. Forged around the circumference of Arte-III to withhold full channel pressure from the mains when it was reopened, it was whole. Undamaged.

Ghulzar called down: 'Everything in order, *ekhin* Flint?'

I didn't realise just how much fear my chest had been holding, squeezed inside, until that moment. I gushed a sigh that became a laugh, siphoning it out. 'Yes!' I called back up to him. 'Girder's alright!'

That queasiness gone too, I monkeyed back up the ropes towards the bridge.

At best, it would be a skirmish. We'd seen that distant group approaching from the erg, so maybe they *would* attempt a first assault on fortress walls. What had Rusper said, sixty? Eighty? Call it a hundred, I rounded up. They'd have reached the walls by now, I guessed. But so would Plamen and his detachments. The entire army Plamen commanded was right here inside this fortress. I almost couldn't believe that I was really thinking it, but fine: *let them.* Let them do it! Let them have their first big push and see what happens! If the next stage of Vorth's defence was to be *that*, a case of warding off Ratheine sapping from hilltop walls that they could never hope to breach – a fortress armed with better artillery than their little poisoned black spears, not to mention the war machines and the chrozite – I could deal with it. I could face them. We just had to get those fusils working properly . . .

The dwarf took the lantern while I slipped my sandals on again, not minding how the foundryman looked down at me, brooding. 'Sure you don't want to go looking for *more* holes, then?' he gibed. But the gibe was hollow, I could hear it.

And I also felt my smile die on my lips. Chest closing, squeezing on that fear all over again, the queasiness washed back in. Hetch peered into my face, folding and unfolding the great lumps above his eyes. 'What's the matter with you, Naemian?' And then, 'Talk, kid,' from Ghulzar.

'More holes . . .' I murmured.

Hetch made a show of looking at the pipes. 'In which one?'

'Kid?' said Ghulzar. Impatient.

I rounded back to the railing. Now that he'd said it, I couldn't look away from the logic. One major channel had been ruptured, why not a rupture in another? Below that girder in Arte-III, the Hub continued to descend another fifty or sixty feet before the floor. Anything could be down there, in any one of the four arterials, where the pipes were still submerged in all that water from the flood. I'd have to go again and check—and this time *all* the way down to the bottom.

Wait. Really, *did* I?

Not caring who saw it, I pulled my sleeve back from the torque and flipped the lion-face lid open. When he saw what was encased and mounted on my forearm, Hetch gave a little gasp—delight: I saw it in the mirror. Shut up or go away, I thought. And concentrated. Brushed the mirror with a finger, just to test, then snapped the lid shut on it. In an instant, the blue glow peeped through the cracks. I closed my eyes, gripped the torque-lever and pulled it.

Tingling coolness. My lungs opened. Force flowed and shook my body like the vertigo sensation the arterials always gave me, only so much stronger. The Sight opened up around me: far too big, ungraspable; as if, while swimming in the sea, the water underneath my legs had gone clear right to the seabed. My awareness floated in it, tiny, just like Ghulzar and his smiths and little Hetch.

Follow the pipes. Water coursed through them, I *saw!* Tamed cascades that tumbled, twisted, looped and climbed. It looked so free, and yet it was only by the will of iron, I supposed, that . . .

Focus! I pinned that focus to Arterial-III and followed its column, downward. Its insides made me tremble even more than its body, but still I plunged; reached the position of the girder. Closed my awareness on the barricade sealing the rupture—intact, just as I'd found it. Passing the curve where the Hub narrowed, I delved down further into whatever lay in wait below the floodwater. Thirty . . . forty . . . fifty feet . . . Light and dark meant nothing here: I knew the space and only space. Drunk on it almost, it became harder to be sure of what should be and what shouldn't. But I saw what *wasn't:* in ugly, splintered, flaking lesions—*another* haemorrhage in Arte-III, ten feet above the base floor of the Hub. Through it were movements. Flitting, darting, *swimming* movements. Swimming up.

And swimming fast.

I jammed the lever, cut the Sight. Finding the solid shape of Ghulzar, I spluttered out 'Another one!'

'What're you talking about?'

'Another hole in the arterial—under the water—down by the floor—broken from the inside like the first!' I swallowed hard. 'They've been trying to get in all this time and now they're coming. They're *coming up!*'

But I could tell by his face and the way he kept glancing at the torque he'd helped me make, not knowing why, that he didn't understand. And how could he? 'Slow it down, kid, take a breath, you're not making any—'

'Rath!' my voice cracked. 'High Commander's got to know!' I set my hands to the ladder's rungs to start climbing, but then froze. Ghulzar turned sharply to the darkness and Hetch took a backstep from the railing. Some of the smiths stood from their work.

We'd all heard it, the splash, and I saw Ghulzar clench his jaw. 'What the . . .' Another splash. Pipes didn't make noises like that. '*Bastards!*'

The bolt of dread shot me up the rungs. Hetch dropped the lantern in his panic and grabbed my foot. Afraid he'd pull me off, I kicked, and the sandal came off in his grip. I flung the other one off too. Metalsmiths hurried in behind him as a guttural echo flew up clearly, then more splashes from below. Hetch kept on grabbing at my ankles, coming up behind me so much faster than he'd gone down. But no sooner did he scramble up onto the second zone bridge than he was shoved aside by the smiths fleeing for the tunnel. He stumbled forward while I rounded on the railing of Zone Two.

Ghulzar hadn't followed. Not moved an inch. Completely still, he stood with his huge hammer in hand and stared down darkness.

With a winded bleat, Hetch ran towards the tunnel but I lunged and caught him by his swathes. '*You're* Plamen's messenger, aren't you! We need soldiers in here right now!'

'They're at the gates, Naemian!' he whimpered.

'They're needed *here!*'

He squealed, pulled free. I let him go.

Down on Three's bridge, the hammer's head slapped into the foundryman's palm. He was crazy. 'You can't fight them! We need to get out!' I pleaded.

He growled low, 'Then get out.'

TWENTY

HIGH WATER

The hammer crashed into the railing of the bridge on Zone Three. Ghulzar struck again, and again, with the strength of mad rage, announcing his presence like a warrior at war drums. It wasn't a metalsmith's tool, but a weapon after all. Between the crashes, splashes echoed; then the patter of wet hands over the pipes. Did it even matter if the dwarf told Plamen what was happening? Who could even guess how many were swimming up right now through that channel?

The first appeared on the north wall, to my left, lizard-like. Glistening-wet, it gibbered into the light of the lanterns the other smiths had left. A second crawled in from the right, grappling among the thinner feeder pipes, and stopping. Freezing in the gloom. Ghulzar saw them, both of them, and held position. I held my breath and took the slowest backstep I'd ever taken. Stilled my body. Membranous lids flashed over the shiny-black stones of their eyes in those pale heads. Knotted tails of hair dangled, dripping. Their mouths were small – I didn't think their jaws could open very wide – but they *were* snarling, baring needles in muddy gums, trailing thick spit. *Just run*, I tried to will myself. By the time any soldiers got to us, it wouldn't be about holding the fortress anymore. Today Antissa could fall and there he stood, one crazy metalsmith— its sole defender. Why *shouldn't* I just run? This wasn't home! I was the borderland boy, just a Naemian refugee.

And—it hit me—more Antissan than I'd *ever* been Naemian. Or ever would be.

The one on the right sprang to Arte-III, from there to Ghulzar's bridge and I nearly *did* run. But it wasn't even that simple: I knew how fast they could move, how far they could leap, and if I ran, I'd only get one chance. Low on its haunches, the Rath wheeled a half-spear.

Before it launched, Ghulzar charged it. He undercut its jaw with a rising sweep of his hammer, which flung its body to the railing.

The other leapt out from the wall. For a sickening second, I lost all sight of it in the shadows, then saw the scuttling of long limbs on a higher feeder. From there it dropped, dodging the hammer, just as a third pair of hands grabbed the Zone Three bridge from below. More black eyes followed.

Spinning from his miss, Ghulzar brought the iron down again and smashed those fingers. A screech tore free and echoed out across the breadth of the zone as that one dropped, hitting another lower pipe and disappearing. Two more replaced it: I saw them clinging, spider-like, to the bridge's under-frame.

The rising numbers made a chorus of fast-pattering hands, and my stomach plunged when I saw the wall of movement seething through the gloom. I had to go now. Had to *run*.

The narrow, sinewy jaws snapped at Ghulzar's fists as he now grappled for his own hammer. He thrust the weapon's handle into the nose of the creature he faced, making it stagger; that gave him time to change his grip and crush its skull, while the new arrival on the sub-frame hissed and launched back through the open. There it latched its legs around another feeder and watched from just outside the light. Triglycerate flickered on its eyes.

'*Pelkh*-spat demons, I'll take you!' roared Ghulzar.

He'd die trying. I knew he would, unless help came. And though it hadn't been my choice, this *was* home now. Another home about to crumble.

My mind raced, scanning the arterial towers. The Sight had done something, I realised now; heightened the way I looked at them—*my awareness of the water,* as if my seeing its true paths had left an imprint in my head! Locking my eyes onto a sub-gauge of Arte-III, suddenly I knew I *could* do something. Buy Ghulzar time. But only if I moved right now. This second. The boy of the borderlands could run. Just not the Chief's boy.

I was running already, before fear stopped me again, but wasn't going for the tunnel. My running jump cleared the railing of the second zone bridge, blackness below, before the sweep of rope-nets caught my fall. I glanced back as the net rocked and creaked under my landing—no followers!—then scrambled up towards the sub-gauge. I'd sealed it once; now with my hands on both its levers, I pulled them hard towards me.

Now down! Don't look, just *climb.*

But the snarls and croaks wafted up and I couldn't help but watch the fight on Three. Ghulzar held his bridge, cursing the creatures as they came. White spear-wielding spiders, they fanned around him. He raised his iron, made another charge and swept two right off their feet with the hammer's handle, then crushed their heads. Another reached him in two leaps, but he was quick; he ducked away from the lunging spear, swung low and broke both of its knees. Disarmed, another dodged a blow to its chest before it followed the others back out into the dark.

Shaking, I scaled my way to the next girder. I dismounted from the net, moved around the column of Arte-III, stepped into gills and started down.

Clawed hands now swiped for Ghulzar's face. The hammer swung again to strike the pipe beside him like a gong, and bodies dropped. From the north, four or five more groped from darkness. The Rath in front of Ghulzar fell, its head shattered and flapping on its shoulders, but now those five at the end of his bridge had turned to eight. Not counting the half-lit limbs that scuttled on the sub-frame.

He gave the bridge up.

Rath on his heels, I watched him sprint to where the cantilever abutted the side of Arte-III, reach for its gills and start climbing towards me. 'Other way!' he bellowed up.

'I have to open the sub-valve on third zone!' I yelled back, shaking my head. 'Could force them—'

'You got some kinda death wish? There's no time!'

Below the man, the numbers thickened, then I screamed as two sets of arms and legs wrapped around him, claws closing fast around an ankle. He booted one in the teeth and broke its grip, let the hammer fly across his wake in an arc that struck the face of the creature behind it and plucked it from the pipe. From the cantilever sub-frame, more Rath sprang onto the surface of the bridge. Five—seven—nine—*too many!* And no longer any way of reaching the gauge on that zone. He was right, there wasn't time, so I turned and climbed back up the way I'd come down. Ghulzar behind, Rath in pursuit.

But I couldn't stop looking down. 'Your back!' I cried. The hammer swept to fling the closest chaser like a toad. Two more leapt in to replace it, but the hammer, rebounding, took them both. The weapon was a pendulum, sacred as every muscle and tendon of the arm that made it swing. As soon as it stopped swinging, I would die.

At least a dozen climbed the arterial and more than twenty were on that bridge.

Then two soared off their haunches, spinning spears in mid-air. They latched onto Ghulzar and, with force, wrapped him in a tangle that pulled him clear of the gills and down, ploughing a path through the upward-crawling mass and sending several Rath skating off the sides. It was over.

But by some miracle, he was still there when I dared to look back down again; swinging from the bridge where his sudden halt had jerked the Rath to his legs. Now they dangled from him, gnashing.

The sacred hammer was gone.

'*Get out! Out! Out!*' he roared at me, grip straining, and I knew there was nothing I could do.

Behind, below, the numbers swarmed.

Then—*snapsnapsnap!*—bolts flew and peppered chalky flesh. Screaming, the danglers let go of Ghulzar, fell and disappeared.

I looked up. Back on Zone Two's bridge, five men discharged a second spray of bolts over the swarm and lowered their crossbows to reload.

Bootfalls, military voices and lights played behind them in the tunnels. 'Crossbows line bridges!' someone boomed into the Hub. 'Hold upper levels!'

My heart leapt as, across the bridge overhead, more men with crossbows filed out and lined the railings. Another troop armed with swords jogged from the tunnels after them in a blur of lantern lights. 'Vortans to lower levels!'

Looking down, I saw Ghulzar haul himself back onto the arterial's gills and start climbing again. Unarmed, legs streaked all bloody, the next Rath to reach him was caught by its shoulders and hurled into the open. The one behind it took a bolt from one of the crossbows in its back and went down after it. But Zone Three's bridge was now crawling, the crossbow-fire merely picking at the edges of the crowd; a crowd that surged into a tight group as the men with swords made their way to the ladders and nets.

Above, on Two, a leading officer raised his lantern and gazed out at the walls of the chamber as if he stood in a bat cave in the moments before dark. 'Drop your lights!' he commanded.

Five lanterns fell. One hurtled past my head, another smashing on a pipe on its plummet to the water. I dared to watch the others, and the Rath that scattered out from them like angry termites—more than fifty around the water and among the laterals of Zone Six. More still rising.

'Open fire on the climbers!' A volley rained out on the Rath, just as a spear flew out of nowhere, right through the officer's stomach. I looked away as he grunted, sword falling with a clang against his bridge and slipping off its side. I grabbed those railings as, in the corner of my eye, the officer's body followed his sword down.

On the nets, bolts pierced the Rath fronting the crowd and delayed the rising of the tide. Some fell, I think, it was hard to see. Others, smitten, kept on climbing. Swords lunged. But even with Ghulzar gaining on my heels, I couldn't move from where I was. Vortan soldiers were still streaming from the tunnel on Zone Two, blocking my way onto that bridge.

A white arm reached for Ghulzar's boot; he rammed it down on the creature's mouth, which pushed him higher. The chaser dropped and I heard its bones crack on the levers of the sub--gauge I'd never reached.

My mind spun back to the day I'd sealed Arte-III and stopped the flood. Arte-III still sealed, the lack of current was allowing the Rath up through its channel. Of course I knew that, I'd *seen* that. But the *sub-valves* . . . they *divided* pressure. Through the flow of jogging legs, I looked towards the tunnel exit. Then up, to darkness. The channel itself could only opened or closed at the mains. That was the floodgate. And I could open it again.

'Hold fire!' shouted new command.

'Vortans engage!'

Swords met the black spears and claws on the ropes above Zone Three. Ghulzar swore and shoved me upwards. 'Enough *overseein'* for a day!' Blood from his nose coloured the dagger of his beard and goatee.

'I have to get to the top!' I shouted at him, clinging awkwardly from the railing so as not to be brushed off by the soldiers.

'What *for?*'

'If we open the mains we can flood them out again.' I didn't wait for his approval; just leaned out, buried my fingers back into the gills of the arterial and stepped clear of the bridge. I went on climbing. Past the crossbows on Zone Two, higher on the column of Arte-III, towards the ceiling. The vicious struggle of men and Rath fell farther and farther below, which helped me master the fear that was rolling through my stomach. I moved with purpose now—a plan—and had almost forgotten about Ghulzar when his hands brushed my soles.

'That as fast as you go then?' he brayed. 'What are you— man or molerat?'

Spurred by his roar, I climbed faster. Saw the four great buttresses that converged around those vertical tubes. There were the arterial summits, their cresting girders and mains wheels.

I risked a glance down past my feet. Soldiers arriving from the access tunnels brought more lights; through their glare it looked as if the vortans had made it onto Zone Three's bridge. The crossbows fired freely now, my heart lifting again at the screeches I could hear through the noise. And still more soldiers poured in, spanning the breadth of Zone Two to kneel a yard apart from each other until the whole bridge was covered. This had all happened too fast to have been Hetch's doing. The High Commander must have believed me after all, and changed his mind!

Another shove from Ghulzar forced me back into my climb and my task, and he stayed behind me all the way to the top. At the summit, he wrapped his strong hands round my shins to hoist me up. I grabbed the mains wheel with one hand on the outer bar, almost slipping, but he caught me. 'Steady!' Gasping, I grabbed it with the other hand as well.

When I was sure of my balance, I made my way to the left side of the wheel. Ghulzar did the same on the right and there secured his footing. Closer snarls echoed up through the clashing and screaming, spitting crossbows, shouted orders. I willed myself to ignore them, nodded firmly and palmed the bar. We heaved together.

No give, no movement. Nothing at first.

Then—*clank*—the bar chugged towards me so sharply that Ghulzar had to lunge to grab my arm.

'Keep on pushing,' I urged him, regaining balance and pulling from higher up on the bar. He was doing the real work, I knew, but I couldn't just hang there and watch. I locked my eyes on his big arms and bunching muscles; the rogue crossbow bolt that had pierced him in the shoulder under the brandmark, blood still running. The arterial's workings began to grumble as we turned. The column shivered.

Officers below cried, 'Narrow fire!'

'Don't let them climb!'

'Fire on the walls!'

I tried to lean forward and look down, but Ghulzar growled me to attention with ice-blue eyes across the wheel. Arte-III's vibrations filled our bodies, its rising moan drowning the cries below our perch. A rapid current filled the column, I could feel its power through the metal; a force too strong to swim against.

But I also heard the crossbow bolts that whistled closer under us. We didn't have long. I kept on pulling at the bar, the shaking stronger all the time as the waking moan became a hiss.

Again that whistle, then a snap. A crossbow volley. When I felt something slip off the metal just below, I knew—*they'd seen us*. I held on tighter, the channel shaking against us. 'It's open!' Ghulzar shouted.

I shook my head wildly. '*All* the way!'

'Leave it, kid, *man* I mean it!'

The quaking jolted me down. I caught the wheel's inner bar just as a white face loomed up and flung an arm towards my leg. Yelping, I kicked on instinct, while Ghulzar swung across the wheel. His boot missed it and, as he swung away again, the white jaws snapped. I kicked it harder this time and felt a tooth snag on my heel. And still I kicked, the panic adding to my strength I had to hope. At my second clumsy, grazing blow, the Rath dropped a short way but caught gills. Poising a spear, it hung there, waiting, glaring up.

The column shook with so much force we couldn't keep hold of the bar. Ghulzar had climbed onto the gills above the axle of the mains wheel, and no sooner had I seen him than he reached for me as well. By my swathes, he hauled me up just as the Rath lunged for my feet. I fell over the metalsmith's thigh.

The spear plunged.

If he cried out, I didn't hear it over my own cry, but I saw him grab the ugly black shaft in both hands and break it off. Blood left his chest in two great spurts as he drove the broken end back down at his attacker. The Rath ducked it with a seemingly impossible movement. Readying to leap, its face distorted in a snarl that made its face look like a baby's, wailing; chalk-white skin grooved deep with a beast's rage. Ghulzar pressed his forearm to my neck and forced me back against Arte-III.

The creature leapt, caught him by the waist. Another one, from nowhere, took him by a leg and dragged him down. I batted after him, falling forward on the axle. My teeth chattered as it juddered through my body while, far below— past nets and bridges—soldiers with their lights had reached Zone Five! White water churned.

But Ghulzar was *still* here, swaying from his one-handed grip on the outer bar. Blood sheeted his stomach and legs and the heads of three Rath that dangled off him like white kelp. I watched him strain against their weight.

Two out of three leapt to his shoulders—that broke his grip. They shrank away, down through the Hub.

I yelled and punched the axle.

Ghulzar was gone.

Below, the battle on Zone Five was now a cauldron of churning. Arte-III's floodgate was open. But two out of three sub-valves were closed, meaning that the ruptured segment was channelling almost all of the current we'd released. Could that hold?

As I thought it, two—three—*six* more Rath hopped into view not far below me. No one to fight for me this time. If I didn't find a way to get off the arterial right now, then I'd be trapped here at the ceiling and they'd have me.

Something exploded. Far below, a massive rivet from a girder burst free and struck a vertical feeder. Water gushed out in a spout that broke the battle on the bridge, thrusting both men and Rath away. The girder *had* started to fail: from here I could even make out the row of jets shooting from its sides. If it collapsed, there'd be no way to flood the Rath out through its haemorrhage! My wrist was burning . . .

I glanced to the Ratheine climbers. One took a bolt in the back. It fell, taking another down behind it. But at least a dozen more of them coated the arterial's sides, coming for me. I looked to the south wall: someone was yelling between the shots he was firing. Ammunition he was wasting to protect me, I knew: 'Get out, boy! Out *now!*' It was Plamen.

My wrist was *burning* . . .

Two of the climbers had been shot, but kept on climbing. Plamen lowered his crossbow and waved his free arm towards me. The Hub was now a storm of clashing steel, straining iron, churning water. And still the pressure *must* increase—I had to flush out any more and I *could* do it.

My wrist was on fire!

I hadn't understood Plamen's warning. The single Rath above me grabbed my swathes and hauled me up above the mains wheel—throat in its hands, face at its *mouth!*—beyond all range of crossbows at this height. Pulling against the monstrous strength of its arms, I ripped my swathes at the collar. That freed my neck and while white claws swiped to regain me, one of my swathe-frogs came unhooked. The cloak went loose. I dropped and, falling, struck the lever on my wrist.

The blaze broke free.

It whirled and swooped, lighting the ceiling—

—and vanished.

What, *where?* These weren't the same gills.

A spout of water erupted. Still through the Sight, above me now, I saw the battle raging close. Right below, the roiling, churning, rising water of the flood. Rath in that water, still more coming. I was nowhere near the ceiling anymore, but all the way down on Zone Five, gripping the gills of Arte-I in a steady spray. The Disc had moved me! *Again!*

I jammed the lever, cut the Sight. Swathes gone, my hair and shirt were soaked, stuck to my skin. How had I even known to *hold* these gills?

No time for that. Arte-I was rocking with the pressure that I'd siphoned, while Arte-III had never stopped its massive quaking at the surge it couldn't take. Its new girder was a ring of leaking fountains; the seething surface of the floodwater, rising fast, telling of the volumes being forced up through its second breach.

And *still* my wrist was burning.

The Rath were in their hundreds, thronging for the nets and scaling sides of bigger pipes to pick off soldiers. Vortans were hurled into the water, some by the Rath, some blown from ladders by the jets.

'Fall back to the second bridge!' shouted Plamen from somewhere in the madness. 'Crossbows on the walls—only the walls!' I spotted his white mantle as he ran across a higher bridge. It was a strangely distant thought that I was simply too far down to get out now; I'd die in here. But I could *still* increase that pressure.

I'd never get back up to the Mains, but just a little more strain on Arte-III from lower circuits might be enough to make the haemorrhage impassable. The sub-gauge of Arte-I was only a short distance above me. I climbed for it, squared up and pulled its levers out. Against my body, Arte-I's vibrations went still and its row of leaks stopped altogether; while behind me Arte-III's groan became a roar. I looked over my shoulder and saw it shake with such a force that Rath were thrown off its flanks.

Then its new girder cracked in half, more iron rivets shooting wide, white fonts of water bursting out. The green wall started to tremble.

And then the column was free-standing. Leaning away.

No, no, no, *no* . . .

'It's giving way!' shouted Plamen. *'Fall back! Back into the Deep!'* At his command, the soldiers turned and climbed and ran for closest tunnels. I watched through spray as, from the bridge where he was standing, Plamen met my eyes. *'Leave the dead and fall back!'*

The column buckled. My body seized and I cried out at the scream of tearing metal, then watched in frozen horror as its feeders snapped like twigs. Bodies fell through the shower of water and metal.

'Look out!'

Another shape was coming down—a ceiling buttress. I threw myself flat between the gauge levers as the massive piece of ancient green masonry hit Zone Two's bridge and broke the line of retreat. As it smashed through lesser laterals and plunged into the water, even huger iron rivets followed it down like metal hail. One split a rope net and sent a clutch of clinging Rath swinging across the Hub's diameter like a long string of garlic. Arte-III groaned past the stone bridge by mere feet, then screeched its way down Zone Two's bridge towards the webwork of cables at the centre, sure to snap or rip them clean out of their anchors.

Another rivet flew from somewhere, spinning straight towards my head, and struck Arte-I as I ducked.

Water blasted me clear—the rivet chased me as I fell.

I gripped my wrist.

TWENTY-ONE

FLAMES

'Little spark . . .'

The voice was thin, like that of a starved man in the cold outside the window. A foggy face loomed at the pane, one finger tapping at the glass.

Glass?

'Come, little spark.' I sensed my body, heard the fire and felt the heat on my skin. Someone was moving near my head. *The voice faded, the foggy face drawing away . . .* another moving into view. Plamen's face. He looked down on me for just a moment, then stepped away and out of sight.

Wherever I was, there was an acrid smell here and sound of shuffling coals. Dragging my mind out of the darkness, I blinked to focus, turned my head. I lay on raised brickwork somewhere in the Deep; the furnace rooms, I guessed, from the roar of flames I could hear through a nearby arch. The High Commander stood feet away, next to a body. I looked at the face of the body, the branded shoulder and broken spearhead still lodged under the ribs. Massive hammer on the floor.

'Wha—' I started, sitting up, but my throat was totally dry and my 'what' turned into '*water?*' Plamen brought me a skin and I drained it, panting between gulps. 'What happened?'

'It's over.'

'How?'

He reached to take the empty skin back and slid it into his mantle. 'Flooded out,' he answered, 'by the pipe you destroyed. Its current filled the Hub Chamber to just below the third zone, then stopped. We're still fishing bodies from the water.'

The memory of the last thing I'd seen surged back at me— the terrific collapse of Arterial-III—and at the thought of the Builders' ancient pipeworks in ruins, halfway flooded, my body tensed all over. 'Are they dead now, the Rath?'

But Plamen didn't answer me. Not until I looked him in the eye. 'The last of those to have entered were shot down in the access tunnels. I now have both tunnels guarded. Should further numbers arise from the broken arterial, they will be seen and dispatched as they surface.' Always so calm. Even now.

'But how . . .' I started, 'how'd I get out?'

As I asked it, I felt what was missing from my wrist, and knew the answer. He raised the torque. 'Perhaps you'd be so good as to tell *me*.'

It wasn't his to know about. Just wasn't. If there was anyone who *should* know . . . '*Rusper!*' I blurted. 'Caliph Symphin I mean—where is he? Is he alive?'

'He is alive.'

'Is he alright?'

'Not altogether.'

'But,' I stammered, 'I don't get . . . how long have I been here?'

He drew a breath. 'It's been three hours. Time enough for the Sanhedrin to convene at emergency notice.'

'Without the Viceroy?'

His eyes widened, slightly. 'He was unfit to attend.'

'I have to talk to him. *Right now,*' I pressed, not even sure why I had to. For what I'd done to the central pipeworks, Rusper Symphin would probably dismiss me from his service. Maybe worse. This was Vorth.

'And so you will,' Plamen said, 'when you have spoken to me.'

I could lie, I supposed, but what good would it do? He would know, he'd find out. He was like that, Plamen. Now he was holding the torque in both hands, at chest level.

'We don't know,' I said small.

'You don't fool me.' So much for that. 'Symphin assigned you the task of discovering what properties it holds, did he not? So then, report. What have you found?'

Eyes on his boots, I ground my teeth. I'd not even had the chance to tell Rusper. No, that wasn't true: I'd had the chance and not taken it. I'd kept it secret from him. Because of that, the High Commander was going to know of it first. And yet, I supposed, had it not been for Plamen—his decision to trust me after all, and send his troops—I'd be dead. He *had* done that.

I owed him something.

'When I . . . touch it,' I said, deliberately slowly, 'it shows me . . . things. Lets me see into places.'

'As does common triglycerate.'

'Not like that,' I rebutted. '*Through* things. Through walls and floors and . . . everything. Anything. I think. When I touch it, I can see it inside my head, like in a dream. But not really a dream. Like a . . .' I huffed. 'It's hard to explain. I just have to look, but with my eyes closed. That's how I found the second hole in Arterial-III, the one the Rath got in through.'

'Which would have been more useful before they did,' he remarked. Not much arguing with that, even though I knew I had tried to convince him before I'd found it.

'Look, I know how it sounds.'

'What else?' he said.

I took a breath; this part was harder. 'It moves me,' I said. 'White light, like a flash, comes out sometimes, from the mirror. I think it's dangerous and can kill things, but then sometimes it makes me disappear and appear again somewhere different. I can't control it, I don't know how yet, but it happened in the Hub.'

'When?'

I thought back, pulling shreds out of the chaos of the attack, and realised that I'd known the answer for a while. 'When I was in danger,' I said. More to myself.

Had he heard me? If he hadn't, he didn't ask me to repeat it. Instead he opened the lion-faced lid of the torque I'd fashioned and looked in, curling his lip as if unimpressed by what he saw. It made me angry.

'You saw it!'

My temper didn't rouse him. Stoic as marble, he put a finger to the metal and stroked the mirror. Testing. Nothing happened. Then he raised it to his face, just as he had in the Captain's office that day and, for a moment, I thought he was going to keep it again. Would he do that?

His eyes slid back to me in the mirror; those pale grey bubbles. 'Considering the ease with which the Rath navigated the city's waterworks, it's clear their kind are able swimmers. As such, they are not dead because they drowned in pipe-water.'

I held still.

'As the arterial collapsed, you—or *this*—released something into the floodwater that killed everything in it. Including many of my men.'

I remembered the falling buttress, how it had smashed into the bridge; how an explosion of water from a flying iron rivet had thrown me off Arterial-I; how I'd opened the torque even as I fell towards the water. And I remembered, through the chaos, that glimpse of Plamen. 'You left me.'

He raised his chin. 'You fell at least fifty feet. The decisions of a commander concern the men he has alive, not the dying or the dead.'

'But I'm not dead.'

'Nor are you a man. Let it not be forgotten that men, vortans, *Vedans*, died because of this.'

He walked away from me again; this time to cover the dead body with a length of hessian.

'Ghulzar's dead?' I said, but knew.

'As you see.'

'He was a soldier, wasn't he?'

'Once, yes. Rank of *marzhal*, a field-officer of the Laudassan Regiment.'

'He died protecting me.'

'Protecting Vorth.' Plamen walked back. 'You should also be dead, child. Yet there you were, alive, in the foundry after my troops retreated. How did you get there?'

'I told you. The Disc, it moves me. That's all I know, I promise.'

A lie. The voice in my head, and the ghost, were still unmentioned. My secret. And that was how I meant to keep them.

'The *disc*,' sneered Plamen, looking down at it again, almost amused. 'The dwarf calls it magic.'

So Hetch had made his report. Some kind of report, anyway.

'Might be,' I shrugged.

With a snort, Plamen shook his head. 'And I thought that I'd been clear when I warned you to keep your people away from the centre of attention. Now again you leap into it yourself.'

'I'm doing nothing!'

Face darting up, he took one step closer to me. 'Acts of national defence do not amount to *nothing*,' he said, intoning the last word like a blade of air.

Tears I didn't understand tightened up my throat; I swallowed them. 'I was just trying to—'

'What you *did*,' he spoke over me, 'was cut off enemy access. Effecting the collapse of that arterial prevented greater numbers from infiltrating the Deep. Without the backwash it caused, Rath could have reached the city surface.'

'What are you saying?'

'What I am saying, *ekhin* Flint, is that High Command can no more deny the merit of your actions in the Hub, than the gratitude owed by Antissa.' I frowned as I tried to work out if he was chiding or thanking me. Gratitude? Shocked by the praise, if praise was what it really *was*, I didn't know what to say. He gave a nod I hadn't seen from him before, a slow bowing of the neck, and snapped the torque's lid shut again. He flung it into my lap. 'Tread lightly, child.'

I swallowed hard. 'I'm sorry.'

'For what.'

'For what I did, if it destroyed Arterial-III.'

'It didn't,' he told me flatly. 'Not entirely.'

'But it fell.'

'Yes, it did fall. But something at the centre of the Hub broke its fall. A vane of cables or some such.'

My jaw went slack. 'The *polymer?*'

His shrug was the slightest I'd ever seen, but I didn't need him to confirm it. The Guild, I knew, had tried to stretch and even cut those strange black cords that we had found right in the centre of Zone Two. Attempts had failed. And yet to think that they had somehow borne the weight of an arterial . . . 'Can I speak to Caliph Symphin?'

'He is with the physician.' Plamen pointed to a bundle near my feet. Of course my sandals were gone. *Another* pair. But someone, somehow, had saved my swathes. 'Don them,' he said.

'They're wet.'

'They'll dry.'

Trying to forget what I'd just been forced to tell him, I put my swathes on and returned the torque to my left forearm. The swathes were only a little damp, but I came through the arch tugging at the collar where the Rath had ripped it wide open. I limped a bit from the bite on my heel, and there was a long slice on my right leg I didn't even remember having happened. It was bleeding, but only a little, and strangely didn't hurt at all, but I still flinched as I remembered that one had had me in its grip. Had me again.

Furnaces raged everywhere, their heat prickling my skin. Near the middle of the rooms, a heap of Ratheine garments and scraps was growing higher. The smiths and sappers dripped as they worked, faces contorted as they stripped the dead white bodies to their flesh. I saw heads lolling and limbs flapping and what looked like the flash of a satisfied smile. The naked Rath were then hauled from the floor to the flames where they crackled and burned. The smell they gave off was horrible; a bit like pork frying in a pan but so much fouler. I gagged, and Plamen shot me a look as if I'd sworn under my breath.

'High Commander!' One of the smiths surged through the hell towards us, dashing the sweat from his face. 'There's bodies here you should see, sir.'

I held my breath. 'I don't want to see them.'

'You should have thought of that before you stepped up to save the city,' said Plamen and strode after the smith. I bowed from the heat of the furnaces and followed him to a table draped with canvas. Back stiff, I put the dance of corpses behind me, only to find myself almost cowering when the canvas flew back. Plamen shifted a bit too.

Four bodies lay on the table; arms at their sides and legs apart. To repel the stink, I forced the air out through my nose. Flies droned and settled on the bodies, though I couldn't think how they had even found their way down here at all.

'Women,' said Plamen. His eyes flashed at the smith.

'That's right, sir. Just these four for now, sir, but we're still dredging from the Hub, sir. May be others, sir.'

'No doubt.' He circled the table, examining. These Rath were smaller and, without that jutting collarbone, also flat-chested. Their skins, now dulled from chalky white, revealed a layer of translucence with only blotches of brighter pigment. Veins stood out black under the surface of the flesh, like dribbled ink. I watched, disgusted, as Plamen handled one of their feet, parting the toes. There was some webbing between them; the same not true of the fingers. As for those blue and purple markings, the water hadn't washed them off. Never more detailed than two or three concave score-lines, they weren't war-paints, as I'd thought, but finely sunken tattoos.

It annoyed me that I found it so hard to look at them like this. They had taken away from me the people I loved; why should I fear seeing them dead, gutted and naked on a table? Why should I care about the dignity they'd had while still alive? The High Commander didn't care and that was right. The Rath were monsters. Yet he'd said "women," not *females*. That was strange.

He gripped a lower jaw, widening a mouth already open. He studied teeth. Sickly, I admired him; touching that face even as its dead eyes bulged back from purple sockets. I dared a small step closer and tried to be as brave as he was; turn my disgust into . . .

No ears, there was that. Where the ear should have been was a weal of chitinous scar tissue. Wondering why, I swallowed my revulsion and laid a hand on its skin. Rubbery, cold. I peeled a sticky clump of hair away from the eyes, then nose, small mouth. Throat slit, gash clean. The body beside it had three crossbow bolts in its stomach. These were the wounds that had killed them.

Or were they? The white blaze from the Disc had killed all that had been in the water, that's what Plamen had said, and I almost felt sick to think how many Vedish soldiers that had been. I'd opened the torque and released the blaze—that had been *me*. So, if the Rath had been killed by its power in that moment, then I'd killed the soldiers as well. And Plamen *knew* that I had.

Just then, he pulled something that snapped: from one of their necks, a strip of tackle or something. He tossed it over to me and I caught it in a clap. 'For your services.'

It wasn't tackle. The cord was twisted from thin strands of dried-out seaweed. Crude charms were looped over the strands; the figure of a man whittled crudely out of deadwood, a strip of hide, a small crab's carapace.

Monsters . . .

I wasn't sure if, in the gift, Plamen was mocking me some-how, but still I pocketed the necklace. Now he turned towards the foundryman. 'Burn these bodies with the rest.'

Another voice hailed the Commander. A new group had arrived, bearing a body.

'Those are martial colours,' Plamen said as he moved to meet the vortan soldiers.

I ran around him to see what he was talking about, but could *smell* it. The chrozite. 'That's him,' I said. They tumbled the phantom's body onto the floor, the ruined head landing close to my bare feet. I didn't jump, or even move, transfixed by the mess of its face. By now, Plamen would have heard exactly what had taken place out on the wall, but the effect of Rusper's fusil was a sight in itself: a morass of bone and blood and leather, all collapsed into the crater. Shattered teeth in half a jaw. I wondered how well Plamen had known Artabh Kathris, the man whose garments the creature wore, but his face gave no clue.

'Sir, the weapon,' said a vortan, offering the Commander the shortsword, hilt first, and taking a step back. Plamen took it and lifted its edge into the light. Blood marked the blade. Kereth and Gareth, and Arras. Some of that blood would be theirs.

Plamen seemed to consider for a while. Then, 'Part the remains from the cloak and garments, and any other article taken from the Artabh. Clean this sword. Send it all to his family.' He returned the shortsword and regarded the smith. 'Another for the pyre.'

A troubled look crossed the vortan's face. 'What do we tell the family, *ekharan?* There's no body.'

'Death in service to the Satrap.'

Even I knew that for a lie. However Kathris had died—if he *was* dead—it hadn't been in obedience to royal wishes. If the Satrap had known about the party he'd led, or anything at all about Rusper's scouts in the desert, sentence may well have been passed that would have brought a far worse death. Now the vortans knelt around the phantom's body. One pulled a boot off, dropping the foot.

The foot was wrong.

Plamen was leaving, but he turned back at the exit. 'Boy.' Ignoring his impatience, I hurried around the ring of focused vortans and peered at the foot between their shoulders. Chalk white, but wrong. 'Wait,' I said.

Soldiers glared at me, a child who'd dared to speak to them. 'Back off,' one said. I ignored him too.

'Spread the toes,' I said. 'Please. Could you spread the toes.'

The vortan huffed as he indulged me; pinched the big and second toe and parted them.

No webbing. We'd just assumed.

'High Commander!' I called.

The vortans stood and made way as Plamen came back and crouched beside me. He studied the foot for himself, then looked up the body to the face. There was no use in trying to peel bits of that mask from the flesh. Instead, he lifted up a hand and turned it over, felt its palm. I could see its stiffness, hear its texture: withered, rough and sandy. Standing and pulling me away, he told them: 'Strip it.'

The second boot was pulled. The cloak was unclasped and pried free from the gangly shoulders, the hood removed in tatters. That gone, the mask was found to reach as far back as the temples. Disintegrating as it came, it freed an unexpected mass of ratty, charcoal-coloured hair. Even the skull was somehow wrong, strange yet familiar at once. And with an ear on each side.

While they cut the garments, a hiss came from behind us in the beds of the furnaces. The first female body was rolled onto its pyre, exciting sparks. The flames claimed it almost completely before I could see any Ratheine flesh curl off bones. Inside the pocket of my swathes, I toyed with the necklace of charms.

It lay there naked now, the phantom. Though it was sleek, the skin all over was grey and sallow and dry, and the body's shape utterly different from both Ratheine sexes. Not only had it a full head of hair; the arms and legs had hair too. No pronounced, jutting collarbone. No blue tattoos. No ink-black veins. Plamen spiralled his finger; the men rolled the body to expose a grey canvas of back, broken only by a scattering of warts, but no scars: battle or lash. I looked at the vortans, who seemed almost to relax at the sight. 'It's not Kathris,' one of them said in a quiet voice, but he sounded sure of it.

'Nor any other of his party. Too thin. And the hair . . .'

'Something's wrong with that skin.'

'Can't be a vortan, or any soldier,' said a third. 'Where's his battalion brandmark?'

'Not a Vedan soldier, at least.'

'Perhaps not,' Plamen said, 'but neither is it Ratheine.' For the first time since I'd woken, his grey eyes looked uneasy. 'This is a human body.'

The lamp-flame wafted, but drew no reaction from him. Not a blink. I stood next to the High Commander and watched while the man who so often chided me for letting my mouth simply hang open, did the same. The hardened cleverness was missing. He looked both childlike and ancient; each crevice deepened in his face, including those around the burn that ran from his left eye to his jaw. Now it glistened with unguent. He was sweating and his hair looked a lot worse than mine did.

The lamp jerked sideways, dragging the flame, but the head tilt came late. 'No,' the physician said as if correcting a pupil. 'Pretending will not help you, Caliph Symphin.'

Rusper made a fist. 'I wasn't pretending. I saw something.' Between their faces at the desk of the Viceroy's quarters, the night was purple-blue.

'What did you see?'

Rusper leaned forward. '*A light.*'

The gowned physician set the lamp in its dish, excusing himself, and approached the High Commander.

'Improvement?' said Plamen.

The man's smile was rueful. 'I've been repeating this for more than two hours, *ekharan*. It seems unlikely to pass. The Viceroy's blindness—'

'Temporary.' This from Rusper. 'I can hear you, Khalyl. And I'm not blind. I can see the lamp's flame, as I said. Vaguely, in blurs.'

Turning back, the young physician called Khalyl spoke with gracious indulgence. 'Viceroy, the chemical from your weapon has caused much damage.'

'Chrozite,' snapped Rusper. 'It burned my face, don't you see. Nothing got into my eyes, only light!'

'That may not be true.'

'*Just . . . !*' He batted for the lamp. Khalyl hurried back to slide it away from his fingers, then scooped it up himself and returned to his seat. At the creak in his chair Rusper seemed to relax a little bit. There was a tray of food there as well, but it hadn't been touched. 'Plamen, report.'

Plamen reported. As he spoke, I watched him closely; now seeing more than a leader, but a soldier who could and would fight for his country.

'The Sanhedrin is uneasy. The viziers, for the most part, wished an explanation of events. That and some assurance that the fortress stands firm. Having led the defence, I was able to put most of their immediate fears to rest. Furthermore, as vortans of the Fortress Regiment alone were called upon, the Caliphs Arif and Omran presented little difficulty.'

The way Rusper stared in another direction unnerved me. Plamen paused, then added a little more discreetly: 'Your own participation at the wall has won acclaim.'

'What did you say of my sight?'

'Only that injuries were sustained in confrontation with the scout. Such was necessary to justify your absence from council. Nevertheless, there is regard for your courage.'

'Fine.'

I almost smiled at Rusper's disinterest in that fact, but stopped myself as the physician glanced at me.

'Vizier Dranz was outspoken,' Plamen continued. 'He called the attack a blatant affront to the throne and maligns the Viceroyalty as entirely to blame. Further, he maintains that your duty as Viceroy outweighs your afflictions at this time.'

Rusper made a sound in his nose. 'He'd be right if I wasn't —' But he must have felt Khalyl's expectant look.

'Ramed supports him,' added Plamen.

'Course he does, the sycophant!'

'As for what took place on the northwest wall, the assailant appears to have acted as a decoy, disguised in the garb of the missing Artabh Kathris to pass the gates.'

Rusper nodded, 'The boy was right.'

I tensed at that but said nothing. Did he know I was in the room?

Plamen relayed what we'd discovered of the phantom's body: that the intruder was not Ratheine, but human. Rusper's expression was hard to read. 'So who was it?'

'Hard to tell. Your weapon did not leave much of his face for inspection.'

'Nor your own, near enough,' Khalyl said boldly.

Rusper slapped the desk. 'Peace!'

'Your pardon, *ekharan*.' Even from the sightless glare, Khalyl bowed his head.

'There were questions,' said Plamen, 'only naturally there were questions, as to how such an intruder might have entered the city at all. I have not divulged that he was human, and maintained that the Rath scout used the same means of entry as the Ratheine force that followed. The breach in the central pipeworks.'

'Agreed. Can't have them thinking he walked straight in through the gate. What of the attack?'

'Regrettably, Viceroy, word of damage to the Hub spread too quickly through the echelons of the viziership for those details to be altered, though I did my utmost to cause no undue alarm in confirming them. A Ratheine force gained entry to the Hub Chamber via a second, heretofore *undiscovered* haemorrhage, and that force exterminated by troops already present there.'

A lie.

Plamen looked at me, seeming to acknowledge the thought, before saying, 'The Sanhedrin is fully briefed in our losses.'

'Which are?'

'Forty-nine vortans of the First and Second Battalions. Six guardsmen. Four watchmen. One foundryman.'

'Who?'

'The metalsmith, Ghulzar.'

Rusper deflated. 'Civilians?'

'None.'

'What of the Ratheine poison?' As Rusper asked that, my eyes shot to Plamen's face, then my own gashed leg. I'd forgotten that!

'In that,' Plamen replied, 'it seems we have been somewhat fortunate. Thus far, no wounds have showed signs of the poison. So it may be that whatever Ratheine spears *were* touched with it before, were cleansed by their time in the water.'

'That is most fortunate, yes.' But Rusper's tone was hollow. 'And Arterial-III?'

'Its collapse was attributed to the attack, as we earlier agreed.'

'*What?*' I blurted. Plamen winced.

Rusper's head bobbed towards me—'Thought that was you'—but Plamen drew my eyes to his and raised a finger to his lips; some fragile moments passing before I understood what he was trying to tell me.

They'd spoken already, Viceroy and aide; Plamen having taken full responsibility for what I'd done in that chamber. Another secret to keep, but another secret that made sense. He might persuade the Sanhedrin that the collapse had been down to some structural flaw, but not the Chief Engineer. And so my actions would be *his* now. Saviour of Antissa or destroyer of her pipeworks, Rusper was not to know how great a part I had played in our defence. And it was all because Plamen was playing by the rules that he had set. Protect my people from attention. And so protect Rusper Symphin.

Rusper's eyes were somewhere else, but his attention still on me. 'You were there, I understand.'

'You ordered me to the pipes,' I answered him.

He was corpse-like. 'I did.'

'But I got out just in time. Thanks to the High Commander.'

'So I see. Or at least . . .'

A boot kicked the door inward. I backed against the wooden bureau, as much from fright as from the flash of blue-and-white that entered. We'd left the door slightly ajar, and now a Shieldman strode in.

'Who *is* that?' cracked Rusper.

But Plamen spoke over him: 'Steady, Jharis.'

The Iron Shield Lieutenant didn't look at the Commander, but locked eyes straight on the Viceroy. Like a prize, he sized him up, then stopped and smirked behind Plamen, not removing his helm. I grappled for my hood but the collar's rip meant that it wouldn't hide my face properly. Instead, I lowered my chin and stood still.

Rusper firmed his expression but also turned his face aside. 'What is your business here, Lieutenant?'

'The Senera Amyra,' announced Jharis, 'to speak with you, Honorary Caliph.'

Dread filled my veins.

Rusper stood abruptly, waving a hand at Khalyl. 'Assist me.' But as he said it, he scraped his chair and fell against the physician, bringing their faces close. When I saw his lips move in that moment, I hoped that Jharis hadn't too. Khalyl walked Rusper over to the chair at the triglycerate oven where the older man eased into the sheepskin.

'Hood away!' Jharis snarled at me.

'Stand down,' said Plamen. But I'd obeyed, and meeting Jharis' eyes, knew he remembered me just fine.

Then a sweet voice: 'Heed him, Jharis.'

Skirt-tails snaked across the threshold, her hips seeming to roll on well-oiled wheels. She wore the skin of the desert, it seemed; a silky sheath of tan fabric that ascended to a bodice of lake-green gems. Every part of her body seemed impossibly perfect: those slender branches of her arms, her olive back, coal-painted eyebrows and lips, the treacle sculpture of her braids that crowned it all; today styled almost flat to her head like a helm of spirals. And yet she'd killed. Murdered her husband, the most trusted of the Satrap. This woman *was* the Iron Shield.

'*Sinarre*,' said Rusper. 'A less than precedented call. To what do I owe it?'

'My sympathies,' she said. 'Only too naturally, *ekharan*. And, of course, my commendations for your brave deeds upon the wall. Such national zeal for a man of your . . . extraction. And indeed, for your years, such fortitude and spirit! Such . . . oh, what is the word? It's on the tip of my tongue.' Her voice was light and bright and buoyant, and her Vedish accent highly refined. And though she faced away from me, I could still hear that she was smiling. 'Mettle,' she said.

Facing the oven, Rusper's body didn't move in his chair. 'Neither sympathies nor commendations are needed,' he said. Amyra looked at Plamen for a moment, and he stared back at her, unmoving.

'Nevertheless, Honorary Caliph, it would appear that your hand grows less than steady over affairs. Not only has the city fallen under direct Ratheine attack, but you failed to appear at the Sanhedrin's assembly. An unhappy oversight, would you not agree.'

'The High Commander was briefed,' said Rusper.

The physician cleared his throat. 'The Viceroy's injuries are no small matter, *sinarre*.'

'Indeed,' replied the woman without a glance in his direction. 'Seated in the presence of our betters, are we, doctor.'

Khalyl stood up.

'Sit down,' said Rusper at the fall of his chair. Khalyl was left awkwardly wavering between two wills before he submitted to the highest, and sat down. Amyra rewarded his decision with a smile I saw one side of, then raised her finely pencilled eyebrows.

'I wonder,' she cooed, 'if the Honorary Caliph, in his eminent capacity as Chief Engineer of this city, might be so good as to indulge a point of lay curiosity.' She paused, for three seconds exactly. 'How is it possible—if you'll forgive me—for a feral, spear-wielding race a thousand years behind our craft, to penetrate a pipe wrought of solid iron?' There was another, shorter, pause as she leaned her head towards Plamen. 'What were the precise words used in council . . . ?'

Jharis answered: '*Torn wide from within*.'

The next silence was like the one I'd heard in council that day, when she had laughed. Rusper, in his chair, was motionless. Plamen didn't move either, nor the physician, or even Jharis. Though it tasted sour to admit, I quickly realised, it was a fair—a *good*—question. How had they done it? Did we *have* an answer?

Skirt-tails rustled again as Amyra took a step nearer Rusper's chair. 'Will you not look at me, *ekharan?*' she purred, almost coy. This one *wasn't* a question.

Rusper's head tilted, face too low to meet her eyes anyway. He growled, 'You are uninvited. You march your strongarm into my quarters and show rudeness to my servants. Do not dare to make demands of courtesy here.'

My eye slipped to Plamen: I thought he'd moved, but maybe not. I was primed, as the silence stretched coolly, for almost anything to happen.

When Amyra spoke again, her voice was harder. Colder. Her true voice, I suspected. 'His Majesty the Satrap demands a report.'

'He will receive one,' said Rusper.

'Directly,' said Jharis.

Amyra looked to her officer and then back to the Viceroy. 'My Lieutenant was present in the tower when the Rath attacked your Deep, Symphin. It may interest you to know that at the sound of the alarum, the Satrap grew most frightfully distressed. A most *harrowing* scene, I'm informed, the full count of his physicians required to restrain him in his torment, as well as potent tonics for the fevers. Such a mercy, he has slept.' She wrung her hands in some gesture. 'But now he wakens, *ekharan*, and calls you to attend him.'

'And as I've said, he will receive me,' repeated Rusper, showing teeth.

My mind was churning like the water that had flooded the Hub just hours ago. Lieutenant Jharis was allowed in the tower of the Satrap, but not her. Not Amyra. The Iron Shield was the Satrap's personal guard, and it was Vizier Zimran who was the true head of that order. Vizier Zimran who was dead, though no one *knew* it. How much was really going on here?

Jharis was looking almost as pleased with himself as when he'd sentenced my finger. 'Thankfully the sedation is one of our strongest Eredian medicinals,' he said. 'Nevertheless, it will subside.'

'And His Majesty's physicians will no doubt be close at hand when it does,' Rusper retaliated in a voice full of acid. 'I trust that's all.'

'For a time.' Amyra's voice was sweet again; thick with honey.

'Then good evening, *sinarre*.'

'Honorary Caliph. High Commander.'

She gathered her skirt. Her slender face, rounding into view, knocked my eyes straight back to the floor. I wasn't sure that she'd marked or even seen me standing there, but I'd seen the smile and it stayed inked into my mind as those skirts whispered past me to the door. She *knew*.

Jharis followed her out; Plamen closed the door, securely. In the chilly, seeping silence, I stepped away from the bureau, while a grey-faced Rusper rose out of the sheepskin. Khalyl took him by the arm and helped him back to the desk. My heart sank at the sound of his voice: 'Plamen.'

'Viceroy.'

'You must go to the Satrap.' His mouth was making the words, but he wasn't fully in them. 'I can't face him.'

'And if your sight does not return?'

'It will return.'

The Commander and physician exchanged the glance of half a second. 'If you'll permit me,' Plamen broached, and Rusper weakly waved a hand, 'I should strongly advise against attempting to conceal this mischance. Announce to the Sanhedrin that you are blind. Tell them—'

'Tell them *what*, that I'm now unable to perform the most basic duties of a Guildsman?'

'For the most part, the viziers applaud your courage. True perhaps, neither your courage nor their sympathy for such an affliction as blindness will buy you the allegiance of Dranz or Ramed. But you may yet placate such men.'

'And just how might that be done?'

'A compromise. Respond with our forces.'

Rusper's laugh was acerbic. 'So, not only should I flout royal decree, I should announce it in council.'

'Approach the First Circle,' pressed Plamen. 'Present the matter at hand as one of immediate urgency and threat.'

'It's what they want!' Rusper retorted. 'There is no *proper* manner in which to controvert the Satrap, Plamen. Only treason! You know this. Behind every vizier who would back a martial course are ten more waiting to hang me for it.'

'The people of the city are already on your side. They chant your name. If you persist in denying that we are at war, you will lose them. Especially now.'

'Royal orders deny that we're at war!'

'You must respond,' said Plamen firmly. 'The Rath have a route straight to the citadel. More than a hundred of our enemy have been in your Deep.'

'*I know that!*' Rusper swiped at the food tray. Missing, he dashed the lamp and dish onto the floor. His face flushed as red as the burn on his cheek and when Khalyl tried to calm him, his hand was flung away. 'I can't, Plamen. Cannot mobilise forces.'

'It may keep you in power.'

'It will put the power in *her* hands.'

My head was darting side-to-side, but the physician interrupted. 'Caliph Symphin, this exertion is unwise. Rest would be better. Eat something, please.'

'I'm not hungry,' said Rusper. 'Flint. Flint, is he still there? You hungry, boy?'

I was starving. 'Um . . .'

'There, take it, eat! It's getting cold. And hold your nose when you drink—the blood of our own now flows in our water!'

Arguing had put a rare crack in Plamen's calm, but now he'd sealed it. Seeming to give up his attempt to advise for the night, he took a breath. 'With your permission, then, I will take my report to the Satrap.'

Rusper flapped a hand at him. Without any further discussion, the High Commander left the room, not gone a second when Rusper rapped his knuckles on the desk. 'Come, again, with the lamp.'

Khalyl relit the wick and waved the flame. It was as if I wasn't even there. 'Caliph Symphin?' I said.

'What is it, boy.'

'Can I sleep . . . here tonight, please?'

I don't know what I expected. 'No, that won't do, Flint. You're a servant,' he said shortly.

'Only tonight. Because of, you know . . . in the Deep.'

'Use the service quarters then.'

'The—?'

'Goodnight.'

It felt wrong, taking his whole meal. So I only took half a loaf of sangak and a small handful of drupes. Then left him in peace with his physician and his blindness. From his quarters, I went to the terrace above the citadel gardens. Back to a pillar, face to the city, I ate the food.

Some servants passed. So did distracted viziers, obviously on their way to meet with other viziers and catastrophise about what had happened today. Could the Honorary Caliph still defend the fortress city of Antissa? Could the engineer-lord be trusted? Was this the beginning of the downfall of the nation of Vorth? I saw Caliph Omran, lost in his mutters as he shuffled along, and realised that I'd started to wonder those things too. Or was it just that he'd stung me then by sending me away? He had been hurt worse than me; I should forgive him, I knew.

He'd saved my life.

Antissa fought sleep, though stars were out bright and deep blue night embraced the city. Out there a humdrum filled the streets: men and their horses, wagon wheels, a woman singing, barking dogs. From somewhere in the Citizen District, chanting went up: '*Viceroy! Viceroy! Viceroy!*'

Out on the walls, torches touched braziers and they went up in towering flames. So high and strong those sandstone walls and yet what had they been good for? The Rath had cut straight to the heart, risen right from under us, and all I could think as I fought my own sleep was how long we had before they did it again. The thousands were out there, somewhere.

Though now I knew it wasn't poisoned, I was doing my best to keep from touching the open gash on my leg, which no one had bothered to ask about and I didn't care that they hadn't. The cut was deep, I thought, but had stopped bleeding, at least, under fragile, squamous clotting. But while it hadn't hurt at first, now it *did:* it hurt a lot. Trying not to focus on the pain, I let my fingers trace the lion-headed lid of the torque. A lot of people had died. The horrors of all the things I'd seen, the killing, blood and savage violence, skittered over my thoughts. Twice today I'd been just inches from my death.

As I pushed that thought away, I realised that I was staring at the lights of the North District; without even knowing it, trying to decide which of those lights was the warehouse lantern.

Other thoughts came on cue. My people would know, now, that we'd been under attack. But they wouldn't wonder where

I'd gone or what had happened to me. Those who had loved me were all dead, and now I couldn't even find Sarah or Erik's faces in my memory.

My eyelids drooped.

Night noises flowed like coloured wind and I tried to let them calm me; soothe some of the pain in my leg and take the place of all that fighting, blood and death. It would be wrong to go to sleep, but I could rest. Just for a while.

The eyelids won. The city sank; its hum of life left me alone. Silence spread with the darkness that lapped where dreams were meant to be.

And in that silence and that dark: *little spark* . . .

TWENTY-TWO

THE BOARD OF XIQOPIX

Zeek had left the note on my workbench that morning. It was in Plamen's handwriting, so the High Commander must have taken dictation from Rusper. Even so, the engineer had covered the list with his own smudged scribbles and circles. The last line read simply, "It should not have backfired." He'd also, clearly, meant to underline the word *backfired*, but had scored it out instead.

Now I stood on the scaffolds of the empty digging level. Only my lantern broke the darkness, but it didn't matter. There was nothing out there to aim at but rock and earth anyway. I'd fired two dozen stones of schot – four rounds from each fusil, as instructed – and now the weapons were hot. Not once had there been anything like the malfunction on the wall. A few splutters, when I'd not dusted off the barrel properly; two out-right misfires from overloading the capsules on the breech; but no backfires. Rusper's weapons all functioned well, and there were holes of my own now pocking the digging level walls. What had seemed at first like magic was now a tool in my hands.

My hands were slick inside their gloves, the mouthguard stifling my breathing and the goggle-strap beginning to pinch my scalp. But I was supposed to be *thorough:* another word Rusper had tried to underline.

So I made the checks he'd showed me: resecured the pyrites, decompressed the ignition mainspring and spun the spindle wheel three times in case the transmission chain was stuck. Then cleaned out the chrozite residue from the chamber and put the weapon in its case. One more to go.

Segment by segment, I assembled the largest of the weapons in his arsenal: the long and heavy "cannon-fusil" he'd hoped to test on the northwest wall. I hefted it into its frame. Barrel locked fast into the gunrest; breech screwed tight between the splines; chamber loaded, chrozite charged, main-spring engaged.

Pulling on the grips, I swung the arm of the jezail frame and presented the cannon to the darkness.

Aim—trigger.

The blast was smart, like a whip's crack, but so much louder. As the hammer struck the pyrites and sparked, lead ripped through gloom and smote the granite. Ratheine faces I'd imagined morphed back behind the showers of dust that drifted back.

Perfect.

Only three days after the attack, Antissa was still shaken to its core. Everywhere I went were furtive looks and nervous murmurs about siege; even in the citadel where people seemed so rattled off their bearings as to forget their normal business. The High Commander had made sure of a military presence on the walls, but rumours had travelled to the people of the city by now that the walls may not be where the Rath would be coming from at all.

Soldiers were also stationed in the Hub: at every hour, vortans on guard along the broken cantilevers. This was a better comfort to me, although the wreckage in that chamber was still a painful thing to look at. Half of the Hub was underwater. Arterial-III leaned across its breadth like a branchless, felled and bleeding tree, while scores of severed minor pipes dangled above the flood like splayed guts. Gashes in the green wall showed where the weight of Arte-III had ripped or snapped them away.

Only *Arterial-II* was untouched by the destruction, and since its few remaining feeders had been sealed off because of leaks, that channel had now become the city's only means of supply. The engineers had closed its routes of distribution in order to siphon output to reservoirs of the districts. Amazingly, it held the pressure – well enough, at any rate, to risk expanding its gauge. Rusper said that this was vital, since outgoing flow had to exceed the source supply to the mains. If it didn't, the flood would rise, spread to the Deep and have everything below its third level awash within a day.

The guilds' expansions to the city's aqueduct network were speedy. In less than two days, delivery lines had reached collection points of the North, Citizen and Mercantile Districts, with further conduits soon added to reach the upper Southeast too. This kept supply going, just about, but it was a shaky supply, and I could only imagine the chaos at the fringes of the North District, where wardens regulated fair ration to the people. Would there be enough?

And what about *my* people? If I could be sure of anything, their shelter's wardens would take the back of any queue for the essentials. And yet this wasn't fish or coal or oats or blankets. It was *water*.

So I kept a close eye on the refugee shelter's manifests, which I still couriered every day, just to be sure that their quota wasn't changed.

The metalsmiths were the spearhead of the emergency plan. I helped with the dispatch and transport of the aqueduct segments from their construction to assembly. At first, I was scared to show my face at their foundry at all, worried they would blame me for the death of their leader. Or that they should. But they didn't. I found no anger or hatred among them; just the same burly comfort in the glow of their work. They'd known him, I realised, and his military scorn for death. If anything burned behind their heat-blistered faces, it was pride.

Meanwhile, the workshop was tense. Manic in his efforts to restore functional capacity to the pipes, Rusper took fewer and fewer hours of sleep, and became scarce above-ground. The Sanhedrin hadn't convened since the attack, and even then he'd not attended. Nor would he see any of the anxious caliphs or viziers who vied to arrange audiences with him. Plamen took the brunt of their constant questions, but even his patience was wearing. I could hear it in his voice when he reminded the Viceroy of the drugs which kept the royal wrath from spilling; a fragile arrangement with Lieutenant Jharis that I didn't understand. Plamen himself had been received by the Satrap's tower once, in Rusper's place. His second visit was refused.

The fact was clear. While the Viceroy sat below the city, waiting for his sight to come back, a less than pleased or patient Satrap was up there, waiting for *him*.

Then, early on the fourth morning after the attack, Rusper persuaded the physician that his sight wasn't lost; not totally. Khalyl had come down to the Deep for *me* at first, having *eventually,* on someone's orders, tended the gash on my leg; stitched it together, salved and dressed it to prevent infection. There'd been no poison in the wound. Besides, he said, it wasn't the kind of wound a spear would inflict. A claw had done it, he said. He checked the stitches, changed the dressing and, once he'd finished, stood and watched as Rusper clearly demonstrated why he wasn't truly blind. With enough light and enough focus, it seemed, he could identify an array of objects set in front of him. He couldn't read or write, or draw, or find his way without a guide. Even when it came to the Transcripts and diagrams he knew like no other of the Guild, he couldn't tell any one page from another. Because of that, he couldn't hope to bring a true and detailed report before the Satrap. Not without revealing his blindness.

So, even more reluctantly than when he'd let me take the dangerous crawl into the Hub, he turned to me: 'I need your help, Flint.'

'Remember what we practiced?'

'Think so.'

'No, you don't *think*, Flint, not here, not now. Upon our entry?'

'I bow and put my back against the wall,' I replied. 'Saying nothing.'

'Why nothing?'

'Because I don't have a tongue.'

'Where are your eyes?'

'On my feet.'

'And your chin?'

'In my chest.'

'So it *hurts*,' he added sharply.

We were on the stairs of the fat tower, and I was leading the way. In his robes, Rusper was slow. I wore a pea-green tunic, long brown leggings, and shoes buffed to a shine. Real shoes this time, not sandals. More valiantly than ever, I'd tried to press down my hair but doubted it lay flat anymore. Under my arm were the parchments, and on my belt a flask of water. I didn't know what that was for. As for the Disc, it was far below us in the workshop, and I felt naked without it clasped onto my wrist. Fifty-seven, fifty-eight, fifty-nine . . . When had I started counting the steps?

Rusper continued: 'When you're required . . .?'

'You'll tap your chair. I bring the scrolls up to the table.'

'No!' he cracked, his voice like a lash at my ankles. 'What did I *say* about the table?'

'Too close, sorry,' I said. 'I should . . . present them at your shoulder, and never . . . never . . . stand forward of your chair.'

'That's better.'

Seventy-five, seventy-six . . . Leaning from ledges, sculpted beasts passed in and out of the view of arched windows: horses and lions and leopards and long-necked lizards with wings. When I stuck my head out and looked up the wall of the tower, I saw the line of great eagles that supported the top parapet on their wings. These were the true heights of Antissa, visible for leagues across the plains.

Rusper was panting behind me and yet somehow his stamina had never looked so formidable. One had only to follow him around the Deep for a day to know he was strong enough for this. Ninety-one, ninety-two . . .

'Take care to watch my hands and movements closely,' he was saying. 'Bring only the parchments I request. Listen always, but by no means appear to understand what is discussed. React to nothing but my signal. Do not speak to the physicians or to the royal valet. Avoid their eyes. Draw no attention to yourself. Do not cough, do not shuffle, do not scratch if you should itch. Touch nothing but those parchments.'

Just as I was wondering who was more nervous, him or me, he tripped on his robes and stumbled badly. I hopped back down and he didn't fight me when I helped him up. 'I think I've got it.'

Blank eyes pinned my shins. 'Let's hope we both have.'

Windows behind, the spiral dimmed. Its air grew close. At the very top was a room full of darting eyes and movements. In purple gowns and skullcaps, half a dozen royal physicians milled in and out of a narrow passage, exchanging decanters, cloths and trays. Another passage veered off left, almost secretly, while ahead was a very solid-looking door that bore the Mooncircle sigil, like a plug. As I straightened my back, Rusper made the hundred-and-forty-fourth step.

One of the purple gowns turned to show a face like dry persimmon. As he recognised the Viceroy, he went to the passage on the right and pulled a cord. Some moments later, the plug-door opened by a frugal crack and a younger face looked out. He looked at the physician, then at Rusper, then huffed and closed the door again. More moments passed. I watched the purple gowns moving about without a word, until the plug-door reopened. Now the young man stepped out, regarded me curtly, and nodded. The royal valet.

355

I nodded back. He glared in answer but then pushed the plug slightly wider open. That was my cue: I stepped away from the wall—Rusper following so close behind me that his babooshes clipped my heels—and curled into the room.

A round room. Of course. And large too, though dark and muddled with fancy furnishings. Rugs, throws, tapestries, latticed screens and patterned panels, an enormous bed. Blinded windows. The air was stuffy in here; it smelled of stale perfumes and camphor.

The valet cleared his throat, meaningfully, and I drove my eyes to the floor. Stepping forward, I bowed fast – although I'd seen no one to bow to – and quickly backed into the wall.

As Rusper stood right next to me, his breaths still laboured from the climb, the valet crossed the floor ahead. 'Your Majesty, if it please you, I present Symphin, Chief Engineer, Honorary Caliph of Antissa and your Viceroy,' he said in a thin monotone, before scuffling away out of the corner of my eye.

Taking a ragged breath, Rusper walked forward and out of sight, his footsteps immediately lost among the other sounds about the room. Chimes and trickling water. Pottering silver. A kind of warble. A muffled clatter, like beads falling on a bread-board. And the faint whistle of a kettle. No, a squeeze-box?

I dared to raise my head, just slightly, and there was Rusper on his knees.

'Worshipful greetings, most high *ekharan*,' he said in a voice I'd never heard him use with anyone before. 'Here before you, true and contrite, your humble servant would beg forgiveness for these four days of absence.'

Not a kettle. Not a squeeze-box. It was *breath*. From here, a latticed screen blocked my view to the breather. Even so, my fingers tightened around the parchments and I felt my thumb burst through a page. It was him: I was actually standing in *his* presence. The breath wheezed in and out behind the lattice divider. Again, beads clattered. I forced calm.

'Rise. Dust those knees,' the breather said to Rusper Symphin. Robes rustled.

And out of nowhere, suddenly, there was a peacock striding past me. Even in the gloom, its lustrous tail-feathers glistened emerald-green.

Again, the wheeze became a voice: 'So. My Shield was mistaken. You can't imagine my relief.'

'Mistaken, sire?' said Rusper.

'Their daft report seemed to suggest that you were hiding.'

'Ah.' A pause. 'No, indeed.' Rusper coughed. 'Allow me to assure you, Majesty, that it was solely due to the demands of civic administration with which I am charged that I could not earlier attend this audience. A great many matters required most urgent attention. I can only trust that the report with which I dispatched *ekhar* Plamen served to allay some of my Satrap's most pressing concerns.'

'Alas not.' A stiff silence. Or it would have been without the warbling of the peacock and other sounds. 'I've little love for the Commander. On his last visit, do you know, he refused every treat I proffered. Rudely.'

'He can be brusque,' Rusper said.

'Brusque!' piped the wheeze. 'The man's a schrod of dry fish. Would it break his face to smile upon occasion?'

'I should beg your grace on his behalf. He means only to honour your Majesty, I am well assured of it, *ekharan*.'

'So I should hope.' The wheezing voice wasn't king-like. Rather it was the voice of someone old and frail living in an edge-of-town cottage, sorely disappointed at how seldom his grandchildren came to visit him. Beads clattered again and the peacock gave a louder warble. And then the wheeze gasped, 'Your *cheek!*'

'Merely an accident, *ekharan*, nothing more.'

'Accident—you're scarred!'

'As your Chief Engineer, sire, my industry will always have its dangers, I'm afraid.'

'Take greater care then, will you.' The beads clattered more fussily. 'If some catastrophe should befall my foremost royal engineer, what should become of our plans? And of the city, indeed?'

'You have me there, sire. And how is your Majesty's health, might I ask? *Ekharan* is markedly pale, it must be said. The headaches . . . ?'

Wheezing filled a pause. Beyond my view, someone shuffled. I looked up, slightly, to see if the valet had moved at all, but didn't think he had. There was someone *else* here, in the room. Behind the screens, near those blinded windows . . .

'They've gone,' replied the wheeze.

'What of the cramps?'

'Yes, gone also. But now my piss is going purple and I've another bad tooth.'

Rusper seemed to consider. 'If I may be so bold, sire, the colour of one's chamber water may be due in part to the sugared *barblars* one so regularly enjoys. Which are, in fact, as it would seem . . . purple in colour. Most likely they are the cause of one's toothache as well. Fewer sweets perhaps, sire? And perhaps, sire,' he continued, 'one might avail oneself of a little more light in these quarters? So many windows here in the tower, such a shame to keep them darkened.'

'My physicians advise otherwise.'

There, that shuffle again! I was sure now—someone else *was* nearby, watching and listening through dividers.

'Well of course,' Rusper said pleasantly, 'I must defer to their judgement.'

'Sit then, and have yourself a *barblar*.'

'No, thank you, sire.' So that's what the beads were, I realised.

'Take one, man.' They rattled again and I heard Rusper's finger find them in space. 'Gorgeous, aren't they?'

'Mhm, most flavoursome, sire.' I cringed for Rusper: he hated sugar.

Then, '*Esha's arse*—the Viceroy's *chair!*' cried the wheezy voice in what was almost a cockerel's pitch.

And Rusper clicked his fingers.

In as seemly a way as I could manage at a pace, I crossed the rugs, just missing the high-backed chair that floated from the right. At the row of blinded windows, I spun on my heel and saw the valet set the chair behind Rusper. No sooner had Rusper eased between its arms than the valet shoved two plump bolster cushions at his back.

'That just won't do,' said the wheeze. At which the valet hurried off to some greater, out-of-sight stockpile and came back with arms loaded with cushions.

Rusper raised a hand. 'I'm quite well cushioned.'

'Shan't hear it, you poor man, that is a miserable chair,' snapped the voice. I caught the valet's look of trapped desperation. Rusper couldn't have seen it, but relented all the same, and by the time the batch of cushions were packed and squeezed down every side, he was all but wedged into place. 'There, isn't that comfortable?'

'Intensely.'

'Have another barblar.'

'Yes *ekharan*.'

'And to the business in hand.' A cough. 'Look me in the eye, Semafin.'

My heartbeat picked up pace. That the voice had called him the wrong name wasn't important, somehow. It was the *tone* of that voice, dropping so abruptly that I'd thought another man had spoken.

'You've kept something a secret from me, Semafin, and even now as you sit here in my presence, you say nothing.'

From this side of the room, I couldn't see the man himself any better—another lattice screen blocked my line of sight. But along that screen, just to my right, I saw a purple-gown approach and peer through the tiny lattice-holes.

'Forgive me,' Rusper was saying. 'I'm not altogether certain . . .'

'Above all things, you know how highly I prize truth from my subjects. Certainly from my foremost minister.'

'Of course.'

'Of course. Curious then, that such a thing should have escaped your report. Nevertheless, it is known. And I believe you know only too well of what I speak.'

'*Deepest* regrets, sire, I do not.'

'Little matter.'

Rusper's shoulders were very high: was he as tense as I felt, or was it simply all those cushions hemming him in? The watching physician was very still. What was this? Was it the blindness, or something else? Something much worse—the thing we feared more than anything?

But as my mind raced through the thoughts of what would happen should he know, the Satrap's cry filled up the tower. 'Don't say I've *missed* it! Your name-day! It *is* today, not so?'

The drop from panic was dizzying, and yes, I saw Rusper's shoulders sag back into the cushions of the chair.

'Why yes, I think it is, *ekharan*. You honour me.'

'And to *imagine* you'd conceal such news from me, your sovereign! Name-day of Semafin, no less! I expect your wife will perform most decadent acts upon your nether—'

'Ah. No wife, sire,' sighed Rusper.

'Then take a whore. One of mine.'

'*Ekharan* is kind.'

'Not me!' declared the Satrap with a chesty chuckle. 'How should I have known if it weren't for that darling Amyra? Sent word to the tower on your behalf, you sly weasel. Been keeping a close eye on you, she says.'

'Her own words?'

'Or something. Isn't she a fox?'

'Isn't she just.'

'Here, another barblar!' he commanded. Whatever dish they were in must have been flung towards Rusper because several of the sweets flew off and over the floor. They *were* like beads: tiny, purple beads. 'Take more than one, it's your name-day after all!' The Satrap's laugh was full and merry.

'Most gracious.'

'Never mind that now. The board!'

The watching physician to my right chose this moment to drift away from the lattice, while the valet hurried forward with a small circular table. He set this down in front of Rusper, then lifted three half-moon panels. A playing board was revealed: a triangular plane of even smaller triangles, painted blue and white.

Again, the valet cleared his throat: '*Ekharan.*'

Rusper started slightly at that, not having seen the valet there, and snatched something out of his hand. 'Will, *ah* . . . will his Majesty play blue today?'

'Of course.'

Dread rising, I couldn't help but dare to watch the pieces laid. Blue in the middle, white in the corners of the triangle. Surely Rusper had somehow been prepared for this to happen. His voice was tight. 'The knuckles . . . ?'

'Right there,' the Satrap said. 'Look, you've put them on the board with your pieces, you goose.'

With a flustered laugh that worried me, Rusper picked up the "knuckles" off the board: four pyramidal dice; two white, two blue. 'Pray, forgive me, *ekharan*. My thoughts were elsewhere but for a moment.'

'Rein them in, man, before me. Forthwith.'

'Yes sire. Would *ekharan* . . . prefer to call knuckles? Only it seems less than fair that I should always call lots. Perhaps one might even the odds on this occasion?'

'Occasion? It's *your* name-day, Viceroy.'

'Nevertheless?'

Teeth crunched a barblar and thoroughly chewed it for a while. 'Hm, yes. Yes I shall!'

I thought I saw a pale, liver-spotted hand reach for the dice, and disappear. Then heard their rattle and clatter as they were cast into the barblar-dish.

'Seven blue and two white. I forfeit.'

As I tried to watch and listen, the warbling peacock emerged again out of the corner of my eye. It flounced towards me, getting bigger, but I couldn't move out of its way—wasn't allowed! And so I stood completely still until it walked right up to me. The shimmering neck bent for my feet and then the bird pecked at my shoe. The hip-flask on my belt sloshed as I bounced back.

Rusper coughed loudly. 'What was that, please?'

'Forfeit, I said! Seven blue and two white. What's the *matter* with you?'

Rusper made his move on the board, while the peacock kept on pecking. It didn't hurt and so I waited until it seemed to lose interest and strut off, sweeping the floor with its brilliant train.

The knuckles fell. 'Two blue, four white. Forfeit again.'

Rusper's hand hovered carefully, I saw; nudged a piece, then took another and set it down in a corner of the triangle. It wasn't the first I'd seen of the game. All through the streets of the districts I'd watched it played by city folk of every class. But folk in the North District had played on flimsy cloths with paint-daubed smidgens of repurposed metal. *This* was a lavish playing table crafted of marble and rich wood, with pieces sculpted into figures that had faces, spears and turrets. Along the outer edge that faced me, I could make out the ancient symbols that made up its name, dating back to the Builders' time, or so I'd heard:

$$\times \cdot - < | \; \mathtt{¤} \; | > - \cdot \times$$

"Xiqopix" - that's what Antissans called it now; a word somehow drawn out of those symbols. *Zick-o-picks*. Symbols of the same kind, I knew, were to be found on Meck's Transcripts. And on his cryptic diagrams . . .

The playing pieces were called "orfin." The player with blue orfin had to defend the "caliph" in the middle of the triangle. The player with the white, outnumbering the blue, had to attack from the corners, break the blue ranks and reach the caliph. And there was another white piece known as a "tower" that could capture more than one orfin at a time. Also other complicated rules about the moving of pieces; terms like "blue fluke" and "white charge" that I hadn't worked out yet. When knuckles were cast, their figures were read as either moving pieces already on the board or deploying new ones from a purse.

As they played their Xiqopix, Rusper broached the important matter of the state of the pipeworks, tapping the arm of his chair to summon for the parchments I carried. When I came forward it was always with my chin in my chest, which kept the Satrap as nothing more than a figment of multi-coloured cushions. I never dared to steal a glance, trying not to think about his fearful likeness in the Dynasty Hall – that beard of coils, dark brooding brow, those tusk-like nostrils, hateful eyes . . .

The game went on. Sheet after sheet, Transcript by Transcript, I brought the diagrams to Rusper in the order we'd prepared, and he explained them to the Satrap. On every sheet, Pintle had added layman's illustrations of the damage in both the Hub and greater circuit. The Satrap listened as he played and sometimes grunted to things.

Then at last he coughed over Rusper's talking. 'A *pelkhish* ploy this is,' he said crossly, 'luring my mind from the board with all these scrawlings, damn you.'

My eyes bobbed up to the Xiqopix board, where two white orfin now flanked the blue caliph. After nearly an hour, and through near-blinded eyes, Rusper had won.

'Well, I am sure there's some mistake,' he said. 'Though perhaps I might beg a moment's more attention—'

I edged forward.

'No more!'

And back again.

The Satrap, it seemed, was a sore loser. 'You've quite over-stretched my indulgence, Semafin. And cheated. Tell me now, in plain words, will the Deep safeguard my people?'

'As numbers stand, yes it will,' replied Rusper smoothly. 'But not with any additional evacuees from the south. Progress has slowed. Damage to the central pipeworks has destabilised fifth level, as you saw, causing critical delays. I have been forced to cease construction. Temporarily, of course.'

'Delays, cessations,' wheezed the Satrap. 'Liberties I call them, when the enemy may be upon us in weeks.'

'I can achieve only—'

'You will *achieve* the completion of the fifth level before the wyle is out, Semafin. Antissa's defences will *not* be breached, and my people *will* have their shelter from the Naemian scourge.'

'A month?' Rusper stammered. 'I beg you to look kindly on me, sire. To open, brace and seal the fifth level in so short a space of time is a feat quite beyond the guilds. We must consider other ways.'

'Other ways, you say to me?' said the Satrap, his wheeze catching in his throat. 'Have you forgotten the fate of the lands across the gulf?'

Now Rusper sat forward from the cushions, or tried to. 'Majesty. I do not believe that if the Naemian prince had delved into the earth of his realm, it would have saved him or his people. Antissa *has* been breached. If it is siege that you fear, let us then heed this new warning. The Rath have beset us, not from the desert but from below, through the pipes themselves. Even now we face further assault from our foundations and should the next force be greater, resistance may come at fearful cost. We stand, sire, to see the Deep of your decree become the enemy's doorway.'

'Then fortify it. Barricade the perimeter.'

'That would deplete our resources.' Though soft, Rusper's voice was a plea. I didn't like it.

The Satrap scoffed, 'Look at him. Chief Engineer of a nation under siege, he wields the craft of my city and the powers of my throne and yet *still* he would resist in the defence of his charge.' He was talking to the peacock. Then, 'You shame me, Semafin.'

Semafin. Why did the Satrap keep calling him that?

'I would honour my charge,' said Rusper, words loud and quick suddenly. 'For that reason alone, I beseech your leave to counter the Ratheine offensive. With newly developed armaments, we may have renewed strength to engage—'

But I didn't hear the rest as the lattice was bombarded with a blue-and-white hail. Game pieces rained across the floor, the little caliph himself rolling under the divider to greet me with a carven blue face.

'*Dare you make such blatant utterance before me!*' the Satrap bellowed. 'I have warned you overmuch. Had not I recalled our forces, no Vedish man-at-arms would live. It was to the *salvation* of this realm that I sounded full retreat out of the north, yet you would undo it with your *bloodthirst*. Oh!—the same *stink* was on Plamen when he knelt here at my feet, I should have smelled it on you when you came crawling up behind him!'

'I swear to you, sire . . .'

Another smack of the big hand sent the whole table and board against the wall.

The peacock flapped.

'*What would you swear?*' the sovereign seethed, a rumbling cough rising in his chest. 'What is there *left* for you to swear unto me when gravest oaths bind you *already* to the will of my throne?' He started coughing but squeezed tight words out through the coughs. 'You wear that *medallion* . . . yet you *torment* me with such base, *foolhardy threats of reckless warcraft . . . such callous mockery! . .* as though I were *not . . . not* heir of the dynasty that forestalled Vorth's *annihilation . . . !*'

The coughs and splutters became violent, turning into an ugly, wet confusion of retching, gagging and gasps. 'It is *because . . .*' he choked, '*because* of my dynasty . . . that the desert has held its head—*held it high!*—from those feeble states of Exelcia Minor, *crawling* in blind servitude to their foolish faiths and false prophets—their soothsaying *Celestri!*'

Cloudy spittle spattered the legs of the overturned Xiqopix table. 'Because of *my* lauded fathers of Aysattah has this great fortress-city weathered the onslaughts of the Lack in ages past. And so too will I—*Szaferis Aysattah, Second Son Of This Name* —weather the hordes out of Naemia!'

'Behind its walls we may all—'

'Hold your tongue, *faithless!* How addled by vapours do you think me? Do you suppose that my wits have unravelled so far in my ill health as to forget your brazen boldness? How upon my confinement you did *twice* refuse to take the burden—nay, the high *honour!*—of that medallion when so commanded? I have forgotten *nothing* of that insult and by *dredth* I shall put you in the erg if you should fail me—why are you standing?'

Halfway out of his chair, Rusper sat; the sweet dish striking his forehead with a crack that made me flinch. Purple barblars joined the scattered blue orfin all over the floor. This was the tantrum of a child!

Rusper sat very still, not even raising a hand to touch his smitten forehead, and the room went quiet. I couldn't even hear the secret shuffles anymore, just the peacock's worried warble and overlaboured royal wheeze.

'Semafin, I love you. Indeed as blood,' said the wheeze, whistling now with only just enough breath recovered. 'As my own, I tell you. Your birth outwith the sands of Vorth is of no account to me, your sovereign. But hear me now. You thwart my edicts on certain pain of your end. You may have *none* of those barblars that have fallen on the floor.'

As if accepting his due punishment with grace, Rusper bowed his head. 'I most sorely regret that I should have invited your distrust, Majesty. Ever do I seek to satisfy your noble wishes, the demands of your Sanhedrin and the needs of your people. I would make only one request, if *ekharan* might still hear me.'

A barblar clacked, squelching a bit. 'Say it then.'

'Time.' He was brave. 'I have here revealed to you the extent of the damage to the greater system, and I fear it is not unreasonable to suppose that the pipes will never again function as they did before the Deep.'

'What drivel you will speak, man. The Builders' greatness flows through the veins of my people! Why now should it fail?'

'It is falling away, sire. Even the finest engineering of the guilds may no longer match the ancient craft of the Builders. The Deepworks will, as you command, recommence and I shall triple the workforce to attain the progress you desire. But I *must* stabilise the pipes. If I fail in this, and they are ruptured yet again, we face the flooding of the Deep. I hardly need remind your Majesty, versed as you are in such matters, that as the Deep is interwoven with the citadel's foundations, such another haemorrhage could—'

'Pipes, pipes, pipes, *pipes!* Desert take it, your ceaseless *piping* could stretch a Lostrian arsehole!'

'Sire.'

'Ten days!'

'I beg your Majesty's pardon?'

'You have ten days,' said the Satrap. 'In that time, do what you must to your *pelkhish* pipes, but know well that you test me.'

A helpless laugh escaped the engineer. '*Ekharan*, please, I must implore you for more—at least a fortnight!'

'In *ten days*, Semafin,' said the Satrap archly, 'I will have a full return to the Deepworks under your ordinance. Should my Shield report otherwise, it will be to my final displeasure with your tenure as Viceroy, a loud betrayal of my will. Rightly, your neck will be shackled and all Antissa will bear witness as you fall from the spire. Because I love you, I will break you before the city you've forsaken.'

Rusper's voice made me think of beaten iron as he asked, 'Who then will finish your Deep?'

Teeth crushed the barblar. 'A truer Vedan.'

Back on the stairs, away from the foyer and physicians, Rusper batted for my leg. 'Give me that flask!'

I uncorked it for him and he snatched it; in three swigs it was empty. He swilled the last mouthful, then seized a window ledge and spat out of the tower. Turning to wipe his mouth on his sleeve, I saw the red mark on his forehead.

'Went rather better than expected,' he said, smirking at my silence. 'Oh, rest assured, I've seen far worse than an over-turned games board. Still.' He sniffed. 'Should've let him win.'

'You beat him blind!' I exclaimed.

'Half-blind,' he corrected. 'No great feat against the Satrap. Besides, it's said the mathematician Azal once drew a game in his sleep.'

'What about the ten days?' I asked him seriously. 'Is it enough to fix the pipeworks?'

'Course it isn't.'

'Maybe he'll . . . forget?'

'Doesn't matter. There were enough ears in that tower, as usual. Ten days is what we have to work with, so we prepare for the worst. What you have heard must stay a secret all the same, understood?'

I scratched my wrist. 'I'm good at secrets.' But as I went ahead and led him down the stairs, I turned back. 'Will you teach me how to play the Xiqopix?'

He scowled, 'Ten days, Flint! Zeek's a dab hand at it, have her show you.'

'Oh, happy name—'

'Don't even try.'

Twenty-three

Deeper Machines

The Satrap's tower: I was back. Through the glow of lamps around the bed, something was flailing. The frame rocked side-to-side, its curtains swaying, while physicians in purple gowns crowded around it, pelted with pillows. A foot struck one of the bedposts and split the wood. Hands forced it down. A purple-gown dropped a spoonful of powder into a cup and brought it to the bedside, but another stroke from the foot sent it flying. Somehow the spoon found its way into the hand of the patient, and from there into the purple-gown's eye.

I fled to the stairs. Hearing a whisper.

The citadel. A door was standing half-open and, through the open gap, I saw two men standing in a room. Dressed in the blue robe and tallith of the First Circle was Vizier Vesh. He spoke in a passion, waving his hands, while Captain Mondric heard him out; arms folded, nodding sagely.

The whisper called me from the room.

There, coiled in a chair so large it made even the tall man look short, was High Commander Plamen; without his head-dress and his mantle, plainly clothed. A small iron coal-fire near his feet outlined the shape of Tazen, who dozed there stretched across a rug.

I saw the courtyard, as though I sat between the stone gryphon's wings. In some dark corner, the dwarf crouched and stroked the horrid little sandrat that he called Heironymus. A fly swooped close to Hetch's cowl and he snatched it out of the air, feeding it directly between the fangs of the rodent.

Men and women, hands and servants, dragged weary feet toward their homes, watched by the guards who stood on duty. Lights shone above the flagstones, from little dwellings in the courtyard wall; above those lights, the high estates.

Following the whisper, I flew up there.

Through the first set of curtains the caliphs of Verunia and Laudassa were dining late. Arif spoke down into his plate while Omran stuffed his mouth with persimmon fruit.

Through the next, the viziers Dranz and Ramed were drinking out of huge cups of wine. Both drunk and bored, they teased and mocked one of their servants from the table.

Through the third was Vizier Basra, lying asleep beside his wife.

My way went blurry. Whisper, faint.

Then there was Rusper at the window of his quarters. Sweat stuck his nightshirt to his chest, hair hung over his eyes, and his lips were moving—but I couldn't hear. With a stagger, he turned his back to the stars and faced the lamplight. It flickered near his pallet and put a sheen on smooth black skin. A bare-breasted woman lay in his blankets, listening. Braids hung loose about her shoulders and her throat was enclosed in a thin band of green gems. Harem-senah.

As Rusper pressed palms to his temples, the woman's lips moved too, and she rose. Rusper looked up, towards her, his face contorted as if searching but unable to find her. Stepping away from the window, he stumbled and, falling, didn't try to stand up.

She was young, but her movements seemed older. She crossed the room on naked feet while Rusper stayed kneeling on the floor, eyes closed, lips murmuring something. When she had shuttered the window, she came to kneel and put her arms around his shoulders like a veil. She spoke slow words into his ear. She touched his cheek, lifted his face. Then smiled and kissed his mouth to stop him saying more. The kiss, it seemed, took some of the anguish from his face, but he still trembled.

From her braids, she took something then. Some kind of green trinket or jewel. A dragonfly. Her nimble fingers twisted away its wings-and-head to reveal a capsule, and only when she raised it to her cheek did I see that she too had been crying. A tear ran down her rich, dark skin and slid into the capsule, before she reached for Rusper's hand and placed the jewel into his palm.

The whisper called me from their door.

Along the corridors, down stairs, through the long grey hall, and further down.

Into the Deep.

There were the smithies at their forges, working late into the night, melting metal.

There in the overseers' rooms, Pintle and Gudgeon cut their pens, taking their coffee, while a girl swept the floor of the day's dust. I knew that apprentice. Taflan. Sometimes we'd run our errands together.

There was the Chief Engineer's workshop. Another boy lay sleeping on his arms at his workstation, one arm stretched forward of his head across the worktop. Blue light was shining through his fingers.

There was the Hub. From what was left of the cantilever bridges, the standing soldiers stared down at the water. Among ripped nets and swaying feeders, Arterial-III was just a shadow. I slipped in through an open lateral and followed the whisper on, and down.

But it was thinning. As it called me, on and down, and down, and down, I felt my waking self. I felt my power over the dream and just how easily I could rise. An open hand that holds a moth and can so easily kill it. Down, down and down . . .

. . . down to green stone and a green tunnel . . . I reached for my quilt . . . *don't lose the tunnel . . .* quilt wasn't there . . . *don't lose the tunnel . . .* felt something firm under my hand. My jaw was numb on a hard surface . . . *don't lose the tunnel.* But I wasn't *in* a tunnel.

My eyelids parted. Just by enough to see my arm across the worktop. The torque was open, and three of my fingers lay resting over the mirror of the Disc. It glowed blue. And as I hazily tried to remember what it was I'd been doing before falling asleep, the sleep pulled me under again. My eyelids drooped . . . *it's not a dream, I was still there . . . still somewhere down there . . .*

Close and perfectly square, the green tunnel flowed on ahead of my sight. I chased the whisper as it grew into a voice, not far ahead. Above, the ancient green stone sank even lower. Walls pressing tight. And soon the way became too low for any man or boy to pass it. Smaller it shrank until I could barely even crawl through anymore.

I didn't have to. Here, I had no size, no body; I was the sight of my awareness, and if I moved at all, I floated.

But was there someone with a body up ahead, standing in the tunnel? Was it the ghost? It vanished then, voice fading with it.

Beyond the tunnel's shrinking square, I moved through cells and cube-like chambers. They were like nothing I had seen; branched left and right and up and down without a way of reaching them . . . distorted walls and angled ledges, fathomless floors, levels and portals that just went on and on and on in all directions. Until the walls began to morph into machines of stone and metal.

A branch of tunnel sucked me in.

It took me down a long, long way into a hollow of the stone: a kind of bubble in the maze. Here, four stone bridges reached inward towards the core of the bubble. And in the core, a golden globe of rings and wheels hung in mid-air. A loop of blades and web of cables seemed to hold it, hanging there, while through its eye a skein of tubes ran up and down, leaving the bubble.

Even though the voice had now gone silent, I floated up through the bubble's ceiling and let the tubes guide me higher. Up, up and up . . . between the bridges and the cables and the pillars . . . four massive pillars in the granite, also rising as I was. Or were they pillars? In their bodies, I knew movement.

Something was higher overhead, growing as I flew towards it, faster. Was it a wheel, a set of gears? Its liquid arcs almost converged around the tubes . . . a shape I knew . . . a shape I'd seen . . . a shape that turned—

And something poked me in the shoulder. I sat bolt-upright in the chair and broke the Sight. For several out-of-body moments I sat there blinking, half-awake, before I saw that Zeek was there. She stood right next to my workbench, wide-eyed and staring at my face. But then she always stared like that. She must have come to douse the lights.

I couldn't focus on her now, or anything else in front of me. Those tunnels, chambers and machines: they were all real. They were real things, and all still vivid. It was the strangest thing to feel, but I could still see every part of that great maze that sprawled below as if a map of it had burned onto my brain. I'd known on sight that golden globe of rings and blades; that looping circle turning weirdly overhead—because I'd seen them both before. In Gaspar Meck's diagrams.

I reached for pen and parchment. '*Builders.*'

Twenty-four

Errands and Encounters

Sanhedrin gathered the next day. I did my best to imagine what could be happening in that hall as I left the citadel, but soon put it out of my mind.

Easy enough. Since early that morning it had been almost impossible to stop thinking about the images I'd dreamed. Though I'd not *dreamed* them, really. I'd *seen* them. Dozing at the worktop with a hand against the Disc's mirror, the Sight had opened. In sleep, I'd reached through space without thinking, or even meaning to do it.

I was exhausted. All through the night and the small hours I'd tried to map the place I'd seen: those sprawling tunnels of green stone and twisted chambers, bizarre machines. Every passage had at first been clear enough to follow from memory, which shouldn't be any more possible. But the clarity had faded, outrunning my pen about an hour before dawn. Of course I'd reopened the Sight and tried to find my way back, but awake it was different. Underlying and enclosing the Deep on all sides was dense rock, vast, unyielding, and to push my awareness down through that sandstone and granite was like searching for a coin in dried mud. I could press through it, very slowly, one tiny fissure at a time, but it took effort and concentration. And I didn't know where I was going. The Disc gave me Sight without direction, it seemed, and no knowledge of the unknown without *seeing* it first. To reach a hidden door that way, I still had to know where to find it. All the same, a tube of six sheets of parchment – my first draft of a hopeful map – hung on a hook in the workshop. I'd need to tell Rusper soon; he had to know what I'd discovered. And *how*, there was still that to explain.

At the gate of the gryphon courtyard, I found myself stopping at the stone birds.

Could it have tricked me? Or lied? The Disc was still such a mystery, but one I knew contained some . . . what? *Will?* If it had a will of its own, could it then have showed me things and places that *weren't* real? Didn't exist? Because, if it *hadn't* showed me lies, then far more stretched under the fortress than the engineers' Deep. And that made it, without the tiniest doubt, the handicraft of the Builders.

Wild possibilities firing my imagination, I got going again and made my way down to the Crop Yard. There I went to the Yieldmaster, who knew me well enough by now to let me sit inside her bivouac and snack on dates while she organised my people's supplies. Like everyday, she burned the message on her brazier. From there I climbed the hill into the upper North District, through busy crowds. Buckets were everywhere I walked, and currents of water travelled over my head through the newly added aqueducts, bound for the reservoirs and collection points all over the city. The City Guildhouse was busier than usual; I drew my hood when I got there, ducking and dodging between the craftsmen.

The black-bearded foreman peered over his reading lenses: '*Ekhin* Flint.'

'Ekh Edish,' I greeted him.

'No drafts today, boy. Ready tomorrow.'

'It's alright, I'm here for parts,' I said.

'Got a manifest?'

'It's in my head.'

'Best be right then,' he said gruffly. 'Last thing I care for is a visit from the overseers 'cos of some squirt who muddled their order.'

'No sir.'

I ran off my list from memory, Edish moving among his shelves of crates and jars he knew by heart, sometimes dispatching an assistant into the adjoining storage rooms of his domain for something hidden a little deeper. 'That the lot?'

'And some sparts for Caliph Symphin,' I added. 'One quadruple lever-wheel, one pin-gear . . .'

'*Grade* pin-gear?'

'Uh, didn't say.'

'Well, if it's anything to do with the lever-wheel he'll be needing a forty, forty-five at a push. I'll give him both. Khopan!' He snatched the arm of a passing assistant—'Pin-gears, forty and forty-five'—and shoved the youngster towards a downward-delving ladder. When the hand returned, it was with two intricate mechanisms of ball-topped pins; one slightly bigger, a little tarnished. Both gold in colour. 'Anything else?'

'A pair of . . .' What was it again?

'Sun's climbing, boy!'

'. . . tallan lenses?'

'*Couple tallan lenses!*' he barked, slapping another assistant on the shoulder. I didn't know what these things were for, nor could I think of anything Rusper needed less right now than a pair of *lenses*. The foreman drooped over his tall counter, propped his own lenses on his head and rubbed his nose. 'How're those pipes, then?'

'Bad.' I shook my head. 'Just two arterials holding pressure. That's why Caliph Symphin's connecting new aqueducts all over the city.'

'Figured as much,' he sighed, adding with bitter sarcasm, 'Take it these scraps aren't for repairs then.'

Trying not to look as guilty as I felt about it all, I smiled back sadly. Edish had hoped to see the Hub in all its glory when it was opened, and now already it was in ruins. Because of the Rath. And because of me.

Two dark cobalt lenses arrived on the counter and I put them into my sling-bag with the rest.

Traffic had thickened even more back at the entrance. As I tried to push my way through the press of moving bodies, I was nudged painfully under the ribs by a badly organised tool-belt, then almost struck across the face by an iron beam as it was turned. All down to aqueduct construction, I guessed, and squeezed free.

All it took was a quick tug while I was squeezing – I felt my sling-bag leave my grip. I made a lunge after its strap but the boy had it—one of the *wild boys*, gutterwaifs!—now zigzagging away through the crowds.

Both fear and anger boiled up together and so quickly I didn't know which one was which, and I catapulted myself after him, yelling something like 'Thief!' I tried to zigzag the way he'd done, but two mules veered towards each other, forcing me back and around. 'Foolish greenstring!' a driver cursed me, but I was too busy making sure I didn't lose sight of my bag.

There! He'd made it round the entrance crowd, bolting towards one of the street-side terraces. I glimpsed an opening —an outer atrium of the Guildhouse that had cleared for just a moment—and sprinted through it, vaulting tables, to stumble out the other side again.

As the waif bounded onto the terrace steps, I grabbed his shirt but it slipped right out of my fingers. He was *fast*. But I could be too and I wasn't going to lose Pintle or Rusper's parts to them, *not them!* When he got to the top of the steps, whacking my bag against the stone, I was right behind him, sandals sliding as I lurched to grab again. This time I got a better handful of his shirt and pulled him back, then quickly grappled his skinny shoulders to turn him round.

Big glaring eyes in sunken cheeks: *not* a gutterwaif. I let go of his shoulders as a big bubble of spit popped at the side of his mouth.

'*Jerms?*'

He dropped my bag and ran for it.

'No, Jerms, it's me! Wait, it's me! Florian!'

I chased him down the length of the terrace but he was even faster now. Over the wall at the end, he jumped, slid down a merchant's canopy and was back in the street before I knew it. I got to the end of the terrace just in time to watch his heels flick another dusty zigzag trail through the mid-morning traffic.

My people's shelter was nowhere close to the City Guild-house, I thought, as I watched him stop to catch his breath by a corner building. Hands on his knees.

He was talking, I saw. Talking to someone out of sight. A green-topped figure curled into view and looked directly at me. Wondering if I *could* make out the milky cataracts from here, I just stared back. Jerome didn't look back at me though, as Loquar took him by the shoulder. Both turned away, around the corner.

For a while, the Builders' dreamy maze of machines melted away. Jerome's huge eyes took their place. I saw that spit-bubble pop over and over.

So he *had* escaped the waifs. He was thin, but not much thinner. Tanned as brown as any Vedan – freckles all gone – which must have been why I'd thought he *was* one.

But alive.

True enough, if there was anything Jerome had always known how to do much better than me, it was run, and now I wondered how I ever could have doubted that he'd made it. He and Con had known how to survive on their own long before I'd ever had to.

The sun was high. Slowly now, I made my way back through the Citizen District, between white, baking walls and up into the citadel gardens. One of the sparts in my sling-bag had broken on the steps, but I wouldn't go back now. Besides, I could see the pillar of smoke climbing behind the sentinel spire: blue smoke to signal the end of council. Horses clattered in the courtyard while, from the colonnaded terrace came the hum of talking viziers.

I sat on the edge of a fountain. Nothing flowed out of the lizards' open mouths, but a little leafy water was in the bottom of the basin. I didn't mind that it was brown and splashed my face a couple times. Then watched the ripples repair the reflection of my face. Frowned at my hair. What had been a tufty black copse when I'd arrived in Antissa was now a thicket and a mess. I tried to press it down with water but even wet hands made no difference.

Why wasn't I more relieved? I *was* relieved, wasn't I? Maybe I hadn't really worried in the first place. Maybe I'd known he'd be alright. He was my friend, though. My family. What was left of it, anyway. So why didn't I feel more . . . happy?

Somewhere, a duduk was playing. The tune was sad, although the hedges all around me made it difficult to tell which way it came from. I closed my eyes and listened, not ready to go back to the Deep just yet. The warmth in my swathes, tempered just right from the mounting heat of midday, was now making me drowsy. The dreamy greenstone tunnel started to form again in my mind's eye, tempting me to follow. Not awake and not asleep, I tried for several minutes, but the images were hazy; now almost as hazy as my earliest childhood memories. Again I wondered if I could trust them. Jerome, at least, was fully real, and now again his honest face surfaced through the half-imagined tunnels.

The music softened and then stopped. I opened my eyes, aware of muddled conversations somewhere else among the gardens' leaves. I left the fountain and strolled the corridors of trimmed hedge, between the pink and white flowers, up and down the shallow steps. How long could all this green last now the pipes could hardly meet the city's needs? Would it all die?

Green. I thought about Loquar. No longer Rusper's assistant, he was still a city engineer. I wondered how the two had come to meet. Had Loquar *saved* him from the waifs, or had it been nothing but chance? It seemed like the old man had been waiting for Jerome after he'd tried to make off with my bag at the Guildhouse, so it wasn't hard to guess what uses he was finding for my friend. My fast-footed, fast-fingered friend.

Why did that sting a little bit? In some way, at least, Loquar must be looking after him, and that was good. Was I jealous? Why should I be *jealous?*—I had Rusper Symphin and he was *Viceroy*, not just the Chief Engineer!

Ashamed to have even thought that thought, I tried to unthink it again.

Between a pair of rosebushes, I leaned on a stocky balustrade. Directly below was a balcony with another stonework pool, hemmed by ivy on the one side, with the Inner Wall straight ahead. A long-legged plover was perched at the pool, dashing its bill, and there was a woman veiled in black standing nearby. Her back to me, she stood overlooking the roofs of the city; the muffled humdrum of the districts wafting to meet her on the breeze. She was a mourner, probably. After the deaths in the attack, I'd seen many Antissan citizens in mourning.

Then a man's voice: '*Sinarre.*'

The plover flapped and took off as a blue-and-white Shieldman appeared from the right. He strode onto the balcony, leading a man in a familiar dark blue gown and tallith. The woman turned her veiled shoulders and, on an instant reflex, I ducked into the rosebushes.

'Vizier Basra,' she greeted.

I stifled a whimper as thorns pierced me in the neck. They hadn't seen me, not yet. But I'd seen *her*—the olive skin and black-lined eyes. Amyra.

'A favourable turn,' the vizier said.

'And deftly played on your own part,' she replied, her charm like silvery oil. 'You see now what can be achieved when the First Circle is mindful of its influence.'

Snip-snip. Someone nearby, one of the citadel gardeners, was working his shears across the hedges. I couldn't stay here, not for long.

'Hm! The First Circle can hardly take credit, *sinarre*. The Viceroy gambled a great deal to appear before the Sanhedrin as he did today. The High Commander may have spoken in his stead while he sat silent, but the matter is all too plain and his affliction all too clear.'

Amyra made a musical sound. 'Perhaps you should take greater care then, Basra. Symphin is shrewder than he appears.'

'I fail to see how. He did not obtain the power he wields by ambition of his own. That medallion is a chain, an anchor cast about his shoulders by a ruler who commands . . . if you'll permit me . . . *digging* as an answer to the threat of war, solely because the man heads the guilds. That is all. And what use to Antissa is a blind engineer?'

I shrank deeper into the leaves and biting thorns. Had I heard that right?

The shears were close. I drew my hood, alert to movements from the closest hedges.

'None of course,' Amyra said. 'But his foibles are only as damning as the First Circle will permit. That is why you and your fellow viziers cannot allow complacency from the Caliphate. It did not escape my notice that dear, sweet Vesh had a heavy tongue. Is he in accord with our agreement?'

Snip-snip-snip.

'The entire First Circle is in accord.'

'Then our position grows firm. You may be interested to learn that I possess information pertaining to the Honorary Caliph's most recent visit to the tower.'

'Indeed?'

Snip-snip-snip.

'His Majesty the Satrap has granted him ten days in which to right the disrepair wrought upon the pipeworks by the Ratheine attack. Then, on pain of public execution, the Deep-works are to recommence at triple the pace. Perhaps you have not yet had the pleasure of observing said disrepair, *ekharan?*'

'I'm keeper of coin, *sinarre*, not an engineer.'

'He will not succeed,' she told him flatly. 'Be it with eyes or without.'

'Ten days,' Basra mused.

'Nine from this day.'

The vizier made a dubious noise. 'Will not His Majesty have forgotten such a pledge by that date? What of the black moods, the hysteria?'

'Well controlled.' This in a different voice: the Shieldman. It wasn't Jharis this time.

'Beg pardon?'

'Most crucial is the timing,' Amyra cooed. 'Remove Symphin now from his seat and we can but expect our next viceroy to be another asphalt-risen Guildsman . . .'

Snip-snip-snip-snap. Ahead of my rosebush, the garden shears poked out of the greenery at ground level. The gardener rounded the hedge and I darted from my hiding place to crouch behind a low stone bench. But it didn't take me long to realise the man's work fully absorbed him; he barely glanced up from the leaves. So, daring to step out from cover, I went and stood near the balustrade again.

Amyra was still speaking.

'Of course, the Satrap is fickle. But, as the watchful eye will observe, the Sanhedrin is far fickler than he. To say nothing of Antissa and its people's famously short-lived and temperamental love for heroes. That is but one advantage. It is within my power to ensure that His Majesty remembers his promise, just as it is in yours, esteemed First Circle, to rouse six caliphs against Symphin. Do not delay the inevitable, nor deny Vorth its rightful due. I have already given you all you require.'

Twenty-five

Wills

My hand hovered an inch above the handle.

'. . . *by other means!*'

'. . . *maintaining order!*'

Rusper and Plamen, arguing. I turned the handle anyway and pushed into the workshop.

'It won't be enough,' Plamen was pressing.

'Enough for *what?*' Rusper retorted, braced in his chair as if to pounce. 'Enough to make of me the sacrificial lamb of the Sanhedrin? How much *less* closely do you think they watch me now Ramed has stepped onto the First Circle?'

Plamen's face swung towards me.

Think quick.

'Uhm, Caliph Symphin, I got your—'

'Flint, wait outside,' Rusper bit off, and I shrank behind the door again. Their voices argued on, leaving me at a loss. I'd already been to Captain Mondric's office; delivered the second part of my people's supplies-dispatch. I'd delivered parts to Pintle. Though of course one was broken, she hadn't sent me back to the Guildhouse. All I had now were Rusper's; those and the wicked conversation I'd overheard in the gardens. I hadn't been supposed to hear that. But whatever it meant, it surely had to be about more than just my people's refuge.

A hand out of nowhere clapped my shoulder. Before I could untangle myself from my thoughts and react, the door was shoved open again and my body barrelled back into the work-shop. A stern female voice over my head said, 'Excuse me, *ekharaan*, but this was right outside the door.'

Hands on hips, thoughts in mid-quarrel, Plamen gave a hot sigh: 'Thank you, *marszalekh*, he's the Viceroy's, you may unhand him.'

'Ah. Sir, begging pardon.'

The firm grip left me and I hurried away to the safety of the middle table. The new arrival was a stout, dark-skinned woman who looked closer in age to Rusper than Plamen; short-cropped hair turning grey. Maybe as tall as Captain Mondric, and just about as broadly built too. She wore open swathes, high quality, with a black-leather tabard and greaves under-neath. I rubbed my shoulder as her brown eyes moved away from me.

Rusper snapped the word, 'Marszal?'

Back straightening, arms behind it, the woman cleared her throat: 'Marszal Savhar, Honorary Caliph.'

Straining, Rusper blinked across the room—he was looking worse by the day—and repeated: 'Savhar.'

'Sir,' she responded.

'The Marszal fronts the Methan Eighth Battalion,' Plamen said.

'I know who she is.'

A heavy pause. True to her martial office, Marszal Savhar stood rooted to the floor without a shuffle. 'I was most aggrieved to learn of your affliction, *ekharan*.'

Rusper's face contorted. 'My what?'

The Marszal went on: 'Your recent bravery in defence of the northwest wall has been no small matter among the Methan Regiment officers. With respect, sir, few soldiers expect such courage from a caliph. Even from a field-engineer, if you'll permit me.'

Silence again, this time stony. Then, 'What's your business here, *marszalekh?*'

'Savhar is present at my request,' Plamen answered for her.

'Yours,' said Rusper. His hand drifted over the worktop in front of him, fingers tripping over parts and tools scattered there. Were those fingers trembling? The room was tense; so tense I felt like crawling under the table.

Plamen took a squarer stance in front of Rusper's worktop. 'Savhar has readied Methan soldiers.'

The engineer's fingers closed around a copper shank and made a fist. 'She has.'

'I'll go,' I said.

'You'll stay,' said both Rusper and Plamen together. The Marszal shot a puzzled look my way, just as Plamen walked forward and leaned over the worktop. 'A single battalion, that is all it will take.' He looked back over his shoulder and nodded a prompt at the Marszal.

'Viceroy,' said the woman. 'It is mine to advise you that the mounted scimitars of my battalion have been placed at your immediate disposal. Under the direction of High Command, the cavalry may be ready to move at a word.'

Rusper's head tilted. 'A word.'

'Sir.'

A vague nod. Something was wrong. What *had* just happened at that council?

'Consider what's at stake,' said Plamen; I caught the clench of his jaw.

But Rusper's voice remained level: 'I will not discuss this further. Flint, did you get me the lenses I wanted?'

'Symphin . . .' Plamen was stern. '. . . this may be your last opportunity.'

'Flint, the sparts please.'

Straightening from the worktop with a strained glance back at the Marszal, the Commander fell silent and I could feel his frustration. Nervous of it, and cowed by guilt for having become the object of attention at this moment, I walked to the front of Rusper's station. Rusper's eyes, when I looked at them, were almost too awful to meet: so red-rimmed and raw that I could barely tell that they were green, or any colour.

'I got everything,' I said and fished into my sling-bag. Piece by piece, I placed the sparts before his hands. Quadruple lever-wheel, pin gears, tallan lenses. And stepped back. The two martial officers watched from behind me, so full of important things to say that I felt the hackles stand on my neck. Rusper had put me before their business—*urgent* business, obviously! —and right now I hated him for it. The silence stretched. Face twitching as he tried to focus his damaged eyesight, his hands explored the objects as if he were all by himself in the room.

Plamen sucked a breath. 'Viceroy—'

'*Under whose authority was a unit prepared for deployment?*' Rusper shouted. He dashed the lever-wheel against the worktop and forced himself up from his chair.

'Mine,' said Plamen.

'These were *your* orders?'

'They were. Deliberation was unnecessary. You would have resisted, when it remains a matter for the High Command of the Mooncircle Army.'

Teeth set: '*I am Viceroy.*'

'And I am your aide, so appointed by Sanhedrin and Satrap,' countered Plamen. 'I have made emergency contact with Caliph Bardon in Methar. Your *ally*. He now knows of the attack on the fortress, as do the caliphs of Shad, Zeidha and

Ospégath. They too have acquiesced to the partial dispatch of their regiments, should needs of state require them.'

'Well that *is* good news,' Rusper congratulated him with venom. 'You have succeeded in appeasing a southern caliph with the semblance of mobilisation, or so you think! And what then? Did you intend to deploy this special unit of yours as soon as I wasn't *looking?* Because that should hardly present too great an obstacle just now, Commander! Well? *Marszalekh?* What were your orders?'

When I looked to Savhar, her eyes couldn't have been any steadier. 'To assemble the company only with your express permission, sir.'

'Preparations have been discreet,' added Plamen. 'I've made certain.'

'Discreet!' Rusper scoffed, spitting a bit. 'You most of all should know better than that. There's a pair of watching eyes for every brick and stone in this city.'

'Yet we have already dispatched scouts. Armed detachments, in the desert.'

'And even *that* was at our peril! How do you expect me to face the First Circle when they discover I'm deploying the army in *pieces?*'

'A single unit of cavalry is all that I ask,' Plamen pressed him. 'At this stage that is all Caliph Bardon will *offer*, lest the Satrap lift his decree.'

Rusper thumped his fist on the worktop, sparts leaping up about an inch. '*Again* I'll say it, Commander, just as I have to all those who would have me undermine royal decree in favour of their caliphies—I will not mobilise forces until the Satrap himself stands before the Mooncircle Throne and makes it known to *all* that he wills it.'

'That will not happen, Symphin.'

'Then nor will this. If your plan is uncovered before it meets with success, it will be a transgression too many. I will be at their mercy. *Her* mercy!'

Her. Senera Amyra. I had to tell them what I'd heard.

But Plamen was speaking again, more exuberantly than I'd ever heard him speak: 'A violation of the Satrap's will awaits us at every turn. A year from now, how many more such waiting violations will royal decree have strewn before us to obstruct the desert's rule? Total submission will *destroy* us, yet this one breach of decree could swing the Sanhedrin in your favour. Even the First Circle. It's what they *want*.'

'It's what they want because it's what'll put my neck in a noose!' Rusper fired back at him. 'Or is that what you want also, Plamen, because I can assure you your neck will be in the noose beside mine. The same goes for you, *marszalekh!* Tell me, please, how this unit was to leave the fortress without the knowledge of the Iron Shield? At the very least, the Fortress Guard would be alerted and when word reaches Mondric, he too will turn against me. What *allies* have I then, I wonder? *Hm?*'

'I am the High Command,' Plamen said again. 'Strings may be pulled to ensure the secrecy of this mission. The Captain need know nothing.'

'Ah,' Rusper smiled, bitterly. 'So you would have me undermine the authority of the very man to whom I should turn when fortune favours us enough to implicate the Senera for her crimes? How *dare* you make a spare wheel of me!'

'Mondric's loyalty to the throne is as steel,' Plamen argued. 'His knowledge of soldiers leaving the fortress will put an end to it.'

'*I* am putting an end to it.'

'You will regret this, Symphin.' Suddenly fierce, Plamen spoke through teeth. 'When the borderlanders your care so much about are marched from the gates of this city, you will regret.'

'Don't threaten me, Commander.'

Marszal Savhar interrupted; her calmer voice a relief. 'Doors are closing to you, Viceroy. On the field of battle, a moment comes when a Vedan of rank must make a decision of daring.

Rash as it may seem, it may spare both his own life and the lives in his service.'

'Is that right.' Rusper tried to look at her, but his gaze fell off-target.

I felt my courage swell. 'You should listen to them,' I said, loud as I dared.

He aimed a glare at me too. 'Well thank you, Flint, for recruiting yourself to my board of advisors, but I've heard enough. From both Commander and Marszal.'

'You have demonstrated such daring once,' the Marszal persisted, warmth in her voice's husk, but also strength. Bravery. Something about her already made me sure that, just like Ghulzar, she would die for the desert if she had to.

'Once will suffice,' said Rusper.

Still she persisted: 'Ultimately, sir, you *will* be drawn back into warfare, whether or not the Satrap wills it. Is it not better that you act of your own accord in martial matters than allow the Sanhedrin to harry you into a corner?'

'Savhar is right,' Plamen rallied. 'When the viziership recognises its power to sway you, the Viceroyalty will no longer protect you from Amyra.' He paused. 'Do this now. Locate the site from which the Rath gained their entry to the pipeworks of Antissa. *Cut them off.* If the mission fails, nothing need ever be known of it again. But if it succeeds—if we break their access to the fortress—you will acquire not only greater hold over the Sanhedrin but leverage to persuade the Satrap into further military action.'

While I marvelled at the words, Rusper laughed. 'You are suggesting we unearth a hidden river in the desert. In nine days.'

'Yes.'

'And *how?*'

Just as eager to know the answer, I looked to Plamen. Whose grey eyes narrowed at Rusper.

'That one so resourceful as you, Viceroy, has not yet proposed that solution is of some surprise to me. From the intelligence we obtained from Kathris' scouting parties in the north, we will easily enough be able to formulate a likely area of the Rath's entry-point. A place to begin, at the outmost. Thereafter, all we will need is the speed of Methan horses, an armed detachment, and the boy.'

I froze. Only Savhar looked at me.

Rusper ground his teeth, and then said, 'What?'

'Your hand, *ekhin* Flint,' said Plamen, 'and the *seeing-disc* he possesses.'

'I don't follow.'

'The boy wishes to be useful to Antissa. So let him.'

Now the engineer simmered through his nostrils: '*I shall be blowing a first-grade steam-flanged* gasket *if someone doesn't tell me what the—*'

'He doesn't know,' I broke in. Rusper closed his angry mouth when he heard me. 'I'm sorry, Caliph Symphin. I know I should've told you before, before the attack. I was *going* to!'

'Told me what?'

'About the Disc. What it does.'

'Yes, *and?*'

This was all wrong. This wasn't the industrious intrigue we'd shared over the Discs before. The workshop bristled with tempers and the wrong people were in it. It wasn't the way I'd imagined this conversation playing out.

'It sees,' I said.

He pushed a sigh. I looked away from his exasperation, trying to squash down the hurt that he would choose this of all moments to treat me like just a bothersome child. But when I looked back, he *was* still waiting. So was Plamen. The floor was mine and it dawned on me that this had probably been in Plamen's mind ever since he had seen the Disc's power in the Hub. When I looked at the Commander, he nodded; I drew my sleeve back. 'Someone speak,' Rusper said.

Plamen was calm again: 'The boy will explain.'

'You seem awfully sure of this, Plamen.' I heard mockery there.

'I've seen enough for myself.'

'But it's just . . . a gauntlet,' said the Marszal, eyes on my arm. 'What does he mean, it *sees?* You said nothing of this before, High Commander.'

I popped the lid of the torque. All eyes—except for Rusper's—were drawn straight to the Disc where, exquisitely and impossibly, each face found a way into its mirror. My own face dominated the lower-right, but I could trace the reactions of all three others as I started speaking; especially that of the Marszal, whose features gave a drama of grave doubt. Plamen's face reshaped under the mastery I knew, though his eyes flicked towards Rusper as he listened, chin raised as one who has heard a story once already. Rusper remained leaning on his worktop, face frozen in a scowl.

In as much detail as I could remember, I reported how I'd come to find the Sight. How far I'd reached using it. What I'd seen below the waterline of the Hub on the day of the Ratheine attack. I kept the voice and the ghost to myself, but told the rest. There was no point or use in keeping it a secret anymore. Plamen had seen the blaze himself and how it had moved me through the Hub. Rusper had seen it once as well. But the *Sight* . . .

'Both hold this power?' Rusper said when I was finished.

'I . . . don't know,' I confessed. 'I've tried to see with the other one, but it never works. Only mine.'

His face then pickled into another, possibly angrier, scowl. 'And so, what else have you *seen?*'

It fell right out of my mouth: 'Underground roads. I don't know what they are, really, but I've made drawings. They're in my scroll case over there.' Plamen followed my pointing finger and retrieved the tube from its hook. 'Under the Deep, under the hill, I think, but I couldn't tell how far exactly. It was part of a . . . a dream.'

'Sounds it.'

'No . . .' I frowned at Rusper's stubbornness. 'You don't understand. I fell asleep touching the Disc. It was a dream, but it was . . . real, too.'

'A real dream.'

With a *schwack*, Plamen extracted my parchments and came back. Opening my diagrams, he looked at them for several studious moments. I felt ashamed of their roughness and a little relieved Rusper couldn't see them too. 'These mean nothing to me,' murmured Plamen as Marszal Savhar came to look too.

'And I'm blind,' Rusper said. All three of us looked at him then. He wasn't leaning anymore, but standing rigid behind the worktop. 'Tell me about these *roads*, then. How do you propose such things could possibly exist when we're still digging so far above where you believe them to be?'

There was only one word with which to answer. When I said it he laughed, but it wasn't mockery. Not quite. Again, I saw him trying to locate me in his darkness.

'So, the Builders left a city under ancient Antissa and forgot to tell anyone about it before disappearing into the desert? I'm going to need a little more than just your word on this one, Flint.'

'I fear I must agree with the Viceroy,' said Marszal Savhar, pushing her chest out as if distancing herself from the subject. 'Forgive me, High Commander, but without proof of this . . . *magic* . . . the boy asks much of a soldier.'

I closed the lid, offended now, and Rusper twitched at the snap. 'This torque you mention.'

'Yes,' I said.

'You have it now?'

'I do.'

His voice hardened. 'Turn him, Plamen. Face him to the door.'

'*Ow!*' I cried as Plamen spun me round. But he didn't have to push. I could hear the clumsy rummaging on the worktop behind me and the door of the vertical cabinet squeaking open. I'd been meaning to oil that.

It slammed. 'Tell me what's inside there. Lowest shelf,' ordered Rusper.

Fine, I thought!

Closing my eyes, I pulled the lever on the torque, and Plamen's hand left my shoulder. The workshop transformed into space made of nothing but blue light; space broken only by the interruption of non-space. There stood Plamen . . . Savhar . . . across the worktop, Rusper . . . and the cabinet. I passed through it . . . the shelves . . . their contents . . . the other Disc wrapped in its cloth . . . and on the lowest shelf, an object. I allowed my awareness of the space to close around it and—

'Flint, please, at your earliest convenience.'

'Flywheel,' I said.

'What?'

'A lightweight flywheel. That's what you put on the bottom shelf.'

Outside the barrier of the cabinet door, I could still monitor the shapes of Plamen, watching, and Rusper who staggered to open it again. He swapped its contents. *Slam.* 'And now?'

'Ball-valve,' I said.

Rummage, squeak and *slam*.

'A clamp . . . a scriber . . . lockpin and hex-plug.'

'Is he looking at the door?' rasped Rusper waspishly, sounding breathless. 'Marszal?'

'Facing it,' she said. 'Boy's eyes are closed, sir.'

I was aware of Plamen edging forward. 'This is futile, Symphin. Surely it is plain.'

'One more,' said Rusper.

Slam.

'A shim . ... no two shims,' I said. 'And a spanner.'

'Hah! *Riveter*,' corrected Rusper.

I both heard and saw Plamen round the worktop and open the cabinet himself. He took the object out. 'I lack your Guild experience in such matters, of course, Viceroy, but this is a spanner, I believe. The boy saw right for every object that you placed.' He set it down.

Fully aware of how still Rusper was standing, my anger flared. How much more did he want? I turned around and glared at him. 'You saw the white light! You *know* the Disc has a magic inside it!'

Glances were exchanged but no one spoke.

So I grabbed the scene I'd dreamed: 'Two nights ago there was a woman in your quarters. A dark woman from the harem with green gems around her neck. She was naked and she gave you a green dragonfly earring. She was touching you and then she kissed you, and—'

'That's enough,' snapped Plamen.

I crossed my arms tightly and just glared at the floor. When I finally did look up again, the blind face had gone empty, and maybe even a bit pale, which made the redness round his eyes more awful. Rusper didn't stare or pretend to look at anyone or anything; he simply stood there, allowing silence to stretch between us. The Marszal broke it.

'Well . . .' she said, stepping forward. And gave a husky, heartening chortle. 'No call for embarrassment, I'm sure, Honorary Caliph . . . *if* . . . what the boy describes *is* true.' She wasn't sure what to make of all this, I could tell. 'Most men of the viziership keep one girl at the very least, do they not.'

Plamen's eyes chided her, but Rusper didn't seem to have heard. Very slowly, he slid his hand into a pocket of his shirt. Withdrawing it, he let a small green jewel fall on his palm. A dragonfly. 'Bring me the torque,' he said.

Anger all burned away now, I was ashamed. But at a nudge from Plamen, I wriggled the leather off my wrist and came forward to place it on the worktop near the sparts. In a small, bruised voice, 'It was in the same dream that showed me the roads,' I added.

'Yes,' said Rusper and sank into his chair. Touching the torque, he passed his fingertips over the lion's head embossed on the lid; then gripped the box and hooked the lid with fingernails.

Blue light.

'*Get your hand away!*' I shouted.

But too late. The whiteness crackled inside like the roots of an explosion, then leapt. A living arm of lightning fury wrapped Rusper's head and threw him right out of his chair. He crashed hard into the worktop behind him, dashing more sparts onto the floor. I flung myself at the source to shut it out —but it was over already. The blaze slipped under the lid. The torque went dark.

Limp, Rusper released the edge of the worktop and slid onto the bricks, while Plamen and Savhar ran to his side. Heart pounding, I made sure the torque was shut—*definitely shut*—before I scrambled under the workbenches to his feet. Plamen knelt and gripped him by the shoulder. 'Symphin?' He shook it. 'Symphin, do you hear me?' He looked at me and snarled, '*What happened?*'

'I don't know what happened!'

'Symphin!'

Rusper's eyes were closed but surely, if he was dead, his head should loll if he was shaken like that.

Plamen shook him again and this time Rusper did move. Only a twitch of his left hand that rolled a washer away. Then his eyes snapped open and I gasped. Two tiny storms of bright white lightning blazed, one inside each of his pupils, burned and gone in an instant. 'Caliph Symphin?'

'Are you hurt, sir?' said the Marszal.

'Yes . . . I am,' Rusper croaked. Then winced, moving his arm and shoulder stiffly. 'Knocked my back *right* on that worktop.'

Slow-feed relief steadied my heartbeat as he gave Plamen his elbow and I took the other arm. We helped him up. But for a while he simply stood there, rubbing the small of his back and looking from face to face, dazed. Then he looked around the workshop as if just woken from a sleep. 'Are you well, Symphin?' said Plamen.

'Yes, I think so,' Rusper said.

And when he looked to me again, his eyes weren't blankly staring. He was looking *at* me. 'You can see,' I said.

'Yes,' he breathed. 'I can, it seems.'

The Marszal ran a hand over her mouth. Then regarded Plamen and me, each in turn: 'What is this power of the boy's, some stray arcanum of Ered?'

'No,' I said distractedly.

'Then what—'

'Savhar,' said Rusper. 'Flint . . .' He blinked slowly, then let his eyes drop to the bricks; glanced leg to leg of the workbenches as if suddenly these were the most fascinating pieces of engineering in all Antissa. He raised the quadruple lever-wheel that he had broken in anger, put it down, then hovered his hand above the torque. 'Hm,' he mused. 'By all means help yourself.' So he *did* recognise the torque from his own wardrobe. The ghost of a smile flickered on his lips, then disappeared. '. . . If you would kindly leave us please,' he said, seeming to find a sharper focus. 'I would now speak with my aide alone.'

TWENTY-SIX

HYPERION'S VAULT

My remaining tasks that day went slowly, even though I worked faster than usual. When I went back to the workshop in the evening for my supper, the place was empty. So, having eaten, I took the ladders and winch-lift down to digging level. No one was down there either. The lanterns I'd hotted this morning were dimming, but there was still enough light for me to scale down from the scaffolds to the floor. Among the rocks and scattered tools around the sleeping rubble-raiser, I sat cross-legged on an outcrop and pulled back my sleeve.

Again, I popped the torque's lid and saw my face stare back at me in ridiculous detail. When that white blaze had launched at Rusper, I'd been so sure it was going to kill him. But it hadn't. It had *healed* him instead, given him back his eyesight . . . In the dark brown of my own eyes, I counted the pinpoint reflections of every single lantern on fifth level . . . *twenty-one.*

'What are you?'

'. . . *spark.*'

Only the hint of a whisper answered; I could have imagined it, though.

I pulled the torque's lever towards me and opened the Sight. Concentrating harder than ever, I pushed my awareness of the space down through the rock of the hill. Wherever a crack opened in the sandstone and granite, I made sure to squeeze in, and through, and down, tracing its route. Most routes stopped dead. And when they did lead into hollows, these were barely wide enough to fit a standard secondary lateral. The deeper I pressed, the tighter the surrounding mass closed in. Real or imagined, all the compressed rock of the hill seemed to exert a kind of pressure on what I was within the Sight, that both numbed and confused me. But I kept at it, kept trying. The Builders' roads were down there somewhere – I'd seen them.

'Naemian.'

For a moment I thought the Disc was speaking again. But this time it hadn't happened in my head. I opened my eyes, cut off the Sight and looked around. Above, on the scaffolds, there was Hetch. Just barely, I thought I saw his sandrat clamber down a scaffold-strut.

'What do you want?' I said, annoyed. My voice echoed through the cavern.

'You,' he said.

'No, *you!*' I snapped up at him. 'I asked for your help and you lied. You told me my friend wasn't at the warehouse!'

'That was no lie, Naemian,' he replied. 'He was not there.'

'Yeah, I *know* that now—but you're *everywhere*, Hetch! You must've known he was with Loquar.'

'Loquar . . .'

'Don't pretend you don't know who that is!' But he only shrugged and made a face I couldn't read inside his cowl. I shook my head, fed up with him. 'Please go away.'

'You're to come *with* me, Naemian.'

'Go *away.*'

'Viceroy's orders.'

Hetch scuttled ahead of me, up and out of the Deep. He led me through the grey hall of columns towards the council chamber doors, and into the same round antechamber in which he'd left me once before. We crossed the chilly little room. The way onto the stairs to the upper balcony was open already, and only now did I realise that those spiral stairs went down as well.

'Be careful, Naemian, it's dark. I shall go slowly for you.' Everything he said was annoying, although the warning was a fair one. Not only was the stairway utterly dark, but the steps were also littered with stony gravel that must have come down from its ceiling; only a little scuffed aside by recent feet. I went at an angle, counting steps: fifty-six of them, and two turns. Up ahead, a prick of light.

Hetch bowed elaborately when we entered. I saw a circular stone table with seats for twelve; six of them filled. The single oil-lamp burned low, but I could see the room was round. A gutter rimmed its perimeter, broken only at the entrance by two stone hawks with necks upturned and beaks wide open.

'Don't gawk. Sit down,' said Rusper. I turned at the sharpness in his voice, now seeing him in the seat that faced the stairs, across the table. Elbows propped and fingers crossed, he gave me a wry smile. 'Any one.'

This room must be directly underneath the Sanhedrin council hall, I thought as I obeyed, my sandals scraping like a gristmill in the hush. I approached the table and wormed my body into the stone seat across from him. The two seats either side of Rusper were empty. Further to his left sat Caliph Omran, irritably patting at the dust on his sleeves. Along to Rusper's right were Marszal Savhar and another soldier I didn't know. Also a woman. This was a new thing to me—women soldiers. She stared at me for a few moments before Savhar leaned at her ear. 'The Elmine, the one I mentioned.'

The soldier's eyes hardened a bit. 'A child?'

Rusper twitched. '*Ekharaan*. I beg your patience and courtesy, if you please. This boy, *ekhin* Flint, is not only trustworthy and astute, he is essential.'

We were waiting, clearly, for something or someone. Now Rusper turned to watch the fat caliph grooming his thobes like a preening pigeon. I could still hardly believe that the Disc had cured his blindness.

'My apologies for the state of the room,' he sighed. 'I don't know that it's been much in use since Satrap Hyphet's time. It was, of course, constructed by Hyperion's guild, as a vault, though I believe the doorway mechanism no longer functions, sadly.'

The fat caliph stopped attacking the dust and looked up. 'Why are we sitting in the dark, please?'

'Because,' said Rusper, 'following the incident on the fortress wall, my eyes remain somewhat sensitive to strong lights. You understand.' As Caliph Omran bit back another question, I saw that in the hours since I'd seen him the skin all around those eyes had gone bright pink and puffy. I didn't like it.

Footfalls echoed on the stairs and Plamen entered like a wind between the hawks. 'Forgive my lateness.'

'*That* I'll forgive,' said Rusper curtly. 'Where's Mondric?'

The High Commander walked with purpose all the way to the Viceroy and leaned close over his seat. '*He is not necessary.*'

'You have my instructions. I won't proceed without him.' Rusper said this with just the slightest hint of warning, then raised a thumb to his mouth and chewed the skin. Plamen straightened. Showing only due respect, it seemed, for the Viceroy's authority in the presence of others, he obeyed; boots returning up the stairs behind me.

This time, as we waited, no one said anything at all. Pretending to look into my lap, I studied the soldiers. The Marszal Savhar, now out of swathes, wore a cuirass and headdress over martial leathers. And the new woman, younger and leaner than Savhar, lighter of skin, wore much the same although her headdress was down. She had sharp features, high cheekbones and long black hair severely bound with hempen cord. Hard beauty.

Hetch toed the gravel on the steps.

When, minutes later, the Captain's voice ricocheted out of the stairwell, Rusper straightened in his seat and put his hands into his lap. Plamen came first, taking a place between Rusper and Omran, while I turned around to see the Captain. That he knew nothing of the meeting until this moment was clear on his face when he passed the hawks. His clothes were plain: a loose shirt, an open tunic and a pair of ruddy breeches. A man off-duty. 'Viceroy.' He said it lightly, but I could hear the suspicion.

'Captain.' Rusper gestured to the seat beside mine, and I winced. Mondric walked heavily, as always, to the table and gave a grin when he saw me.

'Tools! Still working your way up the old ladder, I see.' I ducked sideways before he could tousle my hair as usual, but then he clapped my cheek instead. Rounded his seat. 'Heard about your part on the wall. Very good. Seems if it wasn't for your *piping* up when you did, we'd be in an even bigger *pelkhish* mess.'

Plamen, who had lowered his forehead into his palm, now sat upright. 'There are soldiers present, Captain.'

'I meant no disrespect,' said Mondric as he flopped into the seat.

'We're assembled then,' said Rusper. There were seven of us. 'Perhaps a *little* more light.'

The dwarf raised a decanter. Tipping it at the beak of one of the hawks, he trickled oil down its open throat and into the gutter. I heard the liquid surround us, wetting the stone. Then he applied the flame from the oil-lamp, a shallow light growing in a border around the table. And even though the rim of the gutter blocked the tongues of the fire, Rusper shielded his eyes and blinked repeatedly behind a sleeve.

'Thank you,' he said. 'Now man the stairs, if you will.'

Hetch spat on the lamp and shuffled out of the vault. Only when his feet could no longer be heard on the steps, did Rusper gesture to the group.

'I thank you all for answering my summons tonight,' he said and extended the gesture to his right. 'Marszal Savhar and Artabh Keda of the Methan Regiment.' Then to his left. 'Caliph Omran of Laudassa. High Commander Plamen, of course. Captain Mondric of the Guard. And my own hand, Florian Flint.' All eyes swung to me, but he pulled them back. 'We are here, *ekharaan*, not to discuss options. Nor, as it may seem, to conspire. We are here, as will be known to some of you already, because chance has presented me with something which may turn the tides of our war.'

'War?' Mondric chuckled. 'I'm sure I don't know what you're talking about.'

'Nor are we here in levity, Captain. You know the part that I must play.'

'I'm not a politician,' he scoffed back. Plamen stiffened again, but this was Mondric's way.

'Let us dispense with preamble.' Rusper lowered his eyes and blinked again with some obvious discomfort, or even pain. I didn't like it at all. Then he looked up: 'I am consenting to the immediate dispatch of a single unit of the Methan Regiment.'

Muscles tightened in Mondric's jaw; as he was right beside me, I heard his teeth clamp down and creak. He regarded both the Marszal and the Artabh, just briefly. 'For what purpose?'

'It is my intention to locate the Ratheine infiltration point,' said Rusper. 'They entered our pipeworks by an underground water-system of some kind, most likely a river that adjoins our aquifer at some level. It has been proposed to me, and wisely, that the choicest course of action would be to discover that river. Such a mission needs soldiers.'

'Soldiers the Satrap forbids.'

'Correct.'

The two men held a stony gaze. Then the silver-haired guardsman folded his arms and exhaled. 'You'll do as you see fit. You are the Viceroy.'

But Rusper shook his head. 'This is not a bid for blind eyes, my good Captain. I've had enough of those of late.' In Mondric's silence, I wondered if he was only now realising that Rusper could, in fact, see again.

'Then why'm I here?' he said. 'You know my loyalty is binding.'

'I want your willing cooperation. Both now, and in the future.'

'Have I not—'

'Yes, Captain, you have. That is, shown support to the Viceroyalty at a time when royal decree has rendered my position all but untenable, and your own distinctly complicated. It has not gone without regard. I am asking for more.'

Plamen's snort, though it was soft, turned more than one head; the other Vedans watching the exchange very closely. Even I had little doubt that the Captain would stand up and leave us right then. But he didn't move. His face was grim and his eyes were locked to the Viceroy's. He wasn't a fool; I'd never thought so.

He loosened phlegm. 'I'll hear you.'

For an explanation of an object that could miraculously move my body across any distance, it seemed, and open eyes inside my mind, Rusper's was drier than I would have thought possible. But he was practical, as always. To my surprise, Mondric remembered the "jewel" his guards had taken that day in his office, thinking me then just a thief and a vandal of the colours. To the claim that it held arcane power of any kind, he said nothing. Merely turned his eyes towards me once or twice. By the end of the account, his gaze was back on the Viceroy.

'And you would have me defy the Satrap for this, what was it . . . this *disc?*'

'We cannot ignore its potential,' said Rusper, looking at me as if in reference. 'Whatever it truly is, Florian's Disc offers us the precise advantage we need.'

Mondric leaned back. 'Send out more scouts.'

'They stand no chance now. We cannot know how many Rath inhabit the point of infiltration, not to mention that the northern desert is crawling with them. Scouts will perish in the search. And so will Florian.'

'Ah!' Mondric puffed. 'So you would send the tool-boy on this mission? Well, you have some enterprising uses for *Elmines*, have you not!'

First I'd heard of it, too.

'The Disc answers to his touch and his alone,' said Rusper. 'Furthermore he knows the dangers and, I believe, the alternative.'

Did I?

'Its power is evident,' said Marszal Savhar. She chose some odd moments to interrupt. 'Not only does it grant this sight-of-mind to the Elmine boy, it healed the Viceroy of his blindness.'

Rusper glanced at me, just for a second.

But then Caliph Omran interrupted. 'Begging your pardon, Honorary Caliph, but your eyes look far from healed to me.'

'They can see and that's enough.' The Viceroy opened his hands on the table. 'Captain, I've nine days at the most. After that, the Satrap wills that the Deepworks must continue, whether or not the pipes are stable, and I will be left with no choice but to continue in the forging of our destruction. Senera Amyra knows this. She will use it to herd the Sanhedrin around me and call for the First Circle to overrule my standing as Viceroy. Now, you may very well arrest a vizier for such sedition, but when the Sanhedrin stands unanimously against me, your power as keeper of the law of Antissa will shrink to but a vestige, little more.'

Mondric's chest rose with outrage, but Rusper raised a calming hand. 'But,' he continued, 'the Sanhedrin is not yet *quite* the nest of vipers Amyra thinks. The absence of four caliphs is felt on the scales most heavily now, and those caliphs would of course place the safety of their territories before the interests of a puffed-up civic council. The caliphs, as always, could sway the First Circle in this matter, especially having as I do the support of the capital's people. They could divide my opposition and weaken Amyra's hold. I have already pledged to do what I can for the middle caliphies by way of military support.' He gestured to Omran. 'Here is the Caliph of Laudassa, with whom I shall begin to fulfil that pledge.'

'Yet you spoke of Methan soldiers,' said Mondric with another glance at the two officers. 'Why not deploy Laudassan men?'

'It little matters to the balance which men are chosen,' Rusper replied. 'Nor is the defence of Laudassa my purpose in detaching this unit from Antissa. As I've explained already. I would unearth the Rath's river, and for that the High Commander has seen fit to detach his fastest: Methan cavalry. The Caliph-Archimandrite of Methar, with whom I closely correspond, is also in accord. Both he and Caliph Omran accept that the arrangement comes with terms of allegiance to this undertaking, for if it remains favourable that the mission be kept secret from the Sanhedrin—'

'If it fails,' said Mondric.

Rusper nodded with grace. 'If it fails . . . we'll need footholds. If, in nine days, the Methan unit has uncovered no underground system in the northern desert, then the cavalry with not return to Antissa at all. It will ride to Laudassa and garrison the clerical settlements there. Caliph Omran, in exchange, swears his confidence and full support in council henceforth.'

'It is as the Viceroy says,' said the fat caliph. 'He has kept his word to me and I have given him mine.'

Rusper continued, gaze pinned to the listening Captain: 'I've sent news by falcon to Caliph Bardon in Chidh Uribb. As for Arif, I will wait for the finding of our river. When the Caliphate is assured of our military upper hand, they will rally behind the Viceroyalty again.'

'Caliph Arif will most assuredly stand behind you,' said Omran. 'The prospect of breaking the Rath's hold on Verunia will no doubt secure both his support *and* regiment.'

Mondric grunted. 'You speak as if the Satrap had already lifted his decree. And here I sit, audience to your treason.'

'Treason?' said Plamen. 'Who is guilty of the greater treason, Captain, when your *loyalty* spares not a thread for the true welfare of the Vedish?'

Hands on chair-arms, Mondric hefted himself forward.

'Steady now,' said Rusper; Plamen duly sitting back.

Mondric was slower to do the same, saying slowly: 'I'll ask again. What do you want from me, Viceroy? Speak plainly and I'll answer. But do not presume to think that all this will simply grind and halt, in whatever mind I should turn from this chamber. I may be a guardsman, but I'm as Vedish as any other at this table'—except for me, I thought—'And I fear for you, Symphin.' His voice dropped lower. 'You've been pushed.'

Again, Plamen sat forward; again Rusper raised his hand. 'He didn't call me a delirious fool, Commander, he said I'd been pushed. It's the truth.' I didn't understand *how* he was so calm. 'And were it not for the Disc, I should still be resisting that push. This has nothing to do with who wears the Viceroy's medallion. We have a chance to protect our city at a time when the walls of the fortress may no longer be capable of that.'

'You evade my question,' said Mondric, arms still folded. 'What do you *want?*'

'I want you to ease the passage of cavalry from the fortress at dawn,' Rusper said.

'How many men?'

At this, Rusper nodded to Marszal Savhar. She addressed the Captain: 'With the approval of High Command and the Caliph-Archimandrite Bardon, I have formed a tactical unit from the cavalry of the Eighth.'

'Mounted scimitars?' said Mondric.

'That's correct, *ekharan,*' answered Savhar, raising her brows at Mondric's knowledge. 'That cavalry is the swiftest of the army, long inured to erg travel. Under the direct leadership of the High Commander, and myself, we believe it will be effective in crossing the northern distances at speed without confrontation with the Rath. You may, if you wish, sir, think of it as another scouting party.'

'That's almost a hundred men and horses,' Mondric retorted loudly. 'I'll have no part in it—scouting party, my arse!'

Slapping his big hands to the table, he stood to leave the vault of stone. No one stood to try and stop him, or even spoke until he passed between the two hawks.

'Then I will halve it,' said Rusper. Plamen seethed; I turned in time to see Mondric stop with one boot on the first step, scraping gravel. I wasn't sure I liked the sound of *fewer* soldiers going out there, but was more worried right now about what would happen if the Captain left us here with half a plan. I already wanted it to work. I wanted to *make* it work—myself.

But Mondric shook his head, sadly. 'Perhaps you're a fool after all,' he said to Rusper. 'With or without me, you are flouting the laws I uphold. And there beside you sits the High Commander of the Mooncircle Army, aide to the Viceroyalty and one man in Antissa who might manipulate the entire

Fortress Guard while I file my nails in the bath. Yet you make me privy to your plans. Why risk it?'

'Because I'm no more a politician than you are,' said Rusper without a moment's pause to think. 'And I'm not the Satrap to whom you swore your oaths, nor in fact any true head of his Caliphate. That Satrap is mad, Captain.'

Postures stiffened all around the table.

'You know this,' said Rusper. 'I am his minister, an engineer burdened with the care of his realm against my will. And I am a citizen of Antissa who would dare to believe in good faith among Vedans. Am I a fool for *that?'*

Mondric took his foot off the step. Inhaling deeply, he propped an arm on the head of a head of a hawk. 'You are,' he breathed. 'It's too many men.'

'That much is fair,' Rusper agreed. '*Marszalekh*, the company must halve.'

Despite Plamen's clear unhappiness, Savhar nodded. 'It is done, sir.'

'Fifty men and horses,' Mondric tallied as he slowly came back to the table. 'The High Commander, Marszal and Artabh, at least a half-score of hands to mind provisions. And the boy. I still count more than sixty.'

'Fifty-eight,' said Plamen, staring straight ahead into nothing. 'Hands have been chosen already.'

'Let me repeat,' said Rusper gravely. 'Regardless of number, the company is to depart Antissa from with no combative intentions. Confrontation will be avoided at every cost, you understand, as it will be possible to outrun—'

'Outrun the Rath, with supply carts?' Mondric blurted.

At that, I sat upright and looked at him myself. '*We* did it,' I said. The combined weight of years bore down on my head as everyone around the table looked at me. I shied from the heat in the Captain's face, but didn't let it scare me. '*We* made it to Antissa in carts. We outran them that night.'

To my surprise, my words were met with a shallow medley of nods. So, I guessed, some of them knew I was a borderland refugee after all.

Mondric leaned on the back of his seat with his wrists. 'All of these promises you make, Symphin, are meaningless to me. As upholder of law, the mission of this company makes no difference once it gets beyond the walls. No matter its purpose, it amounts to contravention of decree, and by the Satrap and your enemies alike, seen as high treason. For all I care, it may try to invade Lostrian Ered.'

At that word he'd said, my blood boiled. '*She's* the one who treasoned!' I shouted.

'Flint . . .'

'You know that, Captain, I know you do!' He didn't answer or look at me. 'I've seen her plotting with the viziers. She'll turn them against the Viceroy. The *Satrap's* Viceroy. And you're going to let her!'

As soon as I heard my voice's echo, my cheeks went hot. Someone say something.

Mondric did. *And* looked at me. 'Which viziers?'

'Huh?'

'*Which viziers exactly* did you hear the woman speaking with?' he asked me calmly, as if my earlier outburst had been no more than a sneeze. Rusper's eyes were on me too, under a different shape of frown.

'I only saw the one actually,' I admitted. 'One of those men who wear blue gowns and those big . . .'

'First Circle,' said Rusper softly. I nodded. 'Do you remember the name?'

I thought hard. 'Like . . . Bassar? Brasta?'

'Basra,' said Rusper and Mondric together, glances meeting without a challenge this one time.

'You are certain?' said Plamen.

I nodded tightly. 'Yes sir.'

The Commander leaned back in his seat, two thoughtful fingers on his lips, while Mondric sat slowly forward and crossed his own on the table. At least two minutes stretched in silence; Caliph Omran dozing now.

Then Mondric said, 'Here are my terms.'

Rusper's brows went up.

'You'll have my help and you'll have my silence in this endeavour you've contrived. But be well warned. Should any of this come to light, it is you—*Honorary Caliph*—and you alone, who will face the wage of your defiance before the throne. I cannot save you from that.'

Rusper bowed his head. 'Agreed, just as you say.'

'The company will depart *before* dawn,' Mondric went on. 'It will use the Trader's Gate to avoid any confrontation with the Shield. My watch will not be removed.' Rusper frowned. 'We *are* at war, *ekharan*, no matter the lies we espouse in the name of civic order, and as Captain of the Fortress Guard I refuse to leave a single fortress wall unmanned. I will delay the changing of the watch and post a proxy in its stead. Men sworn to silence.'

'Men I can trust?' Rusper put to him sternly.

'Leave that to me.'

'We'll need a signal,' murmured Plamen, almost completely to himself.

'Crop Yard wall,' said Mondric, seeming to have anticipated this. 'There's a row of four lantern-posts. Know it?'

Rusper nodded, 'I do know them.'

'When all four are shuttered, open the gate.'

The dozing Caliph Omran suddenly jerked in his seat and mumbled something about wafers. Plamen sat still, cool eyes on Mondric. Rusper sat back. 'It's settled then.'

'Not the choicest words,' Mondric grumbled, narrowing his eyes. 'Don't make me regret it.'

'Four lanterns before dawn,' answered Rusper, as if that were any kind of response. 'Artabh Keda.'

'*Ekharan?*' said the new woman-soldier.

'You'll remain here at the fortress. In six days, send out a falcon to ascertain the company's position. Then ride to rendezvous and muster the Laudassan cavalcade.'

'Yes sir.'

'Flint.' Prepared for orders, I looked up. 'You, I trust it's clear, are the mission's central component. Its success or failure depend on what you can discover through the Sight of that Disc. Thus, in order that you may better guide his company through the north, I am placing you in the High Commander's care. Report to him. Understand?'

Guide it, he'd said.

I looked to Plamen—still, grey eyes—and back to Rusper. 'Yes, Caliph Symphin.'

Nodding, 'Between your departure and the re-routing of the unit for Laudassa,' said Rusper, 'you're to find us a Ratheine river.'

Twenty-seven

Four Lanterns

As Rusper hustled me back, I had to jog to keep up with him. Even with that swollen red trail around his eyes, from the Disc's blaze, it was as if he'd never been blind in the first place. There was vital purpose in his stride. Purpose we shared, I wondered if he knew that.

'Show me your sandals,' he said in the workshop. Hopping on one foot, I pulled one off. He took it, flexed at its hide, then passed it back. 'That should last. No, don't put it back on, I'll have Zeek heat you a bath.'

'I took a bath yesterday,' I said.

'Well, take another. It'll be your last for a while. How are your clothes?' The red eyes roved over me now as if for the very first time since the restoring of his sight.

'Fine I think. Except for this.' I plucked the collar of my swathes. The tear wasn't all that bad, really, but it meant the cloak hung slightly loose. As the engineer frowned, I saw him guess how it might have happened.

'There'll be sandstorms in the desert, so no, that won't do at all. Take them off and I'll have them repaired in a few hours. As it is, you won't sleep long.'

Zeek brought warm water, soap, a towel. Puffy-eyed herself, I could tell that she'd been woken for the task. I mouthed a 'sorry' to her; washed in my chamber, then pulled on breeches and slipped under my quilt. There I lay awake until Rusper came down a short time later. Just as he'd done on my first night in the Deep, he gathered my washing and stopped halfway up the steps. 'There will be dangers,' he said.

'I know.'

He turned. 'I didn't ask you—'

'Didn't have to.' There, I'd said it.

And it was true. What difference did it make now, anyway? They'd told us Antissa was our refuge, that we'd be safe behind its walls. Erik and Sarah had believed that. But how could *they* have known it wasn't? Borderlander though I was, I now knew Antissa from within and its walls weren't the protection we had thought, or had been promised. The Rath had been here, ready to crawl up from the Deep and, ever since, I'd known full well that no one here was safe. I knew it better than Rusper Symphin—when had *his* home been taken? Ours *had* been, twice over. And one way or another, after that, I'd run away from them. My people: last living Naemians in the world. Guilt for having made that choice still tasted bitter everyday. But *this* choice was easy. I could make it right. For them *and* Rusper and the Vedans. If there really was a river somewhere under the northern desert, secretly linked to the city's pipeworks, we had to find it. *I* had to find it.

Rusper was standing very still, so I looked away from him and up at the old sealed pipe above my bed. 'I don't need to be safe,' I told the pipe. 'I don't think I even want to be. Not anymore.'

He didn't comment on that; just stood there quietly for a while. Then went back up.

I lay awake for a long time, turning things over in my head. Restless, my skin had gone all itchy and the mattress felt too soft all of a sudden. It was too hot to try and sleep under the red-bird quilt tonight.

I flung it off, onto the floor.

Borderlands at dusk. The huts looked smaller, but our own home was the same: the reeds and mats, pallets, brazier. There on my pallet was Sarah's box, whole again, its treasures waiting for me. Except for one. I emptied the box out on the pallet, reached in and tried to find it. Reached my whole arm in, to the shoulder. It must be there!

Desperate now, I upturned the box to shake it out, then held it above my head and looked up. It was dark; so dark inside that I couldn't see the bottom. But there was something *in there. Something like circles—golden circles—and they moved. Wheeling and turning.*

The box closed in around me then, transforming into walls all veined with pipes, but those golden, turning rings above me grew only larger and larger. I was rising now again; rising towards them.

Faster, I willed. Faster! Rise faster! But I couldn't. My rise was slowing; the golden circles going dim.

They disappeared and then I fell.

I plunged an impossible distance, an impossible depth, as if inhaled by the earth. And there wasn't any landing when it ended; only the discovery that I'd landed, and was somehow still in one piece.

There were people all around me: standing together, still and silent, hundreds upon hundreds of people. All gazing up. And I wasn't scared when I saw their chalky hands and chalky faces, black beetle eyes, long wispy hair. They stood erect. Their hands were still, their faces grave, their dark eyes steady. Their wisps of hair were tied in tails, and they weren't wearing scraps of cloth, but rather sleek jerkins of hide. These weren't the Rath as I knew them.

When I followed their gaze, I saw another, taller figure stepping forward on an overarching rock. That was a man, a slender man with charcoal hair swayed by the wind that somehow reached us at this depth. He wore a mask.

Was he my ghost?

I stood, surrounded by the Rath, and waited for him to say what I knew he would; watched him place a hand over the mask and start to peel it from his skin.

Yes, he was speaking, I knew, even though I couldn't hear the words he spoke. Couldn't hear the call . . . not this time. There was no "little spark." No voices at all, until . . .

'It's time.'

I sat up and rubbed my eyes. He was a shadow.

'Get dressed. There's food on your workbench. When you're ready, meet me at the goods depot on the west side. I'll be with a cart and driver.' Blearily, I nodded and the shadow was gone.

For a few minutes I just sat there on my mattress. As I slowly woke up, I found the little round of charms that had been taken from the corpse of a Ratheine female; somehow it had got under my pillow in the night. I toyed with it: the deadwood man, the strip of hide, the hollow crab. Not so unlike Sarah's necklaces all those years ago. And out of nowhere, I wasn't sure I still wanted to be part of a mission. Or go out into the desert.

Shake it off, I told myself. Fumbled my shirt and sandals on. My swathes were on their hook: true to his word, he'd had them mended, and a scarring of red twine coloured the collar. Like a true Antissan, I had them wrapped fast round my body within a minute.

Upstairs, he'd left a box-lantern. By its meek light, I ate my tashi, doubts shrinking smaller with each mouthful, and then got ready to leave. I took the torque from my sling-bag and secured it on my left forearm, slung the bag across my body, then found a simple folding chib – a keen, flat blade and grip of bone that fitted snugly in my hand. Wouldn't be much as a proper weapon, but it was something, so I tucked it into my swathe-belt.

The moon symbol hung low on the clepsydra's dial. There was no sign of the sun symbol, or even the beak of the gryphon that climbed before it. I looked around once more. A tan-brown cloth was looped over the arm of a machine. To keep the hair out of my eyes, I tied it tight around my forehead, then swept my hood up, took the lantern and left. Closing the door.

The Deep was ghostly. At least an hour earlier than I'd ever been up for hotting lights, its emptiness felt much more threatening. And so it should be, I thought, if it weren't for the soldiers at its core all through the night. My lantern beams played eerily with brickwork and pipes, joining a game of even taller shadows at the top of the rubble-shaft spiral. My own shadow made me jump, looming against the Deeping Door like a tree.

My steps were soft over the stone. As I passed the grand citadel doors – still closed, this early – I heard the mutter of some guards. I passed the empty, silent kitchens and from there took the stairs that led down into the underpass roads.

Night air touched my skin. Head low, I hurried into the sprawling goods depot, ready to cloak my light at the first sign of movement anywhere. But there were no guards to be seen as I moved among the rafters, timber posts and sleeping carts and wagons.

Two shadowy figures stood by a cart by the entrance of the depot. The harnessed donkey gave a snort and shook its head; one of the figures set its hand against its neck. Guild-ring glinting. At the crunch of my sandals in the straw, Rusper turned and glared out from a headdress. The skin at his eyes looked no better. 'Into the cart. Quickly now and keep that hood up.'

He joined me aboard. The second man, our hooded driver, hoisted himself into the front and flicked the reins immediately. The donkey walked, cart rolling out of the depot and veering left into the underpass. Hooves clopped, wheels trundled and this all sounded far too loud.

'Her name is Javairea,' said Rusper after a little distance.

I looked at him. 'The donkey?'

'No,' he blinked. 'The woman. The one you saw.'

'Oh,' I said.

A long pause. 'We've known each other some years now.'

Even though I'd never meant to—it had been the *Disc* that had showed me—I knew I'd invaded his privacy by seeing them together in his quarters. I waited for him to say something more, but he didn't. 'She's . . . harem-senah,' I said, 'isn't she?'

'Yes, from Ospégath. Brought to Antissa very young, as is tradition. She became a prized jewel of the harem. But our relations are no longer bound by Antissan harem regulation. She's not my *girl*, you understand. We care for each other.'

Hearing him say that both warmed me and shamed me at once. 'I'm sorry I spoke about her in front of the Commander and the Marszal.'

He met my eyes. 'It's alright, Flint. You needed my attention and you got it. Besides, the wittering rumours had already begun.' Looking aside, he shook his head while toying with something in between his fingers.

Javairea. It was the most beautiful name I'd ever heard in my life. 'Why don't you marry her?'

His laugh sounded mechanical. 'Because she *is* still bound by regulation. It is against the law of our land to wed a harem-senah. They belong to the Satrap.'

'Like everything,' I said softly, but still hoping he heard.

We rounded the hindquarters of the citadel, our cart passing through faint bars of reflected light from the higher estates. One by one, we overtook the soldiers leading their mounts at a stroll. All were cloaked darkly as well; too darkly for me to tell how many of *them* were women too. The company had been instructed to assemble very slowly through the small hours, so drawing as little attention as might be drawn by their movements. These must be the last ones, I figured.

Passing underneath the council hall and then emerging from the darkness, we travelled alongside smaller estates beside the citadel wall and past the turret that branched from its southern side. As we neared the low wall of the gravel yard, voices sounded ahead: 'Soldier'—'Shieldman.'

'Stop. It's the Shield,' whispered Rusper.

The driver halted the donkey and turned slightly in his seat, speaking low. 'We are close to the Iron Keep, *ekharan*.'

'Not that close,' Rusper replied, then turned and vigorously signalled a halt to the soldiers walking behind us. 'Must be a wide night patrol.'

We listened, sitting very still. Farther off, some guards were talking, but there were no more nearby voices; only the breeze and languid clop of hooves approaching.

Rusper nudged me. 'Run ahead. Stay low and keep close to the shadows. Signal back if it's clear. *Go* boy, be quick.'

I tugged my hood and hopped down to hurry out across the cobbles, quickly closing the distance to the gravel yard wall. There I pressed my back against the stone, took a breath and peered around the corner. The yard was empty and the Deeping Door was shut. As I knew. To the right was the narrow gate that led into the lower Southeast District: *that* gate was open. The hooves clopped closer. A mounted figure appeared and, before I could duck behind the wall, looked straight at me. Then turned his horse, raising an arm.

One of ours, then.

I looked back and waved to Rusper's cart. It moved forward, Rusper coaxing to the soldiers behind, and as it veered into the yard I climbed beside him again. We lowered our heads from the gust of wind that swept the gravel yard, then met the eyes of the cavalryman at the gate. He dropped his mouth-guard:

not a he. Marszal Savhar. 'Viceroy.' Her face was barely distinguishable in the black headdress.

'Shield?'

'Yes sir, opposite gate. Just one. Moved on.'

Rusper's nod was uneasy, and no more words were spoken. Our little cart trundled down into the broken Southeast District. Here was where some of the Verunians had been given shelter after their evacuation; the lower part was derelict. The Marszal and last soldiers, now also mounted, stayed close behind us. I heard the district gate close, and then another pair of riders came to join us from ahead. They remained either side of our cart until we reached the Crop Yard, where I would daily come to arrange my people's supplies from the Yieldmaster.

I'd never seen it at night: a barren space where so much crowding was by day, though maybe *those* might be the pegs of the Yieldmaster's bivouac, outlining the old crone's humble office in the middle. The Crop Yard gave onto the back gate of the city, or Trader's Gate, which would take us down through the farming quarters to the foot of Antissa's hill.

Now the square was alive with the quiet movements of seventy soldiers and their horses. I dismounted from the cart, my eyes drawn to the row of lantern posts above us, jutting right out of the fortress wall like four long javelins. Their diffuse triglycerate shone a murky, milky green over the place. Behind their glare moved silhouettes. Watchmen, I hoped.

Rusper melted into the shadowy confusion of men, women and beasts. Three other carts, these ones much larger, were being loaded by some servants. And there in his saddle was Plamen, black cloak concealing the white.

Minutes passed in the early cold before I heard the first scrape of metal; a shutter dropped over one lantern. Murmurs grew furtive, movements brisker. I heard short orders to the servants, and as I started to feel like I shouldn't be here at all, Rusper wafted out of the throng.

His fingers clicked at my face. 'Open your sling-bag,' he said sharply and stood quite close. When he grasped my shoulder I thought he was going to pull me into a hug—I don't know why —but of course he didn't. Instead he reached into his cloak and produced an object wrapped in hide. As soon as I felt its solid weight, I knew it.

I gaped at him. 'But—'

'But nothing, boy. I want it back.' The second lantern scraped shut then, leaving the Crop Yard darker by half. I buried the fusil and its holster in my bag. 'You'll find three capsules of schot, though I don't intend you should need them.'

I looked up and offered a shrug: 'Dangers.'

'Yes.' Patting my shoulder, he looked up and the third lantern went out.

'Your honest faith in the Captain seems to have been well-placed after all,' remarked Plamen as he rode up beside us. Behind him, the soldiers were mounting and moving into formation round the carts.

Rusper addressed him from the ground, his voice discreet: '*Do not engage.* Not unless absolutely necessary. I want fifty men posted at Chidh Eshipas before nine days are out.'

'So you shall, Viceroy.'

Plamen veered the great shadow of his horse away from us and Rusper ushered me towards the supply-carts. Before I climbed into the seat, he gripped me tightly by the shoulder. 'Under no circumstance are you to place yourself outside the protection of this unit, do you hear me?'

'Yes, Caliph Symphin.'

The breath he pushed out made a cloud. 'Do what you can for us, Flint, *only* what you can.'

He let me go, and as he did the yard went black. Sitting beside the vaguest outline of a driver, I could make out only heads and dim movements. Plamen's voice sounded out just loud enough from somewhere: 'Open the gate.'

A figure jogged towards the gatehouse; soon enough I heard the grind of a winch and the slow crank of lifting iron. Against the deepness of the dawn I saw black teeth rise out of earth.

The shadow at the head of the group wheeled his tall horse before the arch and called attention. The column moved. Our own horse whinnied and, with a pull, got our wheels turning. I was leaving Antissa.

Something poked my shoulder. When I turned to look back, behind my seat, someone was there among the canvassed-over cargo. Slim and very dark. I guessed, one of the hands. 'You're the Elmine?' A young male voice.

For a moment, I hesitated. *You're Naemian*, she'd said. So many times. *Naemian*.

This I would do for them, my people . . . my . . .

My people! A tremor juddered through me. How could I be so distracted, forgetful and *stupid?*—who was going to arrange for their supplies everyday now I was leaving the city? With frantic eyes, I panned the Crop Yard behind the shadow of the boy, but there was no longer an engineer standing there. Rusper was gone.

'Yes,' I said, the panic strangely numbing. 'I'm the Elmine. Who are you?'

'Kobi,' he said.

I shook the hand he held out – bony and rough, but still quite warm despite the chilly morning air – then turned around and hugged my swathes. Over the heads of fifty soldiers, a blue desert stretched towards me.

To conclude in

Volume II
Tools of War

from

VOLUME TWO
TOOLS OF WAR

'Enemy sighted!' came a cry under the ledge.

We looked northwest into the passage of the plain. Blanching in the heat and searing sun, I blinked away the tricks of the glare and saw it: a smudge of something moving against the bands of darker earth. A smudge of *Rath,* about a league off. I felt my hand against the fusil in its holster on my hip. No use in that.

'How many?' Shafra murmured to the woman beside him.

'Seventy, eighty. Could be them that's returning to the caves,' replied the soldier.

Our party didn't have a scope, apparently. Not that we'd need one for long.

'Where's the boy?' snapped Shafra, louder.

'Right here,' I said, from his knees.

His thin eyes darted to my face, and from my face to my wrist. 'Well?'

'Got to be the same ones, *telmadekh*,' I nodded, completely sure. 'The lowest cave was really big. Big enough for a hundred. The pelkhas must've cut them off from getting back here.' At my use of the old Vedish word, or maybe how I'd pronounced it, he almost smiled.

Breaking eye-contact, he looked northeast towards Calvallagh. So did I. The cavalry had reached the level plain; now it was rounding the cliffs, Plamen like a white flag at the head. One horseman parted from the column and rode towards us at the mound. As he stopped, veering his horse, I saw him throw his arm up high. A sudden flash glanced over us, then flashed again.

'Orders to hold position,' said Shafra grimly. The signal was repeated three more times before the rider wheeled back again to join the moving cavalry. 'We garrison the mound. If indeed that rabble dwells here, then it can be staved off and chased back to wherever it came from. With luck, our river.'

'And the High Commander will follow?' I piped.

'If he can. Three more to the scarp! Stand ready to corral and secure the horses. The rest with me. Boy, you'll . . . boy? *Hey,* hey there, *boy!*'

I heard him well enough behind me, but didn't stop, hopping down from the ledge, then running up across the front of the cave-mouth and climbing fast between the crags. As quick as I could, I found my way around the north-facing wall of the mound. It would be harder from higher up, but I had to try. I had to master the Sight or there wasn't any point in all of this!

Drenched by sweat at the top, I fell against the first big rock. Facing north. Even with the torque closed on my wrist, the plain wheeled around me in orbit as if charged up by the thrum of distant hooves over the earth. I could see everything from up here, and hear Plamen's voice as it carried. The cavalry was slowing in the middle of the passage, some five hundred yards or less from the foot of our mound. A mile, maybe, between the horses and the oncoming Rath.

My finger touched the torque-lever, my eyes slamming shut on instinct. But this time I was prepared.

The vastness spun and tried to throw me, but I pinned all of my awareness to the sounds of my target – pushed it *hard* towards the source – until I found myself caught up in rapid, blurring movements. White, black, brown—the galloping legs of forty horses. For just a second I saw the faces of men and women in their saddles; then I was flying, shooting ahead, across the dust, faster than horses. As I flew, I scanned the gypsum until the black eyes blinked out. I strained to hold them in my focus, resisting the pull of the plain.

Chalky bodies loped into my sphere of awareness. Sun--scorched and peeling, caked yellow with dust, they seemed to crawl out of the nothingness at me. They weren't the monsters I knew: not dying, maybe, but withered and weakened by the heat. *Fifty-four*—it was felt without having to count them. Others straggled behind that number, but no more than a dozen. I saw no spears.

My focus snapped. Spinning away through the open, I batted back the lever, clenched my teeth and swallowed vomit. *Couldn't do it.*

No, that wasn't good enough. I climbed up on the rock and looked out, without the Sight. A lick of wind touched my fore-head with wordless shouts from the cavalry down there. It was hard to see much through the dust they'd churned up.

Then they divided. The two halves of the cavalry veered, north and south, a V-shaped trail in their wake. White robes gleamed down the centre. Plamen hadn't joined either half, but rode head-on with three—no, four—other riders.

When next I looked towards the Rath, the bigger group had slowed and stopped, each creature suddenly seeking some escape from what was coming through the passage. Both halves of the cavalry formed and straightened as they rode, parallel with Plamen and now overtaking him. The Rath could only run back now. I heard their screeches, broken gibbers, terror driving them to panic.

But they didn't flee: they loped *forward*.

Plamen and his four fanned into a line. Bright metal glinted; I heard, above the drum of hooves, the shout to open fire, but couldn't see how many Rath fell through the blur of running feet. Only saw the line of crossbows break in two and ride to join the columns.

Up went a shout from the south column, then both the columns veered at the same time. Steel flashed, hooves drummed even harder, and the columns passed by the rabble, brushing the Ratheine flanks. Shrieks carried up to me again. It was all too clear we could destroy them with a single head-on charge, but *no*—we couldn't do that! *Plamen* couldn't! We had to force them to *retreat!*

Taking separate directions and leaving the harried Rath behind them, the two columns withdrew from the middle of the plain.

And still the rabble didn't flee. The Rath were terrified, confused, but moving forward all the same, and now the smaller group of stragglers crossed the gap in worried twos and threes.

Choppy commands drifted up from the north column as it rounded northwest and circled back towards the Ratheine rabble. Plamen had taken the frontline of the south column and was now arcing in this direction, leading back towards Calvallagh. The columns slowed to a halt then: one facing in from the north, the other out from southeast.

At that, the rabble transformed. Seeming to bleed what was left of their strength, they broke into a feral sprint towards the southeast formation, many running on all-fours just as I remembered from that night in the borderlands. They closed fast. Plamen held his ground and pointed his sword high in the air. I caught his words—'*Sidelong all columns!*' and '*Charge now!*'

They advanced. Leaving the passage wide open for the Rath to retreat, they rode hard from both ahead and behind. At less than fifty yards, I guessed, both columns narrowed and swerved to charge alongside, slashing at the edges of the group.

And the group broke. Abandoning all the safety of what was left of their desperate cluster, they scattered and fled for the mound and their caves. Towards *us*.

It hadn't worked.

Below my perch, Shafra's party quickly moved towards their horses. But even as the enemy scampered closer to the scarp, I held position on my rock. Hand on the fusil's grip again.

'Rally!' a voice blared. It was now Savhar's sword in the air. Her column rode around the escape and regrouped behind it, while Plamen's number wheeled away from its northward charge and returned. As he called the last order to charge, the two half-columns reunited.

Forty riders stormed towards me over the already beaten ground, their front line widening. The mound vibrated through my sandals. Rath rolled and tumbled under legs, crushed and devoured by those hooves. Others shrieked in defiance, spinning to face the wave once more before it ran them to the ground.

The charge turned east, hewing the last.

A cold disgust filled up my insides as the dust lifted, and cleared. Still on my rock, I stared down at the swathe of dark marks in the earth below the mound. They looked, from here, just like squashed ants.

My finger lifted off the trigger.

ACKNOWLEDGEMENTS

Thanks to Alexander Milne, Ben Collier, Caitlin Mackie, Carl Holden, Chris Churches-Lindsay, Deborah Dooley, Hayden Westfield-Bell, John Shaw-Stewart, Kit Crane, Kristiina Kotkas, Lisamarie Lamb and Peter Muego for your valuable input at various stages of this project.

A special pair of thank-you's to my two Marys — Mary Marsh and Mary Shaw — for your support and precious friendship throughout the long formation of what has become *The Cycle Schyluscient*.

And to the incomparable Nataša Ilinčić: words cannot convey my gratitude for your extraordinary work on the cover art and design (not to mention your patience!) which has brought to life so huge a part of this dream.

Jay Campbell was born in Cape Town,
South Africa in 1987.

The two volumes of *Deep Mettle* form his
first published novel and first instalment of
The Cycle Schyluscient.

He lives in Edinburgh, Scotland.

Deep Mettle Vol. II
available from Amazon:

1 June 2023

For more information and updates on
forthcoming titles by Jay Campbell,
visit his author page *Worlds by Jay*

voidstep.com

And to view more original artwork by
Nataša Ilinčić, visit her website

natasailincic.com

Printed in Great Britain
by Amazon